CINNAMON GIRL

ALSO BY DANIEL WEIZMANN

The Last Songbird

A PACIFIC COAST HIGHWAY MYSTERY

CINNAMON GIRL

DANIEL WEIZMANN

MELVILLE HOUSE
BROOKLYN · LONDON

Cinnamon Girl

First published in 2024 by Melville House
Copyright © 2023 by Daniel Weizmann
All rights reserved
First Melville House Printing: February 2024

Melville House Publishing
46 John Street
Brooklyn, NY 11201
and
Melville House UK
Suite 2000
16/18 Woodford Road
London E7 0HA

mhpbooks.com

@melvillehouse

ISBN: 978-1-68589-115-2
ISBN: 978-1-68589-116-9 (eBook)

Library of Congress Control Number: 2024931243

Designed by Beste Doğan
Printed in the United States of America
1 3 5 7 9 10 8 6 4 2
A catalog record for this book is available from the Library of Congress

CINNAMON
GIRL

1

I parked by the newsstand across from Canter's Deli and headed for the Shalom Terrace Retirement Home in the morning sunlight. The streets were fresh, softened by the night's rain, and the old neighborhood looked young again, washed clean of memory. Me, I was edgy, crazy restless. I was calling on Charles Elkaim, my former piano teacher, now pushing ninety. Crossing Fairfax Avenue, looking up at the neon chef delivering pastrami, I cautioned myself: be kind and hear him out. *Operation Get-This-Over-With.*

Elkaim had phoned out of the blue with what he described as private troubles—"tsuris of a sensitive nature." It wasn't like we were still close—a million years ago, he lived across the street from the house I grew up in. In the Thursday afternoons of my awkward childhood, I sat beside him on the black bench and practiced Hanon scales. Elkaim was a taskmaster. His motto was "Better to play nothing than touch the wrong note." Still, they were happy times—he liked me, and he was more than teacher or neighbor, he was also my late uncle Herschel's only real close friend. Hersch was gone now, buried out there near Whittier Boulevard, and we hadn't ended on good terms. Odds are, Elkaim knew that.

There were other hesitations as I made my way around the corner to the retirement home in the brisk morning. Elkaim was a survivor—of death camps, of war, and finally, of America itself—his teenage son Emil had been killed in prison some thirty years ago, shivved by a gang member trying to get rep. In our neighborhood, it was forbidden topic numero uno—*the tragedy*. Nonetheless, you felt the silent sorrow of it around Charles Elkaim, even at the piano. In a very real way, it was Charles Elkaim who'd been taken down.

This dark and fading presence, this Moroccan Israeli widower with a phantom for a son—what could he possibly want from me?

Through the glass doors of the Shalom Terrace, the empty lobby was as vintage as the residents. A fake pink crystal chandelier dangled over mustard deco wall-to-wall carpet. Elegant umbrellas sat unused in a brass holder at the door, and a pair of tall smoked windows let in a wash of hazy morning light. It all stirred up the peculiar feeling that time could be stopped at will, the way a hasty croupier might bring a roulette wheel to a sudden, premature halt. I asked a janitor pushing an industrial vacuum if he knew where I could find Elkaim, and he pointed down the hall.

Nobody was in the room, but a crappy Casio sat on the bureau so I knew I was in the right place. I couldn't resist. I flicked on the keyboard and started poking out the melody for "And the Angels Sing" with one hand, and just like magic, he appeared, clunking in on an old steel walker.

"Zantz, this is you?! You still play too fast! Who told you fast was good?"

"Mr. Elkaim," I said, grinning.

"Zantz the fast!" He stopped to wag a finger. "You must be a terrible disappointment to your lady friends."

This was a running gag, and we joined hands to share it. His touch was bony, fragile, all warmth. He was skinnier now. The years seemed to have darkened him, too, even more than I remembered, and when he let go of my hand, something remote glowed through his out-of-fashion glasses—a certain aloneness. All at once, I saw what Uncle Herschel used to say about him— what I never got as a kid—*"This is the real thousand-year-old man."* He'd come to America late in life, too late to shake off the patina of human history.

"I have not seen you since you were this tall," he said, tapping the walker.

I pointed a thumb over my shoulder. "The whole block has changed."

Elkaim made a quick hand gesture—*gone to dust*. Then: "Come. There is a courtyard. It's more private." He turned the walker and I followed, lumbering behind childlike the way we do around the elderly. He led me out of his room, past the nursing station where he insisted on introducing me to Miranda the administrator and Nurse Rosa. Then we moved slowly down the hall, past pale old bodies in various stages of disappearance—some lying down stunned before televisions, some bent asleep in EZ chairs, some nursing a slow tea in a paper cup as if that might ward off the Angel of Death.

"So it's true what your sister Maya tells me?" he said. "You are making a living as a private investigator."

"A living? No. I drive Lyft. Do you know what that is?"

"You lift things?"

"I'm like a taxi driver. But I'm studying for an investigator's license, a college extension course."

"But she sent me by the email—you solved a real case."

"That was just a fluke."

"Fluke, shmook, you're a mensch," Elkaim said, hobbling along. "That's what counts."

Then he stopped, turned, placed a fragile hand on the lapel of my coat. "I have had a visitor. And I need your help."

Elkaim pulled aside the old orange curtain and led us out through sliding glass doors to a small fountained courtyard. We dragged steel chairs into the morning shade. A solemn, topless Greek lady made of white stone poured endless LA water from the big urn on her shoulder. I had the uncanny sensation she wasn't the only other presence gazing down upon us— somewhere Uncle Herschel was looking too.

Elkaim wiped the lenses on his glasses and put them back on. "I was very sorry about what transpired between you and your uncle."

"I know, Mr. Elkaim."

"Still, you should have visited."

"I know."

"Fathers and sons," he said matter-of-factly, then sighed. "Forty years we benched together at Etz Jacob. We were the last holdouts for havdalah on Saturday night."

"I know that meant a lot to him."

"Herschel was the glue—the minion fell apart not long after he died."

I tried to do the compassionate nod, but the family talk was plucking at my nerves.

I said, "Tell me about your visitor."

Elkaim breathed deep with some labor. Then he asked me what I was afraid he'd ask. "What do you know of what happened to my son?"

"A little," I said. "But I was very young—and it's been a long time."

"Yes. In any case, you are a grown man now. And there should be no secrets between us. I came to this country in 1979 on an employment visa. My late wife's cousin got me an accounting job—at Globus. *B pictures.* I . . . we wanted our only child to grow up in a more peaceful country. And Emil— loved it here."

"That I remember," I said.

Then I blurted, "I adored him."

Elkaim nodded without approval.

But I wasn't exaggerating. To a little kid such as myself, scooter-riding up the block looking for the world, sixteen-year-old Emil Elkaim was something to behold. Tall, shoeless, with dark longish hair and a scruffy almost-beard, he *looked* like he just walked over from the Holy Land. But he wasn't solemn. A wisecracker, a daredevil skateboarder and fence-hopper, it was like one day Emil just appeared out of nowhere—the teenage prophet—and all the kids flocked to him. On Saturday afternoons, these neighborhood hangdogs of every race and haircut all gathered at Fairfax High to chill on the bleachers with Emil strumming Beatles on a scratched-up acoustic, the whole gang singing around him.

"I believe he babysat you and your sister," Elkaim said.

"A few times. He and his girlfriend took us to Disneyland once."

Elkaim half-smiled at this long-lost memory. Then he spoke the facts flat and plain, like someone in a spelling bee.

"Emil turned eighteen on March 28, 1984. He was arrested April 10. He was not convicted—but he was the primary suspect in the murder of a drug dealer named Reynaldo Durazo. My son was awaiting trial in county lockup when an inmate murdered him—allegedly on the orders of the victim's cousin."

I could not find a word to say.

"A revenge slaying," he went on. "And Emil's girlfriend—"

"She—ran away?"

"Yes. A few months later. And she died of an overdose." His black eyes bore into me like a telescope scanning for something just one yard away. "In 1987."

"So awful, Mr. Elkaim, I am so—"

"In any case," he interrupted as if to go on—but then he

reached into his brown coat pocket and handed me a folded-up printout of a scanned photo: a fading Kodak shot of Emil and his girlfriend Cinnamon on the Santa Monica Pier, arm in arm outside the Skee-Ball Arcade. Emil was shirtless in flip-flops and cutoff jeans, his grin teenage goofy. Cinnamon was laughing too, in a white-and-yellow minidress that blazed bright in direct sunlight. But they looked more like sixties teens than kids of the eighties. It wasn't quite how I remembered them.

"What year was this taken?" I asked.

"1983," he said. "In the summer. Her real name is Cynthia. *Was* Cynthia."

"But everyone called her Cinnamon," I said.

"That's right."

His old man's nod packed a punch—regret, loss, guilty-feeling erotic charge, and the peculiar wistful hands-off pleasure some fathers get from seeing their sons with pretty girls. Then, as if to back off it, he said, "She . . . loved to sing with us. Shabbat, at the dinner table." But she *was* something else, reflecting back the sunshine. Even from this faded printout scan of a faded snapshot, the feeling came back to me: these two were gone for each other, you could practically see little birds flying around their heads. I returned the printout, and he refolded it.

"Three weeks ago, a man came. On a Saturday in the morning. I was not expecting anyone. I came out of the shul here and sat with him in the lobby. He called himself Devon Hawley. He was perhaps in his fifties, maybe more. He claimed that he had known my son in high school. I did not remember him, but I had no reason to doubt him. He gave me this."

Elkaim dug into his coat's other pocket and pulled out a folded newspaper page. He opened it for me, a page-long article torn from the *Downtown Courier*—"Miniaturist is City Dreamer." In the center of the article was a black-and-white photo of a cheery-looking bald man hovering over a mini-skyline like a middle-aged Godzilla.

I scanned quick:

> For Devon Hawley, Jr., the creation of finely detailed tiny cities is more than a hobby, it's an obsession. In just the last three years, Disney, NBC/Universal, Pixar, and Netflix have all called upon Mr. Hawley and STEAM-WORLD STUDIOS here in DTLA, to design and photograph the backdrops for over a half-dozen blockbusters.

I looked up. "Did this man harass you?"

"Not in the slightest. He was very polite. Tall like the day is long." Elkaim made a reaching gesture. "He was apologetic for having interrupted me and so forth. Quite nervous."

"What makes you say so?"

"He spoke in a halting manner. He seemed to have a hard time looking me in the eye."

"Isn't it a bit strange that you didn't remember him?"

"No, no, I don't think so. My son had a life of his own—especially as a teenager."

"Okay," I said. "But what did this Hawley guy want?"

"He told me . . . that he could prove my son's innocence. He said he *figured things out.*"

"Wow, all these years later?" I sat up, on instinct. "Did . . . did he say how?"

"No." Elkaim pursed his dry lips, tallying some invisible calculation. "No, he would not tell me how he knew, but my lifetime of suspicions were confirmed. I always knew it was a mistake. My son was not capable of murder."

"Of course, but—"

"The night they arrested Emil, he wept to me, he told me he was innocent. He would not lie to me about such a thing."

I took it in—I knew I was on shaky ground. Everybody's son is innocent.

"So . . . this guy just came here out of the blue, without any notice and—"

"But he was not rude about it. He simply said that he wanted to introduce himself and set up a time to speak, to share certain details. He asked if he could return the following Saturday—to take me to his studio, I gather to show me his . . . his files, his evidence. He begged that I tell no one. As I say, he seemed very nervous. But respectful about the whole matter. And then—" Mr. Elkaim raised his palms to the heavens. "—a *no-show.*"

I scrambled for words of comfort, came up short. "Maybe he got the dates wrong?"

"At my age, one does not have time for such delays."

"I understand, Mr. Elkaim—"

"No," he said firmly, "you do not understand. A cancer eats my pancreas. The doctors say I have three months, six at most."

A bright, vivid silence—

"*Ninety days,*" he added without self-pity. But his dark eyes held me in place.

"I want to help," I said. "Anything I can do. But . . . I'm trying to get a full picture. Can you tell me *exactly* what this man said?"

"Word for word, no. I was in a state of shock. I . . . I was shaken, I did not want to press him, I—"

Elkaim hesitated and, before my eyes, his yearning morphed into a peculiar self-scrutiny. His longing for justice, for last-minute redemption was high, wild, out of control, and he knew it. It made both of us uncomfortable, this intensity of hope. I caught myself glancing at the glass door. Like more than one visitor to a nursing home, I yearned for the clock to move quicker.

Uncle Herschel is watching—

"Mr. Elkaim," I said gently, "people do prey on the elderly—we know that."

"He did not ask to be remunerated, if that is what you mean."

"That doesn't mean he wasn't setting you up for some kind of scam," I said. Then, gentle as I could: "What happened to Emil is a matter of public record. For all you know—"

"Yes, for all I know, this Hawley is a pranker. But *he set a time*, he was to pick me up at ten. I put on my suit, I told Nurse Rosa I was going to leave for the day. I waited at the door—early, but there was *no such animal*. Ten o'clock came and it went. I searched for this Hawley on the computer—I found the address of his shop, the telephone. I called many times. Nobody answers. Now? I cannot sleep. First I become enraged, then I am full with self-pity. In the night I beg the Almighty to have mercy and kill me off once and for all." He shook his head. "Pardon my foolishness."

"No, I get it, Mr. Elkaim—this guy made promises, it touched a nerve. But level with me, do you . . . like, have a lot of money? Would somebody . . . maybe somebody who knew about your condition . . . would somebody be interested in making a grab for what you've got?"

"I always saved."

"Yes but . . . who would know about that?"

"Today? Anybody can know anything."

I wrestled with the last bit of resistance surging in my chest.

"And you do understand," I said, "I'm not a *real* licensed investigator."

"Your credentials mean nothing to me. You are Herschel's boy, and I always trusted you. Your uncle loved you too—even when he could not show it."

"Okay but . . ." I raised pleading hands. "What is it you'd like me to do exactly?"

"*Find this Hawley person.* Do not scare him away. Just see

who he is and talk to him. Something possessed him to visit—
try to find out what changed his mind."

"You say he was a big guy?" I was trying to be comical.

"But gentle," Elkaim countered. "This man is not the war-
rior type."

I took it in. Right then and there I told myself to be as blunt
as possible. This was my last chance to slip out of the land of
family obligation.

"Mr. Elkaim, I can look into this guy, I'm happy to. But I
want you to know I'm pretty sure you've either been the victim
of some kind of scam, or this guy is just some weirdo. I mean,
even if he *could* prove Emil's innocence . . ." I tried to weather
my words with pleading eyes.

But Charles Elkaim wasn't listening, he was already digging
into the inside pocket of his old brown coat. He grabbed my
hands and pressed a crisp fold of bills into my palm with fervor.

"One thousand. For an honest day's work. Find him. Talk to
him. One time. This is all I ask."

"No, I don't need this, I—"

"Please." The confidence of his gesture made my heart sink—
I made a mental note to deliver a full refund.

"I can't promise anything, Mr. Elkaim, I . . ."

He took off his glasses and showed me his dark eyes, hum-
bled by time.

Then you'll help him, the ghost of Herschel whispered in my
ear. *God in heaven, I knew you would.*

2

Clouds were moving in over the noisy street as I made my way back to the car. I shrouded my eyes from the last of the glare and walked to where I'd parked off Fairfax. Outside the musty womb of assisted living, here in the sunlight zone, the world suddenly seemed hypercharged—with false exuberance. Was there really any sense in this poor dying man dredging up the worst tragedy of his life? The thousand bucks stuffed into my jacket pocket said *doubtful*, but the daytime crowds with their counterfeit busyness screamed *yes! why not? everything is possible!*

I got into my dinged-up 2016 Jetta, hit the ignition and fired up Google Maps: Steam World Studios in the City of Commerce was forty-eight minutes away. Hawley sounded like a nice enough guy, but what I knew about him wasn't much— he made miniature sets for the movies and freaked out old men in nursing homes with outrageous claims.

And it wasn't like I could save Charles Elkaim. Nothing was going to *save* him—this creaking thing, the last friend Hersch ever had—Herschel, who adopted me at twelve, saved me from state proceedings—Herschel the Good. Even now, driving past Farmers Market and all the bus benches of my youth, the memory of Herschel's disappointed gaze slaughtered me. Herschel who gave me everything so I could pay him back by flubbing college, botching a music career, messing up every job, every relationship.

But I never cried. Almost, which is worse.

Why couldn't I?

Because in the debit column of the spirit, I knew I still owed him. Yup. Jewish guilt tax, unpaid.

Now in the midday gridlock on Wilshire heading east, I cursed my late uncle out loud—*"Nice going, noodnik!"* He was operating from the great beyond, dangling absolution like keys to the family car, but would I ever really be off the hook? The impossibleness of our bond followed me like a tracking device. I'd wanted to please him, wanted to be him, wanted to best him, I wanted . . .

Crossing Western, a ginormous SUV cut me off and I slammed the brakes.

"Go fuck yourself, doucheface!"

I was way too jumpy for 11:45 in the morn, crackling with burdens. Had I even loved my uncle? Probably, but the thicket of *other* complicated feelings camouflaged the love part, so that now, stuck on this godforsaken river of metal, even now, years after the funeral I didn't attend, I couldn't even just miss him without the tinted lens of failure—my failure, the failure to make him proud. No, I'd always be what he called me— "the king of jumping ship"—the picture of financial instability, rocky love affairs, crazy, grandiose dreams.

And in the end?

He was used to it already; he viewed me from the protected space of deep irony, but laced with a drop of pity, too. I was the *shlumiel*, the sad-sack bluffer who continuously promised to go straight and do better but always ended up in another *situation*, begging for a hand, and for forgiveness.

Traffic lurched and crawled. I dialed Steam World once,

twice, three times. No answering machine—had to be a land-line. Someone tried to make a left onto Sixth too late, setting off an orchestra of honking horns and public yelling, but this time I kept it zipped—agitation sent me inward. No, I couldn't *just* mourn Herschel, *just* love him—not before getting past the traffic jam inside, bumper-to-bumper family shit. Seeing Elkaim brought it allllll back, full force, the unanswerables: Why couldn't it have been different? Why couldn't *I* have been different? Either/or. Why couldn't he have gone easy on me or why couldn't I have had the common sense to stop angling for the gold badge I'd never get? And why on earth didn't I stop turning to him for money? For at the heart of our protracted battle was *money*, the stink of it: how to earn it, save it, *not* spend it. Depression-born Herschel was on a first-name basis with scarcity. Money gravity was *the* gravity—part of the way you stood right by God. Fair enough. But in the middle-of-the-middle-class safety zone he built for us, I seemed to come to the conclusion that money was a kind of kryptonite. Hold onto money and it could define you, envelop you, a fate worse than death.

I turned south on Vermont, remembering our last hours together but we didn't know it—I'd changed batteries in the remote, put it in his hand.

"It smells of coffee," he'd said, back hunched in his worn olive wingback chair.

"I made some."

We watched TCM, *The Sundowners* with Deborah Kerr. Sheep farmers, not the world's most exciting flick. But this was the only home I ever knew: me and Herschel and reruns in Technicolor. Yeah—seeing Elkaim stabbed me right in the heart.

I dialed Steam World again. More nothing, the phone rang and rang. I'd have to show up unannounced.

Traffic finally opened up. Washington Boulevard snaked through downtown, then skid row, then it dipped under freeways bathed in decades-old graffiti, curving into a long artery of industrial nothingness. The city outskirts stirred up my already hollow mood—not a body on the streets, not even a homeless tent. Ancient factories lay rusting on giant lots like felled robots, and all the unused train tracks headed nowhere, mourning the Machine Age in the dingy daytime gloom. I passed a truck graveyard crowded with refrigerated big rigs, where all the city's frozen peas bide their time. Where the hell was this place?

The address came into view—a long, low, aluminum Quonset hut sandwiched between two anonymous-looking data processing centers. No windows, but a small, hand-painted wooden plaque out front read STEAM WORLD in old-timey letters. Something ominous fell over me as I got out of the car and stood before the place, but what was I gonna do—go home?

I tried the steel front door. Locked. I knocked hard. Nada.

I stared up and down the lonesome strip.

A Salvadorian man in his early sixties walked backward out of the adjacent lab and onto the street, hosing down the cement walkway. He was short but burly, and his wide arms were flecked with white scars. I'd seen those kind before—hand grenade shrapnel.

I said, "You know the guy that runs this place?"

"I know him."

"You know where he might be?"

"He's usually in there."

I said, "I tried the front door."

The man thumbed his hose and spritzed the hard sidewalk like someone who didn't want to get involved. Then he said, "He prolly can't hear you—bang on the back."

"He have a pitbull back there or anything?"

"Pitbull?" The man laughed. "Naw. He wouldn't want no dog pissin' on his models."

Something about the man's tone gave me the impression that he didn't like Hawley, but I couldn't let that stop me.

I walked around the hut toward the back entrance. A massive ridged-metal curtain painted red was three-quarters open, and two older guys were carefully wheeling out a giant steel table covered with an elaborate miniature—what looked like a chunk of the Palos Verdes Peninsula. The reef came up to my shoulders, a rocky coast sloping down to crumpled vinyl sheets of ocean blue. The details on this model were insane—the pristine lighthouse with gated balcony among swayed trees, unruly fields of green, and white luminous deco mansions, each no bigger than an egg carton. And all along the cliff, a little slatted wooden walkway, winding before the horizon.

I said, "That is awesome."

The men stopped, with blank looks.

"Is Mr. Hawley in there?"

"He took off." The heavier bald guy spoke in a British accent. "Maybe I can help you with something?"

"What time you think he'll be back?"

"Can't help you there."

"Any idea where he went?"

The other guy chimed in. "Think he said he was stopping off at home on the way to the studio."

Hawley's home address was listed at Lobdell Place, deep hills of Echo Park. The house was one-story Spanish, ungated. A mint condition light blue Impala with yellow on black plates was parked in the sloping driveway. Just as I pulled up, a man stormed out of the house, closed the front door behind him, and moved fast to the car. He looked like he was in a panicky rush—I sat there watching, frozen and unnoticed. Had to be Hawley, the baldy from the *Courier* article, tall and gangly in a dark, expensive-looking gray-blue Hawaiian shirt and fit slacks, expensive felt sneakers—the picture of the successful Hollywood man. Yet his gait, his body language, was nervous as fuck. He seemed harried, unapproachable. I thought of coming back later as he got in the Impala, revved the engine, and peeled down the mountain, but then curiosity got the best of me and I hit the ignition and followed, a half-block behind, through the winding, lush Silver Lake streets.

Soon we were onto San Fernando Road, poverty row at the foothills of Glassell Park—fenced bungalows, Mexican supermarkets, autobody repair shops. Hawley pulled up to a taco stand. I circled the block and parked just out of sight, grabbed the binocs from my glove box.

The taco stand looked closed—maybe permanently, I couldn't tell.

A slight, white-haired man sat alone with his hands on his lap, waiting patiently at the umbrella'd plastic bench. As soon as he saw Hawley, the old man stood up abruptly with a pleading look in his eyes. Hawley got out and started doing some pleading of his own. They were arguing now, explaining, gesticulating. Hawley tried to give the old guy an envelope—literally tried to push it onto the guy, but he wasn't having it; it fell to the ground. For a split second there, I thought Hawley might smack him—he tensed up for it— but the old man started to back off, palms up in the air as if to entreat mercy or reason.

Their disagreement, whatever it was, didn't last long. Hawley dropped his long arms. The old man's face colored with determination. He said something final. Soon he was fumbling into his dilapidated gray '96 Toyota Corolla hatchback and not looking at Hawley, who was still staring at the old guy, affronted, shocked immobile. The old guy, for one swift second, shook his head for no one, then turned the key and drove off.

Livid, Hawley picked the envelope up off the ground, then

swiftly kicked the hubcap of his own car, raging full-on. Then he got in behind the wheel and started to cry. He was still in tears as he started the car and drove off.

I followed, too confused to assemble whatever I just saw, but maybe I could use it somehow, approach him at the next junction, ask if he was okay.

Darker clouds rolled in as Hawley rode San Fernando into Burbank, turning onto Alameda. Suddenly, at Cahuenga, he made a fast left and cruised right past the tollbooth into NBC/ Universal Studios with a hand wave.

I pulled up to follow but the security man stepped out with a look of keen displeasure. He didn't like having to leave his cozy booth.

"You got a pass?"

"I'm with the guy that just cruised in. Uh, Mr. Hawley."

"Well, you tell him to call your name in for a drive-on. Otherwise—*vamoose.*"

I nodded and reversed, took one last look at the studio gates. I'd been locked out of the Hollywood gates before—a familiar feeling, not even worth snickering over. Then, as if on cue, the thunder cracked and the rain started to fall in swift diagonals. There was nothing to do but beat it. I pulled out onto Cahuenga and set my windshield wipers in motion.

3

Defeated, I drove back into Hollywood in the pouring rain and turned on the Lyft app, zigzagging the shiny streets looking for a customer. Rainy days in Los Angeles were unpredictable for business. The carless panicked, threw backpacks or freebie newspapers over their heads, uplifted jackets, and raced under marquees praying the alien space invasion would pass. I kept a roll of Bounty up front—my first customer beamed with joy when I handed it to her. I dropped her off at one of the big Century City scrapers, then meandered back to the airport where I caught a young couple heading for the Mondrian on the Strip. They seemed affronted by the weather, like they might write a bad Yelp review if only they could figure out who to blame.

I dropped them off in the causeway and headed east, picked up an old lady coming out of the 99-cent store on Pico with a big, see-through umbrella that she tried to shake out before getting in the car. She wanted me to wait for her in the Vons parking lot while she gathered the week's groceries. I tried to explain that it would be expensive to keep me on the clock, but she pleaded— *"I can never figure out this damn phone!"* Of course, while she shopped, the guilt kicked in and I turned the meter off. Then I took her home and had to shlep the bags upstairs to her apartment. The TV was already on when she opened the door.

"It keeps me company," she said.

Back in the car, I called my sister Maya—technically my cousin, Herschel's daughter.

I said, "You wanna grab lunch?"

"I'm in chambers, waiting on a judge."

"You'll never guess where I just came from."

"Where?"

"Daddy's retirement home."

"It's a bit late for that."

"Not funny. I saw Charles Elkaim."

"Oh good, he called! How'd it go?"

"Not great, he's near the end." I told her the story—pancreatic cancer, visitor Hawley, the big promises, and Elkaim's jittery request.

"That's so sad, Adam. That poor man—still holding on all these years later? *Awful.*"

I said, "I don't know, the whole thing just seems . . . a little futile to me. I mean, what does he hope to get out of all this?"

"Closure, obviously."

"Maya—you think there's even a *chance* Emil was innocent?"

"Welllll . . . he definitely sold weed when we were kids."

"How do you know that?"

"Because we saw him do it."

"I never saw shit."

"You're too young to remember."

"Like maybe once he met someone at the bleachers or something."

"Not *something*—he was a dealer, Adam."

"Maybe. But that doesn't mean he was a murderer."

"No, but dealers deal with crooks. And when you deal with crooks, bad stuff happens."

"But the guy Emil supposedly killed, Durazo, was he a real crook?"

"I don't know. I think they said he was a gangbanger, 18th

Street or White Fence or *I-don't-know-what*. What does Mr. Elkaim want you to do exactly?"

"He's paying me a grand to shake Hawley down, see what's up."

"Adam," she said, suddenly measured, as if addressing judge and jury. "First of all, you're not *shaking* anybody down. Don't do something stupid and lose your one shot at getting licensed."

"Yeah? Maybe you should have thought about that before you gave Elkaim my number."

"Second of all, I don't know how much I like the idea of you taking a terminally ill man's money."

"I *know*, I don't like that either. And I don't *want* to get tangled up in this but—"

"This is Daddy's dearest friend we're talking about—you cannot jump ship."

"I *know that*."

"And he's *dying*. Please don't screw this up, Adam. It's a simple assignment. You talk to this Hawley, you relay whatever information he gives you, you humor Mr. Elkaim—he's practically our family."

"There's that word again."

"What word."

"*Family*. People only ever seem to use it when they want me to do shit I don't want to do."

"And *third*."

"What."

"When we send our pros out on these kinds of things, there's due diligence. You don't just walk in ready to get sandbagged. For all you know, this Hawley person is a raging loon. And, ya know, just *showing up with an outstretched hand* might not be the happy surprise of his day. Oh shoot—judge is here, gotta go."

She hung up and I stared at my phone in sudden disbelief—the grand master of getting my goat got it once again. Leave it to Maya to hand me a performance improvement plan before I even started a job I didn't want in the first place.

But—she had a point.

Before I knew it, I was parking in the underground lot of the downtown public library and crashing through the swinging doors. Up the escalators I rode, into the giant belly of paper knowledge. I pulled out my phone and googled *Hawley movie sets*. An IMDb list came up first, thirty-eight credits under "Art Department." I recognized a few of the flicks. One was a Hugh Jackman thing, *Tokyo Nights*. A few reposts of the *Downtown Courier* article, and under images a handful of press shots of Hawley Junior posing with his crazy city models. But there was very little about the man himself—no Wiki, no website, no bio, no socials. On the very last search page, there was a reference to the March 2014 issue of *PERSPECTIVE: The Journal of the Art Directors Guild*—"Gulliver in Wonderland: The Set Designs of Devon Hawley Jr."

A cute blonde with red glasses held down the desk at Collections. She looked up from some giant yellowing tome. "Can I help you?"

"I'm looking to pull some old mags and newspapers," I said.

"Some of our resources are online, some of it's bound, some of it's in the process of being converted from microfiche."

"Wow," I said. "Microfiche—keeping it real."

She tried to hold back a smile as she closed her book and slipped me a stack of mini-forms and a three-inch pencil.

I filled out my orders—the issue of *PERSPECTIVE* and *LA Herald-Examiner*, Local News January 1983 through December 1988. I was just about to hand them over when I said, "Do you have a system for tracking obituaries?"

"I can search on a name," she said, "but if it's common, you might get back a whole database."

"Let's try." I scribbled *Reynaldo Durazo* on another slip of paper and slid it across the table.

She said, "Give me a few minutes," spun her chair, and walked away nice and smooth. I envied her peace in this high-ceilinged room. All around, across the giant windows, the falling rain made dramatic trails of silver.

Minutes later she came back with a great big bound black book. The word PERSPECTIVE 2014 was embossed on the cover. I thanked her and shlepped it over to a reader's table, thumbed to March. Page thirty-two, a six-page photo spread of some of the incredible, elaborate city miniatures I'd seen, so vivid they looked realer than real. There he was standing among them, the bald, affable creator in another Hawaiian shirt—this one orange—hovering over his mini-world like the sun, holding up a tiny milk truck in a pair of tweezers.

Alongside the photos, they ran a Q and A column.

HAWLEY: It's more than a work style, really. It's a phi-
losophy . . . miniaturism.

PERSPECTIVE: You got a taste for set building very
young, apprenticing with your father.

HAWLEY: I wouldn't call it an apprenticeship, 'cause he
wasn't bossy. And he wasn't exactly a teacher. He was
more of a jack-of-all-trades, my dad.

PERSPECTIVE: But he worked in the art department at
several major studios.

HAWLEY: Sometimes. But when his contracts for Globus
and Paramount ran out, he would do anything. He
sometimes conducted the Steamer trains in Griffith
Park.

PERSPECTIVE: The kiddie train?

HAWLEY: Yup—he wore the hat and everything. Anyway,
they had a mini-town there at the entrance, no bigger

than a baseball mound, but that little town became
my obsession. Then when he saw I dug it, he took me
to Disneyland—we studied the Moby Dick ride, the
Storybook Land canal boats. We rode it over and over.

PERSPECTIVE: Today, with CGI, so many directors are
opting for real-time urban footage. But in addition to
the work you've done for Sam Raimi and Michael Bay,
you still build miniature cities for pleasure.

HAWLEY: That's right. I have a series I'm working on. I
call it The Spirit of Los Angeles 1943 to 1979. It's kind
of a labor of love.

PERSPECTIVE: And it's Hollywood?

HAWLEY: Well, it started as just Hollywood but it's
grown—Chatsworth to Dana Point, Santa Monica to
Palm Springs. And I'm working on adding Pedro, the bay.

PERSPECTIVE: Wow. But this isn't for a shoot?

HAWLEY [LAUGHS]: Not that I know of. I just wanted
to capture . . . not just the design aspects but the . . . the
quietness of city life back then. It was a more serene time,
even when we all thought it was full of noise and action.

PERSPECTIVE: Interesting. Can you say more on that?

HAWLEY: Well, there used to be this wonderful sense, even
in the big city, that life had its moments of solitude. I'm
trying to make a model that captures that feeling.

PERSPECTIVE: Beautiful. Everybody needs to see these!

HAWLEY: Thanks. We aren't exhibiting The Spirit of Los
Angeles just yet . . . but I've been talking to MOCA.
My dream is to expand it into a walk-through installa-
tion that fills a whole museum wing. Like, the greatest
model train you ever saw.

I closed the big book and stared out at the reading room. Two
tables down, a homeless junkie in five layers of dirty black was

nodding off into a copy of *Bon Appétit*, mesmerized by the food porn. The world's greatest model train—it all seemed so painfully innocent, from this man I'd just seen weeping in his car. He was sentimental. Deeply.

And maybe he did know something about Emil Elkaim.

I went back to the desk and gave the librarian back her book.

"Nothing too exciting?" she said.

"You said it."

She reached under the desk and brought out a square blue bucket with twelve small plastic-lidded film cannisters. "You know how to work the machine?"

"Better if you show me," I said. "I'd hate to mess one of these things up."

She took me to the far end of the room with six old-fashioned-looking blue microfiche gizmos, each with their own private station. I took a seat and fumbled with the spool. She leaned in to help, close enough for us to exchange awkward smiles.

"You turn the wheel like this," she said, reaching over me.

"What *will* they think of next?"

"That's a lot of *Herald-Examiner*," she said. "You looking for something specific."

"You wouldn't believe me if I told you."

"Try me."

"I'm a detective, investigating a murder that took place in the early eighties."

A little skeptical, she said, "Good luck, Sherlock," and walked away, stealing my gaze.

Then I faced the music. I started turning the spools slowly, in search of the killing of Reynaldo Durazo on April 7, 1984, followed by the slaying of Emil Elkaim in prison and the disappearance and death of Cynthia Persky. With every crank of the wheel, the past glowed up in illuminated black and white, stories about the upcoming Olympics, the space shuttle

Discovery, Michael Jackson's hair going up in flames—and then I hit pay dirt.

. . . the high school–aged Latino was reported to have sold narcotics to . . .
. . . nicknamed "Rey-Rey" by his street gang . . .
. . . was heard to call out the notorious gang provocation, "Where you from?" . . .
. . . neighbors called in the incident at approximately 11:00 p.m. . . .
. . . officer on duty examining the crime scene noted . . .
. . . the weapon, discovered in the trunk of the teen's MG, revealed traces . . .
. . . the victim's parents have openly condemned . . .
. . . Police Chief Gates calls for expedient . . .

My pulse quickened. I picked up the pace. One spool later:

LA HERALD-EXAMINER, JUNE 17, 1984
EMIL ELKAIM, PRIMARY SUSPECT IN
DURAZO SLAYING, KILLED AT MEN'S CENTRAL
. . . at a time when the California Department of Corrections is under scrutiny from the U.S. Department of Justice, the circumstances surrounding the 18-year-old's death provide yet another stark portrait of the inadequate staffing, policies, and . . .

And then, with a turn of the wheel, that was it—two lives, gone in a flash, without an afterthought.

I spooled on, hoping for something, anything. More Olympics, "Council Dilutes Workplace Smoking Law," Ronnie Reagan giving the thumbs-up. Then it slammed me:

LA HERALD-EXAMINER, NOVEMBER 21, 1984
CHEVIOT HILLS RUNAWAY STILL MISSING.

Cynthia Persky, the young woman who went missing shortly after a fatal altercation in her parents' backyard in April, has not been found, according to the office of Police Chief Daryl Gates. She was last seen wearing dark jeans, a light-colored blouse with long sleeves, and white sneakers. If you have any information concerning this person, please contact your local FBI office or the nearest American Embassy or Consulate.

My heart skipped two beats and I scrolled forward, frantic, like someone racing to the end of a scary dream, and then, three spools later:

LA HERALD-EXAMINER, NOVEMBER 26, 1987
CHEVIOT HILLS RUNAWAY, DEAD AT 21

Cynthia Persky, the local teenager who fled her home after a murder took place in her parents' backyard in spring of 1984, has been found dead of a heroin overdose in Mendocino County. Called "Cinnamon" by family and friends, she is survived by parents Herbert and Marjorie Persky.

Behind the microfiche light was her photo, the Cinnamon I knew, a doe-eyed beauty of the eleventh grade with skin as pale as winter sunlight, a straight-haired redhead whose freckles seemed to float in the ether of her rosy cheeks, and all at once, it came back to me in a rush, our day at Disneyland. Emil's beat-up MG Roadster broke down about fifteen minutes outside Anaheim, and after much tinkering, we only entered the park in the very late afternoon, just as a light rain started to fall. Disneyland was otherworldly under wet gray skies, near empty, with half the rides shuttered. Maya and I couldn't care less—we were in the presence of the Golden Teens and every minute was paradise. I couldn't remember what rides we rode, but I remember Cin's warm smile under the Tomorrowland awning as she held my hand, her laugh when Emil went goofing off with some dancing Mickey Mouse in a see-through plastic poncho. She loved him so, she—

Then another memory flashed—that night, almost home. Just before they dropped us off, Emil said he had to run a quick errand, meet some guys near the high school, it would only take a minute. Now, Cinnamon, Maya, and I sat in the MG and watched as Emil exchanged some bags and some cash. Just who was paying and who was buying wasn't clear, but when he got back in the car, he turned to us and said, "We don't need to talk about this to my parents—or yours."

I looked around the vast, quiet library. Outside the big windows, the rain was falling steady. Something told me to keep scrolling, desperation or a hunch. And then:

LA HERALD-EXAMINER OBITUARIES
DECEMBER 10, 1988
HERBERT ALFRED PERSKY, STUDIO EXEC WHO TWICE RAN FOR CITY COUNCIL, IS DEAD AT 62

Herbert Alfred Persky, the Columbia Tri-Star CEO who was responsible for dozens of Hollywood's most popular "teensploitation" films, has died of a massive coronary. He is survived by his wife, Marjorie Persky.

I clicked off the whirring machine and pulled out my cell phone. A Google run on Marjorie Persky coughed up an Intelius page—she was seventy-eight and still the listed owner at 2825 Medill Place, scene of the crime. Something about the street name hit me funny and then I scrolled back on the phone.

Goosebumps.

Devon Hawley Junior had two listings—Steam World Studios in Commerce, and the pad on Lobdell in Echo Park.

But Devon Hawley *Senior* lived at 2821 Medill Place, two houses over from Marjorie Persky.

A chill passed over me, juiced by the LAPL heaters. Devon Hawley Senior, eighty-six, lived kitty-corner to Marjorie Persky, Cinnamon's mom.

They were next-door neighbors.

That meant maybe—no, *likely*—Devon Hawley *Junior* grew up across the street from Cinnamon. And if he did, he had to know her. And if he knew her, he knew Emil too.

Forty years later—he shows up out of the blue. *"I can prove he's innocent."*

I checked my watch—it was almost 4:30. I'd let the day get away. With just an hour of daylight left, there was no reason not to drive to Medill Place, see it for myself.

I got up and was about to leave when I remembered the Durazo obit. I went back to the desk. The librarian was scrolling her database with a pout on her cute mug.

"I'm really sorry," she said. "Amazed to say there's not one single Reynaldo Durazo obituary in our whole system."

We exchanged a knowing look: nobody'd written one. They'd effectively wiped him out of human history.

4

It was just before nightfall when I arrived at Medill Place—the yellow diamond DEAD END sign hit me funny. I parked on the curve of the cul-de-sac and got out. The rains had slowed but the sky was still silver. Three midcentury sprawls faced each other. Number 2825 on the right was the biggest. White curtains hung in the two big windows over a two-car garage, with twin staircases that wrapped around either side to the double front doors. Two of everything—even the bell ding-donged twice. A housemaid wearing earbuds opened the big doors and turned off her vacuum cleaner with a keen look of interruption. She yanked out an earbud long enough for me to ask for Mrs. Persky.

"Is she expecting you?"

"Nope—but she'll want to speak with me."

It was a bit of wishful thinking and the maid seemed to know it. She disappeared and Marjorie Persky came in from the open-air kitchen with guarded curiosity and a crossword magazine in her hand. She was striking for seventy-eight—even the pearl granny glasses dangling from her neck were part come-on.

"How can I help you?"

"I'm sorry to intrude like this, Mrs. Persky, but your phone number's not listed. My name's Adam, ma'am. I'm an investigator working for Charles Elkaim."

"Oh." The name chilled her. "How is Charles?"

"Not that great," I said. "He's getting up there . . . and he may not have much time."

"What can one say. When it's one's time, it's one's time." She spoke sternly, but her face fought the natural veer toward empathy. "And what do you expect I can do for you and Mr. Elkaim?"

"That's a good question," I said. "Truth is, I'm not sure. Right now, I'm just trying to get a better sense of . . . what happened here."

"Murder happened here," she snapped. "Right here on my property, thirty-eight years ago. And it destroyed my family."

I wanted to tell her that I'd met her daughter—long ago. That we'd gone to Disneyland in another lifetime. That she was my first monster little boy crush. But I knew it would make me sound like a crazy person.

"I do know that, Mrs. Persky, I—"

"Well then, what on earth gave you the gall to come here?" Her voice went shrill all at once. "You do also know my daughter is dead?"

The maid reentered and shot her boss a concerned glance.

"I'm *fine*, Alba. Please give us some privacy." Alba smiled a fake one and split—Mrs. Persky watched her like a general. The commanding allure of these older broads tumbled by the Hollywood machine was a force to be reckoned with. "Now. What does Charles Elkaim want from me?"

"Mrs. Persky," I said, "please don't hold my visit against Mr. Elkaim. This wasn't his idea."

"I don't blame Charles for what befell *all* of us—*Adam*. But I certainly don't have any comfort to offer him."

"Maybe it's not comfort he's looking for," I said. "If you ask me, I think he's desperate to let go."

A wry, wicked smile crept over her face. "So he's having trouble letting go, is he?"

I nodded. I'd touched a nerve.

"Let me show you something, young man. Come, follow me."

Mrs. Persky led me through the house, past the ancient living room with its polished black piano resting alongside an easel with a blank canvas. She flicked her magazine onto the couch as we passed.

"Do you play?" I said.

"Rarely," she said with restrained malice.

I followed her up a curving white staircase and down a white hall. We came to a door covered in big pink and baby blue dots.

"Here's the last of my pretty Cinnamon—same as the day she left us. *That* is called not letting go."

She opened the door and we stepped inside a shrine to pop art, blazing with color. Posters of Lichtenstein's *Drowning Girl* and Peter Max's butterfly and Brian Jones of the Rolling Stones handing a child a balloon covered the walls. One corner over the bed was a crazy makeshift collage of pages torn from *Vogue* and *Cosmo*, but all from the sixties—Twiggy, Jean Shrimpton, Catwoman, Mary Ann from *Gilligan*. And interspersed with the slinky models were covers torn off a comic book called *Little Dot Dot-Land*, a little girl pouring polka-dot maple syrup over polka-dot pancakes, taking a polka-dot bath, walking in the polka-dot rain. On the lime-green bureau sat a polka-dot box of 45s and a rinky-dink one-piece Fidelity record player.

As if reading my mind, Mrs. Persky said, "I know, strange for a child of her generation. But my daughter loved vintage fashion. She was absolutely *obsessed* with the nineteen sixties."

"Maybe because you were her age in the sixties."

"I don't think so." She scanned me for sensitivity. "Cynthia was born to the wrong era. Like her father."

"How do you mean?"

"Herbert was a *homosexual*." She enunciated the word with a kind of clinical accuracy. "He wouldn't come out. But everyone around him knew it. Certainly I knew it, and I did everything I could to make him understand it didn't matter. But, after a lifetime of hiding in his own skin, he lost his baby girl and his heart couldn't take it. My husband quite literally died of heart failure."

"And you? How have you managed to survive?"

"I found strengths I never knew I had. And I come here—to spend time with her spirit. We . . . communicate. I know that sounds a bit odd but it's true."

Mrs. Persky pushed a chair away from the rolltop desk and dragged out a medium-sized scratched-up red trunk. I caught a glimpse out the window: the backyard was green, pastoral, the pool slim and clean, but that's where the papers said the dirty deed went down. *Murder by bludgeoning.* She took a blue ceramic pitcher off the desk, shook out a key, and opened the trunk.

"I certainly hope you aren't expecting to solve any crimes," she said. "Emil paid the price for what he did. And if there was anything here that constituted a clue, the police would have found it years ago."

"Police can make mistakes," I said feebly.

She ignored the remark. "Did Charles tell you that my husband engaged lawyers to help Emil when he got arrested?"

"He didn't mention that."

"Of course not, why would he? They accomplished nothing— they never got a chance. But, okay. If Charles thinks he has the courage to rip open the old wounds, more power to him."

I almost mentioned Hawley's visit—then I thought better of it. "I guess Mr. Elkaim wants to give it one last try—you know, to prove his son's innocence."

"He's punishing himself," she said. "It's the punishment he really craves."

I knelt to the trunk and tried to stave off disappointment—there wasn't much. Ten or twelve LPs. Iron Butterfly, *Something New* by the Beatles, the soundtrack to *Mary Poppins*. A little lime-green Easy-Bake Oven with the metal part rusted over. A stuffed gray rabbit with blue button eyes. A folded faded pink taffeta dress, a pair of little girl's black patent leather tap shoes, and a pair of cream leather gloves that used to be white—the little leather bluebirds sewn into the palms were losing their stitching. There were also three super-old copies of *Teen Magazine*, all midsixties. The articles they promised on the covers had the afterglow of dark premonition: "Demon Eyes—For the Devilish You"; "Root of It All—Hair Color Hints"; "Promises Promises"; "Keeping Secrets"; and "Report from Death Row: A Condemned Man Reflects on His Teen Years." There was also a copy of a rock magazine called *Flipside* from 1981 or 1982 with some kids holding a picture of Manson on the cover, and tucked inside the mag was a flyer for *Mod Night at the Bullet Club*. The address was Argyle, off Hollywood Boulevard. A band called The Unknowns was going to play; tickets were three dollars.

"She was quite the collector," I said.

Mrs. Persky winced. "I'm not sure Cynthia intended to save all this. She merely left it behind." She lifted a glove, considered it. "By the time my baby ran away, her childhood was already long gone." Her words had the odd, scripted quality of someone who has repeated a confession to herself a thousand times. I wanted to press against her comfort zone, crack open the truth. But you can't bully your way to candor.

I said, "Mr. Elkaim gave me the impression that Cynthia was . . . not really some crazy runaway. He said she was really a very good girl."

"She was too good. And too *knowing*."

"Yeah?"

"Yes, unquestionably." She sat herself in the desk chair. She was relaxing around me in little increments.

"What did she know, exactly?"

"What kind of a marriage her parents had, how terribly restless I was. *Now* I understand that it shut her down—having a mother so . . . *wanton*." She said the word flat, without guilt or boast. She idly picked up the bunny rabbit, touched his blank button eyes. "But when she was here . . . I didn't *see* her, not really. And so she did what any invisible person *should* do, she ran. But I still didn't grasp how badly her heart was broken— I . . . I had to identify her body, up north. It was only then that I understood how badly I had failed her." Then, as if waking from a hazy dream, she turned to me and said, "Young man, just what is it you are trying to figure out?"

"Mrs. Persky, *why* do you think Emil Elkaim killed Reynaldo Durazo? I mean, are you sure he did?"

"I didn't see it happen. But I would be lying if I said it was impossible. It's taken me years to admit that—because I adored Emil."

"Really."

"Absolutely. Emil was *marvelous*. He was just what this house needed. He was *all life*. Health. Vigor. Even Herb could not deny—he was infectious." Again, there was something not quite spontaneous in her tone, and she sensed that I sensed it. "If you want to know the truth," she went on, "I think all three of us were a little bit in love with him. Well, *she* was madly in love with him. But Herbie and I each were crazy for him in our way too." She smiled for the first time, almost blushed at the memory. I surged with the desire to tell her I agreed, but she was on a roll. "Oh, Emil was a mess. *Sometimes* he wore shoes, sometimes he couldn't be bothered. Sometimes his hair was combed back, sometimes it was all over his face like a shaggy dog. He knew immediately that my husband was different—and he didn't care one bit. He was utterly without judgment. He flirted with me, too. Wildly."

"Not too fun for Cinnamon."

"That's what *you* think, but she loved it. Because he was *hers*, totally. Believe me, for all my faults—and I was never a saint—I wouldn't have dared steal her happiness."

I didn't remark that somebody did.

"How about Durazo," I said, "the victim?"

She shrugged the apologetic shrug of progressives. "*I didn't know him.* Later, of course, I learned he was a troubled boy." And then, conspiratorially, she added: "Is it possible to be sixteen and not be troubled?"

"Sure, but . . . did Emil have any kind of reason to kill him?"

"I can't imagine. I still get letters from the victim's cousin—she's a professor at UCLA, a very persistent woman."

"Letters about what?"

"Well, she wants the police department to reopen the case, of course. As if that's going to bring back our loved ones." With this, Mrs. Persky bent and reached under the folded sweaters and miniskirts and pulled out an old purple lock diary. "Here," she said. "The pièce de résistance."

"Do you have a key for this?" I said.

"It's been broken for years. Open it."

No words, just sketches—cat-eyed teen girls in miniskirts and mod poses.

"Not a very scintillating read I'm afraid," Mrs. Persky said. "But teenage girls *are* like cats. They feel things but they don't know why. They purr. But they haven't yet got the words." She shot me a deep look, loaded with pain. "Some of them never find the words."

"You're talking about Cinnamon."

"In this house? She never got the chance to find her voice."

"But you don't blame yourself?"

"Of course I do. Her father and I gave her a *show*. Today, everything would be different. Today, we could let her *in*, let her know we knew what she knew and—"

"Okay, but that's not the reason she ran away."

"Isn't it? Her boyfriend was the only piece of reality she'd found. And his family took her in. Why do you think she was hooked? Emil was real—and they were a real family, probably warm and loving in ways Herbert and I could never be. From the day she fell in love with him she just *transformed*. She was alive as I'd never seen her before. And when she lost him, I knew she would lose them too, it was inevitable. I told her, '*Cynthia, nobody will ever look at you the same again—especially not Emil's parents.*'" Mrs. Persky tugged at her granny glasses, checked herself. She had opened up more than she intended. "I don't mean to be rude, but I'm attending a book club this evening. I've got to be on my way—"

As she stood, I shuffled quick through the LPs one last time in a cursory way—*Mary Poppins*, Beatles, *Brahm's Concerto No. 1*, the Bangles, Ian & Sylvia *Four Strong Winds*. The last record caught my eye—RAINBO TEST PRESSING. A white label—all caps in faded Sharpie:

> Customer: THE DAILY TELEGRAPH
> Title: DEL CYD
> Comments: PIONEER RECORDS
> Date: 11/14/83

"What's this?" I asked.

She shook her head, impatient. "I have no idea."

The cardboard sleeve was worn, slightly burned at one end,

like someone had leaned the LP against an electric heater—a toasted relic.

"Was your daughter in a band?"

"No," she said. "But I believe Emil might have been."

"He was?"

"Yes, but—you know, just high school boys. I don't think they made a record."

"Do you know who else might have been in the band?"

She made a lemon face. "It's been thirty-five years."

I had been holding back all afternoon, but I came out with it. "Do you know the Hawleys—your neighbors across the way?"

She glazed over, raised an eyebrow. "Sure, but we've never been close. Now look, I don't want to be rude. But I really must go. Alba will let you out."

Marjorie Persky took off down the stairs and I followed, with Alba closing the door behind me. Mrs. Persky moved swiftly into her champagne Lexus and exited the cul-de-sac in a rushed three-point turn. I was halfway to my car when I got an idea, turned around, and knocked on the door.

"Alba—*so* sorry, I left my cell phone upstairs."

She nodded and I made the dash. Once up in Cinnamon's room, I quickly tore off my jacket and pulled the test pressing from the trunk, wrapped it under my arm and skipped down the stairs and out the door.

As I hustled to the car, LP under my arm, I glanced back at the Hawley residence—a gent in his eighties was watering the lawn, could've been Hawley Senior. He was trim, clean-shaven, with the crystal blue eyes and wry jaw of an aging male model, waving his spritzing hose over the grass with regal self-amusement. But as he watched me get into the Jetta, his lids grew heavy and he tightened up.

Whoever I was, he did not like me.

5

Fourteen rides in four hours—the rains had stopped and the evening shift breezed by, working the hotels along Pacific Coast Highway. All the while, the LP in the trunk was tickling at my conscience. I had a wave of regret about yanking it and getting in deeper, but now that I had it, I had to at least listen to it once. There was just one problem: I didn't own a record player and I racked my brain about who did. The only person I could think of was my sometimes ride Ziva, a painter who lived off Crescent Heights on the Westside. I knew the record player because she'd once insisted that I come in and listen to her favorite vibraphonist. The music had been superfast, almost comical, but Ziva said, "Isn't it relaxing?"

I knocked on the door to her small cottage and to my surprise a beautiful young woman with auburn hair falling over her shoulders cracked it open—her crystal blue doe eyes almost made me lose my bearings.

"Hi . . . is Ziva here?"

"Can I tell her what it's about?"

"I'm Adam. I'm her Lyft driver."

"She didn't tell me she was going anywhere."

"No, no, I . . ." I lifted the LP, held it like a shield. "I want to see if I can borrow her record player for an hour."

The young woman gave me a curious look. "And you're her *Lyft* driver?"

"Well—" I smiled. "We're friends, too."

"Okay, one sec."

"Are you Ziva's granddaughter?"

"No."

"New tenant?"

"Not exactly, I'm her caregiver. Let me ask her . . ." She hesitated, then gently closed the door in my face and I heard the lock turn. Fair enough.

A few minutes later she opened the door and said, "She'll see you in the back house."

I made my way through the living room past the little kitchen. I'd only been over a handful of times before but felt strangely at home here in this elf bungalow. Ziva's husband had died about seven years before and he'd been an electrician, a Black guy from Baltimore—you could still feel his presence in the old-school light fixtures, the high stack of soul LPs, the driftwood coffee table he sanded down smooth. Ziva once told me *"He was my world, my everything,"* but he must've been pretty long-suffering, too, because even before her accident, she had to have been a handful. Ziva was one of those Spanish-speaking Jewesses whose parents fled the Nazis and landed in Argentina. In Ziva's art, her cooking, her disposition, she was a real *porteño*—Buenos Aires born and bred—but past that she was a balabosta all the way, wildly affectionate and high-strung, too generous and too demanding, cynical, outspoken, and very protective of her painting life. Her closest friends called her Lady Blunt.

This caregiver was not her first lodger. It was a curious arrangement. Ziva lived in the guesthouse of her own home, just three feet out the back door, with the deal that visitors could come through the main house. There was never any chance that she'd disturb the tenants—Ziva was paraplegic from the waist down—my trickiest rider. I'd hoist her into shotgun and toss her folded chair in the trunk. She'd had a terrible freeway accident in the midnineties and hadn't walked since. This didn't keep her from her life's work, though. The old master slept under a thick bungee cord with dozens of paintbrushes attached by hangwires. A special bed-friendly easel had been built by a carpenter who admired her work. At the end of each night, or sometimes at the stroke of dawn when she was done with her day's painting, she'd yank a black-tasseled rope and all the color-tipped brushes would crowd at the far end of the room like scurrying trapeze artists.

I came to her open door, LP in hand. From under the home-stitched comforter on her king-sized bed, she glared at a canvas with impetuous fury. Ziva was no charity case and no hobbyist. She'd been written up in *Artforum* and had solo and group shows around the world. Many nights a week, friends and students gathered for one of her bedside salons, to pour her chardonnay and hear her soliloquize on Love, Death, Art, God—all the biggies. Tonight she was alone.

"Knock, knock," I said. "Hi, young lady—I hope I'm not disturbing."

"Adam." The look of shock dissipated off her face. "I was lost in paint. I didn't recognize you."

"God forbid you dozed. It's practically midnight."

"So what," she said. "Push the wheelchair, let me heat you some leftovers."

"Please, don't move—I'm beat. I just wanted to see if I could borrow your record player for an hour."

"To play what?"

"This thing. What are you painting?"

"I'm not, that's the problem. I'm *conceptualizing*. And I just wasted half the day having a tantrum about a wrinkled canvas."

"It's the humidifier. You've got it on full blast."

"Yeah well, *I'm* on full blast. A nuisance to everyone who dares get near me."

The beauty appeared in the door behind me. "Everything okay?"

Ziva said, "Better than okay—Endi Sandell, this is Adam Zantz. He is very dear to me. Will you heat him the cauliflower latkes and—"

"No, no," I said, "really, it's okay. I just want to give this thing a spin. I'm sorry for the late intrusion."

Ziva propped herself up. "Adam understands me; we're night owls. Isn't that right, Adam? You two kids listen to your crazy music. I have to get back to this."

"Goodnight, Ziva."

On the way back into the house, I said, "Endi? Is that like *the end*?"

"Initials—for Nechama Dina. Kind of a mouthful."

"Are you from Israel?"

"No, Far Rockaway."

"Raised orthodox?"

"Conservadox."

"Ah," I said, "my best friend is observant."

"Yeah? Me, not so much." She pointed at the old Pioneer turntable. "You know how to work that thing?"

I smiled. "I do. You sure I won't be disturbing you?"

"Not at all. What is it?"

"I . . . uh . . . it's a test pressing from the early eighties . . . for a record that never came out. The Daily Telegraph."

"Cute—never heard of 'em."

"I don't think anybody did."

"Are you, like, a collector or something?"

"Me? No, I'm—" I scrambled for a fib. "I was asked to write about them . . . for this British mag."

She said, "Cool."

I wasn't exactly sure why I was lying, but it was bad enough being a penniless Lyft driver, I didn't also have to announce that I was the fake Sherlock Holmes. As I pulled the wax out, a yellowed cutout slip of newspaper fluttered to the floor. She bent to pick it up and we marveled at it together. A photoless ad for the Natural Fudge on Fountain Avenue, listings for the week of July 13–19, 1982. There they were in the Wednesday slot, The Daily Telegraph, opening for someone who called himself Bill the Balloon Man.

"They opened for a comic," I said.

"That's weird," she said. "Usually the comics open for the bands."

"Totally," I said.

"Maybe these guys were a joke," she said. "Like, even to themselves."

She handed me the slip of newspaper and was about to walk away when she spotted a Little Martin acoustic guitar on the couch and picked it up with one hand.

I said, "You play that thing?"

She gave me a droll look and didn't answer, retreated to her room and closed the door.

Alone now in the tiny living room, I placed the vinyl on the platter and lifted the needle gently onto side one. I turned the big volume knob on the amplifier down to three, just in case it was really gnarly, but the music came on rinky-dink, a rickety attempt at a sixties kind of guitar pop, with tinny little reverb guitar splashes and a simple riff that looped and looped. They were garage amateurs, for sure. But the words were eerie, mystical, heartfelt.

Runaway sunshine
Through the dangling trees

'Cross the morning breeze
It's callin' out to you, there's nothing you can do
You can never ever catch
the runaway sunshine

Whatever it was, I liked it. Song by song, I floated on the rocky
waves of garage-y teenage sound—you could practically hear
the guitar cables snapping into the buzzing Sears amps. I didn't
know what instrument Emil played or if this was really even
his band. But the songs were real songs, a little spooky, imper-
fect harmonies cascading with intense emotion, and I couldn't
tell if it was because of the passage of time or the murder in the
backyard or the late hour of night or because they *meant* it that
way, this spooky-ookiness from Cinnamon's trunk in the land
of brightly colored dot-to-dots. Just before the third song, Endi
passed through the room, stopped, and smiled.

"They can barely hold it together," I said apologetically.

"Yeah . . . but . . . yet, they kinda *do*. It's good. Turn it up." I
did, and she backed into the funky old lounge chair and curled
up on it and we listened together. I was grateful for the company.

Polka dot princess in the land of nod (ahhhh ahhhh
ahhhh)
She's got a little dot that's a line to God (ahhhh ahhhh
ahhhh)
Princess fair don't lead me on
Tell me when you're coming on
We'll ride a battleship into the dawn, oh yeahhhh

Our eyes met. Endi said, "Wow," and we burst out laughing.

When side one came to an end she said, "Ziva has some
wine in the fridge if you want."

I said, "Sounds great," and I got up to go pour some glasses.

When I came back, Endi had crossed the room and was kneeling on the couch, flipping the wax back and forth, tilting the vinyl to the dim orange lamplight.

"What, scratched?" I said.

"No, no. You know how they engrave things into the run-out groove?"

"The what?"

"*You* know, the glossy band right before the label."

"Oh, that thing? Show me."

"See. This is awesome, look—" I leaned in but not too close and squinted over her shoulder. "T-D-T-4-3-V-3-R" she said. "The Daily Telegraph forever."

"Wow. You're right."

Then she flipped the LP. "But check out the other side."

It read LAZERBEAM scratched in all caps next to a string of numbers.

"Maybe a serial number," I said.

"No, read it." She handed me the vinyl. I held it under the bulb: Lazerbeam 0 0 0 1 2 1 3 6 6 0 2 8 9 5 0 0 0.

"That's not a serial number," she said. "That's a 213 phone number."

"Holy moly," I said. "You might be right. Should I call it?"

"Maybe not this late."

Side two was one long track—a strange, creaky psychedelic jam-out that sent Endi to dreamland with her hands on her lap and her wine glass still half full on the table. Quiet as a mouse, I let myself out with The Daily Telegraph's freaky magnum opus under my arm.

6

I woke in my studio apartment with Endi's laughing smile on my mind, but the reverie was broken by the crinkle of the envelope I'd stuffed under my pillow—Elkaim's cold hard cash. With a heave I sat up and groped for the cell. I was living in the upstairs storage space of Santiago Sound Labs, now complete with futon bed, mini-fridge, hot plate, and a rolling rack of clothes—my wardrobe didn't quite fill the thing. One little window overlooked a three-space parking lot, but it caught the morning sun. I dialed Steam World. After one ring, a man answered. "Yallo."

"Hi, wow, somebody there—finally—can I speak to Devon Hawley?"

"That's me."

"Howdy, hi—my name's Adam, I'm a friend of Charles Elkaim. From the retirement home?"

"Oh man, so glad you called, hold on a sec." His voice was friendly, relaxed, and for a flash I felt a little guilty about having spied on him. "Man," he went on, "I felt *sooo* bad about standing Charles up—I did phone the nursing home a couple times but they said he was busy and then, you know . . . I just wanted to get my ducks in a row before bothering him again."

"Your ducks? You mean, like, about Emil?"

A pause. Then: "Did you know Charles's son?"

"I grew up across the street."

"Oh. Wow. Well—why don't you come by the studio. I'm on a deadline, but I should be finishing up by five or six."

I said, "I'd love that," then I made a thing of taking down the address even though I already knew where it was. Energized, I dressed, started the coffee, and nuked a breakfast burrito. Watching it spin in the microwave, I got a notion and pulled out the vinyl, held it to the sunlight. Then I dialed the number in the run-out groove. A man's squeaky voice answered.

Create new paragraph, beginning with "Collectibles....." "Collectibles." Create new paragraph, beginning with "Hi....."

"Hi. Is this . . . *Lazerbeam*?"

Some kind of rattling, pots and pans. Then: "Who is this?"

"My name's Adam. I'm interested in learning about The Daily Telegraph."

"How'd you get my number?"

"There's this test pressing I found, I—"

A woman's voice started raging in the background. "I *told* you I need the *goddamn* phone!"

"Hey, man, uh, I'm kinda strapped right now," he said. "Why don't you fall by after lunch."

"Where are you?"

"Centinela Trailer Court. Tell ya all about it."

Two appointments booked before breakfast—maybe this gig would be easier than I thought.

I planned to work a six-hour Lyft shift, but by 11:00 I found myself back at the Shalom Terrace Retirement Home, with its mustard carpets and wall-fastened Purells. I was eager to share the good news. Charles Elkaim wasn't in his room, so I asked the nurse at reception where he might be and followed her to the rec room sing-along. Elkaim was hunched in a chair, playing his Casio, accompanying a singing guitarist, a handsome square-jawed entertainer guy in his fifties, a real leading-man type. Together, they led the wheelchair-bound through a heart-crushing rendition of "The First Time Ever I Saw Your Face," with everyone singing in about eight different keys. The guitarist kind of waltzed around the long table, strumming his pristine sunburst Martin acoustic with a twinkle in his eye, crooning person-to-person, trying to cheer up the dying with melody, and it worked. Big smiles on their upturned, yodeling gray faces—they adored him. When Elkaim saw me with the nurse, he pushed the keyboard aside and reached for his walker. I hated to interrupt—all eyes followed us out into the hallway.

One thing about these places: they drew very few visitors . . . a lot less than you'd think.

I said, "I'm sorry to interrupt, Mr. Elkaim, I won't be more than a minute."

I helped him to a yellow couch by a glass birdcage. Inside, trapped little finches darted around on hanging wooden swings. "Have you brought news?"

"*Good* news," I said. "I'm going to see Devon Hawley this evening. At his studio downtown. I thought you might want to come along."

His lip trembled; he considered the birds. "No," he said, "no, you go without me. The journey is too much. Whatever this man has to say, I will hear it from you."

"Okay," I said, "understood. I'll try to bring back a full report. There's one other thing, Mr. Elkaim, I was just wondering . . ."

"Tell me, *nu*."

"Was Emil in a band?"

"A band?"

"Like, you know—a musical group."

"I don't think so. He played his guitar with friends, but they were kids. Then again, he certainly didn't share everything with me. A teenager is like this."

"Okay," I said. "Anyway, not important. Now please, let me get you back to the singing. I hate to keep you from what you love."

"No, no. I don't feel like music anymore." He stood and grabbed the walker. "Help me to my room. I must rest."

"What about your keyboard?"

"Leave it. The entertainment director will bring it to me later."

We clambered down the hall in half-time. As we turned a corner, a bearded man in his thirties approached. Elkaim introduced him as Rabbi Peretz. He was an odd duck—stocky but almost effeminate in a bolo tie and monkish curly hair around his dome. I hated to be cynical about these people that made a career out of acts of kindness, but it was hard to picture this guy anywhere else but here.

"Rabbi," Elkaim said with great official pride, "this is Mr. Adam Zantz. I have known him since he was a child. He is like a son to me. And now he has volunteered to help me get my affairs in order."

The rabbi shot me a skeptical smile and said, "Very good" but his hard eyes had the faint air of disapproval, like he saw *me* as the scam artist.

"It's my honor to *volunteer*," I said, "and that's why I can't accept Mr. Elkaim's pay." I dug for the envelope in my pocket, but Elkaim stopped me.

"Don't insult me," he said. "The money is for expenses."

Rabbi Peretz took it all in. The skeptical smile didn't budge. Elkaim kept moving and I helped him into his room. He sat on the bed and poured himself water from a brown-and-white plastic pitcher. He asked me to turn on the television—channel 4.2, COZI-TV, *The Rifleman*. Chuck Connors was talking to an Indian boy, with captions. Elkaim was asleep inside five minutes.

As I made my way out, I took one last peek into the rec room—the handsome entertainer was solo now, giving it his all, leading the geriatric gang through "Sing a Song," by The Carpenters. My belly tightened again—one of Uncle Hersch's favorites. I could picture him sitting there, humming along in that low croak of his, rumbling under the squealing crowd like a man in prayer. I couldn't always picture my dead uncle, but I pictured him in this instant, in his last days, singing alone among strangers.

And I'd barely visited him.

Too late now, schmuck.

With a few hours to kill, I decided to visit Emil's grave. I looked him up on FamilySearch.org. He was out at Home of Peace in Whittier. Herschel was buried there too—where I didn't know, and didn't want to know.

Down through East LA I drove, past *lavanderias* and *ferreterias* and a movie marquee announcing that *JESUCRISTO ES EL SEÑOR*. Then—the long brick wall. I turned right, passing under the high metal gates. Inside, the place was empty, silent, palms shimmering among the tombs. I parked beside the only other car, a black Chrysler Pacifica with the strange tilted metal *S*, the modern Hearse. In the hazy, gloomy noon light, I hoofed it northeast reading the names along the way—Katzenelson, Greener, Wise—a quarter-mile of dead Jews, but no Herschel Berman. I was grateful for that. Then I came to two markers in the grass, side by side.

EMIL ELKAIM   CYNTHIA "CINNAMON" PERSKY
אמיל אלקים   BELOVED DAUGHTER
MARCH 28, 1966–JUNE 16, 1984   MAY 31, 1966–NOVEMBER 20, 1987

I almost lost a heartbeat when I saw it—sweethearts, together forever.

7

Early afternoon I parked across from Centinela Trailer Court in Inglewood, a jammed lot of thirty-odd mobile homes guarded by a fence any junior high schooler could hop. At the opening of the gate, under a ratty orange beach umbrella, an elderly Black man in a blue windbreaker sat on a low stool, flipping through a glossy real estate freebie without irony.

"What can I help you with today?" he said, mock official.

"You ever hear about a guy who lives around here that calls himself Lazerbeam?"

He smirked. "I ought to—I'm security of this property." Then: "You a bill collector?"

I said, "No. He get a lot of those?"

His smile was a yes. "You can hear his wife hollerin' about it twenty-four seven."

"Where can I find them?"

"Eleven and twelve, on the right."

I nodded and he scooted to let me through. He wasn't much of a guard, but then again, who'd want to rob a decrepit trailer park? I moseyed on down the dirt road in the midday heat, counting tin homes. As I approached #11 I heard AM radio blasting, KSRF—"My Little Runaway." Had to be the place. I knocked and the music cut all at once. A door cracked and a voluptuous older woman in a light purple terry cloth bathrobe popped her head out.

She sized me up. "What can I do for ya?"

I said, "Does . . . *Lazerbeam* live here?"

She burst into a cackle, her stringy dirty-blond locks shaking over her eyes.

"*Larry*," she howled, "it's the guy from the phone."

Larry "Lazerbeam" came out from behind the mini-kitchenette—pushing sixty-five, short, chubby, in thick glasses, with wild salt-and-pepper hair and a thick Rip Van Winkle beard. He wore military tags over a faded Stones tongue tee, an unbuttoned thrift store Oxford, and faded camouflage cargo pants. And like old Rip, he looked like he'd either just woken up or he'd been hibernating for a hundred years. And he wasn't a hunchback exactly, but there was something permanently wrong with his posture, an odd forward lean that made him seem even shorter than he already was.

"You showed," he said, not looking me in the eye. "Here's a guy says he's gonna show and then he shows."

"I hope it's an okay time," I said.

"We're a little disorganized at the moment," he said, "but come on into the palace of love and peace, man, don't be shy."

The woman gave a snort and waved me in. Side by side, these two round, late middle-agers were like teddy bears. Yet there was a distinctly non–teddy bear energy in the air. The place was barely lit, tiny, crammed floor to ceiling with dusty memorabilia, piles of LPs, precarious towers of stacked cassettes and eight-tracks and CDs and boxed sets, magazines strewn over nearly every conceivable spot on the chipped vinyl floor, alongside rolled-up, rubber-banded posters leaning against the walls, signed and framed T-shirts, an RV mantel overflowing with knickknacks and bobbleheads. One sad-looking marijuana roach sat in a Harrah's Club Reno & Lake Tahoe ashtray on the built-in coffee table.

"Sit down, sit down, man," he said. "I don't got much to offer. You want some wine? It's not very good. Or coconut milk?"

I shook my head and took a seat on the built-in couch.

"Well, forget all that," he said, "but it was good of you to pop on by, you know what I mean? 'Cause I'm better *person-to-person*."

"Larry," his wife said, "will you shut the fuck up and let the kid get a word in edgewise?"

"Oh, no, it's okay," I said, shifting in my seat, "I'm okay, I just—"

"Larry's not my real name, by the way," he explained. "She just says that to get my goat."

"But it's not Lazerbeam, is it?" I said.

"It's La-*zar*," his wife said with undisguised contempt.

"*Lazar Lawrence*," he said. "That's my birth name. But it just confuses people, so everybody calls me Larry Lazerbeam."

"I see."

"This guy doesn't care about your name," his wife said. "He isn't from the census bureau."

"Right, right," Lazerbeam said nervously. "This guy wants to know about The Daily Telegraph." He turned to his wife and pointed. "I told you their time would come!"

"Actually," I said, "I'm looking into . . . Emil Elkaim. I'm working for his father."

"Ohhhhhh, I see. Reality TV stuff. Yeah, well—you won't find the dirt on poor old Emil here, man." He let out a low moan. "What can I say? *Tragedy*."

"But . . . was Emil *in* the band?"

"Sure was," Lazerbeam said.

"He was the guitarist," his wife chimed in. "Good-looking boy."

"Were . . . *you* Pioneer Records?" I asked.

"Well, yeah," Lazerbeam said, mock-humble. "We practically invented the indie thing."

"*Oh boy, here we go,*" his wife said.

"But you see," Lazerbeam said, unruffled, "If we're talkin' Telegraph, what you gotta understand is, these were high school kids. *Young* kids. And they wanted to be part of this bigger scene."

"What scene is that?"

"Oh, the *paisley underground,* man, the *mod* scene, the big revival."

He pulled back into the space next to me and threw his dirty sneakered feet on the small coffee table, reached into his musty shirt pocket and pulled out an orange Bic mini-lighter.

"Mind if I make like Bob Marley and light a fire?"

I shook my head, but his wife let out an exasperated sigh and took off for the bedroom.

"Don't mind her," he said, reaching for the roach in the ashtray. "She's got issues."

He sparked up and sucked the last life out of that tiny thing. It was a darn small space to be smoking—I braced myself for a contact high—but he didn't blow much smoke.

"The 'Graph is what I called 'em way back in the day," Lazerbeam said. "And when I say these were *kids,* man, I mean they were really practically children. Ambitious for their age, but there was a lot of excitement going on then. And they wanted in on the action."

"This . . . paisley underground?"

"That's right, you never heard about it?"

I shook my head.

"It was *the* thing, man—"

"And it was all about the sixties?"

"That's right."

"But this was during the eighties."

"*Exactamundo*," he said, offering me a hit. When I shook my head, he licked his big, calloused thumb and put the roach out. "We wanted to *stop the wheel*, you see what I mean? We didn't *like* the eighties. We didn't like where things were heading."

"So you—"

"So we turned back time, man—with religious *fervor*. We didn't just want to *ape* the 1960s. We wanted it to *be* the 1960s, for all eternity."

"So was this, like, a psychedelic rock kinda thing?" I asked.

He shook his head every which way in frustration. "The music wasn't even half of it, man. We were about a *sensibility*. A resurrection. We collected *verification of our correctness*— 'cause we *knew*. And we studied our archives like they were scripture—we *believed* in the past, you know what I mean? And not the ancient past, mind you. We weren't *classical music snobs*. We believed in the *recent* past, like, twenty years out of reach."

I thought of Cinnamon Persky's bedroom and a chill ran through me.

"So where does The Daily Telegraph fit into all this?" I said.

"Oh, it was just destiny, man," he said, his big, red-tinged eyes aglow like fireballs. "From the second I heard 'em. You see, my old man owned the newsstand on Hollywood and Las Palmas, heart of the heart. So I was, like, used to being *on the cultural edge*, if you know what I mean. And working the newsstand—that's almost like being onstage, right? My pops had all kinds of side hustles. He used to deliver *Variety* and *Hollywood Reporter* to Screen Gems over in Burbank every morning, 5:30. When I was seven, eight years old, someone talked Pop into the *extras* game—in sixty-five, he started helping to drum up dancers for the *Shebang* show, you know, scouting the teenyboppers, and Dad was quite the salesman. He talked up every cute chick that walked by that newsstand,

and I just sat there amazed, watching him work." Lazerbeam's eyes glossed with almost tears. "Can you dig it? My dad made it happen, man."

During the course of this impassioned monologue, Lazerbeam's wife had meandered back to the tiny kitchen. She was pretending to look for something in the cupboards, but she was in no hurry to find anything, and I could vibe her taking us in, wanting and not wanting to participate.

"So," I said, "then *you* helped spark this sixties revival. And The Daily Telegraph were part of that."

"You got it, kiddo. I learned how to put my ear to the ground. In fact, Pioneer was going to put out the original Bangles single back when they were called The Bangs but—"

"Oh, *please*," his wife interrupted. "You had one conversation with one Bangle for, like, three minutes." And then, to me: "It's pathetic. For a man who considers himself some kind of world-class historian, Larry *misremembers* every damn moment he ever actually lived through."

"Not true," he protested. "A deal was discussed."

"These days he can't even remember how I taught him to stack the dishes."

He breathed in her venom, his cheeks rosy but his eyes tired with the strain of tolerance. In a slightly lower register, he said, "I'm not saying we were the only game in town, okay. A lot was going on. But we did discover some great acts and The Daily Telegraph was definitely one of them."

"Discover?!" She held a piece of orange Tupperware like a weapon. "What did you discover? You *attended*. You were on the outside, Larry, just *dying* to worm your way in."

He frowned. "I'm just trying to paint a picture for this young gentleman, okay. You don't have to be so hostile about it."

"Larry likes to make it a big mythological thing," she said. "The golden age! Let me tell you, I was there. Yeah, it was fun. But it was small-time."

He pulled the joint from his pocket, but it was too smushed and minuscule to relight. "Anyway," he said, "one man's small is another man's glorious."

"Ha! So small is glorious?" She stepped into the slim door space that separated the mini-living room from the mini-kitchen. "Look where we live, asshole. Is this what you call glorious?"

He shrugged, cowered. Yet, it was a nonplussed kind of cowering, rebellious to the core. They'd had this argument before, maybe 365 times a year. The really uncomfortable one was me, the rope in their tug-of-war.

He turned to me. "Big, small, whatever. To me, the paisley underground was the greatest thing that ever happened to American culture. And The Daily Telegraph were *it*, man. *The best*. When the scene was over, I . . . I almost had like a version of PTSD, you know what I mean? Not from the LSD or anything. But once you've, like, been a part of the *music*, really shared that incredible magic dream, man, civilian life just . . . seems kinda crazy."

"Good excuse, Lar," she said with a snort. Then, to me: "Anyway, just so you get your facts straight, Pioneer put out three damn records. The Cherry Pops, The Cave Ghouls, and Billy Byron. All flops. And The Daily Telegraph didn't exactly make the news either, no pun intended."

"But Emil did make the news," I said softly, careful not to fan her flames.

"Yeah, well," she said, backing down. "That was horrible. *And I don't think he did it.*"

"Why not?" I asked.

But she didn't answer.

Lazerbeam said, "Whole thing was a fuckin' *shame*."

Husband and wife exchanged a dark glance. For the first time, they were both quiet, allies. Lazer got up to open the metal door and air the place out.

I said, "You wouldn't happen to have any, like, memorabilia from that time?"

"You kidding?" he said. "I got all kindsa shit. Baby, you got the key to next door?"

"He has so much crap, I have to rent a second trailer," she said. Then she turned to him in a terse whisper. "Why don't you charge this character for your time. If you're such a font of valuable information . . . *archival research fee*?"

"Honey—can I just have the damn key?"

"Listen," I said, trying to ameliorate. "I would certainly pay to see some Daily Telegraph stuff . . ."

He wasn't paying any attention to me. "Angel, I can't charge this young dude—he's trying to help relatives of one of the *victims*. Wouldn't be right."

She rolled her eyes. As she fished for the enormous keychain hooked to her hanging purse on the wall, she talked to herself, maybe for my benefit. "*A goddamn second rent* I've got to shell out to store his crap. This isn't punk rock, it's *plunk* rock."

When she gave him the key, he went sheepish and considered it like it was a foreign object. "Sweetie, what do I got back there anyway?"

"Well," she said, seething like an impatient babysitter, "you've probably got the cover art, for starts. And I think you have some flyers."

"That's right, that's right," he mumbled. "But no tapes."

"Hawley's got the tapes," she said.

I perked up. *"Hawley?"*

He said, "Dev Hawley, the keyboardist. Nice guy but he's a little scattered."

"*He's* a little scattered?" she said.

Larry the Lazerbeam waved her off, grabbed a yellow pack of American Spirits off the clamorous coffee table and shook out a cigarette. Then he walked out the front door, leaving me alone with Persephone of the Trailer Court.

8

Devon Hawley did know Emil. They were in a band together.

How could Charles Elkaim not know that?

"I'm Marie, by the way," Lazerbeam's wife said, but she didn't give me a second look, and when I said, "I appreciate you guys having me over," she just nodded and retreated to the kitchenette to restack dishes in silence, as if her rage was useless without her husband in the room, and so there was nothing left to say.

From nerves, I grabbed a mag with a blonde shaving her foamy face on the cover and pretended to browse, but I watched Marie in glances, trying not to be obvious. Under the seething was something else; there always is. She was gravely disappointed, stunned even, to find herself in this aluminum half-a-home. Maybe she shared Lazerbeam's passion for the sixties revival, or at least maybe she understood it—once. But I bet she always knew they were running against the grain of time, and maybe she secretly hated that she let herself get dragged along.

I didn't think she was all wrong, didn't see what all this hyper-nostalgia could amount to.

On the mantel was a framed photo—I put down the mag and stood off the couch to take a closer look. It was the two of them, high school aged, in front of a fake night-sky backdrop.

"Is this you?" I asked.

"That's our prom picture," she said with a trace of sadness. "As you can see, we'd already gotten the bug."

In the gold-framed photo, Marie was wearing a fancy white wedding dress that had been hemmed into a tight miniskirt, showing off her sexy, plump curves. Her heavy Egyptian eye makeup was right out of *Swingin' Roma*, Fellini a-go-go. Lazer was skinny then, without a whisker on his chin, cocky in a satin top hat, white tie, and corny velvet tails, with a bright multicolored scarf for a belt. Together, they looked sassy, sophisticated, maybe too sophisticated for high school kids.

I sat back down, checked my watch—2:25. In a few hours I'd be meeting Devon Hawley—*the keyboardist*.

Finally, Lazerbeam came back, jolly, bedraggled, cigarette butt dangling from his lip, with an armful of old poster boards and a big stack of flyers and some xeroxed and stapled fanzines and a VHS box. Smoke was pouring off his curly gray head as he spread his finds all out across the coffee table, hacking and winded. He dropped the butt into a blue water glass and it fizzed out in an instant.

"I *found* it," he said, singsongy.

"Found what?" his wife said, standing in the bedroom doorway.

"Some *won*-derful stuff!" It was hard to believe this bearded old man and his torqued posture was the kid in the prom shot, but the enthusiasm was the same. He reached for the VHS and held it like a trophy. "Right here—the Seeds on *Shebang*! And I was *there*, man, eight years old!"

"Oh Jesus, Larry, he doesn't need to see that."

"Now hold on a minute, woman," he said—his first act of open defiance. "I'm trying to give this guy *context*. Daily Telegraph covered 'A Thousand Shadows' by the Seeds—*why*?

'Cause I suggested it. And you know why I suggested it? 'Cause I saw the original taping when they premiered it on *Shebang*, 1967. My daddy booked every dancer on that show!"

"For fuck's sake, Larry, the VHS player doesn't even work."

"The hell it doesn't." He dropped to his knees and crawled behind the TV, started wrangling with cords. "Incredible clip! You *do* need to see this."

As he fiddled, I said, "What is it I'm going to see exactly?"

"Maybe the greatest moment in all of human history. It was like *American Bandstand*, only insteada Dick Clark, the host was Casey Kasem. *I* turned the 'Graph onto this track, man!"

His wife groaned. "You should probably get a Nobel Prize for that."

He ignored her, scrambled for the black slab of plastic and clutched it like a prayer book. "Fasten your seatbelts, my dearies."

I said, "Don't undersell it," and Marie gave a snort.

He said, "Douse the Edisons, babe."

Marie reluctantly drew the little yellow window curtains and turned off the lamp on the couch-side table. All I could see was the foothill of his crooked back now as he slid the VHS in. He mumbled, "Machine better not eat my tape." Then he stood and thumbed at two remotes like a gunslinger.

With a click, the widescreen went navy blue. Primitive digital titles appeared:

SHEBANG! dancers / Seeds "A Thousand Shadows" U.S.
CBS-TV NETWORK, May 11, 1967.

Straight to Kasem, bearded, talking to a group of teenagers. " . . . new record is called 'A Thousand Shadows' and it's done by the Seeds."

Music: a hammy church organ and a whispering melodramatic singer—*"I did it all for her, my flower child . . ."* And then:

Lost in your dreams!
Said the ride's so long and the night's so black
A thousand shadows can never look back

As the song kicked in, the dancers boogied in couples around a set that was really nothing, but it was a futuristic nothing: long rows of blinking multicolored orbs and a staggered stage designed to look like the rec room on the Starship Enterprise. The screen zoomed into a primitive double-exposure showing, at the same time, a smallish crowd of teenybopper dancers, and superimposed before them, one highlighted couple, strictly from Squaresville. The boy was a long and lean varsity type in a suit with a blond comb-over and the girl was cheery, straight-blonde, miniskirted, with a big, embarrassed smile. Their left hands were joined, like fox-trotters fallen from an earlier era. In fact, most of the high school–age crowd behind them looked square, suited, restrained. Hair was long in front but not long-long; dance moves were more enthusiastic than erotic. This wasn't the nudies having a freakout at Woodstock a few years later. These were "the good kids"—could've been a Catholic school cotillion.

Three minutes—it zoomed by, but I was getting restless with the history lesson.

"Kind of like something out of a Tarantino flick," I said.

"Yeah, but this was *real*," Lazerbeam said, with a little too much rancor. "Maybe we better watch one more time, so you can really understand what the 'Graph was trying to be."

I nodded—what choice did I have? I was being held hostage in the land of footage. We watched again, three modern people in the dark, staring at the past. But the punch line was, the future, which we were now in, somehow hadn't really managed to supplant the past at all.

Which used to be the future's main job.

"If I put this baby up on YouTube," Lazerbeam said, "I'll prolly get a hundred and fifty thousand views and a shitload of likes."

"If you put this up on YouTube," his wife countered, "you'll get sued. Oh, and you'll get one comment—*This sounds way too much like that other song of theirs.* Signed, oldiesgeek number four thousand!"

"That's what *you* think," he said, but he was half-laughing with her. "The sixties are like Dracula—they just keep comin' back! Slap on the hashtags and *voila*, fifty million watchers, *enthralled*."

I said, "That's roughly 49.9 million times the original audience."

He silenced me. "*Watch the magic!*"

I turned back to the screen. The dancers danced. The music swirled. The past was all up in our grill, grabbing us by the eyeballs. Lazerbeam considered the angular couple grooving on the screen as if grading his father's work. "Nice-looking girl. Pretty sure we tried to hire her for a *permanent* but she never came back. She wasn't a great mover—but you want a mix of normal kids and lookers and whatnot. That's what a dance show is, man. It's a show saying, *Hey, normal kid, you are us and this is you.* You see . . . what guys your age maybe don't get is . . . back then, life itself was . . . a *different* kind of contest."

"It was?"

"That's right. Who's the *freest*."

This caught my attention. "The freest?"

"Today, people don't compete over that so much, but back then? It was the *main* thing. You were either *uptight* or you were *outta sight*. It wasn't how rich you were, how powerful you were. It was, can you really be *free*, man? Like, in your vibe, your spirit? That was everything. No greater shame than not being *free*."

As he spoke, I eyeballed the remotes in his hands. He was rewinding, about to play the clip a fourth time.

I said, "Listen, man, I gotta split soon. Any chance I could take a look at that Telegraph stuff?"

"Oh yeah, of course, man, of course."

He turned off the television and put the lights on. We turned our attention to the mess on the table. He started shuffling through things, fighting distraction. Then he pulled out a great big poster board with a tissue overlay held on by white tape—it had to be about thirty inches long and more than a foot wide.

"This was it, man," he said, and then, more quietly, "Greatest failure of my life. They . . . didn't want me to put out the wax."

"They?"

"The band, man. After everything. Plus, I didn't want to exploit the situation."

"Oh *right*," Marie said. "Johnny Virtue over here."

"Believe me," he said, "there were some jackasses who thought I should take advantage. Put the newspaper stories on the album cover. *Drummer murdered, film at 11.* No go, couldn't do it."

"Wait," I said. *"Reynaldo Durazo was their drummer?"*

Lazerbeam looked at me incredulous in the afternoon trailer stillness. "Of course. Him and Hawley were the main songwriters. Then when Emil was killed—I knew I had to leave it alone."

"Oh, it was awful," Marie said.

"Awful," I repeated, blindsided, as he peeled back the tissue and then there it was, improbable that it had survived *but it had*:

a mocked-up album cover, front, back, and spine, laid out on graph paper with penciled printer's instructions along the side.

DEL CYD THE DAILY TELEGRAPH

My heart thumped at the sight of it—a thing of crazy beauty. On the right, the front cover, a haphazard collage—cutouts of Cyd Charisse dancing in white, in repeating echoes, surrounded by wide-eyed tropical fish swimming in every direction, xeroxed moons, hand-drawn Twilight Zone swirls and grinning Cheshire cat heads . . . handmade psychedelia redux on a budget. You could still see the mucilage smears on the sides of the collage.

And on the left, the back jacket—a single large photo of the United Nations of Skinny Teenage Boys, with the hills of Bronson Canyon behind them laying supine like a resting woman. You could picture a B-movie flying saucer coming over those curvy slopes. But these guys had no quarter with sci-fi. They dressed like characters from a 1960s TV Western and stood in poses of strange casual mock seriousness—a dome-haired guy, a frizzy-haired Black dude, a blond saturnine boy with golden curls, and a Hispanic kid so young he looked like he'd accidentally wandered into the frame from the local soda fountain.

And then—Emil, the Emil I knew, with an interrogating half-smile. The handsome bastard—a ripple of heartbreak ran through me.

I tapped the photo gently.

Lazerbeam pulled at his beard. "Yup, that's Mr. Emil, the Elk. He played guitar." Then he pointed to the young one. "And that's Rey, the drummer—the one who . . . you know. This is Jeff Grunes on bass, we stay in touch a little. He works for the LAUSD. And this is Mickey Sandoz, the singer."

There was something jarring about skinny dark-dome-haired Sandoz—he was menacing, disgusted, deliberately *elsewhere.*

"Mickey was a trip," Lazerbeam said. "Fucking ego like you wouldn't believe. You know, he basically thought he could replace the whole band and it would still be . . . *him*, the main attraction. And he didn't even write the songs, man. They don't call it lead singer's disease for nothing."

"Where's he nowadays?"

"Where else, doing hard time—ten years in Banning for moving meth."

"*Worst* kind of junkie," Marie said with tight apprehension. "Just a user through and through."

"One time," Lazerbeam said, "*years* ago, I saw him turning tricks on Santa Monica and Crescent. I wanted to pull over, ask him if he needed a meal or something but . . ."

Lazerbeam gave an apologetic shrug.

"Wow," I said. "And . . . whose this one . . . with the blond curls?"

"That's Hawley, the keyboardist."

I said, "Where's he these days?" in the flattest voice I could muster.

"Oh, he's a big-timer. Set design, features, television. He really made it."

I faked casual, sleepy eyed, but my mind was going off in three directions at once.

"What about Cinnamon, Emil's girlfriend?" I asked. "Did you two know her?"

They looked at each other questioningly.

"*Cinnamon?*" Lazerbeam said. "I don't remember anyone by that name."

Marie said, "Wait, was that the neighbor girl?"

"That's right," I said. "Cinnamon, Cynthia. She lived across from Hawley. You guys never crossed paths?"

They glanced at each other again, some quick discomfort crackled between them.

"Look, we stayed out of their personal lives," Lazerbeam said. "Our thing was the music."

I stared at the back cover , transfixed by the band, their easy oneness. Durazo—eyes of innocence.

"But why," I said, "why would Emil have killed his own band member?"

Marie said, "We don't think he did."

"Okay," I said. "So . . . who . . .?"

"Nobody knows," Lazerbeam said. "And it broke our hearts, man. Because we really *did* see them as our discovery, ya know? And we were gonna work hard to take them places."

"It's not like they were some kind of a *pro act*," Marie said. "They didn't shop around; nobody'd even heard about them."

"It's like—rock and roll–wise, they were *our kids*. And we were gonna bring them to the world."

Together, they stared at me like children themselves, the abandoned kind.

I nodded, took a last look at the LP cover, breathed it in.

"This was . . . great, man, both of you, I'm so glad I got to meet you guys. The *paisley underground*—amazing history lesson."

Lazerbeam grinned with pride. "Anytime, man, anytime."

"Just call first," Marie interjected.

"And come by with that test pressing," Lazerbeam said. "Let's grok it together, man."

"I'd like that," I said. "Say, is it okay if I take some pics? Like, on my phone?"

Lazerbeam looked to his old lady for permission and she gave a cool nod. I took some cell snaps, of the album cover, front and back, and a few random flyers xeroxed on blue-and-yellow paper, long faded. Then I fished out Elkaim's roll and lay a hundred on the table, thanking them both.

Marie tilted her head and said, "Good luck, darlin'. You're wasting your time, but good luck."

At the door, Lazerbeam shot me a look—the hapless, nervous gaze of the henpecked husband. He knew it all made him seem a little ridiculous, the nostalgia, the cowering, and he worked overtime to fend off self-pity. But beaming from his pupils was something else, a trembling beyond panic, beyond shame: *Please don't judge me. I can't let go of the dream.*

I myself was in a kind of dreamy shock as I got back in the Jetta and drove off. I couldn't put a shape on the feeling until I came up over the mountain, and then it hit me full force, larger, louder than the HOLLYWOOD sign across the basin.

Emil Elkaim, Reynaldo Durazo, Devon Hawley Junior.

They weren't strangers or even just acquaintances.

They were a band.

At the bottom of the hill, I cut east and headed for Steam World.

They were . . . a band.

I tore down Washington Boulevard in a late afternoon daze.

Like a family—a band.

I pulled up to the Quonset hut.

This time, Hawley's baby blue Dodge was parked out front.

9

I banged on the front door—once again, no answer. Then I walked around the building—the red-ridged service entrance was half-open. I leaned into the brightly lit open warehouse and yelled, "Hello in there." Still no answer, but he had to be in there somewhere.

I ducked to enter, then froze, hypnotized in my tracks. All around, bathed in the glare of open-faced halogens, miniature sets rose up off wide steel tables, city neighborhoods stretching into opulent SoCal skylines. There had to be a dozen of these crazy things—Hollywood, Santa Monica, downtown, Boyle Heights—and none more than five or six feet high. Hot white beams cut through the room, lighting up the hustle-bustle like electric suns, giving the perfect enamel paint a vaporous glow. These were not ordinary models. Each neighborhood seemed to be constructed with a year or an era in mind. Culver City late '40s, Sunset Strip '66, Bunker Hill of the Roaring Twenties, and so on. Through the glare I yelled "Hello" again and when nobody answered, I moseyed up to the edge of mini-Hancock Park and hovered over it. The touches were mind-blowing. I'd seen some bitchin' dioramas before but this was something else—vivid, rough around the edges, like a vintage photo come to life. My eyes traced the frozen traffic on the 101 over the Cahuenga Pass, down through the Hollywood Bowl—insane. I spun around: moony twilight glistened on the shiny silver-blue Malibu bay. You could practically hear the waves lolling. They were strangely comforting too, these models—they weren't fixed. This was urban chaos as shrunken head, the world in motion, everything floating by, flowing, overflowing, shimmering with the fumbly-bumbly hyper-real weirdness of a miniaturized normal day. I stood there slack-jawed and looked around, tried to shake off the dream stupor.

"Mr. Hawley? Devon? Hello?"

No answer—some green screens formed a kind of partition at the far end of the warehouse. Maybe he was working there.

"Mr. Hawley, you back there? It's Adam . . . I called earlier today . . ."

No sound but the buzzing lights—I headed back there slowly, keyed up in a kind of miniature-land ecstasy. I wanted to take it all in. I stepped gingerly through the winding path, turning 360 in near-total hypnosis. Mini-freeways formed bridges between islands, connecting neighborhoods like a walking maze, the kind of thing you might see at a World's Fair—but how would you move it?

I came upon a model of the RKO Studios building, circa 1930-something, complete with the corner globe topped by a telegraph shooting electric bolts. The words R-K-O RADIO PICTURES were painted red. I never knew that. I'd only ever seen the thing in black and white. And at the little studio gate, a tiny milk truck sat, no bigger than a stick of butter. I knelt to take a look. In teensy-weensy letters it said, DRINK "HOME MILK"—IT'S BEAUTIFUL! And on the opposite corner, a fire escape in ornate grating, a windowed little flower shop with buckets slightly misarranged, a pretzel vendor's pushcart—one of those jeweler's magnifying glasses sat beside it, looking gi-

ant. I pivoted to the adjacent table, also under construction—
Hawthorne Boulevard circa '63, complete with an AAMCO
Transmissions Shop, a Foster's Freeze, and a Hughes Car Wash
with motorized spinning sign. No cars yet, but a Go-Pro faced
down the mini car wash tunnel layered in splashes of white
acrylic to look like spritzing foam.

As I knelt there, studying it all, mesmerized, soft music
began to creep through the whirring of electricity and AC,
gentle and small, from some faraway speaker. I got up and
turned around slowly. I moved in the direction of sound until I could make it out—more KSRF, golden oldies—Friends
of Distinction, "Grazing in the Grass." Cheery, but played so
quiet it sounded like a lonely echo from a faraway time. Music
meant somebody was here, though . . . or at least planning to
come back.

Louder this time I said, *"He-llooooo?"*

I heard a rustling and then what sounded like a low moan
from behind the green screens. My heart thumped.

"Mr. Hawley?"

The moan got louder.

I cut through the models, around the partitions, banged into
a silver cart rattling cupped paintbrushes, the cramped space
cordoned off like some kind of makeshift office—a desk area,
clipboards stuck by magnets onto a great metal filing cabinet,
a big industrial shelf with cutting and painting tools and parts
and glue, hundreds of little mini-wheels and bricks and poles.

And on the floor, Devon Hawley Junior.

"Oh my God, oh my God," I said, "don't move! Stay still."

He was on his belly, crawling slowly, eyes closed, mouth
open, slack in the legs, hands tied in thin rope behind his back,
his feet thrashing listlessly. He'd been crawling, from the belly,
trying to pull himself by his chin, a great big oil spill of blood
across his big bald head.

"Oh fuck!" I said, then double-taked, but Hawley twitched, and I dropped to my knees. "Don't move, *don't move.*"

I untied his hands, looked around, jittery, paranoid. His grip loosened, hands trembled.

"Stay, stay."

He moaned.

I knelt.

He grunted something, two syllables; it sounded like *be hard* or *be hurried* or something.

I shook my head in confusion, insisted "stay" and pulled the cell, punched 911 as Devon Hawley Junior groaned with fading powers and lay his broken head down on the dirty, cold floor, one arm flopped over, the skin sickly yellow like curdled milk.

He looked up at me while the phone rang. Behind his bent glasses, the faint twist of life disappointment corkscrewed in his fading gray eyes.

"A man's been badly injured, he's—"

"Where are you calling from?"

"Steam World Studios, it's a warehouse on Soto, he's got a head wound, he—"

"Is the injured bleeding?"

"Yes, bleeding, very much so."

I rattled off the address and she repeated it, spoke steady. *"Ambulance should be there within the half hour. Please do not move the injured."*

"Yes, I understand, please hurry."

This rant set off another moan, and I turned back to him.

"Do not move, they say do not move."

But he couldn't move anyway, he only grunted from some darkening half-state.

"Oh shit, oh shit, oh shit." I didn't know where to put my body, let alone his—then I remembered we were half-hidden, and I pushed the green screens open, half an eye cocked on the writhing man. Even his moans were slowing down.

"*Come on come on come on,*" I said to no one, dashed past the partitions, then: "Don't move. I'm not leaving you. I'm not going anywhere," as I opened the front door and dragged a small trashcan to hold it open.

I shot glances up and down the street—only my car and his, not a soul in sight. I dashed back inside. Hawley's eyes were fluttering—I dropped and held his twisted wrist, felt the weight of his cold hand.

"Do not die on me. *You will not die on me.*"

10

Inside an hour, Devon Hawley Junior was stretched out in the back of a Good Shepherd Ambulance headed for County General, and I was in the back of a cop car, uncuffed and heading for God-knows-where. The two policemen up front spoke to each other like old pals.

"They find a weapon?"

"Blaylock's on detail."

"Lotta detail."

The two-way buzzed. "Unit 81-46 reporting."

"We gotcha. Site is roped, vic is on the way to CG triage in critical. Voluntary wit with us, en route to N-E-W."

"Thank you, officer."

The box clicked off, they left-turned onto some shadowy south LA street—barbershops and florists all gated up.

"Looks like robbery to me—hit and quit it."

"Ahhhh dunnno." Then: "Nobody can steal that erector set. Plus, there's a fifty-thousand-dollar Varicam on a tripod sitting in the middle of the place untouched."

"Chief notify next of kin?"

"Couldn't find one yet. Next-door neighbor says this guy was a serious loner."

I chimed in. "That neighbor's the one who told me Hawley keeps his door unlocked."

Cop in shotgun: "Too bad about that."

"Just where are we headed, anyway?" I said.

"Newton Community Police Station."

On impulse, I pulled out my cell and shot a text to Ephraim Freiburger, aka Double Fry, my lawyer and best bud.

headed for newton station
emergency could use your help

I stared at the cell for the rest of the ride and got no answer. I couldn't get the image of Hawley's gashed head out of my own head as we parked in the middle of a fleet of black-and-whites and walked into the grimmest-looking civic building on Planet Earth. And it bugged me that they dragged me along—I had already told two cops at the scene why I'd been there. But when the LAPD says ride, you ride. The station waiting room was a kind of decrepit antechamber with two very old wooden benches and an oblong standing reception desk. A cop in uniform watched me register. He said, "Please take a seat. Officer Lanterman will speak to you shortly."

I sat on the bench. The clerk behind the desk busied himself playing Angry Birds on his cell. Beside me, a couple, homeless looking, were excoriating their toddler for having a tantrum.

"*Quiet,*" the father said, "you get us in trouble."

But by the looks of them, they were in trouble enough already.

After an interminable hour, I got up and asked Mr. Angry Birds what the holdup was.

"We need to get all relevant reports before we can let anyone go. Please have a seat."

I grumbled and returned to the bench. About a half hour later, a new officer stepped out and called me to the desk. He introduced himself as Officer Lanterman. He was tall with a razz of jet-black cropped hair, and he seemed majorly pissed off for no reason I could make out, other than maybe facing urban blight for a living.

"If you'd step inside, I can take your full report."

"Okay," I said. "But for the record, I just gave a full report. Isn't it in the system?"

"We would like *our own* report—for *our own* purposes."

"What purpose is that?"

He bristled. "Mr. Zantz, my understanding is you discovered the victim?"

"Well, yeah, and I'm happy to cooperate," I said. "I'm just trying to, like, find out what happened to the first report I gave."

"Do you want to spend the night in lockup for breaking and entering?"

"No, of course not, I just—" I raised hands. "Look, if I'd have done anything crazy, would I have called the police?"

"Sir, you are a material witness to a violent crime, and I'm going to need you to give us a complete deposition. Tonight."

"That's *fine*," I said. "I just want to make sure that this isn't leading to some kind of arrest. Because if I need to call my attorney—"

As if by divine providence, in sauntered Double Fry, unshaven in a blue Marina del Rey sweatshirt, OP shorts, flip-flops, and Grateful Dead knitted yarmulke dangling off his curly-haired head.

"My client has been waiting for me," Fry said, in bluff mode supreme. "Anything he has said prior to my presence was spoken under duress and will have to be considered inadmissible."

Lanterman sighed the sigh of city officials. He had us pegged for a couple of hipsters, wayward arts 'n' culture types, and it made him sore.

"*Please* step inside, gentlemen. So we can all get this over with before midnight?" His slightly agitated insouciance was there to intimidate—and I was intimidated. I turned to Fry, who nodded, and we were on our way.

"What's happening here?" Fry whispered in the hall.

"I found a guy that got brained," I said.

"On a job?"

I didn't have time to answer. Lanterman led us to an open office with five or six desks, all occupied by cops doing intake. As we grabbed seats and Lanterman cracked his laptop, I felt the closing off of breath, the first flashes of panic, and silently posed a question I have often asked myself: Why are some people just so naturally menacing? Why do some seethe in a way that makes you tremble without ever knowing why? Lanterman and I were about the same age, probably from the same city, the same world; we probably grew up hearing all the same songs on the radio. But unlike me, he hadn't been taken in—not by the melodies and definitely not by the lyrics, those flighty matters of the heart. No, his grip on the facts had not been loosened.

"Ohh-kay," he said, clicking away at some form. "Let's start at the beginning. How do you know Mr. Hawley."

"Well," I said, "I don't."

"Ah. Then what was your business at the shop this evening."

I looked at Fry who stared right back at me.

I spoke carefully. "I was doing a favor for a family friend. Hawley had visited this friend recently. At his nursing home. And . . . and Hawley promised a return visit. And when he didn't show, my friend got worried. And wanted me to see if he was okay."

I skipped a few details—the thirty-year-old murder case and the nine one-hundred-dollar bills in my pocket.

"*I see*," Lanterman said, with a little ring of dissatisfaction. "So you were doing a favor. For an elderly person."

I shrugged. "That's right. A family friend."

Lanterman's saturnine look said he didn't buy it. "And what is the *name* of this . . . family friend?"

Fry raised a hand. "My client does not have to disclose that information at this time. Mr. Zantz was on a personal errand; let's just leave it at that."

"Yes," Lanterman said, "but this is a violent crime. Mr. Zantz's *friend* may be in danger."

I said, "It's just that—"

"Zip it, Addy," Fry said. "My client chooses not to disclose that information at this time."

Unlike me, Fry knew how to intimidate back—he was like Bugs Bunny in a yarmulke—and Lanterman was starting to boil over.

"Fine. So you arrived at the studio and—"

"Well, nobody answered at first. I knocked but there was no answer. So I went around back."

"You . . . *let yourself into the shop*?"

"Well, my elderly friend has been very concerned. You see—"

"Addy." Fry raised an eyebrow, pulled the imaginary zipper across his lips.

"Okay, okay," Lanterman said, sitting upright, clasping his hands before him. They were big neck-snapper hands, and he wanted us to see them up close. He directed himself at Double Fry. "Let's forget about this . . . friend for a moment. What I'm trying to establish is—why *your client* just *happened* to drive to Mr. Hawley's studio today of all days. And why he chose to let himself into a building he had never been to before."

"My client just told you. He tried the front door. When no one answered, he let himself in the back."

"Yup," I said lamely. A trickle of sweat was itching at the back of my neck. "And it's a lucky thing I did. For Hawley, I mean."

Lanterman took this in. Matter-of-factly, he said, "Mr. Zantz, this is a violent assault, California Penal Code 240 PC, and although we are grateful for your call, you are officially a person of interest. So you'll want to be as candid as possible."

I turned to Fry: "Does that mean I'm a suspect?"

He paused. "Not yet."

"Look, when I got to the back—" I was about to explain that the studio door had actually been half-opened, but I didn't finish the sentence. All three of our heads turned to watch two men in uniform gently escort a jittery older white man to a nearby desk—I recognized him, the man who lived kitty-corner to Marjorie Persky. He was a wreck now, thin and sallow in a hastily buttoned maroon cardigan, designer dungarees, and pajama shirt—the cops had obviously roused him from sleep. He eyeballed the four tables with suspicion and shot a special flash of disgust Fry's way. Fry had that effect on people.

"Now what is going on here?" the man said tersely. "I'm too *old* to be kept up all night, for Chrissake."

A uniformed Hispanic cop got behind the desk to face him, empathic but very firm.

"Mr. Hawley, I'm so sorry. Your son was taken to the hospital tonight."

"I already heard that. How long has he been in intensive care?"

"Just two hours, Mr. Hawley. Please have a seat."

Hawley the senior did as they asked, but he was fidgeting like a man waiting on terrible news. "Now what the hell happened exactly."

"Your son was brutally attacked."

The skinny old man transformed—his face elongated like someone who just swallowed a fast-acting poison. But he shook his head, shook it off. "By who?"

"That's what we're trying to figure out."

"I . . . I . . . I haven't seen or spoken to Devon in many years. We . . . aren't close. Anymore."

The admission was so awkward, the policeman pinched his lips.

The old man said, "Was it . . . some kind of thief?"

This returned decorum, the cop exhaled. "We're still trying to determine that. But it appears that someone hit him over the head with a metal object, likely a pipe."

The old man's face crinkled into a sharp frown. "Where did this happen?"

"At his shop in the City of Commerce."

Now the old man let out a fragile groan, buckled like an animal that had stepped into a hidden trap. Then he looked up, stared back at the police, frightened.

"Well, what the hell am I doing here? Tell me what hospital he's in."

"We will take you to County General just as soon as we're done. Mr. Hawley, you say you haven't been in close contact with your son. Have you spoken on the phone lately?"

"No. A little. Last year. *Will somebody tell me what the hell I'm doing here?*"

"As I explained, the assailant is still at large, and we're trying to get a handle on who your son's active associates were. Is it possible that he had dealings with criminals or—"

"Of course not."

"Did he express any fear or . . . *apprehension* to you recently?"

"I told you, I haven't seen the boy in ten years. I talked to him on the phone last Christmas. He was . . . it was . . ."

"What's that, Mr. Hawley?"

But his thoughts went adrift, just as a policewoman came in and called his interviewer from the desk. When the cop returned, he said, "I'm very sorry, Mr. Hawley."

Hawley looked up at him bug-eyed.

With a single, pained nod, the policeman said, "Your son died in operation."

Mr. Hawley let out a wail that pierced the noisy room. Then, through tears, he scanned the somber cop faces all around and pulled himself into a twist of fleeting reserve.

"*Devvy is not a crook,*" he said. "*He's a sensitive boy, a special boy.*"

"We understand, Mr. Hawley."

But the old man wasn't listening. He was bawling now, falling apart, mumbling something about his son's bad obsessions, and how the boy's mother was an ice queen, and how there was some kind of a talent show he lost, and how his son was born to be taken advantage of, a grown man, no wife, no kids, nothing but the tinkering and the sickness and—I couldn't make all of it out, and I didn't want to be too obvious about clocking him, but the long and short of it was this guy thought his poor dead son was a mark.

11

They cut us loose at 3:00 a.m. with a ride back to the Jetta and a warning: *Return our calls same day and do not leave town.* I took the wheel; Fry got in the passenger seat. Under a waxing crescent moon, we shot down the 10 in the few hours that aren't bumper-to-bumper, heading for the ocean.

Sparking a doobie, Fry said, "You look like you've just seen a dead man."

"That . . . was fucking horrendous."

"What were you doing down at the guy's workshop anyway?"

I explained the situation, the history, the band, everything.

He said, "Well, we don't know if there's a connection. And you need some rest."

"Can I crash on the boat?" I said. "I'm too freaked out to go to the studio."

"By all means—let's have a snifter of grog and chill. It's been a hell of a night."

A little nervous time passed in the car and then I blurted, "They're not gonna, like, come back at me with an arrest, are they?"

"Right now? You're not even a suspect. You're just a schmuck that walked into the wrong room—it's on them to establish

motive, means, all of it. But . . . I don't want to sugarcoat, Addy.
They're going to be watching you, so no funny stuff."

I nodded, still shaken.

We pulled up to the marina and made our way around the
dockage. *The Shechinah* rested in a pay-by-the-week slip, lolling in the late-night waters, the last of the paint-chipped Grand
Banks. I clambered on board and flopped on the ratty couch.
Fry poured cheap Don Pablo Tawny into tin camping cups.
Then he poured some milk for his tabby cat Howard, who
cruised past me with a pitying look and a squeaky cat hello.

Fry said, "Tell me what you know."

"Other than what I already told you? Not much. I thought
this was half a joke, man. Ya know, run a little errand, humor a
family friend. Which would've been fine, but now it's on record
that I'm the idiot who tripped over a dead body."

"No, you're the *concerned citizen* that tried to save him."

"Whatever, even that's more than I bargained for. And I
don't have my investigator's license yet."

"I don't see how this would screw that up. But you've estab-
lished that this Hawley guy definitely *knew* Emil Elkaim, right?"

"Without a doubt. They were in the band together, all of
them. Durazo the drummer is the guy Emil supposedly killed
a million years ago."

"And then Emil was killed himself in prison?"

"Right—some kind of a revenge thing, like, Durazo was
in a gang or something. The *story* is that a drug deal went
south—Durazo ended up dead, and Emil was the main suspect. Does that even sound like something that can happen
between band members?"

"Welllll? Yeah, why not? But . . . you don't think Emil did it?"

"His dad doesn't think so, and allegedly Hawley didn't either.
But—" I shrugged.

"From the kishkes."

"I mean, I *loved* the guy, okay? I worshipped him, coolest cat on the block—but honestly? I was eight or nine; he was a teenager. The truth is, I barely knew him."

"What about the girlfriend?"

"She ran away after Emil died and then she OD'd a few years later. I don't know if it was suicide or what."

"Wow." Fry sighed. "Brutal posse."

"Fry—level with me. For real. Do you really think it's a coincidence? Tonight, I mean? This guy comes to Charles Elkaim with some theory about his son's innocence and two weeks later he's tied up and brained?"

Fry's eyes tracked runaway thoughts like a Talmudic scholar. "Look, the bad news is—you're in this, like it or not. And it's ugly. And whether or not some old band has anything to do with what happened tonight probably won't matter to the homicide detectives in the LAPD. But either way, they are gonna drill down and find out what you were really doing there—that's inevitable."

"Okay," I said, "so what's the good news?"

"I don't know yet, I'm working on that. Meantime, just lay low, and let the cops catch the bad guys, okay?"

After a drink and a long pause, I said, "I can't."

"Why not?"

"Because Charles Elkaim isn't going to be around that much longer. And he hired me to find out what Hawley knew."

Fry considered. "Okay," he said, "but that's a long shot now—"

"Yeah, I know that, but I've got to *try*."

"Okay, okay—but at this late date, why is it so important?"

"*It's important*," I said, a little too vehemently. "It's important. Because . . . he was my uncle's only friend, ya know?" I made a hand gesture like stabbing my own heart.

"All right, fair enough—but can you do that without poking your nose into another crime scene?"

"Yes. I think so."

"Know so. You stay away from the workshop, Hawley's home, his current associates, any of that. You're investigating the band, and Emil Elkaim, there's nothing wrong with that. Just stay off of tonight's business."

"I gotcha." Howard the cat hopped into my lap—a vote of confidence.

"What about the rest of the group?" Fry said. "Anybody you can talk to?"

"Well . . . the bassist is a guy named Jeff Grunes, he works for the school district. That should be easy enough. But the singer is a guy named Mick or Mickey Sandoz, and he's incarcerated, up at Banning."

"What for?"

"Meth—selling, I think. Getting an actual sit-down with him might not be that easy."

"I can look into it," Fry said, "but that ain't his real name."

"What makes you so sure?"

"'Cause—Daily Telegraph, lead singer—he's a psychedelic rock guy. Sandoz was the lab Hoffman worked for."

"Who?"

"Albert Hoffman, the Swiss chemist who discovered LSD. Sandoz Pharmaceuticals. Before it became illegal, they pumped out a million vials of the stuff under the name Delysid."

"Oh, Jesus," I said, "the LP they never put out is called *Del Cyd*."

"Told ya."

"Fry—how come you know everything?"

He sang it: *"They call me mellow yellow."*

I said, "Quite rightly," but he was already reaching for the beat-up laptop, pulling down his reading glasses, frantically clicking away.

"Oh shit," he said. "Oh boy."

"What?"

"Holy moly."

"What?"

"Aye caramba."

"Come on, dude, it's late."

"Real name's Michael Sanderson, age fifty-nine."

"How'd you—"

"Banning database," Fry said, scrolling the page. "This mofo is a serious drifter. Drug busts, psychiatric treatment, six counts of larceny, two convictions, two violent assaults. Before lockup, he also had a restraining order."

"From who?"

"His wife?"

"Where's she?"

"Weird address—two numbers and no street name. It's some kind of annex to his father's ranch up in Coulterville."

"Where the hell is that?"

"Mariposa County, up past Fresno. Apparently, when he wasn't slugging her, Sanderson and the wife liked to deal a little heroin together."

"How romantic."

"They were apprehended in a joint investigation of illegal narcotics activity by the Mariposa County Sheriff's office back in 2016. Didn't stick, but the California State Bureau of Investigation charged the lovely couple with felony possession with intent to sell a Schedule I controlled substance—also in possession of drug paraphernalia."

"Gotta have paraphernalia," I said, "otherwise, what's the point."

"Right? This database also says Sanderson's got four Crime Stoppers' reports."

"You mean like . . . finks?"

"I'm thinking maybe . . . call-in tips from junkies he burned."

"Wow," I said, "the Lazerbeam dude I talked to called it lead singer complex. But this guy sounds like a serious asshole."

"Sure does. But . . . if he's doing hard time at Banning, it's hard to say how helpful he'll be anyway. We'll have to ring up a visitation officer, and there'll probably be a ninety-day wait." Then, he closed his laptop and said, "This band was cursed."

"And I'm beat. Blankets in the trunk?"

Fry killed his port and started digging through the trunk. "Blankets, pillows—I'm Conrad Hilton of the marina." He was a goof, my old friend, a lawyer without a firm who made his living as a paparazzi, but I was damn grateful for him at this moment. There was something comforting in Fry's big Cossack face, his black eyes, and mouth of crooked teeth, half-smiling as if about to share a bad pun. Funny thing is, it was a tragic-*looking* face—in another epoch he could have been some snow-blinded pogrom survivor—but here on the boat, shaking a fresh blue sheet across the cot in his Bermuda swim trunks and flip-flops with early fog creeping up over the horizon, he was just California mellow.

I thanked him, sounding a little sheepish.

"Addy," he said, stuffing a pillow, "it's gonna be okay. You stay here, you clear your head and *cool out*. You see what you can find for Mr. Elkaim, but you do it straight and narrow."

When he tossed me the pillow, I said, "Should I tell him about tonight?"

"Elkaim? You have to, it's your ethical obligation."

I groaned. "Charles Elkaim thought this guy was like the return of the Messiah or something."

"Yeah, well, Hawley can't help him now."

We exchanged a look.

Fry said, "You gotta tell him."

I said, "Fun."

I got into my cot and lay there in the dark.

"Fry," I said, "they were just, like, some crappy garage band."

"Yeah?"

"So—*why* were they cursed? Who wants to kill off some hinky-dinky little band?"

He shook his head and made for the cabin, lights out. Now there was nothing but me and the sound of the night tide and the rocking boats and the fog passing under lonely, glistening stars.

Memories came in lurches.

The old neighborhood, the Fairfax District—Uncle Hersch called it The Big Matzo Cracker—Melrose to Pico, Highland to Doheny.

The Elkaims—first Israelis on our block. But they weren't just Israeli, they were North Africans, Moroccans, as different from us schleppy American Jews as the local cholos, Crips, surfers, and new Armenian immigrants. They brought gravity, the tides of war.

Mr. Elkaim, Charles Elkaim—back then he must've been fifty-something—regal, too wise for the hood. Tough, diffident, suited. Even talking power steering with Hersch, he carried himself with the quiet discerning air of a foreign ambassador in a crisis.

The mom, Dvorah—dark-eyed, chatty, a voluptuous presence. Gone almost ten years now—but even before the tragedy she seemed to be in hesitation mode, watering the wildflowers, eyeballing passing cars as if she was not yet sure the move to America had been a smart one.

Then . . . Emil. Sixteen. Shoeless. Cutoff jeans and a Hang Ten tee. Wisecracker, daredevil—Emil was just . . . rock and roll, its swift and natural all-consuming fire.

The Elkaims—father and son up front, me and Maya in the back, headed for a drive-through McDonald's. Charles

Elkaim's used '74 navy blue Dodge Dart Swinger had a toy-like plasticky interior, the smell of cigarettes and vinyl and hot metal and gasoline, with loose black seatbelts nobody used. The single band AM radio played oldies but goodies in a fun-nel-like mono—"We'll Sing in the Sunshine." Charles Elkaim hummed at the wheel, coasting through the Melrose-Fairfax intersection. Then—to Emil: "What does she say?"

Emil, funny smile, slight head shake—he talked euphemisti-cally to protect us kids. "Well, *Aba*,"—the Hebrew word for father—"you know, a man and a woman meet, shake hands. They, uh, go into a tent together. And then everybody goes his way."

His father said something admonishing in Hebrew, glanced back at us, and Emil burst out laughing.

But even at eight, nine, I got the gist, and Mr. Elkaim's curi-ous displacement: even the spirit of sex, it seemed, was different in the New World—no shades drawn, no melancholy desire, no sin. How could the thousand-year-old man find his way in the land of pink bunny ears and brightly lit gas station pit stops? How would he survive this brave new bubblegum world?

Flashes now, on the cusp of sleep—

Emil on the bleachers at Fairfax High, strumming Beatles on a scratched-up acoustic, neighborhood teens singing around him. *"You say goodbye, and I say hello."*

Emil on his red-and-black Duane Peters board, sidewalk-surfing past Sam and Ruby's Kosher Butcher and the Judaica gift shop with its gold-plated menorahs and wind-up *Fiddler on the Roof* music boxes . . . *flying* by.

Emil dancing with Mickey Mouse in the rain to the music of Cinnamon's glittering laughter.

Herschel's whisper, riding on the cool marine layer—*"Don't jump ship."*

12

Next day I headed back to the Shalom, praying for the bad news to go down easy, but I found Charles Elkaim in faded light blue pajamas sitting on the edge of his bed, looking eager for good news. I took the one seat in the room and, in the gentlest possible words, I told him about my night.

He shook his head in confused disbelief. "But—you found him like this and—"

"And I called the ambulance," I said. "But it was too late."

For a moment, Elkaim looked like his circuits might overload, and I wondered if maybe I should have kept it from him—then his expression hardened, fight or flight.

"Do the police suspect someone?"

"They wouldn't say, not yet. But . . . there's something else."

"Tell me. You must tell me everything. We agreed there would be no secrets."

"Devon Hawley did know Emil," I said. "Without a doubt. In fact, they were in a band together—and Reynaldo Durazo was in the band too."

"How do you know this?"

"I found a record they made, a test pressing. I spoke with their producer. They called themselves The Daily Telegraph. It seems like they were just getting started but . . . without Reynaldo and Emil, the record never came out."

Elkaim raised his bony hand to his trembling mouth. "I swear *on my life* I didn't know about any musical group. That Emil played the guitar, I knew. With friends, as a . . . a hobby, for fun."

"So the guitar wasn't a secret."

"No, no—I bought him the guitar, in that big noisy place on Sunset Boulevard. He was in heaven—'*Thank you, Aba, thank you.*' And at home he had the . . . the box, the—"

"The amplifier?"

"Yes, the amplifier. Three times a day I asked him to turn it down. Where he got it, I didn't ask."

"But nothing about a band?"

"To us?" Elkaim shrugged his frail, bony, pajama-covered shoulders. "He said nothing."

"Anyway," I said, "I'm sorry to bring this awful news about Hawley. I know how much you wanted to hear what he had to say. I did too."

"And I am sorry," he mumbled, looking grave. "Sorry you had to witness such a thing."

But there was something absent in his dark eyes; he was still plugged into the past. "How *off* I was, in my own little world, crunching the numbers. I *felt* we were close. Our Sabbaths, our camping. I . . ." He looked up at me. "But maybe I knew."

"Knew what?"

"That my son kept his life in the shadows. I knew, of course I knew. A parent always knows. And refuses to know."

"But why would he be so secretive about a thing like that? I mean—not telling your parents that you have a . . . fun little band that's gonna maybe put out a little record? For a teenager, that's kind of a big deal."

Elkaim shook his head; self-admonition was seizing him up. "It's because of *us*, his mother and I—how we were."

"How were you?"

"*Prrrimativi.*" His *r* sound rolled like a rattler.

"Primitive?"

"No, like, on television—*Beverly Hillbillies*."

"You mean, like, country bumpkins?"

"Yes, yes, bumpkins."

"But I didn't see you that way at all. I thought—"

"But he *did*. Most certainly he did. He knew his father was from the mellah, the ghetto for Jews in Casablanca. His mother, may God bless her soul, her father was a fisherman—" Elkaim scoffed with compassion. "He smelled of sardines from head to toe."

"Yeah but here you were—"

"We were, like you say, *bumpkins*. And Emil with the music and the skateboards and the car without a roof, he knew he understood this place better than we did. He was hungry for it."

"Like, he wanted to be more American?"

"That's right, a real American."

We shared a moment of silent wonder at the futility of it. Nurse Rosa came in, rolling Elkaim's lunch under shrink-wrap—chicken, gravy, cooked carrots, compote. When she was out of earshot, I said, "Ya know, whoever Devon Hawley was, isn't it good to know that someone out there thought Emil was innocent?"

Elkaim looked at me, affronted, his eyes hard with anger. Then he tore off the plastic and said, "Emil *was* innocent."

"I believe that, too, Mr. Elkaim, it's just—"

"It's not a matter of belief. It's a fact."

"Yes, of course, but don't you think—"

"*I don't think. I know.*" He pointed at me, clearly heating way up. "And now I am more convinced than ever."

"How do you mean?"

"These were his compadres, his people. My son could not have killed a stranger, and he *certainly* could not have harmed one of his own team."

"It's not that I don't agree with you, Mr. Elkaim, I just—"

"My son was *framed*, do you understand? My family was destroyed."

He was red in the face now, frantic, trembling with fury. I'd never seen him like this. Mortified, I tried to reach out to touch his arm and he knocked my hand away. "*Destroyed*. And I could not find one person to tell me why, not one. Instead—*salt in the eyes*. And now another innocent man has been silenced, *you do see that*."

"If that's true—"

"Of course, it's true. You must find out what this man knew—talk to those who knew him, anything. You must. I can pay you more, I can—"

"No, no, Mr. Elkaim it's not about money," I said, getting firm. "I don't want to disappoint you."

"My days are numbered, Adam," he said tersely. "It is not possible to *disappoint* me." Then he reached for my arm, ameliorative, he breathed and downshifted. "Soon I will join your uncle. I will be gone from this room. But I will not rest in peace. Unless I know why."

Heavy silence. Hawley's last moans hung in the air.

"I'll try. That's all I can promise."

"You will bring me the music to listen?"

"The music? Of course."

"Before I leave for the world to come, I would like to hear my son play his guitar."

I left his room, spinning with fresh guilt and resentment, the two-sided coin. Why did I have to be the person to drag ugliness and horror into this poor old dying man's last days? Seriously—why me?

On the way out, I bumped into the entertainer and Rabbi Peretz pinning up flyers in the hallway—*Tuesday Is Popcorn Night (Leave In Your Teeth)*.

"Jensen, meet Adam," the rabbi said. "Charles Elkaim's friend."

"So I heard," Jensen said, and we shook. "Charles was just bragging about you—he says you're an old student."

"Yeah," I said, "long time ago."

"You should join us for the sing sometime."

"I saw you guys play yesterday. Really nice—you were working wonders out there."

"Well," he said with a sad look of recognition, "folks around here need all the comfort they can get."

"Too true," the rabbi said, tacking a flyer: *Morning Tai Chi 7am in the Courtyard.*

I cast a worried glance back at Elkaim's door. "Speaking of which," I said, "could you guys do me a huge favor and check in on Charles later today? I had to deliver some bad news—"

Jensen said, "Nothing serious I hope."

I sighed. "I dunno. But . . . like you said, he could probably use all the comfort he can get."

Back in the car I twisted with frustration, pulled between the bloody night and Elkaim's somber conviction. The long shot just got longer. Still, I had a good enough excuse to see Endi again, that was something, so I headed home, picked up my laptop, a couple of cables, and the LP and drove back to Ziva's little cottage.

Endi greeted me at the door looking radiant, slightly preoccupied in a sweatshirt that said *hell no cardio* and gray pedal pushers. She was barefoot, and only some of her toenails had been painted. "Oh, hi, um, she's . . . she's giving a lesson right now."

Her smile made all the bad burn away like sun through morning fog.

"I'm sorry to bother," I said. "Any chance I can steal another hour in the living room? I want to rip a copy of this thing."

She looked over her shoulder. "Sure, why not? Go for it."

"I won't be long—scout's honor."

She watched as I fumbled at the couch with the cables.

"How've you been?" I asked.

She shrugged. "Good question. I'm not even sure. This town is intense."

"How long have you been here?"

"In LA? Just three months. I guess I'm still getting used to the place."

"Nobody ever gets used to this place," I said, and she laughed.

"You find out anything more for your article?"

"My article?"

"About the mystery band."

I paused for a beat. I couldn't remember why I'd lied, but now I had to stick with it. "I heard the bassist became a school-teacher," I said. "I'm trying to track him down."

"Wow, well, good luck. What a fun assignment."

She split for her bedroom and closed the door. I sat at the end of the couch with the laptop beside me, burning one long, slightly scratchy MP3 on Audacity, then I sliced and tagged the files with patient wonder, all the while marking up the insert.

DEL CYD / The Daily Telegraph, 1983
    (Pioneer Records, unreleased)
SIDE ONE
Runaway Sunshine 3:41
Fair-Weather Freaks 3:05
Polka Dot Princess 4:51
Launch the Lightning 2:50
A Thousand Shadows 4:28 <—Seeds cover
SIDE TWO
Auguries of Innocence 0:55
Sea Green Shanty 18:33

Mickey Sandoz—Lead Vocals
Emil Elkaim—Lead Guitar
Jeff Grunes—Bass Guitar, Vocals
Devon Hawley Jr.—Keyboards, Vocals
Reynaldo "Rey-Rey" Durazo—Drums
Produced by Lazar "Lazerbeam" Lawrence
Engineered by Martin Anawalt
Recorded November 11–13, 1983, at RainBo Records,
    Santa Monica

This time around, after seeing Hawley in his final hour, the sunshiny blue melodies played more sorrowful, the last flash of innocence from the island of doomed teenage boys.

> *You're not ready for the night when I—*
> *Launch the lightnin'!*
> *Launch the lightnin'!*
> *Light UP the sky!*
> *Fight fire with fire!*
> *And don't ask why!*

For all their plugged-in electricity, they were human-sized, and it brought back Hawley's strange remark in the interview, about moments of solitude in the big city. A dazed feeling came over me, like someone straining to hear the ocean in a seashell. My heart pulled to know him, to know why someone had it in them to—

Endi cut my reverie, moving through the living room quickly to hand me a yellow flyer—*Angela Elsworth at Van Gogh's Ear It's Free (2 drink minimum)*—with a little cropped photo of her strumming the guitar.

A big smile spread across my face.

"Wait a minute—this is *you?*"

"Next Friday." She shrugged. "It's just an amateur hour thing. *Only* if you're not busy."

"Oh, I'm there, are you kidding? Nice stage name."

"It's my . . . *counter-persona* or something," she said with a deadpan smile. "I'm doin' this undercover."

I thanked her for the flyer and did not tell her that I'd just seen a man die the night before. Then I made my way back to the car with a freshly burned CD—it lit up the car stereo as I considered heading for Southwest College. I'd been taking a certification course in private investigation—today was Intro to Data Mining—but after the night I'd had, another lecture on workers' compensation fraud just seemed a little inconsequential. Plus, I had a paper due in two weeks—how to establish probable cause in order to file for a search warrant—and I hadn't even started the research. Trying to motivate, I pulled into Mobil to fill her up when a college girl at the next pump turned her baseball cap backward, exposing the letters UCLA in gold on blue.

That gave me an idea. Madame Persky had mentioned that Rey Durazo's cousin was a UCLA professor. A quick phone search told me Professor Socorro Durazo, PhD, taught "How to Read *How to Read Donald Duck*," for the César E. Chávez Department of Chicana/o and Central American Studies at UCLA. From the online syllabus, I picked up the gist: *Professor Durazo's class takes a close look at the legendary 1971 essay by Mattleart and Dorfman exploring Disney's anti-communist propaganda in the form of pro-capitalist comic books, distributed throughout greater Latin America.* It was Donald Duck as mindfuck indoctrination and political child abuse, pure evil. As luck would have it, class started 4:00 p.m., Haines 39.

I paid up and headed for North Campus.

13

It was my first trip to UCLA since I'd dropped out twenty years prior, and it blindsided me. The campus, with its chipper youth and brick towers in the classical mode couldn't stop the memories from flooding in waves of ache. Wanting to please Uncle Herschel, I'd given this place the college try, but my heart was wrapped up in song, and I couldn't concentrate. Grandiose MTV daydreams dogged me at every turn. Playing the clubs seemed ten times realer then—*now* it felt like I'd been tricked, hypnotized by the neon lights on the Strip like Pinocchio at the carnival. When, for a third semester, my grade point average dipped like bad stocks, I tore up Uncle Herschel's tuition check and told him I was quitting. Naturally, he was furious.

"You want applause for this?" His droopy frog eyes swelled with fury. "This is the biggest mistake you will ever make."

"Uncle Hersch, it's my mistake to make. Please. Let me suffer the consequences."

"What did I work for all these years?!" His hands locked in a spasm of grief. "I swore to your mother, may she rest in peace, this *one thing*. An education is something nobody can take away from you—and you throw it away."

The packed auditorium made it easy to blend. I took a

seat in the back, maybe the sole person over thirty besides
Professor Durazo. She was majestic, striking—but very rigid,
like somebody'd struck her with an arrow and the poison was
taking hold. Her jet-black hair had streaks of forbidding gray.
She ignored the opened notebook at her lectern and spoke
with grave parataxis, only ever moving to click through the
giant overhead PowerPoint: comic book panels, voting stats,
questionable headlines *en Espanol*, photos of the massacred.

"You may have noticed. In these comic books, there are no
fathers. No sons. Only uncles, cousins. And yet, in *reality* . . .
how . . . are children oriented? By *mother*. And *father*. So . . .
so what are we seeing here? A bold act, of distortion. The Walt
Disney Corporation . . . has created . . . an *alternate* reality.
The ultimate capitalist reality. *Without blood hierarchy*. In the
duck world, the *only* hierarchy is possession. Competition, at
every level. And yet . . . your smarts don't count. Your *efforts*
don't count. Without luck, no social mobility." And then, she
added, with fake sorrow and acid sarcasm, "No social mobility,
for the ducks."

When it was over, I waited for class to file out, as the last
of the students chirped their questions at her. Then I made my
move down the steps to the podium.

"Professor Durazo, hi. I'm Adam Zantz. Do you have a few
minutes?"

She looked at me but didn't answer.

"I'm a private investigator looking into the death of your
cousin Reynaldo."

She surveyed me now in that brain-churning way particular to the academic intellectual. Wryly, she said, "Aren't you a
little late?"

"Better late than never?"

Again she didn't answer. She closed her notebook, gathered

papers, fussed with her laptop. When her briefcase was packed, she said, "I have a meeting across campus. Walk with me if you like."

You can tell a lot about a person from how they walk. Socorro Durazo moved through the great quad with an animal sense of purpose that underscored her power and made her impossible to ignore. I couldn't help but wonder if some of these college dudes shlepping backpacks hadn't enrolled in her class just to breathe the air around a woman like that without really caring too much about Marxist theory and the cultural exploitation of Latin America.

"Do you remember Reynaldo well?" I said.

"Who hired you?"

"Charles Elkaim—the suspect's father."

"I know who Charles Elkaim is. You know you're not the first Dudley Do-Right to try and tackle this?"

"So I've heard."

"They've been throwing their money at it for years."

"Who's they?"

"All of them. Anything to clear the names of their precious children. And of course, Devon Hawley—the most deluded of them all. He pisses away half his life savings paying hacks like you—he can't let it go."

My belly tightened. "Is that right?"

"Yup—last one was an ex-cop named Gladstone, one of these so-called experts in closed-case investigation."

"What happened?"

"I'm guessing *zilch*."

"So . . . you *know* Hawley."

"Not exactly. We met twice to compare notes."

"Notes?"

"That's right. I've been conducting a little investigation of my own."

"Really."

"Oh yeah. I spoke to all of 'em—I even went to county lockup to talk to that white trash piece of shit singer."

"What . . . what is it you're trying to figure out exactly?"

She stopped to face me. "Who killed my cousin—obviously. Because it sure as shit wasn't Emil Elkaim."

"No?"

"Of course not. Rey-Rey *loved* Emil. They were *best buds*—thick as thieves. Rey called him the Israeli Keith Richards—they had a band together."

"I heard that."

"They had *big dreams* together. People don't kill their own dreams."

"So they were really close," I mumbled. For one moment the whole campus seemed to go into slo-mo. Then she smiled a fake one and kept walking and I followed.

"To answer your question," she said, "I think about my cousin Reynaldo every fucking day. Too much maybe. I see his face in all these young men."

"What was he like?"

"Rey-Rey? *Enthusiastic*. That's what got him killed."

"Enthusiasm gets you killed?"

"Absolutely. People like their Mexicans lazy. Rey had *gusto*. Too upbeat and they take you down." When I didn't comment, she said, "He was my angel, my guardian. When he was alive, I mean. I looked up to him."

"How old were you—"

"When Rey was murdered? Eleven years, eight months. I remember it like yesterday. I suppose I was in love with him in a way. We all were. He was the family hero."

"I read a newspaper article that claimed the whole thing was over some drugs."

"Don't talk to me about what you read in the white man's

newspapers. It's unreliable now, but then? They wrote about us like we were gerbils."

"I don't doubt that. But are you saying Reynaldo wasn't a drug dealer?"

"Whatever he was into, it was small potatoes. Rey was not some big mover of contraband. At most, maybe he was a pot smoker who . . . who *proselytized*. In his backpack, he kept some herb in a plastic camera film container; I can remember the smell of it. Tell me, who on *earth* murders a seventeen-year-old, five-foot-five kid for three joints?" She kept walking but her eyes blazed with age-old indignation.

"What about Reynaldo's gang? They took Emil down."

"It wasn't a *they*, it was a *he*, a person with a name—Frederick Castillo. Just some psycho trying to get into Sureños. He wasn't even in the fucking gang."

"So it wasn't—"

"Sick piece of shit just *used* my cousin as an excuse to slay Emil and make a name."

She had stunned me quiet—we walked in silence.

"I'm sorry," she said, "as you can see it's still fresh for me. My world caved in the day they told me Reynaldo was gone. Everything after that morning has been one long aftermath."

"So if it wasn't a drug deal—"

She stopped under the arches of Bunche Hall. "It was a lover."

"A lover?"

"Absolutely. Or a jealous spouse—of course it was."

"But who?"

"My cousin was handsome, like a Latino Monty Clift—with dazzling eyes. He was a powerful drummer, too—all muscles. And he had serious game—too many conquests for me to keep track. But he told me stories—to entertain me, and to make me jealous."

"What kind of stories?"

"Oh, there were local girls and high school girls. In junior high, he screwed his art teacher, Mrs. Nicola. And there were others."

"Do you think he was sleeping with Cynthia Persky?"

"I *know* he was sleeping with her mother."

"Marjorie Persky?"

"Yes. And he told me he couldn't shake her off. He was fond of expounding on the hypocrisies of married women."

"But—*she* told me she barely remembered Emil even had a band."

"Yeah well, she lied to you, okay? How could she not know? Madame Persky was a mover and shaker in the music biz. She used to be a teen DJ or something on KHJ."

"And she had an affair with Rey?"

"That's a stone fact. I don't say she killed him, not with her own hands anyway, but she was having her way with him and not just once. I think she even conducted a little three-way with Rey and the singer."

Professor Durazo turned into the giant building and I followed her, upstairs, down the fresh-mopped corridor reflecting dreamy sunlight. *The hallowed halls.* She stopped at an office door that bore her name.

"Now, if you'll excuse me, I have papers to grade. I'm sorry I couldn't be more help."

"Professor—who *do* you think killed your cousin?"

"*Somebody* killed him. Somebody that went unpunished."

"Okay, but—"

"But nothing. Reynaldo's death tore my family apart. Nobody was ever the same again, least of all me." She glanced down the hall bitterly. "Sometimes I wonder what he would have become if he had lived. For all I know, he would have been an alcoholic FDA inspector like his dad. Or a valet attendant who sleeps with old white ladies for cash. That's what I tell myself to get through the night."

"But you think that he might have been sleeping with Marjorie Persky and—"

"Why not? Read the history books—her husband was lavender as they come."

"What did Reynaldo say about her?"

She shrugged. "We were kids. We were into *La Revolucion* and Rey-Rey just *embodied* it, because he was so free-spirited. I think this lady was part of that—showing a grown-up white woman what's what."

"So," I said, "you think her husband might've caught Rey and—"

She smirked with displeasure, her back to the door as if she was blocking my entrance. She said, "You think it's funny."

"That isn't true."

"No—but what I mean is, if he hadn't been murdered, you *would* think it was funny."

"Why? What makes you say that?"

With an angry yank, the professor hoisted the valise over her shoulder and opened the door. "The young Mexican hombre and the horny gringo lady, the MILF. He brings around the loco weed, she seduces him. It's like a bad eighties movie."

"When you put it that way—"

"But it's not funny. It's not funny at all. Don't you see, *that* is where the crime begins."

"Maybe you're right, maybe I don't see. How does murder start there?"

"Because whoever she was, she had all the *power*. A young, short guy like Reynaldo, with his whole being tied up with machismo, Mister Drummer Man, the Mexican Keith Moon, out to *prove*—no, don't make a face. I have thought about this for *years* now, decades. I don't know if Mr. Persky killed him or some other goon did or what. Just because Herbert Persky was gay doesn't mean he wasn't possessive—she was his wife. Or maybe it was the daughter, Little Miss *Cinnamon*, the band's little mascot. Or the singer—not a well man. But *whoever, however*—Rey-Rey was *already* put in a compromised position just being there and *that* is on Mrs. Lily White. She was no *grown-up*. She didn't give a rat's ass what happened to my cousin the minor. She just did the white person thing and said, '*My pleasure comes first.*' He was her gardener, literally—*at your service.*"

She opened the door and stepped inside. "That's right," she said over her shoulder. "The expendable amigo—she set him up for the kill."

"Professor," I said. "*Ms. Durazo*. Devon Hawley Junior was murdered last night. I went to see him, I . . . found his body. The police are . . . I was questioned, they . . ."

She stared me down, near frozen—her upper lip trembled once.

Then she slammed the door in my face.

14

On Thursday morning, I went to Devon Hawley Junior's funeral uninvited. From the nearest faraway bench on Forest Lawn's long green slope, I peered through mini-binocs over my shoulder as little black-clad bodies gathered on the tilted horizon, nestled by a very man-made running rock stream. The day was hot but overcast and the crowd was light—maybe twenty people in all. All I could see were the unfocused backs of heads. The black-robed priest gesticulated like a listless car dealer, pitching his prayer like he was selling the extra-long black box. For a man who loved miniatures, Devon Hawley had been a giant. Maybe that was the point.

No weepers that I could see—the whole affair played like a have-to ritual. This peculiar distance brought me back to the day of my uncle's funeral, how I couldn't bear to see him lowered into the ground so I hid at a coffee shop counter, jittery and bewildered. And it was bewildering, this life that ends in death, this game of hot potato. Here I was, stalking a total stranger's funeral, incognito and alone, yet now I could sense Herschel beside me, looking over my shoulder surveying the scene. The dead don't go far. They hover like nurses on-call. With some, you can get closer than you ever could in life.

A team of Mexican laborers in matching long sleeves approached. How they bore the heat was the real mystery. Shovels caught the sunshine as they thudded ground. Goodbye, Devon Hawley Junior, builder of cities, player of songs.

I got up and leaned on a tree for a better angle. Nobody familiar, no sight of Hawley Senior or Marjorie Persky or Socorro Durazo, but one old reed of a cocoa-toned guy caught my eye because of his gray Jew-fro and his rock-and-roll threads—black Harley Davidson tee, black jeans, black Converse, silver dog tags. As the crowd dispersed, I shoved the binoculars in my windbreaker pocket and moseyed slow down the hill, hoping to line up with him and get a closer look.

"Excuse me." I pointed. "Are you Jeff Grunes?"

He stopped in his tracks, went skeptical. "Who are you?"

Flowing fields of plaques surrounded us in every direction. His dark skinniness cut a dramatic figure against the green. He was early sixties at least, an aging half-Black, half-Jewish rock dude in thick prescription glasses, but the spark of life in him was still jumpy, youthful, looking for a place to spread. Behind the heavy lenses he had the kind of learned eyes you know have read *everything*—cognitive theory, poli-sci, *The Life Cycles of Empire*. No *People* magazine for this guy.

"I'm Adam," I said. "I'm a Daily Telegraph fan."

"No, you aren't," he said, matter-of-factly.

"Well—I'm working for Charles Elkaim."

"Ah, one of those. Good luck on that." He turned and made for his car in the glaring sun. I followed.

"Must have been a rough day today," I said, "saying goodbye to an old friend."

"Yeah, not exactly. More like . . . a lifelong enemy."

"Really?"

"Everybody's got one. Hawley was mine."

"So you two haven't been in touch?"

"Not since Bush Senior was president."

"But how did you know about the funeral?"

"I kept tabs. Old band members do that." He snorted. "What the hell's the internet for, anyway?"

"Mr. Grunes, if you would just—"

"You know you're like the eighth person that's tried to figure this shit out, right?"

"So I've heard, but—"

"*Everyone* wants to talk about 'em, the teenage killers, slaying and dope and runaways and all that fun stuff."

"Right. But you don't see it that way."

"The world didn't stop in 1984."

"For Charles Elkaim it kind of did," I said.

"Yeah well." The funeral crowd was dispersing. Grunes turned to face me, then changed his mind and started walking away again, and I followed him in silence to an unwashed gray Prius. He clicked the fob to unlock his car and turned one last time to look me over. He wasn't pissed exactly, but he didn't know what to do with me, and I couldn't be sure what he saw. Maybe an opportunist, maybe a sycophant. I zipped my lip and stood for inspection. He considered the long hill of graves and something human in him turned over.

"Listen, man," he said, getting into his ride, "I stay *away* from the past, you know what I mean? Took me *years*. Now, I work with the actually needy. You know, as in—*reality?*"

He started up his engine and rolled down his window.

"And as far as *Emil* goes—" He shrugged at the wheel, drank deep from his own scorn. "Sure, I miss him. I miss all of it. But it ain't coming back."

I leaned on the open car window so that he couldn't drive away without knocking me over.

"Jeff," I said, speaking low and serious, "I'm the guy who found your frenemy."

"Yeah?"

"It was the worst thing you could ever imagine." Our eyes met. *"Who do you think did this?"*

A long pause and then, "I don't know."

"But you have guesses."

He scanned the fields. "Where's Mickey? Why isn't *he* here?"

"But . . . Mickey's in prison."

"Bullshit. He's been out since last August."

"He has?" I let go of the car window and stood.

"Last I heard he was living in Tent Town over on Ohio, under the 405. When he got out, first thing he did was hit me up for cash, *as usual*. Wanted to talk old times, *as usual*. Stuck in the past, *as usual*. Now back off, dude. I got kids to take care of—and they're stuck in the present."

Grunes began to roll his window up and I stepped back, watched him drive away over the dotted green hill.

Outside the Forest Lawn Flower Shop, I called Fry and asked him to meet me at Newton Station.

"Addy, I told you to stay away from the Hawley scene. Dude, I'm trying to keep you from getting indicted."

"I know that," I said, "but this is too hot to ignore. This Sandoz character has a serious criminal record, and he's been out and about for *months*. Don't the police need to know about that?"

"Not really, and definitely not from us. Besides . . ."

"What?"

He hesitated. "The department's already got a sus—"

"They do?"

"They do. They made an arrest late yesterday. And frankly, their guy's a little closer to the action."

"Who is he?"

"I don't have a name. Hispanic male, early twenties—living in his car four blocks from Hawley's studio. They found the crowbar and Hawley's wallet in the trunk, okay?"

"No way."

"Adam, he sounds like a keeper."

"Come on—"

"Apparently that stretch of Soto's notorious for break-ins."

"So you're telling me some random guy pulls a robbery and just happens to commit murder along the way? I don't buy it."

"Why not? It plays. Hawley was a big guy, thief panics, it happens."

"And then he keeps the weapon? After not stealing anything but a wallet?"

"Look, maybe they can hang it on this guy, maybe they can't. I'll be watching it closely. But I'm betting the cops wouldn't even look into . . . *this Sandoz character*—and you'd just make yourself sound like a crazy person taking it to them."

"*Really?*"

"Think about it, Addy. From an official POV, it does sound crazy. Forty years ago, some nothing rock band—so what? The grown-ups are looking for motive and means, right here, right now. And even if Sanderson was a viable suspect, the cops are not going to be happy about *you* meddling. Like everybody else on this planet, they got *I-me-mine* fever." Then he started singing: "*All through the day—*"

"Please don't. And if they aren't gonna look into it, I am. I gotta talk to this Sanderson guy."

"Dude, I don't advise that at all—he sounds like a total jackass."

"I'm not going to go shoot meth with him, I just want to meet him."

"With what protection? *Addy*—this is a hardened criminal."

"Fry, I cannot go chickenshit now," I said. "I cannot be the king of jumping ship once again. I'm looking into Emil's band. And you don't know a band till you've met the lead singer."

"I'm not joking; you need to exercise some caution here."

Silence.

Then: "Let's go together—I'll look into hiring some security to accompany us."

"Security. Yeah, that'll really encourage the guy to open up."

"Adam, you're not thinking straight on this. Once again, you've got ants in the pants. I mean, really—you can just picture Officer Lanterman."

Fry went into his hyper-rigid authority figure voice. "Who gives a flying fuck about some crappy unknown garage band from a million years ago that could barely play and never even put out a record?"

I looked out past the grass, the graves, the freeway under streaking skies.

"I do."

"Well," Fry said, sounding exasperated, "then don't be reckless about it. The sun's about to set. Come by in the morning, we'll go at rush hour. Together. Okay?"

I grumbled and we signed off. Back in the car, I headed into the city and worked a shift—Torrance to LAX, LAX to Burton Way, Doheny up to Santa Monica, then down to Third. The customers came and went—long, fat, short, tall, talky, morose, hurried, drowsy, seatbelted into a low mood or gazing out the window looking for something nobody could find. All the while, I played The Daily Telegraph low on the car stereo and nobody complained. Some songs were already stepping out, announcing themselves. "Fair-Weather Freaks" when the blistering guitar solo kicked in, played wavy and stiff all at once, like you could hear Emil's vision outracing his fingers in real time. And "Polka Dot Princess"—pretty, breezy, music for a teenage kiss. It made me think of Cinnamon buried alongside her true love. Also, the crazy opener of side two—"Auguries of Innocence," William Blake recited like a TV horror movie host with the voice going from left channel to right and back again against wind chimes, wide open sound, building and falling like the surf.

They were specious, elliptical, goofy, fake erudite, hyper-charged. They were teenagers.

> *To see the world in a grain of sand*
> *And heaven in a wild flower*
> *Hold infinity in the palm of your hand*
> *And eternity in an hour!*

Then the goofy spoken word segued into the last number, the long one—

> *Swords are drawn*
> *As you walk the plank*
> *you're through*
> *The sirens are singing*
> *a sea green shanty*
> *for you*
> *'Cause your shiiiiip . . .*
> *. . . has sailed!*

This corny, creaky record—I was hooked.

Things slowed down after the dinner rush, and I was only blocks away from Ohio Ave under the 405, so I drove there, just to see. No harm in seeing. The freeway columns were graffiti'd in up-slanted black.

EVERYTHING
    YOU
        WANT
           IS
              HERE

I drove right past the village of ratty tents that covered both sides. The place was busy enough, like a Yosemite campground as the fires dwindle. I parked up the street, heart thumping. I didn't like the idea of dragging Fry into this—it wasn't his gig and it wasn't his problem. In a split decision, I cracked my wallet, put the big bills in the glove box, shoved the rest in my pocket, and hoofed it back into homelessland, dry Santa Anas blowing through the underpass at 11:00 p.m., the delta of LA night.

15

At the lip of the underpass, bicycle parts were piled high alongside shopping carts sitting in dark metal solitude, far from home, overflowing with trash like cornucopias from hell. I walked wide of the metal, ducked and passed through a kind of cardboard portal with nervous unease, thrust suddenly into their skinny homemade alley, faces hijacking, flashes of eye light, low ghetto blaster bleeding into mind window, a street poem of faces signaling danger, voices in midnight negotiation:

" . . . old lady dress, fuck that . . . "

" . . . back to Sacto, I don't need no cutthroat . . . "

" . . . says 'I love you'—*bullshit* . . . "

" . . . Yeah, I went out. But then I came back. Don't forget that. I came right the fuck back."

" . . . told him, brother, I can't stand no more darkness. I. Just. *Can't.*"

I moved through this rummage sale of death, shooting over-the-shoulder glances with a jagged pace out of silent movies, fear probably written all across my face.

"Howdy, excuse me, yeah, you hear of a guy named Sandoz? Mickey Sandoz? Sanderson? You know a guy, you ever meet a guy—I got an old picture right here (hoping nobody jacks me for the phone) see this guy, yeah, I'm looking for him—"

Sallow expressions, shaking their heads, broken America saying no, the dream decimated for all time, and who was I, anyway, with these useless questions? Some Lyft-driving bottom-feeder—wasn't I maybe two paychecks from joining them?

That's what Uncle Herschel knew about me—that's what he couldn't ignore.

And yet these people didn't see me that way. Even near midnight, even in my wrinkly hoodie and worn-down jeans, they could tell from a mile away I wasn't one of them.

Then a woman's voice: "Yo—*goober*—whattaya looking for?"

Her laughter was sudden and caustic. I stopped, turned to face her. She was my age, sitting on a lawn chair, stringy blond hair dyed light green, tatted-up track marks, T S O L inked across her right-hand knuckles, not quite beaten looking but she positioned the chair so her face was out of the lamppost glare. Behind her, a filthy Snow White dress on a hanger had been set up as a door to her torn Coleman Two-Person Sundome, same shade of lime as her hair.

Homeless camouflage.

"I *said* what you fuckeen *looking for*, dude?" In the dark of tent alley, she vibed scar tissue.

"I'm looking for a guy named Mickey Sanderson. Or Sandoz maybe. Older guy—used to sing in a band."

Recognition. "What do I get if I take you to him?"

"I dunno—ten bucks?"

"Cheap ass. Hand it over."

"Let's see him first."

"And then you ditch? No fuckeen way."

"How do I know you aren't taking me around the corner to get jumped?"

She rolled her eyes. "You fuckeen civilians are all alike. *Whole world wants to jump you in the dark*—believe me, bro, if I wanted to whomp your ass I'd do it right here under the lights."

"You have an accent," I said. "Orange County?"

She half-cackled. "I do not."

"Fullerton?" I said. I pointed at the dress. "Uniform?"

She smiled—this was trust enough. I dug a twenty out of my pocket and quickly slipped it to her. "What's your name, anyway?"

"Salty."

"No, it's not."

"Fine, call me Stormy then."

"Okay, *Stormy*. You gonna do something stupid with this twenty?"

She gave me a fake-disappointed look. "Straight into my arm."

"Where is he?"

"You didn't even need to pay me, stupid. Half the fuckeen people here know Karaoke Mike."

"That's what they call him?"

"Feck yeah, he puts on little shows here."

"No way."

"He's kind of like . . . our very own Sinatra." She goofed at her own joke.

"Who is he to you?"

She shrugged. "I geezed with him a few times, but he's just too weird. Brageen about his escapades and shit."

"What kind of escapades?"

She changed the subject. "He wanted to, like, give me a ride back to Anaheim. He tried to talk me into going back to my grandma. I wasn't having that."

"Why not?"

"She's a bitch. My mom's okay but she's in Anchorage. I'm not going back *there*. If I die homeless, I'm gonna do it in the sunshine—Jordan. *Jordan*."

A bloated, shirtless older Black man came out from behind

an adjacent silver tent. He wore Coke-bottle glasses and his teeth were crooked. He had some kind of lesion near the center of his belly. I tried not to stare.

"What this guy want?"

"He's bugging me," she blurted. "He tried to molest me."

Jordan stepped to me—way too close. He almost pushed my shoulder. "Where the fuck you think you are."

"I'm *kiddeen*. He's looking for Mickey."

"Check the gallery."

"Where's that?" I said.

"*Take* the motherfucker there."

She said, "I'm not going in there alone!" and he shot her a look.

Stormy stood up—she was slim, still brimming with vitality in her black windbreaker and torn jeans, but her fists were permanently balled up like a tae kwon do student. Jordan led and she followed, turning back to me.

"Just . . . follow us, dork."

I followed. Jordan and Stormy led me through the tent village out to under the off-ramp and down a narrow side alley. The more alone we got, the more my heart thumped, stepping around the alky puke, bologna wrappers, nasty hypos. They ducked into the mouth of a construction site—rusty infrastructure, crisscrossing metal behind black netting caked in spackle.

"What's in there?"

"You wanna see Mickey or not?"

I pushed through a rip in the fence and followed.

"Watch out," Jordan said as we entered the guts of the unfinished apartment building. "Some of this shit is loose. I saw a beam come down and almost hit a dude."

"We're fuckeen idiots for even being here," Stormy said. "They haven't worked on this place in, like, *years*."

All around us were stacks of metal planks, tiles, drywall panels piled on high.

Jordan put his knuckles to his mouth and whistled once, loud and swift. Grumbles returned from a dark corner.

Two skeletal white guys were nodding off under an open purple single-person sleeping bag. One was barefoot, his filthy blackened feet creeping out from the far end of the crumpled gold zipper.

"Where Karaoke at?"

No answers, just dead eyes.

"Well, when was he here last?"

Half a shrug. "I heard he went clucking."

"Where, though?"

"Sorry, boss, he didn't leave no forwarding address."

Low laughs, two or three stragglers came out of the shadows.

"This guy's looking for Mickey."

"Mr. Karaoke?"

"Skinny motherfucker, Rock and Roll Mickey, he up in here somewheres?"

"White Flight's hidin' like a bitch." The guy laughed—his front tooth was gold. My pulse was just lowering to almost normal when a super-tough-looking, tattooed and aged Viking, shaved head, gray tank top, stepped from the shadows.

"Whose *this* fuckwad."

"He's with us," Stormy said. They exchanged a knowing look.

"I don't care who he's *with*, who the fuck are you."

"My name's Adam," I said. "I'm looking for Mickey Sandoz."

Stormy and Jordan went tentative—they were no match. The guy was a motorhead or batshit or both; he went right up to me like we were already mid-brawl. "I don't like your face."

"I'm not crazy about it either," I said. "But it's the only—"

He pushed me hard. "Don't get fuckin' funny with me, Jewboy. I don't like your fuckin' face."

"*Yo.*" Stormy tried to intercept and he moved her hard with his arm. She went stumbling back into the rubble.

"Fuck you, asshole!" she howled as she pulled herself up.

Now the guy was revving, walking me backward over piles of garbage. "Don't fuckin' come around here looking for *shit*, Holmes, stay in your fuckin' lane."

Jordan said, "Dog, you need to get a grip."

But this psycho wasn't listening. "I want my fuckin' money, little bitch. You find Sandoz, you tell him I'll get paid or I'll shoot the both of you in the fuckin' head. Bam! Bam!"

"If I find him, I'll—"

"Shut up, bitch." He pushed me again. He liked pushing me, it made him smile. "Lotta people can't stay in their lane. Learn to stay in your fuckin' lane, bitch." To accent this concept, he *almost* gave me a fast elbow to the chest but I dodged it, which sent me backward and I fell over some kind of concrete stack. Now he was standing over me. He put his gray-sneakered foot on the slabs of concrete to demonstrate its proximity to my face.

"You can't stay in your lane, you get stomped, bitch." Then he reached down and pulled me up by my sweatshirt. The junkies looked at the two of us like together we were a unicorn or some other half-mythical creature they didn't yet believe in. I was trying to raise my hands, to say something like *"I'll leave,"* but the wind was knocked out of me and I hadn't even taken a punch. This crazy fuck wasn't finished; he was positioning himself to give me a beatdown. Trying to come to my aid, Jordan almost blocked him but this only sent the guy into gonzo fury. He started ranting about how Sandoz had burned him and how he knew all kinds of shit about Sandoz that could put him back behind bars forever where he'd be somebody's bitch and about how he was gonna kick my face in *tonight* if it was the last thing he did, maybe right this second.

I saw a pyramid pile of thick pipes, and in one swift move I scrambled to grab one, stood and held it out—it was heavier than I expected.

Jordan groaned.

Stormy said, *"Put that down, idiot."*

But I ignored her. I said, "Let me outta here, dude. I don't have any beefs with you. I just came here to tell Mickey Sandoz some bad news."

"What kinda news is that?"

"His good friend is dead—*was killed.*"

"Who?"

"You don't know him."

"Who?"

"Hawley." And then I looked at the pipe in my hand and lost a breath and trembled, and it dropped to the ground with a clank. "Devon Hawley."

For a still moment, my attacker and the homeless posse behind him stood frozen. And then he buckled, half-lunged at nothing, balanced on a metal beam and vomited, long and hard.

When he lifted his face, he was pale as death and bawling.

Stormy put her arms around him. "Oh, Mickey, I'm so sorry."

16

It took Sandoz about an hour to piece himself together, hunched over on a concrete slab with fits of shivering and tears. The muscles, the tattoos, the hard leathery shell had released, gone slack, and he looked weak, disoriented, in the throes of sudden mourning and maybe also some kind of drug comedown. He tried to apologize for what he called "rassling" me, said he'd thought I was a debt collector, said incarceration had turned him into a monster, that he hated himself.

Then he said, "Is he really gone?"

I nodded. "When was the last time you saw him?"

"Ah, Dev cut me off a few weeks ago."

"How come?"

"Usual arguments, stupid shit. He was always on a mission to straighten me out." Sandoz bristled, clutched himself. As the wayward crowd around us finally dispersed, he looked at me from the corner of his eye. "You don't think I'd hurt him, do you? That why you're here?"

I spoke in a terse whisper. "I don't know, man. You tell me."

He stared at me through watery eyes, rocked with pain, gasping jagged at the unleaded night air. "I could *never* hurt Devvy, man. That'd be like killing myself. Worse. I . . . Dev was my brother. *And we didn't even say goodbye.*"

The tears started streaming again, and I felt compelled to put an arm around him—this strange, wizened tough guy that had only just threatened to shoot me in the head.

He looked up at me, emptied of life, corpse-like. "The dream is gone, man."

I took it in and said, "When was the last time you ate something?"

We drove down Santa Monica toward the ocean until we reached a revolving sign—RICK'S CHARBROILED: BURGERS "IS" US. We ordered and I picked up the tab. Then we took our grub to a dirty, scratched-up, blue-green Formica picnic table outside the shack, surrounded by bumper-to-bumper drive-through, late-night burger freaks. Between bites of the greasiest chow on Planet Earth, he said, "I just don't see who would do this."

"I need to tell my lawyer about the band and everything," I said. "He's not sure it lines up."

"And you are?"

"I don't know. But two weeks ago, Hawley went to Emil's dad, saying he could prove Emil's innocence. And then . . . this?"

Sandoz morphed for a third time before my eyes. First, he'd been rough street animal, a chain swinger. Then, suddenly, he was broken, the aging addict, a wreck. Now something else came through, somebody who still cared about something.

I said, "Mickey, I want to understand exactly what happened to your band. To Emil and Reynaldo, all of it."

"It's a long time ago. I don't know where to begin. Plus . . ."

"What?"

"Man, by the time we made the recording, I was already high. That's when I really started using, maybe right after that, and then there were some heavy-duty sessions, a high-level recording studio or some shit, but I swear, man, other than that, I do not remember one fucking thing."

"But you remember that Reynaldo Durazo was killed."

"Honestly? I *know* it in here—" He pointed a bony finger at his temple. "But that whole time is just one bad blur." He popped the top off his strawberry shake and considered the cold pink foam. "Only thing I really remember is how unhappy I was."

I said, "The papers wrote that Reynaldo was a drug dealer. Was he the one you were scoring from?"

Sandoz rolled his eyes as he shook out fries onto a bed of ketchup. "Rey-Rey was no *drug dealer*. Rey-Rey was just some dork we went to school with."

Sandoz gave me a weak smile.

"Couldn't keep a beat to save his life. He *begged* to be in the band, told us he had a kit. That was good enough for us. '*You're hired.*'"

"But did he and Emil have some kind of beef?"

"No way. Elkaim was Mister Mellow. I never saw him have beefs with anyone, ever. He wouldn't have punched Rey, let alone *kill* him. Emil was kind of, not our leader exactly, but he was the courageous one. We ran through a lot of guitarists before he showed up, but once we heard him play, it was over, man; he was the heart and soul of the band."

"So what the hell happened?"

Sandoz whispered, "I don't *know*, man."

He ate his Double Chili in a kind of meditative stupor, but he was slowly coming back to life. The right burger could do that to an Angeleno. I watched him and wondered what he was remembering, or trying to remember.

I said, "Is it true you had a thing with Marjorie Persky?"

"Who?"

I raised eyebrows.

"I knew Cinnamon Persky—you mean her *mother*?"

"Yeah," I said, "that's who I mean."

"I didn't know her."

"What about after the band. You served," I said, pointing at the tags.

"Yeah. Wrong decision number five hundred fifty-two."

"So why'd you do it?"

"After all the shit went down, losing Rey and Emil, I quit high school, I tried to sober up. Then I enlisted. I was totally lost. I didn't think there was gonna be a real war. All of a sudden, Desert Storm, I'm stationed in Mina al Ahmadi, driving a T-72—the skinny rock dude who *never* should have been sent into combat."

He laughed, but under the goof, the permanent wound to his safety vibed through.

"A long way from The Daily Telegraph," I said.

"After what happened, there was no Daily Telegraph."

"I got your LP."

He groaned. "I haven't heard that piece of shit in years."

"But it's great."

"Come on, man—we maybe did five gigs. We stunk. Never shoulda left the garage, what fucking hubris." Despite the words, talk of the band lit him up even more—the death glow fell off like dried lizard skin. He reached for his strawberry milkshake. "If we made it to the end of a song, it was like a minor miracle."

"And you and Hawley stayed close?"

"I wouldn't call it that. I tried to stay close. He just, like, tolerated me."

"I don't get it."

"You know, man, when a band breaks up, it's like a divorce. Hawley got insular, cut everyone off. He didn't want to jam, hang out, nothing—total blackout. I lost my whole world in, like, three days." Sandoz breathed deep, eyes fragile. "You really found him?"

I nodded. The night air around us seemed heavy, thick with exhaust. Sandoz looked at the last of his food but didn't eat. Mourning was creeping back up on him. He reached into his pocket and pulled out a pint of Classic Club gin, emptied it into his milkshake. Then, from his other pocket, he fished out a pre-scription bottle—he shook out two pills, then a third, gobbled them and slugged the loaded shake.

Then he said, "Dev was what people now call *obsessive compulsive*. But we didn't have a name for it."

"What makes you say so?"

"Oh, he was fixated, *totally*. He could not let go of the past."

"That's what Grunes said about you."

"Yeah, well, fuck that guy—*Methinks he doth protest too much.* I *reminisce* but Devon was *doing* shit. He was even in touch with Durazo's cousin, hounding her night and day."

"So he was actually trying to find out who killed Durazo, like, this whole time?"

"Yup. He had this big, like, wall collage, filled with what he called leads—I saw it. It looked like a lot of BS to me. Recently, he even hired this pro detective, but the guy only got so far."

"I heard the guy flopped and gave up."

"Bullshit—he didn't give up; he quit. And Hawley freaked. He was *real* upset about it last time I talked to him. He was all, like, '*It doesn't make sense; it doesn't make sense!*' I think Dev thought the guy got bought off or something."

"By who?"

Sandoz shrugged.

"Did Hawley tell you the detective's name?"

"Gladstone. Martin Gladstone—when he quit, Dev practi-cally had a nervous breakdown." Long pause—Sandoz stared out at the gasoline vapor. "Like finding out who really killed Rey would change anything."

"Wouldn't it?"

"No. Absolutely not. It's *done*, man. Our youth is *gone*—into the black hole."

Energized, Sandoz got restless, held hostage here at the fast-food shack, trapped between the scratched-up blue-green bench and tabletop. To blast free, he poured more gin, took another pill, and started lecturing me. First about his bad marriage and the treachery of living under his father's thumb. Then he digressed on why being in a band is for people who need a real family. But then he monologued himself into an anti-rock tear. In twenty years, he had not placed a single rock track on his Pandora, not classic rock, punk, alt, or otherwise; he hated all of it. He was a karaoke crooner now, a jazz convert, but he didn't seem that happy about it. Then he started thrashing the internet, a familiar riff. He said that hard drugs were healthier than Facebook. Pointing ketchupy fries at me, he insisted we were on the precipice of complete cultural dissolution, which didn't stop him from loving Rick's Charbroiled. Then when he finished eating, he tossed his wrappers in the trash and returned to the table to tear Grunes and the LAUSD a new one. Sandoz wasn't homeless by default; he insisted he chose it. He only felt at home with crazies, bangers, and the permanently wayward.

"I've come to know a thing or two about human personality," he said, "especially teenagers. *Now* I see—I should have guessed what was going to go down with our band all along."

"Really? What were the signs?"

"Cinnamon was on fire. She was looking for trouble; it surrounded her. She was way ambitious. And she was *fast*."

"Because of Emil?"

"No, no, the opposite. Elk had to race to keep up with her. She was out on the Strip every night, hanging at the Whisky, the Roxy, handing out acid, these great big sheets of perforated tax stamps she kept rolled up in her purse. And she always had some coke on her, too. I won't say she was a groupie, but she was some kind of ambassador to all the British bands that came through, Tin Tin Duffy and all that eyeliner bullshit."

"What was her role in The Daily Telegraph?"

"Her role? Well, she was kind of our de facto manager. She had big plans for us. Actually, I didn't know how in-crowd Cinnamon was till I bumped into her at one of the Mind-Life Potential seminars."

"Mind-Life Potential?"

"Yup, it was a *thing* in the eighties." Sandoz put on the anchorman voice. *"Harness the power of aggressive positivity through Mind-Life Potential."*

"You did the seminar?"

"Yeah, we all did. It was supposed to make you more self-aware, more confident, all that bullshit—they had all us high school kids walking around like zombies, spreading the gospel. Somebody in the A/V club hustled me, and I signed up. I was a high school nerd with bad acne, ya know? I craved me some major guidance."

"What about your parents?"

"My family scene wasn't too cool. My dad was a fireman; he only slept at home, like, one in three nights. My mom was morbidly obese. She couldn't hardly get off her ass to change the TV channel. Of course, today I understand she was depressive, but back then, like I said, we didn't have the right words. Man, I'd go anywhere after school instead of going home."

"So, Cinnamon showed up at this thing, too?"

"I *thought* she was the squarest girl in school. A *preppy.*"

He said the word with true contempt.

"You know, a drill squad girl in purple Lacoste and over-priced sneakers. But no, she shows up, and lo and behold, she's the It Girl, knows everybody. She was dressed different than at school, too. She wore this super-short miniskirt and all kinds of bangles and stuff; all the dudes were drooling over her, including me. At the seminar, I didn't dare speak to her. But afterward, I got the courage to offer her a ride home. I had this killer Vespa P200E that I bought with money I earned being a movie usher. Cin very politely turns me down. And then . . ."

He took a slug from his shake, impatient with himself.

"*This is what really blew my mind.* Just as I'm revving my scooter, up drives these two slick older dudes in this convertible red whatever, probably a Mustang or a Camaro or something. And they are there expressly *to pick up* Lady Cinnamon. I froze in my tracks. And that's when I realized who these guys were—they were famous DJs, these two big-timers. I'd seen their faces on billboards, man. I stood there like an idiot and watched the three of 'em drive away and, I'll never forget this, Cinnamon turns back and waves goodbye to me and she says, 'See you in homeroom, Mickey.' Just like that—*whoosh!*—they're off to the races. Here I was, thinking I was the cool cat on campus, and this ultra-square girl is being chaperoned by, you know, *icons.*"

"You saying she went out with one of them or—"

"Those two hound dogs? You'd have to ask them. If they're still alive. They've been off the air since forever, but the thing was, back then, they had the most popular oldies show on K-Earth. They were, like, city heroes. And they had this thing—*Can YOU Spot the K-R-T-H DJs? Catch 'em if you can!* You'd call in and if you could correctly identify the whereabouts of these assholes and the car they were driving, you'd win a trip to Disneyland or Knott's or whatever. So you see, I had a dilemma. I could hit the nearest pay phone and say I had just spotted these guys, but then they'd announce the winner by name and Cinnamon would know it was me and . . . it just didn't seem like the thing to do. So I didn't. Next day, she leans over to me in homeroom, talking to me at school for the first time ever. And she goes, 'Did you cash in?' And I said something sarcastic like, 'Do I look like I want to join the Mickey Mouse Club?' and she just raised a very approving eyebrow and that was that. It was nothing, two tiny little events. But it changed me forever."

"So, two old DJs gave her a ride somewhere," I said. "I don't get it, what's the big deal?"

He sucked the last of his shake through the pink paper straw like a man taking his last drag before execution, but the color had returned to his cheeks once and for all and he was buzzing. It was like he'd morphed into his former heart-hurt kinetic teenage self, complete with odd-tilted posture. "Well, it *was* a big deal. Because . . . because I realized right then and there . . . I saw . . ."

He blushed.

"What, tell me."

"Because it made me *realize* that there really was no such thing as *cool.* This thing I'd been trying to be since the age of ten, it didn't exist. There was only one real law and that law was *sex power.* Period. Sex power. The world . . . was just a game of . . . *sexual checkers*, jump and capture—the only law. It overrode *everything.* Still does. And it was a shock to me, man. With my two parents flyin' off each other like magnetic Scottie dogs, I never thought of sex that way—as a *power.* My dumb ass, I really thought sex was *Can you get the pretty girl to love you?* But when Cinnamon Persky hopped in the ride with those old dudes, *I saw the light*, right then and there. And it seemed so cruel. *Sex power.*"

He chewed his straw with ferocious concentration. Then he said, "Much later I heard she brought our demos to them, the DJs, but they didn't do jack shit for us. Soon after, everything went to hell—but I never forgot that afternoon, all my life. Couple years later, I was stationed in Khafji and I thought I was gonna die; we were down in a desert bunker and they were rocketing the shit out of us, hot metal flying everywhere, and you know what? I remembered that moment, the feeling, seeing Cinnamon ride away, how it stung me. Actually, you know what? It made me less afraid of death."

We sat, not speaking, listening to the sound of traffic around us, the car radios and horns and the drive-through intercom crackling through mixed-up orders. We were stranded, stranded on Cheeseburger Island.

"Who were the DJs?" I said.

He shook the last pill in his bottle into his palm and frowned. "Kip 'n' Rog."

Then—

"Man, you know what I just remembered? I know where Hawley hid his key."

"What key?"

"To his pad—*I can get us in there.*"

"I—no, that doesn't sound like a good idea."

"No, no, actually it's a *great* idea." He downed the final pill with the dregs of his strawberry shake. "I'm an old friend; I know where the key is. He let me in there all the time."

"I can't do that; I'm a person of interest. I'm not breaking into—"

"Nobody's breaking *anything*. There's stuff in there, all the leads he collected and whatnot. I mean, you want to figure this shit out or not?"

"Not like that, I can't. My lawyer—I can't."

His brow hardened, eyes sliding into a mean squint—the tough guy resurfaced, buzzed and pissed. "Fuck your lawyer—you're taking me down there, bro. I just opened my fucking heart to you. *Quid pro quo*—fucking ride's the least you can do."

"Mickey, for all we know there'll be cops all around the place; it could be roped off—"

He stood. "*Get up*—we're gonna go find out."

17

We pulled up to Hawley's place on Lobdell—lights out, empty driveway.

"See—no cops, *goofball.*"

We got out and Sandoz moved quickly, up the little walkway to the potted alocasia. He slid it, lifted a brick, dug around, squinted.

"Shit—key's gone. Fuck it, follow me."

We walked around the back, over some old rolled-up hose and a tin trash can. Sandoz pressed open the gate.

I whispered, "What are we doing here? We are *not* going to break and enter—"

"This ain't nothin', man. We're visiting."

He pulled a ratty-looking handkerchief from his pocket and was wrapping it around his fist. "Once I robbed a Winchell's with nothing but my hand in the pocket—*stick 'em up!*"

"Don't," I said, "don't break anything, please, we're—"

But it was too late; Sandoz rammed his fist through the back door window and was reaching in to jimmy the lock. No alarms, no lights. We cut through the dark laundry room, the small kitchen, into a big empty dining room/living room combo—old Spanish, 1930s style. The place was sparse—hardwood floors, antique furniture, a round table straight out of some old King

Arthur flick, and one big framed painting of red flowers in a vase—it looked like something you'd pick up at a garage sale.

"*Psst.*" Sandoz was hyped, eyes darting. "Follow me."

He led me down the railroad hall and opened doors—a home office with a drawing board and sketches of models, a green-tiled bathroom, pristine. Then he cracked open the door to Hawley's dark and lonesome bedroom—the first thing that hit me was the bed, a perfectly made single beside an empty nightstand.

"This guy ever have spouses?" I said. "Girlfriends, boy-friends, anything?"

"Nope. He had one thing—*the dream.*"

Sandoz flicked on the light and spun me around by the shoulders to face the inside wall—a massive cacophony, thumb-tacked on corkboard.

I stared, breathless, pulse racing: The Daily Telegraph and nothing but—lyrics, flyers, undeveloped photo shoot strips, a demo cassette cover, and Polaroids: a classroom full of intent-looking eighties teens, yearbook pages, Guitar Center receipts, same cutout listings ad from Natural Fudge that was left in the test pressing, all of it overlapping, hastily unarranged, the cornucopia pouring.

And dead center: Emil's Fairfax High ID card—hopeful Emil, rosy and bright-eyed.

"Told you he was obsessed."

I reached for the ID to get a closer look.

"Don't touch!" Sandoz said, grabbing my hand. "Fingerprints, dum-dum."

I nodded, dazed. Then I pulled the cell phone and started taking photos, but as I did, Sandoz went kinetic behind me. He was getting busy, grabbing a pillow one-handed, shaking it out of the pillowcase.

"What are you doing?"

"*Research.*" He started bagging things—the dresser full of

old watches and pens and batteries, a hanger full of ties—then he dashed down the hall and I watched him stuff an unmatched pair of dinner candelabras into the bag, and he was digging through drawers, grabbing handfuls of silverware.

I tried to get tough in a hard whisper. "Dude, I thought we came here to get info, not pilfer."

"Hawley don't care anymore—he ain't got no quarter with the material world."

I heard clanging and shuffling as I scurried to photograph every corner of the collage. Sandoz came back down the dark hall wagging a book.

"The Holy Bible," he said like a gospel preacher. "Been looking for one of these."

He tossed the book into the pillowcase and shook it like Santa. "Locked and loaded. I'm outta here, bro. Come on—*front door's faster.*"

Shaking my head, I followed him out, taking one last look at the gloomy place—a lonely man's home, lonely no more.

I jammed the ignition as Sandoz flopped into the passenger seat. As I tore down the hill toward Sunset, he burst out laughing, his wide mouth showing off chipped meth teeth. "We did it! Nice work, cowboy."

"Yeah, great," I said. "We robbed a dead man—really cool."

"This is what Devvy would've wanted, bro."

Then he reached into the pillowcase and pulled out a black spiral datebook, slapped it on my lap.

"Happy birthday, amigo. Now cruise by Sixth and Arapahoe."

"Oh no," I said. "Not a chance. I am a licensed Lyft driver. I'm not taking you on some kind of a drug run."

"Dude—I'm *sick*. I'm addicted. You do get that, right? You don't want me to throw up all over your car, do you?"

Disgruntled, I cut down Santa Monica to Hoover—it wasn't the first time a rider wanted me to go there. Dark figures phantomed the corner, parking garage duckers, porch hiders. I idled, tense as fuck, staring down the rearview for cops while Sandoz traded the candelabras for a silver foil ball. I had half a mind to tear off and leave him there, but no. Then he was back in the car and thumbing the shit up his nose, looking damn content.

I said, "You . . . need a place to crash or anything?"

"Take me to my tent, Holmes. I can't get a good night's sleep anywhere else."

We made the rest of the trip in silence. I pulled up to the 405 and parked before the columns. Sandoz said, "Home sweet homeless."

Then he got out and came around to my side of the car, leaned in and placed a weak hand on my shoulder. "I'm glad to know you, brother."

I said, "Are you scared?"

"Far from it. The Daily Telegraph *lives*, man."

"I'm not so sure about that."

"Well, you care. That's what counts. And you gotta figure this shit out."

I nodded.

He said, "You find something, come by and let me know."

Then he walked into Tent Town with the rest of his loot, head bowed like a pilgrim.

I drove home and showered off the night, nuked a burrito and tried to watch the news. How inconsequential it seemed! The Earth was a planet with its children living in tents and empty homes and nobody understood shit. I finished my burrito and got up the courage to flip through Hawley's datebook. It stopped cold on October 6—blank pages spelling death. I went backward page by page, slow and methodical.

Tuesday, October 3—the day I followed him, the day before the day he died—*Gladstone @ Taco Miende*, circled.

September 30 storyboard conference 11423 Burbank, Model 48b/16E33.

September 10 CE and then the address at the Shalom. *CE*—as in Charles Elkaim.

August 29 Paramount Model 517j-unmotored. Call for refrig truck.

August 18, Gladstone to Fountain Grove. Again circled.

Other than that—a lot of deadlines, studios, addresses, model numbers. Hawley had some kind of tracking system I couldn't make out, but it was precise.

Then: *February 21—Martin Gladstone int*, circled.

I flipped back and forth—from what it looked like, Hawley met or hired detective Martin Gladstone in February. On August 18, detective Gladstone went to someplace called Fountain Grove, and on October 3, I watched them argue. Maybe Gladstone dropped the case.

I looked him up—easy trace. He was a retired LAPD policeman living at the Ravencrest on Los Feliz Boulevard, Unit 2. No listed number.

Then I looked up Fountain Grove. Closest local match was a tony retirement village in Laguna—

> *Southern California's premier active lifestyle community for people 55 and older. Just 10 minutes from the beautiful Laguna Beach coastline, the Village is nestled on 3.8-square miles of rolling hillsides in Orange County, California, offering a Utopian alternative to the traditional aging process highlighting advanced memory care, body rejuvenation, connections of the heart, and spiritual awakening. Come let us bring health and joy to your penultimate years in an atmosphere of sensitivity and enlightenment.*

The place was sponsored by a pair of aging celebrity DJs—Stan Kipler and Roger Paulsen, aka Kip 'n' Rog.

18

I slept in and woke up heavy, disoriented. In dreams, Herschel had warned of blind alleys, mazes. He was worried, displeased, getting panicky—I tried to shake it off. By the time I got out, it was early afternoon. I vowed to put in a regular Lyft shift, but once I got behind the wheel it felt like every other passing cop car was giving me the evil eye. I'd stumbled over a dying body, broken into the dead man's home, taken off with his possessions. I was an unlicensed investigator with an unreleased LP for evidence, and I wasn't even sure what case I was trying to solve—a murder that took place forty years ago, the brutal slaying of some guy I never knew, the history of a long-lost band nobody cared about, or the sudden disappearance of the man who'd been put on the job before me.

Then there was Emil Elkaim. It was like there was a silent understanding out there among almost everyone involved that he'd been framed, and I was starting to think they were right.

And Devon Hawley Junior *did* know something—I was sure of that now.

Before the sun waned, I drove to Los Feliz to try to speak with errant detective Martin Gladstone. The Ravencrest was one of those old dilapidated two-story mods with the burnt palm courtyard and an egg-shaped pool in the middle. A tilting FOR RENT sign stuck out of the dirt out front. I went in through the unlocked gate and knocked on the door of Unit 2, but nobody answered. I peered in through the smoke-stained window curtains—a bare, cream-rugged living room and a tiny yellow kitchen. I walked back out onto the street and dialed the number on the sign but got a machine. I was about to leave when I spotted an old lady stepping out of Unit 1 in a bathrobe, swim cap, and blue plastic flip-flops. She dropped her bathrobe on the lawn chair and was carefully descending into the pool in a frilly one-piece as I came back in through the gate.

"Hi," I said. "Sorry, sorry to bother. I'm an old friend of Martin Gladstone's." I thumbed his apartment. "I was wondering—do you know where he is or—?"

"Ya missed him, hon—Marty's moved."

"Wow. I had no idea."

"Just last week, gone down to Laguna."

"*Laguna*. Did he leave a forwarding address?"

"Super might have it, but she's never here. She's duckin' me 'cause I want the damn washer-dryer fixed."

"I see."

She ran her wrinkled, pale hands over the shining water and said, "Marty musta come into a pretty big chunk of change to be leaving this dump—lucky old fool." Then she gently lunged into the blue.

As I headed for Double Fry's, the Jukebox Id kicked in. Not everybody had the Jukebox Id, but if you had it, you knew it—song fragments spun in your head, nonstop. This one was a kind of rock thing with wild man drums, but sung to the tune of "He's So Shy" by the Pointer Sisters:

Private eye
Private eye
He's the guy who blew the case sky high
Private eye
Private eye
He took off just like a butterfly

Not good. So bad. But even the bad songs had a way of connecting the dots. At the boat, I caught Double Fry polishing his camera lenses on a big black towel.

"Before you get mad," I said, "I want you to know how much I truly cherish our friendship."

"What have you done?"

I told him about my night's adventures and where I'd been.

"But . . . you didn't get caught."

"No, thank God. We, uh, slipped through the cracks."

He shook his head, laughed through his teeth. "Well, thanks for listening to your lawyer's advice, *schmuck*."

"I know, I know—but I think this might be a real lead."

"So what you're saying is this detective guy went to investigate a retirement village, then he dropped the case and *moved* there?"

"Yup, that's what it looks like."

"Okay—but it might not be the way you're framing it. Maybe he just . . . wanted to retire and his work happened to lead him to the right place."

"I don't know about that," I said. "This place looks pretty upscale for an old snoop—Fountain Grove Estates. I mean, is it assisted living or some kind of . . . *group* or what?"

"You mean like a cult?"

"Not a cult-cult, but the web copy is ridiculous. *Utopian alternatives, let's all light some incense and play shuffleboard in the raw.*"

Fry grinned. "I get it—heavy sixties ethos. Mindfulness,

all natural, love and peace, vegan, holistic, hemp bathrobes, a little THC bar. Of *course,* public nudity's on the menu."

"Yeah, but something's off-kilter. They have all this ad copy about dying with grace on the website, with all these euphoric, blissed-out aging faces."

"Self-actualization for grandpa and grandma—nothing off-kilter about it. Ten zillion boomers are about to check out. They want it to be as groovy as Woodstock."

"Okay, *that* much I understand. But where do the DJs fit in?"

"Corporate sponsors—they lure the target market."

"According to Wiki, these guys were the kings of Boss Radio. They held the coveted Saturday night slot on KHJ—you know, AM for the cruisers."

"Well, yeah—a hundred fucking years ago. *Now* how are they gonna earn some bread?"

Fry closed a case of black lenses embedded in black foam. Together, we pulled the awning across the deck and Fry opened the laptop. Howard the cat hopped on my lap—whatever was on that screen, he wanted to see it too.

"Check this out," I said. "*Seventy-two thousand fans—* clockin' their every move."

Kip and Rog had their own Insta with links to YouTube videos of their air checks, and the talkbacks were loco:

> Bring back the dynamic duo!
> Teen town lives!
> americka ended june 16, '92—the night Kip/Rog went
> off the air

"1992," I said.

"I'm amazed they made it that long," Fry said. "I guess the lucrative world of oldies but goodies kept them in business. But let's play the old-school shit."

I reached over and fired up a YouTube: *Kip 'n' Rog 93 KHJ Wednesday 22nd December 1965.*

No movie, just a still black and white of the two hepcats. Their air check slogan pumped in like a megaphoned battle cry—*"Teeeeeeeen Towwwwwwn Tunes IN!"*

Then one of them started talking—the fastest silver-tongued DJ spiel you could ever imagine, riding over the sound of snapping fingers. *"Wigsters, digsters, geepies and groovers, you're cooking with K and R, the caper cruisers from coast to coast, the hosts who don't have to boast, we're wailing with the wax and shuttin' down the shushers on that twisting river of electric light known as Everystreet, Anytown, U.S. of A. Sooooo fire up your hot rod, jack up your jalopy and go, baby, go!"* Then, the sound of revving engines and screeching tires as the opening riff to Sonny and Cher's "The Beat Goes On" kicked in.

Fry shot me a droll look and we both burst out laughing. But as the laughs died, we sat there listening like two men in a kind of séance. It quickly became apparent the fast one was Kip, the cool one was Rog. They spun 45s, took dedications, ran bombastic ads for swimsuits, razors, and something called Gorilla Milk.

"You'll go ape for Gorilla Milk—now featuring strawberry malt . . . it's hairy!"

Then, over an orchestral bass drumroll, Rog said, "Fasten your seatbelts, swingers, it's time . . . for . . . *the Pickup Line Parade!*"

A Salvation Army–style band romped up behind the clang of an old-school ringing phone. Then Rog, in that easy half-southern drawl of his, said, *"All you fine people out there makin' it with the modern sound, we've got a very special guest today right here in the studio with us, we just met her right out there on our way in, window-shopping on Fairfax Ave, a lovely young lady right here with us at radio station KHJ, she's sweet sixteen and impossible to ignore, folks, finalist in the Miss California Pageant—you shoulda taken that trophy, darlin'—Miss Marjorie Hirsch."*

A cacophony of trumpets and kazoos and then—

"Hi, Kip, hiya, Rog." Flirtiest voice on the planet, pure sunshine. *"Can't believe I'm really on the air!"*

"You really are, darlin'—is this a pretty girl or what? Now—tonight, as promised, we're gonna take some calls, let the boys make their pitch, and you decide. You know how the Pickup Line Parade works?"

"Of course I do—I'm your biggest fan."

"Wait a minute," I said. "Wait, wait a minute—play that again, like, half a minute."

Fry toggled back.

"—she's sweet sixteen and impossible to ignore, folks, finalist in the Miss California Pageant—you shoulda taken that trophy, darlin'—Miss Marjorie Hirsch."

"Hi, Kip, hiya, Rog. Can't believe I'm really on the air!"

Pointer finger trembling at the screen, I said, "That's Marjorie Persky."

"Who?"

"Cinnamon's mother—the lady with the LP. Sweet sixteen—Jesus."

"Quite the ambitious teenybopper." Fry leaned in to focus. Kip and Rog were leading a series of nervous teenage boys through phone-ins, each one trying to make their voice sound deeper, more suave, more commanding than the last:

"Hi there, miss—just wondering. Are you a magician? 'Cause whenever I look at you . . . everything else disappears."

"Hey, baby, let's go to the mountaintop . . . 'cause after we make love . . . you'll see flowers in the snow."

*"Excuse me, ma'am—do you have a map I can borrow?
'Cause I'm getting lost in your eyes."*

After each phone-in, that same haranguing rave-up of trumpets and kazoos. And after the last caller, Kip said, *"Okay,
Miss Hirsch, that's three for three."*

"What do you say?" Rog piped in. *"Any of these fellas stand
a chance?"*

And then, Marjorie, this "female guest," so obviously a paid
actress, said, *"Caller number three, I liked your style best."*

Kip, gone frenetic: *"We have a winner, folks! The jury's
in! So—Miss Hirsch, are you saying you would willingly give
caller number three your phone number?"*

*"Well, I don't know about that. But . . . I might hear him
out."*

Rog, in full *menefreghista* mode: *"You heard it here first,
callers—when addressing a pretty gal, try the softer touch.
Thank you very much, Miss Hirsch. The boy who catches your
heart is a lucky fellow indeed."*

Kip: *"Caller number three, you'll be getting a pair of tickets
to Knott's Berry Farm Christmas Jamboree, where we'll be on
hand to spin some sides and blow some noggins. And now—
Duane Eddy taking out the . . . 'Trash!'"*

Over the twanging cowboy guitar, Fry said, "Man, the
world was cuckooballs then. *I'll make you see flowers in the
snow?"*

"Yeah," I said, "but—those two DJs have thousands of fans
right now. Can you imagine all those people listening to yesterday's radio like it was on today?"

"Actually?" Fry said. "I can. Think about it. It's just like
listening to the cantor sing a prayer that was written two thousand years ago. People want to be"—he whirled a finger—
"connected in time. People *want* endless repeat."

I scrolled on. "Look—they still have a show—on Sirius. No, wait—they *had* a show. It's canceled."

"Well, there you go—two old geezers, taken off the air, sent out to pasture. Now they're the face of Fountain Grove Estates."

"Okay, okay, let's connect some dots here before I go me-shuga. Marjorie knew Kip and Rog, and so did her daughter, Cinnamon, whose boyfriend was in the band with Hawley. Cut to the present—Hawley hires a detective and now Kip and Rog run this strange retirement village. But why does Hawley's detective go down there—*and stay there?*"

Fry said, "That's what swingers and hipsters want to know, daddy-o." He was staring at me with that terrible glint in his eye.

"You can't just show up at a place like that," I said. "They'll throw up the gate."

"Well, if you show up and say, '*Hi I'm investigating a murder,*' they might. But there are other ways."

"Such as?"

He swooped up the cell phone.

"Freiburger," I said, "whatever you're about to do, please don't. I've had enough shockers for the week."

He raised a shushing finger.

"Yeah, hi, is this the retirement village in Laguna?" He turned his back to me. "Great—*my name is Adam.* I have kind of a . . . *situation.* You see, my uncle Marty's a newish resident there, and he asked me to come down tomorrow, but he isn't great with a phone and he forgot to tell me his unit."

When Fry signed off, his eyebrows did a little Groucho Marx wiggle of triumph. "Uncle Marty's expecting you to-morrow at noon."

At the wheel, driving home, I was still marveling at teenage scenemaker Marjorie and how her sweet daughter Cinnamon seemed to have picked up the baton, only to discover it was a lit stick of dynamite. That's when I suddenly remembered Endi's amateur hour gig. I pulled over and got the folded yellow flyer out of my glove box. *Van Gogh's Ear, 8pm*—my watch said it was already quarter past, but I was only ten minutes away.

19

The joint was a gutted bait-and-tackle shop on the Strand in Venice, more like a coffeehouse than a nightclub, but it was jam-packed, with a tiny stage about three inches off the ground. It was dark in there, and Endi was nowhere to be seen as I maneuvered through the crowd to the last empty seat, trying to be inconspicuous. Onstage, an undernourished college guy in a mustard-colored beanie was lecturing the crowd. "Just a reminder—you get *three minutes total*. It's not much so let's give everybody a chance, okay?"

The audience groaned in unison like students who just received news of a test. I looked over my shoulder. Still no Endi.

Personally, though, I got the guy's point. Three minutes was high pressure, and the comics and singers and skit teams came and went faster than you could hate 'em. The first guy sang a Billie Eilish song I didn't know, then a straitlaced comic did a rant about the Dutch and their wooden clogs, then the next guy cracked jokes about the perils of being a Black ski instructor, then a crazy-eyed young woman merely chanted, *"You are not my people, you are not my people"* over and over again, pointing at the audience—strangely enough, she got laughs. And then, from the dark, Angela Elsworth, aka Endi Sandell, tripped onto the stage, guitar in hand.

She was transformed from demure lodger into a vision in an antique-sage velvet wrap dress with a yellow carnation in her hair, quick-tuning her guitar with a slightly nervous look in her big eyes. She said, "This is a Sarah McLachlan song" and then she started playing, singing quietly, beyond intense, like having a stranger whisper in your ear. I tried to be cool but I was transfixed. Ruh roh, I was flippin', even harder than I had already flipped. Because there was something extra about her onstage—magnetic and mysterious. What she lacked in confidence, she made up for in just being open about it, this stranger so far from home. My ex was a singer too, a songwriter and a performer, but so different in every way. Kerrylyn was born to take the stage, she couldn't hide it, whereas Endi was tentative up there, clutching a reluctant inner something that peeked out at the world. But it drew you in, drew me in, the whole room. The song ended, she opened her eyes. A moment of silence, then big cheers, and she smiled. Stepping off the stage into their applause, she was blushing, nervously pulling the flower from her hair. Halfway through the next act, I craned my neck, searched the place for her—she was just outside the door, talking to some friends. I got up and went out to join them. At the sight of me, she made a big gesture.

"You're here!"

I said, "That was . . . *wow.*"

"You liar, I was a mess." Her color was still high.

"No way," one of her entourage said. "They *loved* you."

"I did too," I chimed in, overeager—one of her girlfriends raised a curious eyebrow.

"We're going down the street for a drink. You should join."

"Oh, that's okay, I'm just—"

"No," she said, "join us." She rattled off the names of her pals.

"How do you know all these people? You just got here?"

"These are Yael's friends. She forced them to be here. Adam

is writing an article on this strange, obscure rock band—all they left behind was this amazing test pressing."

"What were they called?" asked the blond guy with the baby face.

"The Daily Telegraph," I said.

"Never heard of them."

"That's the point," said Endi. "Nobody did."

Half-reluctant, I ambled along with the pack—Endi, blond Cliff, a dreadlocked guy named Eric who claimed to have participated in some kind of Wu Tang Clan remix project, curly-haired Yael, a tall skinny poet named Pablo, a real stunner named Onnalisa "with an O," and two others whose names I didn't catch. We went to the Lincoln and took the long table. I nursed a Scotch at the far end and listened to the banter, a little out of place but enjoying it. Cliff had auditioned for a horror movie that morning and described what it was like to scream at a video camera in a brightly lit room. Yael and Endi both went to the social work program at Cornell together. Eric gave a soliloquy on how he'd produce Endi if given the chance, gesticulating a big screen—"What you need is to bring the elegant—horns, strings. No, I'm serious, shine a big light on what's already there." They were a little younger than me, this gang, Endi too—that hadn't quite dawned on me before. They were chatty and ebullient and all of life for them, it seemed, resided somewhere in the not-very-distant future. Except for Pablo, none of them had grown up in Los Angeles. They were the fresh and the hopeful, and every year brought a new wave of them, rolling in like seaweed on the Venice tide. They laughed, they ribbed, they flirted, humble-bragged and concocted capital *P* Plans for the lives they yearned for, but a silent question hovered over them, as untouchable yet as present as the fluorescent lights that flickered through the colored bottles along the bar: *Who will make it here—and who will not.*

For some, the dream was a child's secret hunger, born in the wrench of being outside, unwanted.

For others, it was just the natural move, quote unquote—they'd been born with gifts, they were sure of it, people told them so, and it would be a modern kind of sin not to go for it.

For some, though, the dream was a way station for the soul—they were lost or maybe never found their way and needed a buoy to cling to until the waters of life settled.

I watched Endi, holding back my crush, trying not to stare, wondering which kind of dreamer she was. She had too much inner life, too much ambivalence or too much dissonance or too much *something* to end up as the B-girl on a sitcom or in some career dotted by music videos. I couldn't take my eyes off her, but that *too much of something*—there's no word for it—could go either way in Hollywood. A protective surge came over me watching her laugh with her friends, and I had to remind myself that I was just an aging fool who should probably keep his mouth shut—what did I ever know except the jangling clanging music of failure?

Nevertheless, I still had Endi's funny, reticent spirit on my mind driving home, humming the song she'd sung. It was just before midnight when I got to my studio apartment and cut up the stairs and into the hallway. Then I stopped in my tracks. My door was wide open. I didn't always lock it, but I usually at least closed it to hide the mess. I stepped in carefully. At a glance nothing was different, but it was like I could tell someone had been there.

I itemized—keyboard, microwave, hot plate, mini-fridge, the old boom box and the ancient iPod, rack of clothes, sneakers, all the worldly possessions. Far as I could see, nothing was missing.

"Yo." My landlord, Mr. Santiago, startled me at the door.

"Somebody come in here?" I said.

"Guy came by—said you borrowed one of his LPs."

"A guy? What kind of guy?"

Santiago shrugged. "I din't catch his name. Kinda plain looking, older. Maybe in his sixties? Anyway, don't trip out. I watched his ass, made sure he didn't take nothing that didn't belong to him. When he couldn't find no LP, he thanked me and took off."

"What . . . guy? Who was the guy?"

"Sorry, dude—I didn't ask for ID. I figured if you'da borrowed his wax, you wouldn't be all that pissed about giving it back."

I shot Santiago a grim look, but he just laughed. He'd seen it all and done it all twice. But it bugged me for the rest of the night. I didn't own any LPs—except for one test pressing hiding in the trunk of my car.

20

After a light sleep, I headed out in the morning, planted the LP on Fry's boat, and took Pacific Coast south, across the Orange Curtain, exiting onto a steep, two-lane road up a beachside mountain. The sky was blue with puffy clouds, and the sea breeze made past and future seem like twin illusions. About an hour in, the Fountain Grove Estates came into view. High hedges surrounded the place, like a movie studio or an insane asylum. The lady in the tollbooth was a seventy-plus gum-chewing Black woman with purple and red beads in her gray cornrows. She looked over the dusty Jetta and said, "You're gonna need to let me take a picture of your license."

"For real?"

"These are the rules, baby. I don't make 'em."

I handed it over. She snapped it with a smile, handed it back, and said, "Now—just head on down to the right. Park in the green spaces, but not the green ones that are for electric cars."

"Gotcha."

She got out of her booth and slapped a yellow sticker on the driver's side window. "This is a seven-hour pass. Eleven p.m. I boot the car and you spend the night."

The thick boom bar lifted and I cruised a much smaller, winding path down to the first foothill, turning into the parking area with the green painted lines. One whole row was lined up with nothing but expensive vintage vehicles—a white '55 Bel-Air, a Citroën, a purple Galaxie, a coffee-colored 1980 Datsun with simulated wood paneling, a convertible Mustang, a super-rare Cortina, and a cream '37 Rolls 25/30 with spotless whitewalls—seven rides, all cherry. Who drove them? Maybe they were like golf carts for the grounds.

I got out and stood for a moment in the breeze coming off the water, gazing down a walking path toward a cluster of Spanish bungalows surrounding a courtyard fountain. The grounds sprawled out, tropical and pastoral, a landscaper's masterpiece painted in green, stretching to a white-fenced cliff and a sweep of ocean blue below. This was not just some dude ranch to get your massage on. This was a theme park for dying, a kind of pre-cemetery where you could skip the hard part and go straight to heaven. Too bad I didn't put Herschel in a place like this. A few elderly couples in shorts were hiking up ahead. Two old guys sat on one of the benches outside the fountain having a relaxed discussion. Another older woman with a wide straw hat took photos of some rosebushes throbbing with color in the beachy sun. Not a soul under eighty.

I started walking, making my way along the path, past unlit tiki torches and posh grass-topped pagodas, groomed overgrowth and twisted banyan trees, benches carved from polished driftwood and little ponds, their waterfalls bleeding into a curving creek. About halfway down, gentle music piped in through the bushes. " . . . *but it's much too late for goodbyes . . . .*" The song faded into "Over the Hills and Far Away," Zeppelin, but soft.

As I got closer to the courtyard, a few elderly heads turned. I approached the men on the bench.

"Sorry to interrupt—do you know where Treehouse 32 is?"

They eyed me mistrustfully, like nudist colony members might stare down a man in a three-piece suit.

Then one of them said, "You see where the path forks? Take a left past the salmon building."

I thanked them and kept walking.

The rushing, man-made creek led around a little moat over which you crossed a dark wooden bridge to one of those ornate beaux-arts Hawaiian Island two-stories, guarded by short palms. "Two Tickets to Paradise" played softly in the distance. Through the arch, I could see several old-timers side by side on the bench in the lobby, probably there for the air conditioning. I kept walking the back road until a little wooden sign came into view: TREEHOUSE COTTAGES. They weren't really treehouses, of course—but the handsome cabins staggered up a foothill, wrapped in thick vines, as if getting tugged back into nature.

At Treehouse 32, I scrambled up the rickety wooden stairs and tapped on the door. No answer.

"Mr. Gladstone?"

Still no answer, but I heard a television.

I turned the knob and peered right into a plain suburban living room—clean avocado carpets, an old light-brown couch, and a great big dark brown EZ chair, its back to me, with *The Twilight Zone* playing on a big TV. On the screen, a hot and sweaty-looking brunette with big eyes was painting a canvas in dark gray splotches.

"Mr. Gladstone?" I said.

A grumble. "Yeah, yeah, one second."

The man in the chair reached for the remote and turned off the television.

The EZ chair spun around slow—the man in it looked me over like he was used to interruptions. And it was him—the guy I saw arguing with Hawley. Up close, he was skinny, beaky like me, with comical, sensitive eyes and a less-than-full head of gray that didn't want to behave. His jaw trembled with frustration. "I didn't order the Salisbury."

I smiled. "Nothing like that. Actually, Mr. Gladstone, my name's Adam Zantz."

Now he looked puzzled, a little frightened.

"I'm studying to be a detective," I said, stepping in, "and I was wondering if I could take a minute of your time to talk about one of your cases." I closed the door gently behind me.

At this, Gladstone's big eyes did a little skip-action like he had the urge to flee, but his body wouldn't take him. "One of my *cases*?"

"That's right, a recent one."

"How the hell did you get on the property?"

"Well," I said, moving to the center of the room with a shrug, "I told 'em you were my uncle."

"Get the hell out of here before I call security."

"*Oh no*, you don't need to do that, Mr. Gladstone." I raised hands with a smile, moved to the orange couch beside him and took a gentle seat. "I'm harmless. Just a student—at Antioch. Studying to be an investigator."

"Well, I can't help you." He wrapped his hand around a gold-topped cane that had been resting on the side of the EZ chair.

"But . . . I think you can. See, I'm looking into a cold case, involving an old musical group."

"And that brought you to me?"

"It did. One of the band members was Devon Hawley—I believe he was one of your last clients."

No reaction.

I angled for a soft connection of the eyes. "And Devon Hawley was murdered last week."

Gladstone took this with a frozen frown and stared down the blank TV screen like he hoped it would turn back on. Then he looked back to me. "Murdered?"

I nodded.

"Why?"

I shook my head.

"Well, I barely knew him," he blurted. "And I don't know about any band."

"But . . . he did hire you."

"Yeah, so?"

"What did he want you to find out?"

Gladstone grumbled. Then: "*Garbage.* He wanted to look into a fellow that was killed in prison a million years ago. And his *girlfriend*, the runaway, she—" He stopped himself, shook his head a little in bafflement, then squinted in disgust. "Hawley was *murdered*?"

"He was." I scooched a little closer. "What were you saying about the girlfriend?"

He tightened his grip around the cane. "Nothing, I didn't say anything. I told you, I barely knew Hawley—"

"But you got here. Is that what brought you here?"

"Huh?" One beat too fast.

"Was . . . *she* here? The runaway?"

"You know you got a hell of a nerve busting into my place and—"

"Yeah, yeah, I know, Mr. Gladstone—c'mon. *This is our racket.* And I'm trying to be a pro—just like you."

His jaw went hard, so did his eyes—he didn't go for these little I-Spy affinities. Through gritted teeth he said, "I got nothing for you."

I scooched closer. "But you were saying something about the girlfriend, Cynthia, *Cinnamon*—"

At the mention of her nickname, his countenance transformed by centimeters, his color went high. The data was uploading to his eyes, hiding behind a firewall.

"Nothing," he repeated. "I got nothing."

"Okay, okay," I said, changing tactics, staying soft. "So maybe just tell me why you came here—and why you stayed."

Staring contest—young Jew vs old Jew.

I smiled. "Spill it, grandpa."

"Why should I?" he cackled.

"'Cause I'm not leaving till you do?"

Now he pointed the cane like a weapon. "First *you* tell *me* who you work for—Hawley?"

I shook my head. "I told you, Hawley's dead." In a swift parry, I yanked the cane from him, put it aside. "And there's nobody here to protect you."

"You don't scare me," he spat out. "You're a wimp."

"True," I said. "But I'm a thirty-seven-year-old wimp and you're an *octogenarian* wimp. Odds are, I can take ya."

He glared at me like a cornered animal—then the cell on the coffee table vibrated and rang: FG SECURITY. We both stared at it, frozen. He reached for it; I grabbed his arm with one hand, grabbed the phone with the other, chucked it toward the kitchenette—it went skidding like a hockey puck across the lime parquet, ricocheting off the oven. He didn't flinch, the composed geezer—another member of the seen-it-all-done-it-all club. The phone kept ringing. I pushed the cane farther away.

When it stopped ringing, he said, "*You* getting any good leads?"

I shook my head.

"*'Course not.* 'Cause there are none." He hoisted himself up and walked himself slowly to the kitchenette, but I got up and blocked him. He gently nudged me out of the way, picked up the phone and rested it on the kitchen island. There was something measured in his movements, like those of a man who had vowed to never do anything sudden ever again. Then he turned to me with a resigned sulk. "What do you *want* from me?"

"Just to know what happened here."

"Here?" He gestured to the avocado living room.

"Yes, as in, what are you *doing* here? They brainwash you?"

"Brainwash? My God, you're a cornball." He laughed, and for the first time I saw the handful of teeth in his big giddy mouth.

"You come down on assignment, for Hawley," I said. "Then you drop the case and you stay. I don't get it."

"What's not to get, kid. Look around—for a fixed-income schmuck like me? This place is Shangri-La. And it's *trimsville*, if you catch my drift."

The sound of a truck in the far distance, and Gladstone raised a knowing eyebrow.

I said, "You gonna scream for help?"

"I don't have to. Listen, kiddo, take my advice and get the hell out of here. This place isn't safe for intruders—*sin vagabundos*."

"I'm not splitting until you give me what I came for."

"What *did* you come for?"

"The scenario. You came here for Hawley. You decided to stay. Now *what did you find out*?"

"I told you, nothing useful. Nothing at all."

"You're lying through your crooked teeth. Why'd they pay you to drop the case? What is it you know they don't want you to know?"

No answer.

"Who killed Durazo?"

He snickered.

"Were the DJs here connected with Hawley's band?"

"What band?" He shot me a droll look—his intelligence beamed strong and sharp for an old guy—everything had aged but the eyes.

"What about *Cinnamon*?" I said.

Again, his answer came one beat too fast: "What about her?"

"They have something to do with her OD?"

For one-tenth of an instant, Gladstone's face went rock solid.

I grabbed him by his bony shoulders. "They kill her?"

"I didn't say *that*."

"Tell me."

"There's nothing to—"

"Bullshit—*tell me*—"

His eyes fritzed, lower lip trembled—pale.

"What?"

Footsteps up the path. "They're looking for you, kiddo—you're screwed."

"No," I said. "You're screwed. Hawley's been murdered. Brutally. If you don't spill the beans, I'll take it up with the Los Angeles Police Department, Newton Station, Officer Lanterman. And unlike you and me, he's no wimp."

His eyes went calculating, REM wide awake.

"Quick," I said. "Before they bounce me outta here."

"She was waitstaff, okay. Big deal. For less than a year, before she split for Santa Cruz and got herself a nasty junk habit."

"And then?"

"Then *kaput*—she overdosed like an idiot, and her mother ID'd the body and it was over. Miserable *shit*."

Footsteps up the stairs.

"They tell you this?"

He gritted teeth.

"It's me or the cops, old man. Did. They. Tell you?"

"You better leave."

"Naw, there's more. She worked here—*and then what*?"

"*And then she disappeared*. Off the books. And you better disappear too." He was seething—hard knock at the door.

"*Mr. Gladstone.*"

Our eyes met in the zone of pressure.

"Take my advice," he said, "play it cool or you're gonna get yourself in some awful trouble."

"Talk," I whispered, holding my ground. "Now."

Another knock. "*Mr. Gladstone?*"

He croaked, *"One minute."* Then he whispered: "They'll kill me."

I said, "I'll play dumb, you tell me what I need to know."

A security man's firm voice: *"Mr. Gladstone, please open the door."*

He went panic-eyed; the knob was turning.

"She wanted to move on, change her name. They tried to help her—changed her name, she—"

"Changed her name? To what?"

He shivered, the door jiggled. Panic eyes, mouthing near silence: *"She's—she . . . "*

"She *what*?"

But the door was open—a muscle-bound groundskeeper stood before us, elderly but taut in leather sandals, white linens, and a nametag that said *Beadle*. Gladstone greeted him as Jimmy.

"Everything okay, Mr. Gladstone?"

"Yes, yes," he said. "This is my nephew—Adam. He wanted to check out the new digs."

"That's wonderful," Jim said flatly. "Adam, our founders got word of your visit. They're so happy you came. And they'd like to meet you personally. Give you a tour of the grounds."

"Founders?" My heart started pounding.

"Yes, Mr. Kipler and Mr. Paulsen."

I looked to Gladstone—he colored with defeat. "Go ahead, kid," he said, "take the tour."

"Please follow me," Jim said. Then, to Gladstone: "You have a massage scheduled for this afternoon? I'll send Kayla."

Gladstone nodded, faking contentment, but something there was frail and broken.

Back down the path I walked in nervous silence with Jim, the new age bruiser. We strolled along the curving river back toward some kind of big Spanish-style community building way up ahead, nestled between high hedge walls. I caught a few more idling seniors standing out under the brown awning, kibbitzing and laughing. Then we passed a newer building, a closed classroom, like a kindergarten romper room. Inside the windowed door, a heavy woman in a pilot's jumpsuit walked around pontificating to seven or eight oldies sitting crisscross applesauce—they *appeared* to be screaming at the top of their lungs, heads to the ceiling, but I didn't hear a peep—soundproofed. Then we passed another brick building—on the third story, an open window. I caught a flash of two older women, naked, standing close to each other but not touching, doing some kind of healing tai chi thing.

"This is a heck of a retirement community," I finally blurted.

"Oh, it's much more than that," Jim said. "Seniors come here for life transformation."

"Sounds . . . expensive."

"Actually, money's not the only criteria for entry. There's an extensive interview process. The committee handpicks applicants who are truly open-minded, because a lot of experimental therapies get their start here."

"What kind?"

"*Amazing* stuff," he said. "Everything from memory enhancement to intuitive nutrition, alt meds, ayurvedic healing, expedited hospice—"

"What's . . . that?"

He smiled. "We're not allowed to get into details with visitors."

We came to the bridge and crossed it, into the lobby. An older Latina woman with a compassionate smile sat behind the main desk. Jim flashed his pass card.

"Is this the young visitor?" she said.

"One and only."

"They'll be a few minutes. Please have a seat, Mr. Zantz."

It tweaked me that they all knew my name, but I took the free bench and waited, looked up at the ceiling—a horrible domed mural. A reaper cloaked in a flowing map of Earth led a naked elderly couple up some twisting lit-up disco stairs. The music was playing softly indoors too—Elton, "Crocodile Rock." I always loved the song but it hit me funny here, narcotic, like musical Thorazine to induce sleepwalking.

The friendly secretary broke my dopey reverie.

"Kip and Rog'll see you now."

21

The big, dark doors opened and Roger "Rog" Paulsen let me in with a cynical grin. He was gangly-tall and toned, another one of these old guys that glows with supreme health. Still, he seemed to want to get it all over with—not just this meeting but the day itself.

"Kip'll be right out. I'm gonna fix us some drinks. You'll try our health shake, I hope?"

"Sure," I said, suddenly keenly aware from his timbre that I was in the presence of radio royalty.

"It's coconut," he said, "good stuff. Sit, sit."

I stepped in and he shut the door, locked it and retreated to a back bar/kitchen area. I was trapped in the lair. All around was lushness, more exotica, big palm fronds drooping over the sunburst furniture, tiki masks, carved shields. And dead center, a framed photo of Kip 'n' Rog seated in a swank restaurant with a slightly puffy, aging Elvis. Any visitor would receive this central piece of information: they had broken bread with the King.

Stan "Kip" Kipler came from another back room brandishing a poster.

"Your uncle tells us you're a fan."

I said, "Absolutely," wondering who told them that.

He unrolled it—a giant ad for *Shotgun Sixties at Six* on Sirius FM. "Proof you met us."

I thanked him—what else could I do?

Rog came out with glass goblets of white liquid and some almonds on a big silver tray. He took his place at the twin yellow arm chairs and now they were side by side, like pilots ready for takeoff.

"Where'd you find that thing?" Rog said.

"It's the next to last one," Kip replied.

"Lucky guy—free poster."

"What? Kid drives all the way down here for Uncle Marty, he's earned a poster in my book."

"If you say so. Just don't sell it on eBay," Rog warned.

"Oh no, I wouldn't, I—"

"He's *teasing* you," Kip chimed in. "Don't listen to this *noodge*."

They were both DJ Handsome—which is to say, good-looking, but with an unevenness in the features that prevents being on camera for a living. Both dressed like they had money to blow on casual clothes. And they both wore gold Rolexes.

But that's where the similarities ended.

Kip was short, like maybe five-four, sprightly, and restless in his seat, full of groom-bearded gung ho, a craggy Jewish troll, a grotto creature, a seeker of shade and moisture, nibbling from his vase of almonds, snickering and munching and exfoliating. Yet as creaturely as he was, he also seemed like the more direct of the two men. Rog was remote, receding into his own tallness, cowboy cautious with a single wave of salt-and-pepper comb-back and boyish blue class-clown eyes that promised big resistance.

Rog was the boundaries; Kip was the action—he pulled out a silver Sharpie.

"Adam, right?"

"That's right," I said.

He was about to sign when he stopped himself and put down the pen.

"By the way, what did your uncle tell you about Fountain Grove?"

"Just that he loves it," I said. "So far, I mean. It seems like a special—"

Rog leaned back. "What we do here at Fountain Grove is—"

"We aren't a high-priced nursing home."

"This isn't a *spa*."

"The really *sharp* older folks come to us for—"

"We like to see it as a kind of late-in-life cleanse."

"But instead of cleansing your abdomen or whatever, which we also do, by the way, here we cleanse the spirit."

I said, "Wow," as if on cue—their banter ping-ponged like they were talking for some third party behind me—*the callers out there, John Q. Public.*

I shot a glance at Elvis and looked back at them. "You know," I said, stretching an arm out to get pretend-comfortable, "it's kind of a funny coincidence, but I actually grew up with a guy who dated a girl who knew you guys during the K-Earth days."

"Zat right?"

"Yeah—Cynthia Persky?"

Long faces, radio silence.

"Her nickname was Cinnamon," I added.

No reaction—cold.

Then, Kip to Rog: "You remember a *Cinnamon* Persky?"

"Cinnamon? A name like that I think I'd remember."

"Wait a minute." Kip sat up. "You don't mean Barbara *Minsky*—teen reporter girl that was on the show. Rog, you remember the Minsky dame—the little blonde with the glasses."

"Pinksy, Minsky," Rog said, "never heard of 'em."

"Cynthia Persky's mom was actually on your show," I said. "She—"

"*Sonny*." Kip pointed at me, cool guy style. "From sixty-three to eighty-three—whole city's on our show."

"Whole town's our best friend."

Kip turned to Rog, went DJ indignant. "I can't believe you don't remember Barb Minsky, *teen town reporter—on the beat*. Kid's one of these high school journalists, but legit—we did a little feature, come on."

Rog went all-out exasperation. "Stanley, how many guests, how many *hangers-on*—" Then, to me: "In '65, *Time* magazine runs a list, the twenty most famous people in the world. You're looking at number seven and eight right here."

"Seven and eight," Kip said, going into a Cheshire grin. "But who's seven and who's eight?"

"I'm seven," Rog said flatly, the annoyed straight man. "You, my friend, are number eight."

"Wait just one minute, Buster Brown . . ."

They had locked into each other on some well-tread material; it was tough to get out from under the memory lane act. But also—they spoke about the past in a kind of eternal present, to the point where it seemed like the past itself didn't even really matter to these guys, not like you'd think. The only thing that mattered was *the show*, here and now and forever.

Agitated, I pressed on. "*Cinnamon Persky*—her mom, Marjorie *Hirsch*, was definitely on your show. I heard it on YouTube, she—she did the pickup lines."

Blank faces—too blank.

"Anyway, Marjorie's daughter Cinnamon had a boyfriend in a garage band. Called The Daily Telegraph. They made a record."

Kip leaned toward me for one last labor-intensive explanation: "*Kid*. Everybody was in a band."

"Everybody shows up with wax."

"*Evvv-rybody* thinks they're the next Rolling Stones."

"Yeah, but the band I'm talking about," I interrupted in a burst of frustration, "The Daily Telegraph—two of them were killed. In '83."

"Killed?" Rog went affronted.

"Maybe you saw it in the papers. Supposedly a drug deal went bad, a—"

"We didn't know from *drug deals.*"

"Didn't need to—in those days? Sharing was caring."

"Just like the sex."

"That's right—*Let's burn one. Make love. Let's connect.*"

"There was no *paralysis by analysis*, you dig?"

I nodded but I didn't dig, didn't dig at all. They were doing anything they could to pull off topic. Moreover, I was unentertained, and it was probably written all over my face. I made one last turn of the radio dial.

"So you guys are sure you don't remember a Cinnamon Persky, or a Marjorie *Hirsch*, or a band called The Daily Telegraph?"

They shrugged in unison—I sighed. "Anyway, it's not important. The main thing is it's great to see Marty in such good—"

"Oh, relax with the Uncle Marty bullshit, kid." Rog stood and shook almond dust off his salmon slacks. "Is this kid a bad liar or what?"

I said, "What do you mean?" My face went hot.

Kip said, "We know who you are, asshole."

"That's right," Rog said. "Don't know what you're looking for—but we sure as shit know who you are."

"I told you, my uncle—"

"*Uncle shmuncle.* We looked you up, *nerd.* Your only *uncle* has been dead for seven years. You're a cheapo investigator-for-hire looking to dig up some dirt."

Kip scratched his belly with satisfaction. "How stupid do you think we are, anyway?"

"Stupid? No, it's just that—"

"I don't want to hear it," Kipler blurted. "Call Luba in here, let's get this shit over with."

Rog opened the door and waved the secretary in. "*Luba.* Get in here, please."

"Is everything okay?" She stood before them in a cream cardigan, gray hair pinned back tight, her ebullient smile flat with duty—but the dark eyes gave off nervous.

"You know who this young man is?"

"Yes, Mr. Paulsen," she said. "His name is Adam Zantz. I've got his driver's license on file."

"That's not what I mean. Do you know what this schmuck *does*?"

She went ashen.

"You *did* look him up, Luba."

She nodded. "He works for Lyft. He also wrote some songs; they're registered with ASCAP but they . . ." She shot me a sympathetic look. "They didn't chart. I didn't think it was worth mentioning."

"I don't care about that," Rog said. "This idiot is a low-rent *detective*, and he just spent the last half hour trying to grill us about some ludicrous BS."

"But I checked the bureau, the—"

"He has no investigator's license, Luba. He's a sneaky little rodent."

"But Mr. Gladstone in Treehouse 32 is his uncle, he—"

"*He has no uncle.* Next time spend five minutes doing a little research instead of watching quilting videos or whatever the fuck it is you do all day."

She trembled, and her chest was heaving. "How did you find out about him, Mr. Paulsen?"

"By *reading the goddamn news*, Luba. It's not that hard. This is the idiot that worked on that Annie Linden case."

"I'm sorry, Mr. Paulsen, I—I—I—"

"You're not gonna cry now, Luba, are you?"

"No, Mr. Paulsen, I—I thought that he—" But she started heaving and sobbing and, *bam*, Paulsen grabbed her roughly, gave her a hard, cruel shake.

I stood and said, "Take it easy, what the fuck."

"You sit down and zip it."

Luba looked at me, her mouth trembling. "*Please*—you caused enough trouble already."

"You can go now, Luba."

"I'm sorry, Mr. Kipler," she said, still shaking with sobs. "I'm sorry, Mr. Paulsen."

Rog opened the door, and she was about to scurry out with her head bowed, but Kipler said, "Wait a minute, babe, wait a minute."

"Yes, Mr. Kipler." Luba dried her eyes with the corner of her silk blouse sleeve and waited for instructions. Rog went nice-nice, petted her bony shoulder.

"No hard feelings, okay? You know we have to be careful."

"I understand, Mr. Paulsen."

"Call Jim back in here. Let's get this snoopy little bitch off the premises."

The door shut behind her.

"You're outta here, sonny boy." Rog winked.

I kept my eye on the closed door. Luba came back with Jim, the organic Jack LaLanne from hell.

She said, "Mr. Paulsen would like you to escort this young man off the premises."

LaLanne said, "Up—now, dipshit."

I said, "Fuck you."

"Ha!" Kip said. "Will you listen to this prick?"

I said, "The Daily Telegraph—they came to you."

LaLanne exchanged a glance with Rog, who gave a single cold nod.

LaLanne said, "Get up or I snap your neck."

I was already in the process of getting up, but he shoulder-pinched me anyway and I crinkled like a Cheeto—he had incredible strength for a silverback. His grip tightened around my collarbone. "Let's go."

He pushed me to the door, but then Rog said, "Wait a sec, hold on. I gotta know something. Hold it. *Just who sent you here?*"

I stared back, silent.

Kip said, "How 'bout we make a deal? You tell us who told you to come here, and we won't shoot you in the head and bury you behind the rec building."

"Go to hell," I spat out.

They burst out laughing, the three of them.

"The balls on this kid!" Kip said from his seat. "We should hire him."

LaLanne grabbed me by both elbows as Rog encroached on me. "Come on now, snoopy dog-dog. Who told you to look into all this Daily Telegraph horseshit?"

"Nobody," I said. "*Your mother.*"

Rog rolled his eyes, unfazed. "Well, who told you 'bout Fountain Grove?"

"Nobody, no one."

I wriggled and LaLanne gave me one hard shake—my arms practically popped out of their sockets. I said, "Let go of me," which he didn't. Then I angled to the bosses: "They came to you, with Cinnamon Persky and a test pressing. Maybe Marj sent them—your old comrade, Marjorie *Hirsch* Persky. Were you gonna put the record out or play it or what?"

Kip stepped to me. "Play it? Is this a nut job—*'play it.'* Play it where? The Daily Telegraph, the shittiest group in the history of recorded music. Who sent you here?"

I said, "Nobody," and Rog smacked me once hard—the side of my face lit up like a gas fireplace.

Kip shook his head—good cop mode. "Roger, please—what is the fuss here?" Then, to me: "Yes, The Daily Telegraph. We heard them, as a favor to Marj—she said her daughter's managing this group, they got a record, we said great, tell her to come by, play us a few tracks. But we didn't *see* it, you dig. We passed, sent 'em packing."

"So you do remember them," I said, my face still on fire.

"What's to remember?" Kip said, "I quote liked it unquote, but—"

"No, no," Rog said, "*I* thought it was okay, you said—"

"Well, you said, okay, they're fun but it's throwback."

"And you said the singer was—"

Kip shrugged. "The singer didn't have it."

Rog snickered. "Whatever the hell *it* is, he did not possess it."

"You remember them," I repeated. "And you remember Cinnamon."

But Rog was furious—he'd overheated and been called out. Through clenched teeth: *"Now what the hell is it you're trying to find out?"*

"Did you see Cinnamon Persky again—before she died?"

"Of course not. Now what are you doing here?" Just like Gladstone, his answer came one beat too fast, one note too hard.

I paused, looked at him skeptically. "I found the test pressing, I talked to Lazerbeam, I—"

"Lazerbeam?" Rog shook his head in disgust. "There's a name I haven't heard in a dog's age."

"Oy vey," Kip said, waving hands in the air. "Not that idiot."

"World's biggest fanboy strikes again." Rog raised a hand and made the letter *L* on his forehead, imitated a high-pitched squeal: *"I was on Shebang! I met Casey Kasem!"*

"Burden on the state."

"Somebody should shoot a laser in *that* idiot's head."

I wriggled against LaLanne again, restrained like a prisoner.

"Larry Lazerbeam," Kip said. "Somebody get that fella a time machine."

Rog faked a microphone: *"Broadcasting live from the Loserbeam time machine, daddy-o."*

They started to laugh.

"What happened to Cinnamon?" I blurted. *"Where did you send her?"*

The DJs exchanged glances of disgust and then Rog grabbed my lapel in one last attempt to be king of the hill. "You listen to me, you nut. What happened to the Perskys was a goddamn tragedy, and it ain't none of your business. Now amscray. If I catch you playing around here again, you'll be very, very sorry."

Kip flopped back in the seat to enjoy more almonds. "Adam," he said half-conciliatory, "you don't look like a guy who's ever had his feet held to the fire. Be smart and keep it that way."

Then Rog said, "Jimmy, get him outta here," and LaLanne dragged me down the hall and out of the building. He didn't loosen his grip as he led me back up the pathway in the afternoon sun. The elderlies looked on like they were witnessing an arrest. Up in one window I saw another naked couple, men this time, doing the stand-close nudie tai chi. I stopped at the sight of them and LaLanne gave me a yank.

"Take it easy, oatmeal head," I said—not the world's cleverest insult, but it made him sore.

At the door of my car, he finally let go of me with a thrust. "Beat it, putz."

I spun around and took a swing for him—foolish. He blocked and returned the favor in two punches, one to the belly, one hard to the jaw, then walked off victorious as I went to my knees, staggering up onto the Jetta, fumbling for the keys, wheezing as I got in. I drove off the property, back up the coast, vibrating with pain.

By the time I got home to Santiago Sound, the stinging was gone, but I was still throbbing in the ribs and face. I parked and made it up the outdoor stairs, pulling the banister one hurting step at a time. I opened the door to my studio expecting to fall right on the bed, but to my surprise Endi Sandell was sitting on my futon couch, plucking at my beat-up guitar.

22

Her face went horrified when she saw me. She put the guitar down and hopped to her feet.

"Oh my God, what the hell happened to you?!"

"Well," I said, tossing my keys in the basket. *"Hello."*

"Were you in an accident?!"

"Of course, you *might* be an optical illusion . . ."

"Adam."

"Naw, you look too good to be an illusion—how'd you get in here?"

"Me? The nice old man downstairs showed me up. I told him I was your sister."

"But—he already knows my sister."

"Well then, he must be very confused at the moment—*what happened to your face?*"

"My face? Oh, yes, my face. I . . . I'm a bit old for skateboarding, I realize that now." I faked a balancing act.

"It's kinda gnarly, Adam. Do you have medical insurance?"

"Who do you think I am, Jeff Bezos?"

"Well, is there any Neosporin in this place?"

"Neo what?"

"Hydrogen peroxide?"

Soon she was seated next to me on the bed, daubing the cut

on my lip with a Q-tip, and we were very close. But her expression was stern.

"You don't strike me as the daredevil type."

"What type do I strike you as—*ouch*."

"Don't smile." She gave me the dubious once-over. "That's what I'm trying to figure out. I looked you up. Not that I'm stalking you or anything."

"Oh. That's . . . I'm flattered. Find out anything good?"

"Well, you *live in a recording studio* for one."

"Yeah—it's, uh, affordable."

"Do you play those instruments?"

I froze. "No. I mean, I know a few chords but, no, they just keep those here."

"I didn't find too many music articles by you, but I did see an article *about* you. They said you solved a homicide?"

"Oh that, that was just—that was a flukey thing, one of my riders. Yeah, that was awful."

"But are you really writing about that band or what?"

"Yeah."

She gave me the big unbelieving eyes.

"Well . . . no, okay, not exactly. But I didn't lie to you, I just—" I scrambled for a half-truth. I knew I had to toss her something.

"Is it for a magazine?"

I paused. "No."

"Are you a journalist?"

"Barely, sort of. Once I was, barely, but no."

"So . . . what's it about?"

"That's just it, Endi, I'm not sure I should talk about it."

"Are you doing something illegal?"

"No, no, nothing like that." Another half-truth.

"Well *tell me*."

"It's," I said softly, "it's just a favor for an old friend, okay? I probably shouldn't say anything more."

For a moment she froze—she was obviously itching to press it but didn't. And I was grateful because, kind and earnest as she was, my gut told me she would not be able to handle it—homicide, breaking and entering, creeping outside the law with known felons.

"You came over," I said to change the subject.

"It's my day off."

"And here you are playing nursemaid on your day off."

"Yeah, right?"

"I'm *so* happy to see you."

Our eyes met—pure, uncut tension—then she kept daubing. "Don't move," she said.

"Okay."

She must have felt the heat because she straightened up, moved back a little, and said, "Let's go out. I'm taking you out."

"Where are we going?"

"You're the native," she said. "Show me the hot spots." She studied the bruise one last time and said, "Yeah, out, definitely. Let's go."

"Cool. And I won't tell the waiter you beat me up."

We drove west and she kicked off her shoes in the passenger seat and we talked and it was just crazy easy—easy like I didn't remember with anyone for ages. She was an open book. She'd been playing guitar and singing her whole life, but she insisted it was a hobby, a secret one. The other night was only her second-ever time onstage. She grew up in rural upstate New York—she called it *freezingly bucolic*. She was the youngest of five siblings—her parents nicknamed her *the afterthought*, but she said they were loving. The sibs were all high achievers—one doctor, two lawyers in finance, and an associate producer for *60 Minutes*. Both parents were celebrated professors, too—her mom taught something about Wittgenstein and law, and her dad was one of the leading authorities on Jewish life in Eastern Europe just before the Holocaust.

"So, like, the decimated," I said.

"Yup—he's the expert."

"Heavy duty," I said. "So you're almost . . . the black sheep."

"I guess so. I was *about* to get my master's in geriatric social work but—I got cold feet."

"I thought you came to Hollywood to hit the big time."

"Me?" She laughed. "That's not me."

"Oh, come on—you're a singer."

"No, no, that's just fun and games."

"So . . . what brought you here?"

"Welllll. I had a bad thing with this guy in Ithaca. I'm still kind of reeling from it, actually."

"He treat you badly?"

"The opposite—he was really good to me, he was great. But I just wasn't feeling it. And I didn't exactly ditch him at the altar, but I let it go on wayyy too long. I mean, we had invitations printed for the engagement party, deposits on the catering, flowers." She shot me that serious-goofy look. "I ditched Mr. Right. I guess I flipped out."

"You made a run for it."

"Totally. I requested an emergency leave of absence from the university and broke up with him on the same day. Six hours later I packed my bags. I just—" She shrugged. "—*carpe'd the diem*."

"How'd he take it?"

"*He* wasn't all that surprised, but my parents went ballistic. My dad went into a major depression, like he was the one who got dumped."

"Well," I said, "you just . . . needed something else. Maybe your music."

"Noooo—that's just . . . like, my private compulsion."

"What do your parents think about it?"

"They don't know."

"*They don't know* . . . that you can *sing like that*?"

"Maybe vaguely, I mean, they've heard me sing, they know I play a little guitar—but they don't know I just performed at an amateur hour. They would die."

"Why?"

"I don't think they'd get it. My father's a very serious person."

"How could you not be, in his line of work."

"Yeah, well—he chose it."

"Did he?" I said. "Maybe it's like singing—maybe he's compelled."

"True, but, still, yeah, no—when I was a teenager, *maybe* I would have gotten up the courage, but now? They'd try to have me committed."

"For real?"

She sighed. "You'd get it if you met them. They're all about gravity."

I glanced over at her wistful expression, her deadpan eyes—despite the topic, I could tell she was having fun and it made me darn happy.

We dined early in a Thai place in the rough part of Venice, one of those mini-malls that break up the homeless tents. It was easy to talk to her about the past, my personal past, my mother's breakdown, being raised by my uncle. I told her I knew what it was like to have high-achiever siblings—my sister was a hotshot attorney. I told her driving Lyft was a temporary thing to put me through some college courses, but this veered dangerously close to the lie, so I spun a big yarn about the few music articles I'd written for fanzines a zillion years ago, trying to make myself sound like the professor of song, and of course I came off like a pontificating doofus. She took it all in, not quite trusting but taking stock.

"You're a real city guy," she said, "but you don't seem as cynical as some I met."

"It's a daily battle," I said, "you'll see. You're still a tourist."

"I know. Actually, more like an impostor."

"How do you mean?"

"Sometimes . . . I wonder if I'm just having a lover's quarrel."

"With who?"

"Myself? My family? The East Coast? It hits me in the middle of the night. Like, you think you're gonna shake off your old self like a lizard skin but—" She stopped herself and shook her head.

"Yeah," I said, "it's more like the new lizard has to make peace with the old lizard and then walk around wearing the old lizard like a top hat."

She smiled, then said, "That . . . is a really dumb image, Adam," and we laughed and hers was the most bubbly, the most musical laugh I'd ever heard. Then she blurted, "Come on, Adam—you *gotta* tell me what the LP thing's about. You got me hooked; it isn't fair!"

I measured the dose. "An old family friend, my late uncle's friend," I said carefully, "his son was the guitarist in that band."

"Did you know the son?"

"A little bit, when I was a kid, he was a teenager—and . . . he died young. Anyway, the father found this old LP and . . . ya know . . . just wanted to see if I could find out anything more about his son's high school band."

"So you're doing this research, like, just as a favor to the family friend?"

"He's really old, he's in his nineties. His health isn't good. I'm just trying to gather a little info—as a gesture, digging through some old newspapers and stuff. The sad thing is I sincerely doubt I'll turn up anything."

She gave me a funny look and said, "That's . . . really honorable," but I could tell she only half-bought the half-story.

"The reason I couldn't tell you," I went on, "is I promised the dad I wouldn't go advertising what I was up to—he's weirdly cagey about it."

"I understand," she said, but her expression said she didn't.

In an effort to regain composure, I flagged the check, then I said, "You ever been swing dancing?"

She shook her head no. "I'm a terrible dancer."

"There's this awesome place just down the coast here—"

She wagged her hands in protest. "Oh, no, no, I don't know how to do all those steps."

"There's no *steps*, it's easy. I mean, the basics are easy—the guy leads, anyway. We're like, minutes away—Rusty's. You've gotta let me take you there."

"Someday," she said.

"*Some*day? What about *carpe the diem*?"

The place was an old Elk's Lodge off the Ballona Wetlands, hot and packed inside with the full Saturday night crowd, a live jumpin' jive band and plenty of diehards in full forties regalia. We took a big red velvet booth and she scooted in next to me, tasted her first cosmopolitan and swayed her shoulders to the music. Actually, she looked like she was having the time of her life, gawking at the extreme nostalgic Hollywood fakeness of it all, but also kind of dazzled, knocked out by the musicians playing to the swinging crowd.

"Look at those sax guys! Nobody's watching them but they're going crazy. *That* would be my kind of gig!"

After much coaxing, I got her out on the floor; she turned beet red being swung around, burst out laughing when I tried to dip her. Then we were out on the club's balcony letting the sea breeze cool us and we faced each other—the warm summer night blew her hair around wildly but the compassion in her blue eyes held steady—and then she wrapped her arms around me and said, "Kiss me, mystery man," and it happened with the big band playing in the background and the crescent moon shining down upon us.

When we separated, she touched my lip and said, "Does it hurt to kiss?"

I said, "Hell no," and pulled her close.

Back at my place we fell onto the frameless mattress and wrestled and rolled around in kisses and heavy-lidded smiles, grappling before she stopped me and said, "Wait, wait, wait."

"Okay."

She breathed out. "Can we take it slow? I like you."

I breathed in and said, "Absolutely," and fell back and exhaled, and she curled up in my arms. One more kiss and then, with eyes closed and a sweet, easy smile she whispered, "You know I know you're not telling me everything, right?"

I said nothing.

"Whatever it is," she said, "I will find out. I'm omniscient like that." Then she fell asleep so peaceful, an innocent in my city guy arms.

When I woke up from the sunbeams, Endi was still there, sleeping next to me in her dress, and my heart zinged. I reached for the phone to see what time it was, but the thing was blinking; I'd missed a morning voicemail from Charles Elkaim.

I sat up and listened—he sounded testy, brittle.

"Adam, I have been visited by police. I would like to discuss—in person only. Please come to the home as soon as you get the message."

Heart pounding, I got out of bed, started scrambling for my sneaks.

Endi said, "Is everything okay?"

"No, I'm so sorry, I—the old man I was telling you about is in some kind of trouble. I have to go."

"Let me come with you."

My mind scrambled. I nodded, threw on a coat, and she carried her shoes as we cut down the studio stairs and into the car. I was still buckling my belt as I turned the ignition.

"Is he going to be okay?"

"I don't know," I said. "He has pancreatic cancer, he—I have no idea."

When I pulled up to the Shalom Terrace, I was braced for cops, but an ambulance was idling out front, red-and-green lights spinning in morning sunlight. As we got out of the car, two paramedics rushed Mr. Elkaim by on a stretcher. He was white as the sheet, and for one brief second I thought he was dead, but he jerked his head in discomfort.

Frantic, I angled back to the staff watching on. "What happened?"

Nurse Rosa said, "Mr. Elkaim have a stroke."

Endi was at the back of the ambulance, speaking with one of the paramedics. "Excuse me, would it be okay if we rode with him?" she said. "I'm a trained geriatric NP."

I rushed over and added, "I work for this man."

The paramedic gave us the once-over and looked back to staff—Rabbi Peretz gave him a nod and he motioned for us to get on board. Using my arm, Endi hoisted herself up first, then I followed as she reached for Elkaim's dark, bony hand and held it in hers. He looked at us with tired, helpless eyes and didn't speak as the siren went off and we tore through the city.

23

Minutes later we were pulling into Cedars-Sinai—Elkaim's gurney folded out and hit the ground running like a soapbox racer, right on through the automatic ER doors. Endi and I followed apace but a nurse stopped us. "Are you related to the patient?"

"Please let us through," I said. "I'm as good as a relation; I've known him all my life. She's a professional caregiver."

"That's fine, but you'll have to fill out some paperwork first." The nurse sent us to a desk where they started in on who his insurance carrier was. I told them I didn't know, and they found his records and his primary care physician, then they had us sign about eight digital waivers.

"Can we go see him now?"

The desk clerk was nonplussed. Panic was her bread and butter. "Mr. Elkaim is in the ICU. There's a waiting room down the hall."

Endi said, "Are they—will he need surgery or . . ."

"I don't have that information here, ma'am."

The waiting room was empty save for a heavyset woman in a bathrobe playing Candy Crush on her phone. Without uttering a word, she conveyed in no uncertain terms that our presence bugged her. We took our seats anyway. CNN played silently on a TV in the corner, rigged to the wall by a metal arm. The news was like a collage of fire. The world, it seemed, was fighting fire with fire, fire, and more fire. But what did the world care about one little old man crumpled on a gurney in the adjacent room?

As if reading my mind, Endi looked at me and said, "Do you pray?"

I gave her a funny look. "I thought you were a nonbeliever."

"Well, I've got problems with religion. But I do pray; I find it really helps."

"Yeah maybe," I said. "I'm just not that good at it. It's like I believe in a higher power but as soon as I start, I picture Him saying, 'Oh, not this schmuck again.'"

She shook her head and repressed a smile. "I do not believe in a god that wants you to be invisible." Then: "Actually, you sound a little like how I feel onstage."

Just then, to my happy surprise, Jensen the entertainment director showed up, guitar case in hand. He still had the faint crease of pancake makeup that hadn't quite washed off and explained that he just happened to be doing a show for children in the hospital when he heard the news.

I said, "This is my friend Endi." She and I exchanged an awkward glance. "Jensen's the entertainer at the nursing home."

He said, "You guys been waiting long?"

"We just got here," Endi said.

"How's Charles doing?"

"We rode over in the ambulance. He was pretty out of it."

"Wow," Jensen said. "I'm glad you were with him." Then, to Endi, he said, "Elkaim's crazy about Adam."

I said, "Endi here's a singer just like you."

"No kidding?"

She shook her head in protest. "Just for fun."

"No, no, she did an amateur show over in Venice last week—rocked the house."

Candy Crush lady raised her head from her cell phone to glare at us.

Jensen said, "You guys wanna go downstairs and grab a coffee?"

"Good idea," I said. "Looks like it could be a while."

We rode the elevator down to the windowless café, got coffees, and found a little plastic booth. Looking out over the fluorescent-lit cafeteria, Endi said, "I really hate hospitals. When I was eighteen, I lived through my father's heart attack."

"Did he make it through?" Jensen asked.

"Yeah, sorta. I mean, he survived. But we thought it would scare him into relaxing a little. Instead, as soon as he returned to work, he got into this long-standing feud and almost lost his tenure. I mean, you'd think at his age he'd want to avoid stupid petty conflicts but . . ." She shrugged.

"That's not how it works," Jensen said sympathetically. "The older they get, the less they back down."

"So true," I said. "My uncle was very stubborn toward the end and . . . we had a falling out. That's one of the reasons I've been trying to help Elkaim a little."

"You mean," Jensen said, "like . . . you're trying to get some peace about feuding with your uncle by . . . helping his friend?"

"Yeah," I said. "I know it sounds crazy."

"Not crazy at all," Jensen said. "But it is a trip; it's almost like . . . the whole purpose of life is really to just understand our parents or parent-figures or whatever."

"You think?" Endi said.

"Speaking for myself?" Jensen stopped to consider—he was older than us by more than a few years, and I got the impression something paternal in him wanted to set us on the right path. "Yeah, definitely. Man, I thought my dad was larger-than-life. Only later did I figure out he was really just larger-than-life to me. My dad did Korea—he was convinced some divine force had seen him through battle."

"What did he do when he came home?" Endi said.

"My dad? He tried to make it as an actor. He had the looks and plenty of charm."

"Did he get work?"

"Eh, a little, a few small speaking parts in some junky TV stuff. Plus, he had a second-billing role in a thriller called *Down a Dark Road*, and after that he couldn't get arrested. I think—well, this is the one thing *he* could never admit. But later, after a lot of psychoanalysis, *I* had to admit that maybe the reason things petered out for him was 'cause he got his shot in that movie, and it kind of proved he wasn't . . . not that he couldn't act, but he wasn't *star material*. The movie's not very good, and he's part of *why* it ain't that good."

"That's awful," Endi said.

"No," Jensen said, "it's honest."

I said, "Did he, like, give up?"

"Yup. After the movie tanked, he worked his way through law school selling appliances at Goodwin's, and he did real good at all that. Not that he cared. I mean, here he was, a middle-class guy, a lawyer with two cars and a two-story home, best part of town, but he was miserable. Or at least he *seemed* miserable to me. All the good fortune in the world couldn't heal that wound—he still thought of himself as a *flop*. He was kind of an ogre, too—verbally abusive to my ma. He could flip on a dime and go off, scare the daylights out of us."

"That must have been so hard for you," Endi said.

"Worst part was he . . . he exuded this real *gnarly* dissatisfaction. Nothing ever seemed to please him, like daily life was a chore or a humiliation. 'Cause no matter how good things got, well—he expected a different destiny."

"My uncle had a little bit of that," I said. "He made it through Korea too. He was a good man, he never took it out on us, but I don't think he ever got over his big band days. And I wanted to cheer him up *so* bad."

"Me too, man!" Jensen said. "I wanted to *turn that shit around*. I wanted to achieve what my pops couldn't."

"Like that would've helped," Endi said wryly.

"It's a child's logic," Jensen said. "Any shrink'll tell you, you can't beat someone at their own game and honor them at the same time. I got close—maybe closer than he ever got. I had a few tunes that were picked up for a silly beach flick, but to my surprise he wasn't happy about it at all. *'Frame the check,'* was what he said, which was just a potshot 'cause he knew they were paying me sub-scale."

I said, "Ouch."

"Anyway, the deal never even went down and he started encouraging me to quit. *'Let's just say showbiz wasn't very kind to you.'* All kinds of subtle, nasty shit."

"Such a bummer," I said. "I can totally relate. I never did save my uncle's good name."

"Yup," Jensen said with a sigh. "It's hard."

"But you persevered," Endi said to him. "And you're still making *music*. And helping people. That's what counts."

"That's right," Jensen said. "I turn to the *art form* for my sustenance. I try to get past the *showbiz*, the liars and grabbers and all that petty ego shit, and just *do the work*. And it isn't about fame. It's about putting a smile on their faces."

"Wait a minute," I said. "Hold on—*lightbulb*! Could Endi come to the nursing home for one of the sings? She really does have an amazing voice and the seniors would love her."

Jensen said, "That'd be great."

"Oh, no, I couldn't, I—"

"But don't you see," I said, "it's a total natural. You're a . . .

a social worker, a caregiver—and a beautiful singer. This could be a new integration."

"Yeah, but I'm not a real performer, I mean, *I have really bad stage fright, I—*"

"Well, there's no stage to speak of," Jensen said. "It's very low pressure. Just fall by tomorrow and join me for a song or two. You'll have a good time."

"I don't know."

"Adam's right—it could be a nice combo of your talents. And if it goes bad . . ." He smiled. "*Most* of 'em won't remember anyway."

We laughed. Endi and I exchanged a glance and she squeezed my hand under the table.

"All right kids," Jensen said. "Let's go check on the old man."

The three of us rode the elevator back to the waiting room. Up at the nurses' station, they told us Charles Elkaim was in the clear but too tired for visitors. They said he would likely be sent back to the Shalom Terrace the next day after tests. Apparently, he was lucky that Nurse Rosa had taken his blood pressure and saw it was sky-high right before his collapse.

Relieved, Jensen bid us adieu and I walked Endi the four blocks north back to Ziva's. At her front door, she slipped her arms around me and we kissed under the awning. Then she said, "Thanks for the dancing lesson."

I made it back to the car around 2:00 in the afternoon, light in my step, still marveling at this blue-eyed angel who seemed to fall from out of the blue. I hit the app and started a shift, but into this beaming mood, one funny phrase kept poking at me, something Jensen said in passing—*the liars, the grabbers, all that petty ego shit.* An image accompanied this harshing of my mellow, a hiccuppy VHS on rapid rewind—it was Lazerbeam telling me with a straight face that he had discovered the band, that they were thrilled to be on Pioneer, and that he did not know Cinnamon Persky *at all*, had barely heard of her.

But Kip and Rog flat-out stated otherwise—The Daily Telegraph were going places, or trying to, and it was Cinnamon who was working the hustle.

The more I got stuck on this, the more I absolutely *knew*—Lazerbeam had lied to me about the band, about Cinnamon, all of it, right to my face. Whatever Kip and Rog had to hide, whatever that kook Gladstone was trying and not trying to tell me—one thing was for sure: Larry the Lazerbeam knew way more than he fronted, and he was playing me for a sucker.

I cut the app and headed back to Centinela Trailer Court.

24

Marie opened the trailer door with a smile this time—I smirked and gently pushed past her. The hairy old geezer was in the kitchen on his knees in a Foreigner T-shirt and cutoff jeans, shuffling through a pile of sleeveless 45s, maybe a hundred of 'em.

"You," I said, "you *lied* to me."

He looked up, caught off guard, tried to play it off. "Hey, it's Sherlock Holmes. What's happenin', pops?"

He started to get up and I grabbed him one-handed by the tee, hoisted him up against the tin wall. The rickety sink creaked with his weight.

"You lied to me," I repeated. "About the band."

His hands shook. *"Whoa, Nelly! Mellow out, guy, you and me are pals, remem—"*

"You ain't my pal." I pressed gentle but firm and stared right into his washed-out gray eyes. "They didn't start with you and they definitely didn't *stop* with you. Something happened— they kept going. Spit it out."

"Okay, okay," he said, "don't *spazz*." He cast a worried glance at Marie.

I let him go and stepped back, and he did a little corrective pull on his shirt.

"I'm sorry," I said, sounding insincere. "But Devon Hawley's dead, I'm the one that found him—and I don't have time for more bullshit."

Lazerbeam fished anxiously for his pack of American Spirits—Marie watched us like someone at a ping-pong tournament.

"I . . . we heard that," he said. "Awful. But you don't think *we* had anything to do with that?"

"Out with it."

"Okay, okay—so maybe I skipped a part or two," he said, lighting the cig. "They shopped around."

"Yeah, I already know that—I've been to see Kip and Rog. *Then what*?"

"They made a demo or some shit. *And then it didn't take.* There wasn't much to it, see what I mean? They couldn't sell it. And then the boys came crawling back to me *begging* to put out the tracks. And *that* is the honest truth."

"The boys?"

He nodded once.

"Don't you mean *Cinnamon*—their manager?"

He bristled; his nostrils vibrated with tension.

"Lazerbeam Larry or whatever the hell your name is, you are a mediocre liar. For one, you had a stake in all this, a contract and a record to put out—your *one shot at glory*, per Kip 'n' Rog. And the band burned you, cut you loose. Don't tell me it was nothing. In fact, I'm guessing you probably *flipped your wig*. Your little paisley fantasy went kaput and probably you couldn't handle the humiliation, no way. Who knows? Maybe *you* killed Durazo, and maybe, when Hawley tried to out you, you killed him too."

"No, no, I—"

"Yeah, you know what? Never mind. Maybe I'll just take all this up with the cops."

He was starting to shake in place, whimpering like a crazed terrier, looking to Marie, his master without a leash.

"Or else . . . you can tell me the truth," I said firmer, "*now.*"

In one move, Marie lunged for the green antique lamp and swung for my head—I ducked but then she swung again the other way, bashed me right at the ear.

I screamed, "Dammit!" and yanked the lamp from her hands, chucked it halfway across the trailer—it crashed into the Formica cabinetry. Lazer spun to his wife with a moan. "Why'd you do that? You didn't have to bonk the guy!"

I had fists up, tae kwon do–style, crazy man in a trailer kitchen—"Don't do anything stupid, either of you." Then I grabbed my throbbing ear and said, "*Fuck!*"

Marie's face curled, her hands raised in prayer. "I'm *sorry,*" she wailed. "I thought you were gonna hurt him."

"*You got some ice?*"

"Get him something," Lazerbeam said, "quick, honey."

Soon I was hunched over in pain on the tiny couch and Marie was beside me, holding a bag of frozen peas up to my ear, caressing my head. Lazerbeam cleared the coffee table of magazines and sat on it to face us. The maternal-paternal awkwardness was worse than getting bonked.

"It's true," Lazerbeam said somberly, "I lied to you. But not to protect us. To protect *you.*"

"From what?"

"Kipler. Paulsen. These are not nice people."

"I might not have gone *down* there if you'da been straight with me."

He stroked his beard with knowing dread. "These are the ugly souls who ruined everything I believe in," he said. "Destroyers of the love generation."

"Laze," Marie said, "please. Just . . . tell him everything already. Stop pretending to be Bob Dylan and help this kid out."

"All right, all right. I am sorry. I—look—the sad truth is—"

Lazerbeam looked up to the framed photo on the mantel— the prom shot. It was his shrine, the source of his courage.

I whispered, "Tell me."

"*They were ambitious.* They wanted things—and I couldn't compete. Cinnamon Persky . . . was not just Emil's girlfriend. She really ran the band, it was her operation, her *thing*. I think she's the one who brought Emil to them in the first place; she's the one who got them shows. She sat in on the rehearsals, gave them all kinds of advice about the songs, the arrangements. Even what they wore. And . . . she's the one who brought them to me."

"So—she was like their manager?"

"Yes."

"Then why would you lie to me about not knowing her?"

"Because I didn't want you to get the wrong idea. It wasn't long before she and I were at odds. First she talked them up, convinced me they were gonna be the best thing that ever happened to the scene. Then, after we recorded, like—days later—she wanted out of the contract; she was sure they were headed for a better deal. I said, 'What are you kidding me? I just dropped my life savings on this.' But she was adamant— and she had the twenty-four-track tapes."

"Where did she think they were headed exactly?"

"Well, look, it's taken me years to admit—but she had good reason to believe she could take them further. Cin's folks had real connections. Not like me and my pops, they were real Hollywood people—*lot appropriate*."

"Okay," I said, feeling like I was finally getting somewhere. "Now tell me where Kip and Rog come in."

"I think it was her mother who set that up," Marie said.

"Course she did," Lazerbeam said. "They went back twenty years. Kip and Rog listened to the acetate, but they didn't hear a hit. They weren't interested but *I believe* they knew someone who wanted to break into the biz, a wannabe producer—someone they were in debt to. The 'Graph might've made a demo with this guy or *started* to make one. You gotta see, I wasn't privy at this point—*obviously*. All at once, everyone went secretive—nobody would tell *me* bupkus. A lot of double-talk on the phone. Anyway, they bought the week to record at Sunset Sound—a fortune at that time. That much I heard. And all of a sudden—"

"He dropped them, right?" Marie interrupted. "The producer dropped *them*."

"*What* producer—who? What the hell was his name?"

"That's just it, we don't know—nobody *we* knew, and not a name guy either. But that's the way I heard it, something maybe went down between this guy and Rey—some kind of bad falling out, I don't know what. Out of the blue the band came crawling back, begging to redo the contract and put our record out with some new tracks."

"But you wouldn't," Marie said.

"Correction—I *couldn't*," he said. "See, I'd already paid for the design of the jacket, the lyric sheet. I was *days* away from pressing wax—I couldn't suddenly change the whole kit and caboodle, I didn't have that kind of dough! And so we haggled and then—"

He made a grim hand motion—the slashing of neck.

"First Rey . . . then Emil," he said. "It was like a nightmare descended. Cinnamon ran off, disappeared. The others . . . never called me again. *I* dialed—Hawley, Grunes—no answer. Sandoz came around one time, like, six months later, asking for a handout, jonesing out of his mind. Marie gave him a twenty-dollar bill and told him to never come back again. We weren't invited to the funerals even. Overnight we became *personos non gratos*."

A brittle silence passed in the trailer. I looked to them, a little sheepish—but I still felt like they were holding back. "So that's . . . the *whole* story?"

Lazerbeam and Marie looked at each other in a solemn, unbroken exchange. The force of their bond vibrated with secrets and shared longing, the hesitation of hiders.

He raised a gentle hand in her direction and said, "You tell him."

"But it's crazy."

"Marie Anne—you tell him, or else I'll tell him."

"Come on, guys," I said. "In the last three days I've been pushed around even more than I was in junior high. Do me a solid—help me out here."

Marie looked to the low ceiling for a worried instant, placed her hands on her knees, then studied them like a scolded child.

She said, "I . . . I thought I saw her."

"Who?"

"Cinnamon."

I took the ice pack off my ear. "When?"

"Four or five years ago."

"You mean, like, you saw her ghost?"

Marie shook her head.

"But . . . she's dead," I said as if I were talking to certified lunatic. *"Her mother . . . identified her body."*

Marie looked up at me. "I know. And I know I sound crazy, I probably am. But I saw her."

"Or someone that looks like her," I said. "Did you speak to her?"

"No. I didn't—we didn't speak."

"Where was this?"

"At an antique store in Palm Springs. The whole thing—was maybe two minutes. As soon as she glanced my way, she made herself scarce. I don't know if she was browsing or she worked there or what, I got nervous, turned away. When I turned back to see—she was gone."

"Which antique store?"

"On Sunny Dunes, it's like—there's a whole mini-mall of 'em."

"We came back the next day looking for her," Lazerbeam said. "No dice."

Marie was wet-faced now, dark streaks down her cheeks. "But it couldn't have been her. How could it? Even if she was alive, she—no, it's crazy. I was seeing things."

Lazerbeam moved to the edge of the couch to comfort his wife, but I looked up at him and our eyes met.

He said, "It was her."

With a shake of the head, I handed Marie back her frozen peas and walked out of the trailer without goodbyes.

I got in my car with the throb still fresh on my ear and sat there parked, stinging and annoyed, mouth wide open. I was turning into one of those Kewpie dolls people poke for thrills. I hadn't worked a full shift or had a full night's sleep in seven days, and suddenly Cinnamon Persky . . . was alive? But who knows what those two old kooks saw, some random lady in an antique shop. No. It was more psychedelia, more fantasia, wishful thinking—*Emil is innocent, Cinnamon is alive, the past is the future, old is young.*

Whereas I clung to the reality before me like someone losing their grip on a buoy. I shook my head, hit the ignition, and then it throttled me—like a go-kart engine. *This* was the funny vibe I was catching at Fountain Grove—from Gladstone, from Paulsen. This was what they wanted to snuff.

Cynthia Persky was alive. And they knew it.

That night at my sister-cousin Maya's dining room table, I tried to share this half-baked vision, sounding a little high-strung—I felt high-strung, leaning across the dining room table in hushed tones. Maya and her husband, Marty, listened with their usual half-patience and skeptical frowns. In the next room, their eight-year-old daughter Stephanie watched *Beat Bugs* as I walked them through my search. I told them about the LP, Lazerbeam and his long-suffering wife, finding Hawley, all of it. I told them about the break-in and Hawley's collage, Detective Gladstone and the trip to Fountain Grove. Recounting all this, my eyes kept drifting to the framed photo of Uncle Herschel over the blue denim family room couch—Herschel seated in a lawn chair at Maya's wedding, her big, white-brimmed hat on his knee, bald, octogenarian Herschel, sagacious behind big glasses in a dark pin-striped suit, thick aqua tie, red rose boutonniere.

He'd put me on this search.

It was for him, because of him.

And it was *right*.

"They said they *saw* her, Maya. And I'm starting to believe them."

"You have finally gone insane."

"I know how it sounds. But lines are connecting—that detective who was on the case before me practically had a seizure when I mentioned her name. She was their manager, they were a band," I repeated, tapping the table, "and they were all *friends*. Close friends."

"So what?"

"So somebody murdered Reynaldo Durazo and framed Emil. And when Hawley figured it out? Pretty sure that someone shut him up too. And I don't say that someone is Cinnamon Persky—but if she *is* alive, there's a reason she's hiding. And she's the best line to the truth."

"Adam," Maya said, the way you'd speak to a child with a high fever, "there's a *death certificate*. You yourself told me her mother identified her body."

"I know, but—"

"No," Maya said, getting up with finality, "this is a job for the police."

I got up too, followed her to the kitchen. "The police don't even think there's a *there* there. They say Hawley was killed by a random thief."

"Which he probably was."

"Bullshit. Tell me, who *robs* someone and leaves behind a fifty-thousand-dollar video camera the size of a loaf of bread?"

Maya didn't answer. In the background on the TV, four little bugs sang "Strawberry Fields Forever." *Nothing is real—*

From the table, Marty said, "Why don't ya tell him?"

"Tell me what?"

"Because it's not relevant," Maya blurted.

"What? Tell me."

She sighed. "Nothing. Just—come on, I'll show you."

Marty stayed with Stephanie to watch the bug quartet as Maya led me up the carpeted stairs, then up a short staircase to the world's cleanest attic.

"I was going over Daddy's finances when the will was in probate," she said, "and . . . I was really shocked. I knew he didn't have much, but I didn't think he had debt. You know how careful he was."

"Hersch thought a pack of ten razors from the 99-cent store was a rip-off."

"Well," she said, kneeling to pop open the black trunk with gold trim, "toward the end, his medical expenses started *really* racking up. I never heard a word about it. I figured Kaiser covered the chemo, but Daddy also took a trip to Texas to be diagnosed by some superspecialist. Kaiser didn't cover that and the bill was insane, like thirty grand, not including airfare and hotel."

"And we never heard about any of this?"

Maya scoffed. "*You* never heard about anything; you were off in la-la land trying to be the Jewish Stevie Wonder."

I joined her on my knees as she started digging through the last of Uncle Herschel's worldly possessions. It was all there—the life of a man, or what was left of it. His old trumpet case, his *Real Book* sheet music binder, a little framed baseball card—*Duke Snider outfield Brooklyn Dodgers*, two commemorative plates—*Annie* and *Gone with the Wind*, a stack of tax return folders dated by year, his engraved retirement clock from the DWP, some old letters and postcards, and a worn paperback copy of *the King James Bible* with the New Testament ripped out. He really was a funny guy in his way—almost too sentimental, yet oppositional to the core. The sight of a diary made my heart thump. I picked it up.

"Hersch kept a journal?"

"Naw," Maya said with a half-groan. "That's just a log of expenditures."

I opened it—long lists of dates and amounts in small, meticulous handwriting. *Band-aid cloth tape $2.99, Tums chewy $2.11, Jumbo Fair slippers $5.00.*

I said, "Captain Coupon strikes again," and Maya smiled, shook her head.

"What's weird," she said, digging in to pull out a rubber-banded brick of folded bank statements, "is that I never heard about all this debt. I mean, for one, I could have helped him."

"That is odd."

"And frail as he was, Daddy actually *snuck away to Texas*? Doesn't that seem crazy to you?"

"It does—but what does that have to do with the Elkaims?"

"Two years before Daddy died, the debt disappeared—and I'm talking, like, a hundred grand, *poof.* That got me wondering, so I started taking a look at these. Well—"

"What."

"Look."

On the back pages of the bank statements in miniature faded xerox, check after check, all from Charles Elkaim—$5,000, $850, $1,200, $2,500, $15,000, and on and on.

"Elkaim just . . . like . . . paid his way?"

Maya nodded. "Till the bitter end."

"So what are you saying?"

"I don't know. He really did care about Daddy. And it's nice that he reached out to you. But this is some scary business you're getting into, and . . ."

"What?"

She slammed the trunk shut and there we were, kneeling like two children at their daddy's coffin.

"I just hope this isn't Charles Elkaim's way of calling in a debt."

25

The next day after lunch, I picked up Endi and her blue acoustic at Ziva's and together we drove to the Shalom Terrace. On the way, she was edgy, stiff as a board.

"You okay?" I said.

"I'm sorry," she said, "I don't know why I'm flipping out like this. I'm a nervous wreck."

"You are going to be great. You're going to put years on the lives of some of those old folks."

"Yeah," she said, "and take a few off my own."

Still, she softened when she entered the place with its soft gray creatures drifting through long halls. Rabbi Peretz greeted us warmly and told us Charles Elkaim wasn't back yet, but doctors said he was in much better shape. Then Jensen showed up and took us to the empty rec room. He set up mics, plugged in his guitar, and started looping a sweet hooky riff while Endi strummed along. Then they adjusted volumes, set up a music stand, and cracked open a songbook. Watching them practice, working their two-part harmonies, I wished for the zillionth time that I could sing better, but these two were pitch-perfect; the last thing they needed was my croony croak in the mix. Besides, I was busy holding down the first pangs of jealousy. It was early to be feeling all that, but I did.

At 2:00 p.m. on the dot, the doors flung open and the crowd shlepped in, some clomping on walkers, some rolling by wheelchair, some leaning on nurses. I took a seat between a man with no teeth and a woman with very little hair. Their excitement was childlike and infectious. As Jensen fumbled with the small PA system and karaoke TV screen, a husky old wiseacre snuck up on the mic uninvited, grabbed it, and said, "Introducing Mr. Jensen—a man with too much talent for this sorry place."

The crowd grumbled, cheered, told the old guy to sit down.

"Actually," Jensen said, half-laughing, putting an arm around the man, "Jensen's my first name, and far as I'm concerned, this place . . . is my *happy* place." Then he introduced today's special guest, "the beautiful and talented Endi Sandell," and she flashed a blushing smile as they kicked into their set, with the whole room belting out the karaoke hits: "Love Me Do," "Blue Skies," "My Favorite Things," "What a Wonderful World," "Stand By Me."

I sang the oldies with the oldies, adding to the general disharmony. From inside this cacophony, though, each song took on a strange new power, a new context of life and death, and Jensen, as if knowing full well the emotional risks of the exchange taking place, did not let a moment of silence lapse—he cracked jokes, addressed the congregants by name, cheered them on, and then he thanked Endi, kissing her hand in a grand gesture before asking her to take five as he launched into a solo number, "All Shook Up," with some fake Elvis moves that had the seniors clapping in almost-time and hooting and shaking the last of what they could shake.

Then Endi was called back for "Send in the Clowns" and they cheered, they just adored her, and *finally* she stood at ease, ten times more comfortable than she'd been at the amateur hour, but when the song was coming to a close and the old guy sitting next to me blurted, *"Don't bother. They're here,"* Endi and I caught eyes and we both had to look away fast to keep from cracking up.

After the big "All You Need is Love" finale, the elderly were gently escorted out, and the nurses and the performers and I were treated to some not-that-terrible square-shaped cafeteria pizza. As Endi was being congratulated by all, I got a text from Double Fry, almost like telepathy: *Beatles double feature at the Vista 4pm?* I showed this to Endi and Jensen and soon the four of us were sitting in the Jetta parked up the street from the movie house, passing around a joint like a pack of teenagers.

"Be careful, guys," Double Fry warned, "this is some *really* strong stuff, nothing like what you citizens get at the dispensary."

Jensen said, "Man, you ain't kiddin'. I haven't done this in years—what a treat to meet all you guys."

"You're in our gang now," Fry said. "Going to this movie is the initiation."

Just then a cop rolled by and the four of us froze up. Double Fry whispered, "Pigs," and Jensen said, "Duck." As the cop car cruised past, Endi said, "Geese?" and we burst into unstoppable laughter. Then Fry pointed at the car clock. "Oh shit, we're late."

We bustled out, passed out Altoids, and turned the corner, last in line for tickets. Up on the marquee: BEATLES FOREVER.

"So much fun," Endi said.

"Not for Pete Best," Fry said dryly and the rest of us groaned.

At the concession stand, Jensen weighed Libra hands. "Raisinets or Kit Kat? Kit Kat or Raisinets?"

I said, "No sane person can decide on *that*."

Endi said, "Will you two get out of my way please," and pushed past to order a huge popcorn.

"See?" Jensen said to me. "They get a taste of fame and all of a sudden it's *outta my way.*"

Soon the four of us were down the sticky aisle, grabbing seats in the theater, with Jensen nudging Fry out of the way to sit next to Endi—I chagrined, took her other side, and Fry frowned. Now we were up close with a coming attraction for *Andy Warhol's Frankenstein* in 3-D up on the big screen, but without the glasses it was more splotchy than scary. We settled in, Fry, then me, then Endi between me and Jensen, and he angled toward us, raising his two hands in surprise.

"Ta-dah!"

He'd bought the Kit Kats and the Raisinets.

Endi said, "God bless you."

The movie started and we all leaned back to face the giant black-and-whiteness and then there they were—George, John, and Ringo, on the run from a pack of rabid teenybopper girls, and they're running, laughing, George falls, then Ringo slips, or maybe Ringo kneels to pick George up, you couldn't tell, but they're moving fast—and here's Paul and now they're hiding in phone booths, photo booths, climbing the walls—*the wanted guys*—and the girls, these supercute messengers of crazed yearning, are screaming and chasing them against this music of ridiculous happiness, the exuberance, the ecstasy jamming up everybody's heartbeats.

From the corner of my eye, I saw Double Fry stunned into ecstasy by the screen, then I looked to Endi, also mesmerized, her beautiful mouth open and breathless, and then I saw Jensen, entranced, stupefied, his eyes welling up *and so were mine*; I got it, liked him even more for this flash of vulnerability as I leaned back to take in the black-and-white tidal wave of joy and brotherhood before us—almost too much for a human to bear.

The popcorn box was passed, candies exchanged hands, and the movie on the screen maintained this shimmering beauty for an awfully long time, and then it kind of went sideways, cuckoo, but that didn't matter—the music was all that mattered. During "I Should Have Known Better," Endi slipped her hand under mine, intertwined our fingers, and I went flush with a happiness I had not thought possible for a very, very long time.

When the credits rolled, she remembered that she had to get back to Ziva's to make dinner, so we excused ourselves and left Fry and Jensen to watch *Yellow Submarine* as we headed back to my car.

Cruising home, she rolled down the windows and let in the nightfall breeze. "That . . . was such a fun day."

"You guys were superstars up there."

"Well—he knows what he's doing. It's actually a big job."

"He really likes you, ya know."

"Yeah, I know." She turned to me. "He kind of asked me out."

"Oh. Really."

"When you went to go help with the pizzas."

"I see."

"I mean, he wasn't gross about it or anything—he just said he'd like to get to know me better."

"And . . . what'd you say?"

She kept her eyes on me, gave me a cautious smile. "I told him I had feelings for someone else."

I got caught in her eyes for one sec too long, then looked back at the road. "Good answer."

"Anyway," she added, "I don't do the *very* older guy thing."

"*Very* funny. I am glad you let him down easy, though. He's a good egg."

"Yeah," she said, "I tell ya, working with the elderly is rough."

"How do you mean?"

"It's hard to give everything you've got to people you *know* are going away."

When we pulled up to Ziva's, Endi reached for her guitar and said, "I can't believe you actually got me to do that."

"It was so worth it."

"I loved that you were there in the audience rooting for me—you stuck out like a sore thumb."

"Yeah?" Then she touched my face and I grabbed her for one of those awkward over-the-gears car kisses that are completely uncomfortable but make life worth living.

She sighed and said, "I gotta go."

"I know—go. Give Ziva a hug from me."

Then she got out with her blue guitar, walked up the little path, searched for her keys, and went inside, and I headed down La Cienega humming the guitar riff of "And I Love Her" like a corndog.

But somewhere around where the boulevard crosses Third, it started to dawn on me that the same gray '22 Subaru Legacy had been behind me since at least Sunset. That just wasn't natural. Thinking back through my half-stoned lovestruck state, I realized I'd noticed that same car in the rearview when we first left the theater. Goosebumps. I slowed down to let 'em overtake me but when they wouldn't, I pulled a radical right just before the piano shop and gunned it through the residentials.

So did they—they were after me.

26

My pulse jacked up as I cut south, eyes on the rearview, and when we hit some traffic I adjusted the mirror for a better look: it was Devon Hawley Senior at the wheel, squinting to see me in the night glare, looking miserable, shaken, deeply disoriented. What the hell was that old geezer doing, stalking me on a Monday night?

Losing him would probably not be that difficult once traffic opened on Beverly, but then it occurred to me that maybe the guy was senile—he was the worst tailer in the world. That's when I got the crazy notion to lead him right back to the cul-de-sac, take him home, so to speak.

I kept my pace down Beverly, trying to not let on that I knew I was being followed. Then we made the long dip down Doheny onto Pico, straight into the curving streets of Cheviot Hills. At his cul-de-sac I stopped and he pulled in front of his home. I got out as he got out of the Legacy in an old khaki trench coat waving a pistol and coming right at me.

"Whoa, whoa, whoa, Mr. Hawley!" My hands went up as I backed up to the Jetta. "Put that thing down!"

"*I'll do nothing of the kind.*" He was stern, vulnerable, face all pale with half-crazed grief.

"Sir—please. Put the gun away."

"You just tell me how you knew my son, and don't forget, I am brandishing a nine-millimeter Rock Island Armory firearm and *I know how to use it.*"

He sort of displayed it for me. It was beyond awkward.

"But . . . I didn't know him, Mr. Hawley."

"If you don't talk straight with me, I swear on Devvy's soul—"

I leaned way back on the car, searching for how to play it. But there was no way to play it. This jittery old fool could go off—

"Whatever you need to know," I said, fake calm, "*whatever I know*, I'll tell you. But I can't think straight with that thing in my face." I kept my eyes on his and slowwwwwly, gennnnntly reached and moved his wrist, getting the gun to point elsewhere.

He scowled. "Why were you there, and skip the official version. You told the cops you're working for some old man—who is it?"

"I can't—"

"Charles El-*kaim*, isn't it?"

Our eyes locked.

"That's what I thought. What the hell does he want?"

"Your son visited him," I said, "and promised to return. When he didn't, Charles asked me to look into it."

"*I know all that,*" he said. "Ma-*dam* Persky already told me all about it."

We both cast a glance toward her house—curtains drawn.

I said, "Then she told you I went to see her."

"*What else?*"

"I learned about your son's old group."

"What old group?"

"The Daily Telegraph. The band he was in with Elkaim's son."

"Oh *that*, that was no group, that was a bad joke."

"So . . . you knew about them."

"There was nothing to know. They played one high school contest—battle of the bands. And they lost. I was there, it was pathetic. I took pictures for their yearbook, big deal."

"I'd like to see those," I said. "And hear more about what happened with them after—"

"Is that all you've got? His lousy band?"

"The drummer was murdered," I said. "Then the guitarist. And then—"

Our eyes met again in the zone of mistrust. I tried to convey real sympathy. It's not easy when the other guy's holding a Rock Island whatever-it's-called. But Hawley Senior caught the vibe and cast a curious glance at the gun in his hand. Exasperated, he shoved it in his trench coat pocket.

"Is *that* why Devvy visited Elkaim? His stupid band?"

"Your son said he could prove Emil was innocent."

"Oh *blarney*. I warned Devvy to get off all that—many times. I told him none of it was anybody's business anymore." Hawley Senior drew a hand across his face. "But he was done listening to his pop."

"Do you remember the other members?"

"Sure I do. Emil. Jeff and Mickey and Rey, they were kids."

"What about the girl across the street, the one who OD'd." I pointed with my chin. "Cynthia Persky?"

"What about her? Trouble for everyone in the neighborhood. Just like her mother."

I let my eyes trace the upstairs windows of the Persky home, then brought them back to Mr. Hawley. "Was she trouble for your son?"

"Cinnamon?" He threw me a knowing look. "That one was out of Devvy's league."

"But my understanding is she helped the band."

"Devon followed her around like a pup."

"Well," I said, "she was the girl next door. Like, literally."

"Too close for comfort if you ask me. Devvy was stuck on her. I mean really stuck." Hawley Senior's shaky hand felt for his coat pocket, as if he might try to shoot his way out of overpowering memories. "I said to him, repeatedly, *'Devon Junior, why are you torturing yourself? This girl doesn't* like *you.'* Devvy would break down and cry. Just like he was a little boy again."

Hawley Senior looked around the lonesome street of giant homes like he was a little boy again, a frightened one.

"I am so sorry about what happened to your son, Mr. Hawley."

"No." His arms dropped and he turned, first this way, then that. The cul-de-sac provided no comfort. "No, I'm the one who's sorry. This has been an exercise in futility. What the hell am I doing?"

"Just what I'm doing. Trying to find out who would be sick enough to harm these guys. Have you spoken with the police?"

"Yes, I know all about the man they're holding—some cat burglar."

"You don't sound convinced."

"Because I'm not. They're lying through their teeth. They haven't spent a minute learning the first thing about Devon. They want it off the books."

"Mr. Hawley," I said, "some people believe . . . or . . . *have intimated* that maybe Cynthia Persky . . . didn't OD. That maybe she isn't even dead. I know that's completely crazy, but . . . is there anything to it?"

I couldn't be sure he'd heard me at first; he stood there like a statue. Up behind the castle turrets of his home, the moon hung, casting a gloomy pale light across his still face. It made the guy look embalmed, but some horror of recognition burned in the blue of his eyes.

Then he whispered, "That's what *he* said."

"Who?"

"My poor son. I . . . didn't believe him, he was trying to tell me—he said she was . . . I got angry, I—"

"What did he try to—"

"—he was chasing her, *still*. I called him an idiot, I—"

"But what did he say to you exactly?"

Hawley Senior was trembling now. "That's what he knew," he said. *"That's what killed him."*

"Mr. Hawley, did he say *where* she was? Where she ran to?"

I was practically shaking, frantic.

"No." He looked up to the Persky curtains again and mumbled, "No, he didn't. He tried. He wanted to . . . tell me everything. And I . . . "

"What? Tell me."

He shook his head. "I hung up on him."

Then the lamplights flickered once and Devon Hawley Senior awoke from his stupor of shame like a man who'd sleepwalked into some random dead end. He turned to me pleadingly and said, "I'm tired. I . . . I must be grieving. I need to rest."

"Do you need help?"

"Help?"

How can you ask an old person if they're lucid enough to take care of themselves? You can't. I said, "Up the stairs, I mean."

His eyes traced the curving staircase to his looming home like it was the on-ramp to an alien spaceship.

"Yes," he said, "I think you better make sure I get in there. And take this—" He nervously pushed the gun into my hands. "I got no business being near this thing."

I walked him up the stairs and saw him in, and he mumbled an embarrassed thanks. Then Devon Hawley Senior stepped inside, into the darkness, and closed the door.

I went down the stairs and back across the cul-de-sac to get into my car. I popped the Luger in the glove box. As I started the ignition, the sight of Hawley's garage door in the lamplight stopped me cold and the full force of time hit me in slo-mo, like a sugar cube refusing to dissolve. *This is it. This is where they played.*

Back home, frantic, I tried to review all the photos on my phone—the shots of the corkboard collage I'd taken at Hawley Junior's Silver Lake pad. I even held a square magnifying glass up to the phone, but it was hard to focus. Finally, in a fit of frustration, I hit the tiny administrative office downstairs and started printing out every snap in multiples—enlarging some, cutting multiple crops, super close-ups, overlapping combos. At some point the color cartridge began to run out and the prints started coming out streaked, tinted, lined, and finally cloudy gray like a fading dream—I didn't care. I kept printing, chastising myself that I'd waited this long.

Somewhere in that collage was what Hawley knew. Somewhere in there was whatever he wanted to tell Charles Elkaim about his innocent son. And I had a feeling—a raging hunch—that he knew something about Cinnamon, something.

Last print, I grabbed my stack of paper and the old Scotch tape dispenser and pushed open the door to my room, took down the big, framed Chaplin poster, *City Lights*. Then I started taping, sheet by sheet, a crazed, fractured quilt of a collage, a re-creation of Hawley's wall, but insane.

It was all there—the flyers, photo strips, yearbook pages, all of it glaring and misshapen in random angles now. I noticed some things I hadn't before—a Polaroid of young Lazerbeam studying a recording console, an ad for *KRTH 101 Golden*

Oldies at 1—didn't say Kip and Rog, but it could've been them. I stood inches from the wall and let the mosaic wash over me. Up close and blown up, Emil's student ID card was more ominous than charming, the backdrop behind him glowing blood red, his eyes cautious, discerning, maybe secretly a little frightened of the brave new world he'd been thrust into. Also . . . fatalistic.

This isn't going to work, those eyes said. *This isn't going to play out legit.*

How did he know?

And on the ID, underneath his pic in a bold box: CARD VOID UNLESS ADMISSIONS OFFICE VALIDATION FOR CURRENT SEMESTER APPEARS ON REVERSE SIDE. The American high school was like a prison in its way—step out of line, you're finished.

I walked around the collage, scoured every corner, every sheet, anxious, brooding.

The Daily Telegraph at the Natural Fudge.

A ticket for "Meet the Bangles at Rhino Records."

A guitar pick that said *McCabe's Guitar Shop Santa Monica* in hokey letters.

Then: *Fairfax High Yearbook '82,* page 64, sophomore portraits, Gregson thru Jeffries. And smack dab in the middle, there was *Hawley, Devon,* looking slightly out of step in his blond curls and Roger McGuinn granny glasses, surrounded by portraits of surfer dudes, Latina chicks with high hair like Vanity 6, one or two scowling close-cropped punkers, one Black girl with cornrows, a headband, and a big stoney smile, and a smattering of so-called normals—kids of all races who didn't or wouldn't or couldn't play the culture game.

I backed up to take in the big picture—the mind-blow mixed-up chaos of it. Sometimes you need the big picture to catch the detail. I backed right up to the futon bed, then I sat like a mental patient on Thorazine and stared the whole thing into a blur.

Who framed Emil Elkaim?

The answer was in here; it had to be.

And that's when I saw a splash of faded yellow—lower right, a printout of a square chunk torn from the Yellow Pages with frayed edges, business listings, and cheapie ads. Ant Man Pest Control, B&P Locksmith, Couch Appeal Upholstery, Dogs of Yesteryear—that name hit me funny. I figured it for a pet groomer, but I hopped off the futon for an up-close, dropped to my knees to see, and got a jolt of electricity. At the top of the scan—*YELLOW PAGES 1998 LOCAL,* and then, in finer print: *Cabazon/Palm Springs/Cathedral City/Palm Desert/La Quinta.*

I pulledout the cell phone and googled *palm springs dogs of yesteryear.*

Antiques and Collectibles, located at Vintage Market, 537 E. Sunny Dunes Rd, Open Tues – Sun 10 am.

The Dogs of Yesteryear.

They didn't wash dogs.

In the morning I showered, hit the road, grabbed Starbucks drive-through, and headed for the desert.

27

Seventy miles per hour under the big black sun—the 10 East snaked through some of the poorest counties in Southern California, flooded by a special kind of heat, the kind that underscores lack. All the way, KSRF-AM played the oldies as I pressed the accelerator against the rhythm. "Judy in Disguise," "Surf City (Here We Come)," "Incense and Peppermints"— songs of innocence. But fifty years later, was clinging to these melodies still innocent?

No, it was more like a salve against experience.

I dialed Endi.

"I'm out for the day—I just wanted to hear your beautiful voice."

"Where are you going?"

"Palm Springs. I got a long-distance pickup." Once again, I found myself fibbing without premeditation, swerving from the unexplainable. "But I should be back before tonight."

"Come over for dinner?"

"If I get back in time, absolutely."

It was high noon as I pulled onto CA-111—twenty minutes to La Quinta Highway. The giant spinning fans at the desert delta were tranquil in the oily heat, but the sight of them whirled me back to the stark, arid present. I was on the hunt for a woman who only one day ago had been dead forty years. And the rumors about her hadn't been good, nothing like I remembered her. The way people talked, Cinnamon Persky came off reckless, dangerously ambitious, one of these operators that breaks hearts and contracts and never looks back. For all I knew, she set her boyfriend up for the prison yard. For all I knew, she faked her own death over the corpse of an actual person. If she was alive—and how could she be—she was running from something, maybe justice.

But dead or alive, she was the missing puzzle piece.

I took South Palm Canyon to East Palm Canyon and parked in a large mini-mall about thirty yards from Dogs of Yesteryear. The hand-painted sign boasted 20TH CENTURY REJECTS in flowing purple cursive.

I pressed my nose to the glass window, shaded my eyes, and peered in.

Antiques, lots of 'em, in multiple displays, each with their own placard. The place was some kind of seller's co-op, eBay for real life. Well—why the hell not. Palm Springs was Boy's Town, Camp Mecca, and finally the name made sense: every object in there, from the Singer sewing machine to the framed authentic replica of the Declaration of Independence, glowed with the intensity of the abandoned. Rows of clutter, Mickey Mouse phones and 78 rpm booklets, boxes of postcards labeled *Hawaii*, *Vegas*, *Pike's Peak*, and studded cowboy name belt buckles in a big pile, green-headed space-age monster dolls in clear plastic bubbles dangling from the ceiling and model WWII battleships placed on a rug-map of the world circa 1498, with a faux fifties living room setup in the middle.

But there were also seven or eight real live dogs sleeping around that living room setup, a bulldog and two labs, a beagle and a few mutts, all kinds of pooches flopped out here and there. They didn't stir much, but they added to the chaos, the endless rows and stacks and corners of shrapnel from America the Great. If Devon Hawley Junior's workshop was a perfect, controlled miniature of the world, this was where you learned the truth: the real world was dizzying, uncountable.

A cheesy little electronic doorbell bing-bonged as I entered, setting off a hectic chorus of canine yelps—they were all over me.

"Poolside," a woman said firmly without yelling. The dogs didn't back down and so she said it louder: *"Pool. Side."* This time, the hounds dispersed. She turned to me and said, "Sorry, I'm a rescue, they won't bite." She smiled. "Not unless I tell 'em to."

And it was her.

I froze in my tracks, ears burning, paralyzed for one long second—

Behind the counter, rummaging through a wooden wine box filled with costume jewelry, it was really her. The freckle-faced teen from the trip to Disneyland, Emil's girl, Cinnamon, now a middle-aged woman. The red luster gone from her hair, she was auburn-gray, looked permanently tired, but she was beautiful.

My heart raced as I turned and did a little fake browse through a rack of "Hang In There" cat posters, admonishing myself for not having a plan, but what kind of plan could I have? An upside-down white kitten stared back at me and the world came to a dead stop, like when you're in the presence of a celebrity you'd never dare approach. With great force I had to yank the pull cord within, to stop the busload of questions rushing forward: *Was she—? But did she—? How did she—? And why was—?* But I did look back at her over my shoulder and she caught me, our eyes met. She had one of those faces, one of those smiles that radiates ease through a wistful little silent inner laugh. It was a Renaissance face—the Madonna, about to crack up.

"Everything over on that right wall is thirty percent off. Lotta cool records and old rock tees."

There was a funny, lilting chirp to her voice. It was a teenager's voice, coming out of a fifty-something woman. Her kindness pained me, and for one brief second I considered turning around and going . . . out the door, home, anywhere. But my heart thumped, and I reached into a discount bin and picked up an orange fuzzy ball with googly eyes, maybe the tackiest thing in the whole damn joint.

"You like that?" she said with a curious grin.

I looked at it and looked at her.

I said, "You're not gonna believe this, but you and I went to Disneyland together."

Crooked smile. "That's a hell of a pickup line."

I shook my head a little. "I'm not kidding. You used to date my next-door neighbor, Emil. Emil Elkaim."

Now she looked right through me, wheels spinning double-time.

Cold: "I don't know that name."

I smiled, to soften the blow. "The heck you don't."

Turning back to her wine box, pulling a long string of fake pearls, she said, "You must have me mistaken for someone else. I get that a lot—"

"We went in a convertible fiberglass MG. Your nickname's Cinnamon. Was Cinnamon."

Through gritted teeth, she said, "*Steno pool.*"

Three of the dogs snapped to attention, stared me down with caution. One started growling—a nasty-looking dark shepherd, hot to show teeth. On instinct, I raised my hands.

"I don't mean any harm."

"I don't know you," she said coolly. "And I think you should leave my store."

"But I know you." I spoke super slow, hands in the air, one eye on the dogs. "You're Cynthia Persky, manager of The Daily Telegraph."

Now out of nowhere, without a command, one fat pitbull got closer to my heel, and the very impatient-looking shepherd knelt to lunge position. My adrenaline was pumping haywire.

"What do you want?" she said with undisguised disgust.

"Please tell these guys to back off," I said. "I've got *no reason* to turn you in or expose you or whatever. That won't help me at all."

"My husband will be back soon. He doesn't—he—"

"I understand."

"No, you don't. He doesn't know anything. You need to leave."

"You've got to talk to me."

"I can't."

"But you have to. Otherwise, I'll have to tell him . . . " I shrugged. "Everything."

She spat out some gibberish word and double-clapped. Disappointed, the hounds slumped away. One cocky terrier wandered past me. My hands dropped and I breathed relief. But she was livid.

Through gritted teeth, she said, *"I can't talk here."*

"Devon Hawley Junior was murdered last week."

She kept one eye on the door. "I heard that. Who are you and what do you want?"

"I'm Adam. I used to live across the street from Emil. You babysat me and my sister, we went to Disneyland in Emil's MG and—I'm from the old neighborhood."

She closed her eyes, shook her head. "Please go away."

All around me, the dogs, my former enemies, struggled to read the moment.

At that very second the bell rang and I angled fast, fake-browsed the Mickey phone. A tall, burly, tattooed man with a long gray beard and a biker's cut lumbered in with a cardboard box. Her whole countenance changed—she moved toward him with fake morning ease, relieved him of the box, and gave him a kiss.

"Baby," she said, "take those to the back room."

"But they aren't sorted."

"I know—sort that shit now, please. And don't get it mixed up with the stuff that's already priced."

The old rebel gave Cinnamon an aggravated, affronted look. "All of 'em?"

She said, "Pretty please?" and he grumbled, made his way to the back, looking harassed. When he was out of earshot, Cinnamon turned to me and hard-whispered. "I'll meet you *later.*"

"Where?"

"Not here," She was edgy, frantic. "The Bootlegger, at midnight. My husband has a night shift."

I nodded cool, pulled the CD from my coat pocket, and handed it to her—*THE DAILY TELEGRAPH DEL CYD* in fast black Sharpie—she held it like kryptonite. Then she made a firm head motion for me to split.

28

The Bootlegger was a refurbish of the old Don the Beachcomber—red and warm and lantern-lit, still crowded with the chatty and the Hawaiian-shirted. Over the loudspeakers, Alex Keack, *Surfer's Paradise*. I took the last empty booth in the far back, ordered a Navy grog, and watched and waited. It was a comical place to sit alone—carved wooden tiki faces loomed from every corner—but I wasn't feeling comical. I was too keyed up for any kind of paradise, surfer or otherwise.

Cynthia "Cinnamon" Persky, now per Google Deborah Summers, owner of the Dogs of Yesteryear, came in thirty-five minutes after midnight in a long brown patchwork coat. She got in across from me and stared me down. Her eyes were wet, eyeliner a little smeared, but her color was high, kinetic, just this side of anger, and she already smelled of drink. She twirled a big, loose button on the coat and studied me.

"I wasn't going to come."

"I'm glad you changed your mind."

"I remember you," she said somberly. "You were just a little boy."

"Cinnamon," I said, "*Deborah*. I don't mean to barge in, and I don't—"

"Why are you doing this, Adam? This is some bad shit you're stirring up—and it's *the past*."

"I know but—"

"What do you hope to get out of unearthing all this ugliness?"

"I didn't unearth it," I said. "Devon Hawley did, and look what happened—"

"Exactly," she said, leaning in. "Which means someone very dangerous is out there."

I leaned in too. "Before he got killed, Devon went to Mr. Elkaim and said he could prove Emil's innocence, he said he—"

A waitress with a bright smile and a giant red orchid in her hair appeared at our table and we stiffened, quickly scanned menus and ordered—a Zombie and another Navy Grog, tropical truth serum. As soon as she was out of earshot, Cinnamon said, "We gotta switch seats, I need to watch the door." We got up and maneuvered around each other. "My husband can't know about any of this."

"You can't confide in him?"

"No. No, I can't. He'd kill if he caught us here."

"Me or you?"

"Let's get this over with. How did you find me?"

"That doesn't matter."

"Well, then tell me why I should say anything to you?"

"Maybe you shouldn't, but—"

"What are you gonna do, Adam? Out me? Put me in mortal danger just so you can speculate on something that happened thirty-five fucking years ago?"

"No, of course not. But Charles Elkaim is dying, he—"

"He is?"

Her voice hit a confused register—memory and surprise. The world had not sat still.

I nodded. "He called on me."

She stared me down with an impatient scowl, almost vibrating with the news. She clutched at the table like she might make a run for it—but she didn't.

"He's not well," I said.

"How not well?"

"Dying. He's got pancreatic cancer. And . . . this is his last request. Even if nothing comes of it, I gotta do something. I owe it to him. And to my late uncle."

A deadly silence passed between us, then the drinks arrived in tiki mugs that frowned at us both. She put her liquor away like cough medicine. I swigged too, let the hard vapor soften my nerves.

Her voice dropped to a terse whisper. "So Mr. Elkaim is really going?"

"Soon."

"And . . . he wants you to look into all this."

"That's right. But if he knew you were alive, I'm sure he would not want to put you in harm's way."

"*You* are in harm's way, Adam—you do get that, right?"

I shrugged. "I won't tell anyone I saw you, okay? No one."

I pulled for eye contact.

"Look, the truth is—this isn't about Mr. Elkaim or my uncle, that's just a bullshit excuse."

"Then what the hell do you think you're doing?"

"Cinnamon," I said conspiratorially, "I *loved* Emil. I mean, I didn't know him like you did, obviously. But he was the closest thing I ever had to a hero. Ever. He was free and fearless and just . . . he was like—everything I ever secretly wished I could be. Forget about Mr. Elkaim—if I don't find out why someone would take down my hero, I will never be right with *myself*."

This little speech only tensed her more. She looked into the eyes of her mug, as if for help, but Tiki, that mocking god of war, was no help at all. She whispered, "Mr. Elkaim is dying?"

"Yeah," I said, "it's a bummer. And he has no peace. Devon came to him, got him all fired up and then . . ." I showed her my palms.

She stared me down hard, measuring for God-knows-what. Then: "Of course Devon was right. Of course Emil could never have killed anyone, least of all his best friend."

"I believe it. But then, what happened? Was Emil protecting you?"

"What do you mean?"

"Were you part of it?"

"Part of *what*?"

"Of the murder of Reynaldo Durazo."

"Of course not."

"Well, then why did you run?"

"I *ran*," she said, "because we were *cornered*. My mother was convinced that Emil was guilty. She *claimed* she saw him fighting Rey in the backyard. She *lied* through her fucking teeth. I was seventeen. The cops weren't going to take my word over hers. It was a nightmare. And it wasn't just . . ."

"What?"

"The story blew up. Word spread, fast, threats started coming—even before Emil was arrested. Rusty Durazo, Rey's uncle, was this big labor union guy and the press went crazy. Plus, Rey's cousin Lucas was a fucking loon from LADS or NASH or . . . some psycho skinhead posse. I got phone calls at three in the morning, got chased out of clubs—I was fucking terrified, morning, noon, and night."

"Jesus. Okay, okay. But why would your mother be so convinced about Emil?"

"I don't know. 'Cause she's a crazy narcissistic bitch? Or 'cause she wanted to push me away? It felt like she was pushing—like maybe *she* wanted to run away. But she was always pushing me in those days, to lie, to sneak. I learned all the tricks from her—when to shut up, when to roll over, play dead. Plus, ya know, far away, I made better material."

"For what?"

"For the Marjorie show, the great pity party." Cinnamon scoffed and drank.

"So . . . you're sure Emil didn't do it."

"*Beyond,*" she said. "He was with me the whole damn night."

She shook her head. "My parents were fighting as usual. My mother—ya know, she knew my dad was gay, right? And she just hated him for it. Like, maybe he couldn't make love to her, but did she have to hate him for it?"

"And she had a lover?"

"Lov-*ers*. So many I lost track."

"I met her," I said cautiously. "Quite a woman for eighty-nine."

Nothing.

"Does she know where you are?"

Cinnamon held the wet-eyed staring contest. Then she said, "My mother is a monster, okay? A beautiful monster. And she couldn't help it, men went insane around her, like apes. Women loathed the sight of her."

"Because—"

"She *oozed* sex, and I don't just mean she was nice to look at. She was *about* sex. Like, she just moved and talked with the . . . the possibility, the promise . . . people just lost their fucking bearings, man."

"Tough for a daughter."

"You can't imagine. The jealousy I went through—by age eleven, twelve. It was like living with a terminal illness. So maybe I had to get away."

"She is . . . a powerful presence."

"By half."

"How do you mean?"

"My mother was a twin. And . . . there was a car accident,

when she was a little girl in Rhode Island. Everybody was killed except her. Her parents. Her aunt. And her twin brother."

"That is a horrible thing for a little girl to survive."

"My mom's brother fell over her, that's what saved her. She never talked about it—not a word. But . . . the way I see it, it's like she spent the rest of her days trying to . . . bring him back. Fucking everybody, trying to rejoin with him, with some missing part of herself."

"Is it true she slept with Rey?"

"She slept with everybody, and nobody could hold on to her—my dad was the only one who could handle her. That's why she married him, she couldn't drive him crazy. Though she sure as shit tried."

Cinnamon eyed for the waitress. Round two came like a pair of tooth-clenched soldiers. She drank. I sipped. The fruit wasn't disguising the potion much.

"Anyway," she said, "the night Rey was killed, I was with Emil, the whole time. Believe me—I've been over every detail in my mind ten zillion times. It's my main occupation."

"Well—what do you remember?"

She held herself with a funny mix of reluctance and the desire to connect. I worked to be still as possible, to let it happen. There's no other way.

Finally, she said, "It was Oscar night. My parents had another one of their screaming matches in the afternoon and Daddy got all tuxed up and went alone. Then me and Mom and Emil watched the ceremonies in the living room on NBC, full color on the Zenith—big wow. Mom was . . . *seething* the whole time. Daddy accepted an award for *Tiger Blue*, he was one of the producers, and just as he got up onto the podium with his cronies, Mom stood up and stormed off out of the living room. And it all was a little extra dramatic because Emil and I had dosed."

"On LSD?"

"Yeah, we were just coming on and it was superstrong."

"Did your mom know?"

"Naw, she was off where she always was—in her precious studio, the one Daddy built for her in the backyard. It was a guesthouse with a piano and her easels and paints and a six-thousand-dollar Italian couch and everything. Anyway, me and Emil went up to my room and by this time, we were just gassed out of our minds, listening to Iron Butterfly."

Then she slugged her drink. "We were *gone*. And right in the middle of peaking—you know, the part where, like, nothing stays still, all of a sudden there was Daddy, standing in my bedroom doorway with his bow tie loose."

She scrunched her face like she was begging for an exit from the story.

"I turned down the music but it was too late, he popped his head in and we were busted. I got up to hug him, congratulate him, and he was all convivial, Oscar in hand. At first he was clueless. *'Hi, Emil, hi, Pumpkin Pie.'* Then he asked where my mom was and like a total freak I started laughing hysterically—he turns to Emil and says, *'What the heck's the matter with her?'* And Emil's cool as a cucumber. *'She's just happy. She got excited seeing you on the television.'* But I wouldn't stop, I mean, I was really off my rocker. Daddy tried to shake me and I started crying. He might've even slapped me or something because I started babbling like a psycho until finally I remember screaming—*'Daddy, I'm scared! I'm gonna die!'* That was the last straw. Like, he finally got it. *'Are you two on drugs?!'* Emil was scrambling to calm him, but Daddy wasn't listening. *'Where the hell is Foxy?'* That was his nickname for my mother. Neither of us answered. Daddy almost, like, tossed me on the bed. Then he went looking for her. And I knew . . . "

"Knew what?"

"She probably had someone back there. I mean, she often did. My dad went up the path to the guesthouse. It was dark. I don't think he'd been there five times in his life, not after his studio guys built the place, and I don't know why he decided to interrupt her this time."

"Because his daughter was having a bad acid trip?"

"Yeah, well, *anyway*—off he went, and I followed him. It was dark but when you're flying on 270 mikes of purple microdot, the colors don't slow down for nighttime. The music was still playing loud or . . . maybe it was just playing in my head. But everything that happened next . . . went *very* fast. Complete confusion. I don't think I will ever know exactly . . ."

She closed her eyes, warding off the juju.

"What?"

"My mother was in a robe, dark silk in the doorway. She was frightened, frantic, explaining something. I could see them but I couldn't *see* them—they kept morphing into shapes. She led Daddy back around the side of the bungalow and I heard a wail—I didn't know what he saw, not yet. I recoiled, back into the house, the kitchen. I never saw the body but Emil, he made, like, a dash to look. He came back to me *freaked out of his fucking mind*—but for real."

Cinnamon opened her eyes.

"You sure you need to hear this?"

I nodded.

"Daddy returned in a blind panic. He gave Emil a weird look, like . . . the way you might look at a rabid dog. '*Son—I want you to tell me what happened out here.*' Actually, no—first my dad grabbed him. '*Marj says she saw you and this boy fighting. Is that true?*' Emil couldn't speak, he was stuttering too bad to defend himself. '*Look, whatever happened with this Mexican boy, I'm sure it was self-defense, a bad accident—*' My mother was behind him, pale as death; Daddy was rambling like a producer pitching a movie—'*This drug dealer came to sell marijuana and . . . and other narcotics to Emil and things went sour and Emil did what he had to do to protect you and your mother and*—' Even blazing on acid, I knew it was wrong, insane. He said he had the power to talk to some people, get it off the books. Then my mom shrieked—'*Herbert, call the fucking cops already!*'"

"So there's a body in the backyard, *Rey's* body, and your parents are scrambling, blaming Emil. And then?"

"And then Emil shot out of there like a wild man—who wouldn't?"

She exhaled, looked around the Bootlegger like it was the flimsiest bamboo hut in a tropical storm.

"Even the next day Daddy kept going on about how it was *an accident*, and he promised me they wouldn't take Emil away—he swore to me he would protect Emil all the way, even while he was accusing him. And my father was a bigshot—he did have power like that. I mean, Senator Cranston used to come over for dinner when I was in grade school; Tom Bradley saved a box for us at the Rose Parade. I really thought he *would* look after Emil."

She looked up at me with a fractured smile.

"And he didn't. He betrayed me. My own dad."

"That is crazy," I said. "So harsh. But I still don't see why Emil didn't try to defend himself."

She leaned forward in the grip of drunken memory. "Two things my father didn't count on, okay. First, Emil was not a citizen yet. Emil did not want to get sent back to Israel, he was draft age. Any conviction could've been deadly. Plus, Daddy thought Reynaldo Durazo was just some sorry Mexican kid from nowhere. You know that soft-pedal racism—the *reason-*

able middle-class kind. It could make you puke. Well, actually Daddy had it all wrong—Rey was from this gnarly family, his uncle was a big union organizer. And maybe Mayor Bradley got a kick out of having a few Hollywood Jews at the Rose Parade, but the Durazo family were not showbiz, they had pull, they were real life."

She leaned back. I put down my drink and pushed it away. "And then you took off."

"And then I took off. In my mom's Civic. It wasn't like now. A person could disappear back then. I used to have these paperbacks all about runaways—*Go Ask Alice, What Really Happened to the Class of '65.* And I was all, like, if they could do it, so can I."

"But why—" I made a hand gesture to the bar. "Why this? Why fake your own death?"

"I just got so tired. Tired of running. Living in crash pads, ducking the cops. Some people hid me out and—"

"Kip and Rog?"

She shook her head once. "It doesn't matter who. Just—someone planted the seed. '*No one chases the dead.*'"

There was a noisy clang of laughter from a booth at the far end of the joint, her eyes glossed, and in a rush of compassion I reached for her hands—ours had not touched since Disneyland, all those years ago.

"You were kids," I said. "What you lived through, what you survived—"

She smiled sadly through a stream of tears and our hands squeezed.

"I'm sorry," she said, wiping her face with the cuff of her coat. "I haven't talked about any of this in years. You've got a kind face."

"I'm glad it's good for something."

"Goofball. Whoever thought you'd care enough to come here and . . ."

"I'm glad I did."

She finished her drink, just a little more peaceful, unburdened. Watching her, thoughts crashed in me like bottle rockets heading for each other—she had been open, candid even, she hadn't lied—but I knew she hadn't really let me in.

Not yet.

"The band," I said tentatively, "you played a big part, right?"

She nodded.

"Lazerbeam told me about the record."

"Did you see Larry?"

"I did. I saw Kip and Rog, too."

"Wow. Good work, detective. What else you got?"

"A broken story. Your mom sent you to Kip and Rog? I don't know if it was some kind of an audition or what, but . . . they didn't bite, and then—"

She gave me a knowing look and didn't speak.

"That's where it gets foggy to me. Kip and Rog seem to have passed The Daily Telegraph on to someone who wasn't really in the music biz, like maybe a wannabe producer? Why, I don't know—practical joke or maybe paying off debts, I just don't get it. So—it's like there's this mystery person that either no one wants to name or nobody *can* name or nobody will name. Who the hell is this guy? Sandoz and Grunes never mentioned him to me. But—the band allegedly made a recording with him? And then—"

She nodded knowingly. "And then *death*."

"Yeah, but—"

"No, Adam, there is no but." She squeezed my hands again. "I get that you want the whole story, and you want to do what's right for Mr. Elkaim, that's . . . lovely. And it's astonishing what you already figured out. But I cannot live with putting one more person in danger. And anyway, we're talking about *the past*."

"So what?"

"So the past . . . is something to let go of."

"Said the woman who sells Major Matt Mason dolls for a living."

She froze, then smiled into a wet-eyed laugh that made me think of Endi's laugh. There's nothing in this world like a woman's surprise laughter—it's a truth detector better than any polygraph, an allegiance beyond vows, lust, all of it, and it emboldened me. I cut to the chase.

"Okay—forgive this. But what makes you so sure your mother didn't kill Rey Durazo?"

"Believe me, I wish she had, it'd make it a lot easier to hate her. But she's just not that kind of monster."

I gave the half-nod. Everybody's mother is innocent.

Sensing my skepticism, she said, "*Both* my parents had way too much guile to kill anyone. In their own backyard? There's no way."

"Well, then what happened to this band, Cinnamon? Who would want to hurt a high school kid like Rey?"

"I don't know."

"Then why was Emil taken down before they even found him guilty?"

"I don't know."

"And why was Devon killed days after he told Mr. Elkaim he'd discovered the truth?"

"*I don't know.*"

"But you know something. You're running from it—for real. I can see it in your eyes."

Just then, another round of olive-green mugs came, stern and forbidding. When the waitress was out of earshot, Cinnamon seemed to measure the invisible line between yesterday and tomorrow. She could get up right now, head for the door. She could never say one more word to me and keep pretending. Instead, she reached behind her head and let down her gray-auburn hair.

"Okay," she said. "Fine. On one condition. You tell *nobody* you found me—and I mean nobody. Especially not Mr. Elkaim. I would die if he knew I was this close and didn't say goodbye."

"Deal."

29

Cinnamon hung her head. The bar was really bustling now, the Keack exotica piped in over the chatter and the yuks.

"All of us," she said, "were part of Dr. Bahari's thing."

"What . . . thing is that?"

"*Dr. Aharon Bahari*—he's a psychiatrist, or at least he was. He ran this workshop, the Mind-Life Actualization Seminar for Teens. He'd written this book called *Aggressive Positivity*, and he was everywhere. '*Harness the power of consciousness.*' For teens. And we—took the bait."

I flashed on Sandoz and the after-school seminar he attended. "But . . . was it a cult?"

"Not exactly. But it wasn't not a cult, ya know what I mean?"

"Not really."

"Bahari's trip was all about . . . changing the way you think. You had to, like, completely embrace the program—no halfway."

"How'd the band find out about it?"

"Mickey was already there, but—" She smirked with humiliation and pointed at herself. "I talked the rest of them into doing the orientation—my dad read about it somewhere and I got all psyched to check it out. The band were mostly into it, too—except Rey-Rey, he thought it was jive. '*You are fucking lost, all of you. And this shit ain't rock and roll.*'"

"Wow."

"Yeah, wow is right, it's like he saw what was coming. Anyway, Bahari *loved* that the guys were in a band. And eventually it came out that he had designs to be in the record business."

"Get rich quick scheme?"

"Oh, he already had money, he was loaded. I mean, he was a big deal back then."

"So what was it about?"

"At the time I thought he was just . . . *getting off on the aggressive positivity of it all*. I was hypnotized. But now I see—here's this guy, all charismatic, he can hypnotize a whole audience. But he's still an immigrant, right? The little man from Cairo. Definitely not *in-crowd*. And I think he craved that . . . that rock and roll glamour, and all that comes with it. He thought—you know, with these cool young dudes, there'll be an overflow—of razzmatazz. They'll all hop on a Lear jet with a bunch of models and head for the Bahamas or whatever, count their platinum records."

"He really thought that's where things were heading?"

"Oh, yeah. Bahari went bananas when he heard them rehearse. He bought us a brand-new Dodge Ram, opened up a charge account at Guitar Center. And he did make it seem like we were going places. He'd study the Billboard charts like they were a playbook and come back to the band with all these big ideas—he could be very seductive. He played us what he called *doppelgangers*—records to aspire to, right? It wasn't *completely* different, that was his genius. He found the place where, like, The Daily Telegraph could be a little more modern, more up. '*No more blues*'—that was one of his mottos, '*The blues are for losers*.' Lame—but he was so driven, it was hard not to get sucked in. And his first order of business was to get rid of Rey."

This landed like a thud between songs in the suddenly quiet bar. She turned to face me.

"Who replaced him?"

Dryly, she said, "A Roland TR-808 drum machine."

"Well, did the band protest?"

"Nope—and I didn't either. I mean, we loved Rey-Rey, he was family, but the truth was, he wasn't the world's greatest drummer. So when Bahari told us he didn't need to be a part of the recording—"

She shrugged.

"Was Rey pissed?"

"Not at first, he didn't have the chance. He just . . . wasn't invited to the sessions. But the other guys were completely sold, and Bahari especially doted on Emil, almost lived through him. The full-on Svengali trip. Two foreigners, taking over America—and it all happened *so* fast. Suddenly one day after school we're in these offices in Century City, up on the fifteenth floor, the next week we're tracking at Sunset Sound like we're Fleetwood Mac or something. I mean, what are you gonna say? No? David Bowie was literally rehearsing in the next room over."

"Wow," I said. "So Bahari was really pushing for the big time."

Cinnamon's eyes went catlike with candor.

She shook her head. "It was me, Adam, okay? *I* was the crazy one. *I* was the one pushing. From the second I smelled fame and fortune, I was transformed. I got them tangled up with this weirdo and worked it one hundred percent, night and day. I fired up the fantasy, sold them his vision—I was relentless."

She pointed at her own heart. "Everything that followed—is on me."

"Okay, wait a sec, you wanted what was best for your band, that's not a crime. And what makes you think this Bahari guy had anything to do with Durazo's murder?"

She didn't answer, not right away. A drunken silence set in between us, a wedge, but I understood—to me this was a story of long ago. To her it was a powder keg of shame right in the here and now.

"Between us?" she said.

"I swear it."

"I don't remember everything." She scooted back into the booth and turned her profile to me, like a penitent at confession. "It's like, I've been over this chain of events so many times, all I've got left is my own playback."

"I get it. That's how it is."

"Anyway, one night, about two weeks before Rey was murdered, I saw him. I was coming back from the recording studio alone, I had this little back entrance to the house, just past my mom's bungalow, like, 2:00 a.m. on a school night. And while I was fiddling with the keys, Rey-Rey stepped out of the shadows—practically gave me a heart attack. I guess he'd been with my mom that night, but now he was *furious*. Raging on me about cutting him out, lying to his face, all of it. He said I'd let this evil businessman change their music, break up the family. I mean, he was totally flipping out. And even worse was I could tell he was *really* hurt. He went on this crazy rant about how he had been spying on Dr. Bahari and . . . he found out about all these supposed questionable businesses—VD clinics, fake arcade games, euthanasia, all kinds of shady shit. I didn't know if any of it was true, but Rey was on a rampage. He said . . . he said he was going to . . . step to Bahari and . . . put him in his place, something like that. He said—"

Just then Cinnamon's eyes went wide—crazy wide, staring past me.

"*Oh, shit. He's here.*"

I turned.

Rambling down the aisle, through the drinking crowd, Cinnamon's husband came at me like a gray bull in ratty, worn leather.

"Who the hell's *this* candy-ass?" He yanked me from the booth and threw me to the floor.

Cinnamon screamed, "Bill, stop!" but he didn't—a boot lodged into my side, then he yanked me up again and planted a right to the no-fly zone between my nose and my ear—I flew onto a table and it tilted, drinks capsizing everywhere.

The waitress was yelling for us to take it outside, somebody else was on the cell phone calling cops.

Customers scurried. Cinnamon tried to intervene. Billy Boy threw her off and threw me forward and I flew back, toppling into a giant frowning tiki, which fell sideways, still staring as Bill straddled me with a raised fist, about to dislodge my nose once and for all when Cinnamon grabbed his arm, and he grabbed her.

"*Who is this punk?*"

"Nobody."

"You're drunk. This your new stud?"

"Don't be ridiculous."

"Then who is he."

He was about to smack her in full view of a gaping audience, half the customers halfway out the door, when she confidently lowered his arm and looked into his eyes. To my amazement, she told the truth. At least some of it.

"He's a private investigator."

"What's he want with you?"

"I had an ex who was killed in prison. *In high school.* This young guy is looking into it."

"Oh." He gave me the once-over, looking chastised. Then he turned back to her, a little sheepish. "Well . . . you help him?"

"Not a whit—I don't keep track of no exes since I met you, William, you know that."

Now leather Bill went through the ingratiation of having to straighten out the place and apologize to the waitstaff and the remaining customers. I slipped into the bathroom to splash some water on my own sorry-looking tiki face. I was getting tired of being smacked around, darn tired of it. I spit a little blood into the sink and caught my sad eyes in the bamboo-framed mirror and at that moment I remembered that my school paper, the one on filing search warrants, was due the next morning.

Oops.

When I got out into the low-lit bathroom hallway, Cinnamon was waiting for me alone with her back up against the wall, a little apologetic tilt to her eyes.

"I'm sorry," she said. "I sent him home. He's . . . sensitive."

"Not to me he ain't."

She reached into her big, brown stitched-leather purse and pulled out a cassette case, thrust it into my hands. It had a picture on it of a stout, bald, dark man with a massive thick honker and oversized glasses, wearing a doctor's white lab coat over a suit and thick tie. In gaudy bold red eighties font, it read:

A. Bahari, PSY.D., DOCTOR OF POSITIVITY
PRESCRIPTIONS
From the Dr. Bahari Spiritual Clinic
- Booster Shots to Increase Life Profits
- Building a Super-Success Plan Step-by-Step
- Remedy for a Life Without Meaning
- Rx for Health, Wealth, and Loving Relationships

I shot Cinnamon a curious look.

She said, "Open it."

Inside: a cassette with a printed label.

TELEGRAPH
1. Big, Wide World 2. Foghorn Nights 3. When I Want
You Too
Golden Harmony Mgmt.

And then a phone number in the 213.

Side two was black, no label.

I said, "They changed their name."

She shrugged, sighed, shook her head a little. "Don't forget our deal, okay?"

I took it in and gave her my word.

"Adam, I'm not joking. You need to leave this alone."

I felt for my hurting cheekbone. "Is Dr. Bahari still alive?"

"Yes. And he's still sketchy as they come."

"Okay, but where?"

"Last I checked he was running some kind of vitamin company in Playa Vista, but—"

"Well, I could just—"

"No, Adam. Last April, Devon found me, and he came here. I begged him not to go digging into all this and he didn't listen."

She raised eyebrows.

"*That's* what happens when you fuck with the past."

"So . . . is Bahari the reason you stayed away?"

Her eyes did a funny dance of apprehension, she shook her head a little and grabbed my hand, put her face close to mine and cut to a whisper. "I stayed away because I knew that every street corner would remind me of Emil's smile. And I'm never going back again."

I took it in.

She said, "Are you going to tell Charles you saw me?"

"Not a chance."

"How much time does he have left?"

"I don't know. Not much."

Our eyes met—hers were pleading. Then she gave me a kiss on the cheek and said, "Get out of here."

The woman who once so long ago ran for her life and never stopped running. The woman who thirty-six hours ago wasn't even alive. Now it killed to think I'd never see her again.

30

Back in the car, I wasn't still drunk exactly, but the night's long, dark glow hung around me like a personal heatwave. I wrote a text apologizing to Endi for flaking on dinner and promised to drop by the next day—no response.

The night sky was vast, twinkling eternal mystery.

I gassed up at Chevron and was about to hit Highway 10 heading for Los Angeles, when I remembered I had a crappy boom box in the trunk, one of those mono-speaker jobs. I'd picked it up on my last case. I pressed play and the little rollers still spun—batteries not dead yet.

I got behind the wheel and popped in the cassette demo as I took the long curve through the desert, past ancient rock formations and cascading mountains, under the wash of stars, glowing like Cinnamon's Chaplin-esque smile, the laughing sorrow of a grown woman full of trapped teenage light.

But *she lived*. And I saw her.

I pressed play. Hard-hitting precision drums, a splash of large wide guitar like a crack of thunder—from the first note, Telegraph sounded different, very. More confident, deliberate, ahead of the beat—and then the voice kicked in and it was *really* different. Maybe it was Sandoz, but it sure didn't sound like him—this was crooner majestic, with just a tint of British and a timbre that verged on pro.

> *The big wide world*
> *it's been sneaking up on us*

I drove in a trance, shooting down the highway night. I cut the windows, letting the big sound mix with the breeze. Gone was the folk rock, the wannabe Dylan strumminess. Gone was Grunes's hinky bass, Hawley's Farfisa organ. This *was* ready-for-radio stuff, cascading and plunging like a waterfall into a smooth lake of harmony. A percolating synth rhythm drove the whole thing forward, pedal to the metal—had Bahari tacked it on?

> *The big wide world*
> *it's been waiting on us*
> *sneakin' up on us*

Emil's splashy guitar had been treated by some special chorus or reverb or something—one of those plasticky eighties pedal effects that maybe sounded modern then but seem old-fashioned now.

> *Just around the corner*
> *into the big wide world*

Then, without warning, his solo erupted like a geyser from the spaciousness, cycloning above the groove, chasing after some secret force. The urgency of his melodic sense, the erotic power of it, pure Emil—thrilling, reckless, thin ice. He built it and pushed it and raced it to the magic high, and the night desert spread out before me as grand and alive and mysterious as

Mars. If this was what Emil was capable of, no wonder—no wonder he won every heart, no wonder they called him the brave one.

And no wonder he was marked for death.

Without notice, the solo made way for the chorus on return, and I knew I had to hear it again, the whole song, so I pressed rewind and play. It was pop, it was slick, glossy, melodramatic, far from the practice garage earnestness that made their unreleased LP so sweet—no, this was . . . grandiose even, but I had to admit one painful and undeniable thing: I liked it.

I liked it and I hated myself for liking it.

Maybe that's why I couldn't stop playing it—from Vista Chino to Beaumont, under fading, taunting stars, I clung to it, one hand on the boom box. As soon as the fade kicked in, I'd rewind and fire it up again and rest my hand on the buttons like a nervous air traffic controller. I must have played it ten times in a row, but I needed to hear it just once more—because it contained some something, some secret code, beyond the case even—the shape of the mystery, of Cinnamon and Emil, of being young and in love, all of it slipping away with brutal quickness.

> *the big wide world*
> *is gonna steal you away*
> *steal you awayyyyy*
> *from me*

Something elegiac in the voice—but determined too. The past, this song was saying, is gone. Time to face the future—the painful, synthesized, synthetic, ice-cold future. To salve the wound growing inside me, I groped for their beginning, their happier times, as if they were my own. I tried to picture it—

he's working after school at Kone-Coctions, she's blushing on arrival. Twisting the scoop, he smiles. She says, *"You go to Fairfax, right?"*

But even then, on the cusp of first love, it's just around the corner.

> *the big wide world*
> *is just around the corner*
> *sneaking up on us*
> *and taking you taking you*
> *far far away from me*
> *into the big wide—*

But did they know this was prophecy, the shape of things to come? Maybe they did. Maybe that's what scared them. The world, with its flying metal and bloodlust and clocks that don't stop was sneaking up—*that* they knew, every seventeen-year-old does. The world was the crowd all around, pushing, grabbing for some ice cream on a hot summer day. People. Too many. Waiting for ice cream and a destiny. Never knowing . . . how close we are to the end of a dream.

With a majestic swoop, dip, and curve, the 10 met the mighty Pacific Coast Highway and all at once I knew. I had to find him—*Dr. Bahari*—I had to see his face. I had to understand why he went so far, mutilated then slaughtered his musical children. With a surge of late-night hurt, the ocean horizon appeared before me like a signpost up ahead—the moonlight zone.

31

Waning late afternoon sun hit the palm trees that surrounded FG Vitamin Laboratories, casting lanky shadows across the lizard green walls. It was a generic-looking two-story commercial building that took up half a block of industrial park, and if it wasn't for the FG logo out front—bold letters on a graphic lime-colored four-leaf clover—I wouldn't have known I was in the right place. Big glass doors, darkened glass windows—there was something eighties-ish about the whole operation. Maybe it had always been Bahari's little spot, revamped for every fresh scam. I parked on the street and tried the door—locked. I peered through the dark glass. The place was soft, pastel, ergonomic. The logo reappeared on the wall inside over a half-oval desk, lime couches, a pile of brochures—but nobody home.

I smarted with defeat. There hadn't been much to go on in Wiki—Bahari was eighty-six, a celebrated headshrinker, motivational speaker, businessman, and one of America's first foreign-born billionaires. Among his current holdings, FG Vitamins advertised *"best-in-class" supplements that address a wide spectrum of needs for men and women over the age of sixty.* It was more wellness juju, all-organic, feel great, and never die. But it didn't make me Sherlock Holmes to guess that FG stood for Fountain Grove.

I dialed Fountain Grove Labs and got a machine. "Yeah, hi," I said, "my name's Adam Zantz. I'm . . . I'm trying to get in touch with Dr. Bahari. If there's *anybody* at all that can get me in touch with him, please let me know. Soon as possible is better, thanks. And tell him I'm a fan of The Daily Telegraph."

I gave my number. Then I texted Endi again—I'd been trying her all afternoon already. After no response, I called and got the answering machine. Maybe she was miffed that I'd flaked, but that wasn't important now, it was time to make a full confession—*I am studying to be an investigator, I picked up this crazy case, things got hairy and I—just . . . wanted to be careful. And I'm sorry I lied.*

Something told me she'd understand; she had to. I fired up the ride and tore down the 405 back into Los Angeles—night was falling again but it was still early enough to pay her a surprise visit. When I pulled up to Ziva's, a cop car idled out front, its lights casting red-blue on Endi's grave face as she spoke to a uniformed police officer taking notes on his tablet. She seemed to be gritting her teeth at my approach.

The policeman said, "You know this man?"

"Yes," she said, but she wasn't happy about it. "This is the one I was telling you about. It's his album they were looking for."

"You leave an LP here?" The cop seemed incredulous to be asking about something so outmoded and breakable.

"No," I said, the blood leaving my face. "No. I played one here, though, but I took it home. Can somebody tell me what's—"

"Is there something particularly valuable about this record?"

I looked at Endi—she did not want to exchange comforts. "No," I said. "I mean, it's rare—but it's not worth money, if that's what you mean."

"Can you give us a few minutes?" The cop's tone was hard,

and so I nodded and walked back to my car and leaned on it, clutching my keys, all twisted with anxiety.

After the police drove off, I caught Endi at the front door. "What happened?"

"I don't feel like talking to you right now."

"Endi—please tell me, I'm worried."

"Not worried enough. A man broke in here today while I was at Trader Joe's. Apparently, he wanted to know where your stupid LP was."

"No."

"Yeah actually—he turned the place upside down and when he didn't find it, he pulled a fucking gun on Ziva."

"*No.*"

"*Yes*, Adam—he gave her the scare of a lifetime."

"*No no no no.*" I was shaking. "Where is she? Can I see her?"

"I don't think so," she said, in full contempt mode. I grabbed her by the shoulders.

"Endi, who was this man? Did Ziva say what he looked like?"

She shook me off. "Don't touch me. You got a lot of nerve, coming around here, pretending to be a journalist, getting us tangled up in your little . . . *unofficial* investigation. And *lying* to me every step of the way. The officer told me you're in their database as a . . . *some kind of a witness to a homicide*? Are you fucking kidding me?"

"Endi, it's not how it sounds. I didn't—"

"How does it *sound*, Adam? Or do you just make things up as you go along?"

"Look, we were just getting to know each other, I thought—"

"First you don't tell me one true thing about your family, your music, nothing. Then you tell me half a story about this—" She hung finger quotes. "—*work* you're doing. It's like you're desperate to obscure who you are—*you* don't even know who you are."

She made for the door but I blocked her.

"Maybe you're right. Maybe I don't know who I am. I just . . . maybe I'm like you, I feel like an impostor. And I didn't want to scare you off."

She turned to me now and gave me the full force of her big blue eyes, but their light was strained with pity.

"Dude," she said, "You're *nothing* like me. I am working overtime right now to keep it real. And I can't afford to roll with *anybody* who needs to put up a front. And forget about me! Think about that old lady in there—the one who can't walk, you remember her? The one who's practically *in love* with you? How fucking disappointed do you think she is?"

I froze up.

She spoke softer now, but with conviction. "I don't think it even occurred to you that you could be compromising Ziva. Who, by the way, happens to be *my charge*."

"Your charge?"

"Yes—that means it's my job to take care of her."

"I know, I know, that was so reckless, *dammit*."

She started for the door again but this time I got out of her way.

"Endi—*please* let me talk to her. I've got to know what this guy looked like. Before he goes attacking somebody else."

Exasperated, she said, "Fine," and swayed her arm toward the little living room with sardonic drama. "Be my guest."

Sheepishly, I passed through the house, the pied-à-terre kitchen, out the back door and knocked on the guesthouse door. Endi watched, arms folded.

Ziva said, "Come in."

"Ziva, I am so sorry, I heard what happened, I—"

I reached for her hand but she pulled it toward her chest.

She was trembling slightly, elsewhere. "A man came tonight."

"I . . . I heard."

"He wanted your record album."

"I know. Who was he?" I asked somberly.

"A man."

"Like, my age?"

She shook her head a little. "Older."

"With tattoos?" I was thinking of Sandoz.

"I saw no tattoos."

"Did he have, like, curly hair? Half-Black maybe?"

She shook her head. "A man. An angry man."

"Was he short, tall—"

"*He was the gestapo,*" she blurted, furious. "In cheap sunglasses." Then she recoiled and said, "Please let me rest."

"Ziva, I am so sorry."

But she looked away and I backed off, as in a nightmare, from the half-painted canvases, the brushes hanging on wire, her aged face, hard with disgust. I turned to Endi—she wouldn't look me in the eye either, and then I was out the door and driving off in a broken daze, almost crying, pulling into the parking lot at Vons. I moved through there feverish and scored an eleven-dollar Tracfone. Then I got back in the car and pulled around to the alley behind the supermarket. I dialed Fry.

"It's me, I'm on a burner—*I got a problem.*"

"Talk to me."

"I'm being followed or . . . *something.*" I looked over my shoulder—dark alley. "Someone broke into one of my rider's houses—"

"One of your *riders?*"

"Endi's client—they must've got the impression the LP was there, and they tore the place up looking for it."

"Jesus," Fry said deadpan. "Someone either really wants that record, or else they really want to scare you off."

"Yeah, well, they're doing a bang-up job of it." I tried to complete a deep breath—a fat rat scurried from under a garbage bin out into the slash of lamplight.

Fry said, "Who are you getting close to? Who are you making nervous?"

"I . . . have a lead. A big one, but I can't tell you where it's from. There's this doctor, a wannabe producer named Bahari."

The alley was dark, dead still.

"Fry—everything bad that happened to that band went down after this doctor got involved. And *supposedly* he kicked Rey out of the group, like, a few weeks before he was killed. And . . . and Fountain Grove—*they're together.*"

"Bahari's with the DJs?"

"They gotta be—it's a program."

"You really think so?"

"A hundred percent. Dr. Bahari runs a bogus vitamin lab—health solutions for seniors, right? First they hook elderly people, people on their last legs, to invest in this crap, they lock 'em into some kind of culty residency at the estates—drain them of their resources, who knows what else. The guy down there, my lovely tour guide, even insinuated they had some kind of . . . euthanasia program."

Fry said, "Wow."

"Wow is right. These fucking guys are pulling the ultimate comprehensive elder scam. And it's more of that same aggressive positivity bullshit—*mind power über alles.* Bahari started with the youth, right? *Teen potential.* But then he saw where the really big bucks were—the boomer set, going geriatric."

Fry went silent. Then he said, "I buy it. But euthanasia's not even illegal here, Addy. And I don't get what any of this has to do with some garage band from a zillion years ago."

"These guys—Kip, Rog, Bahari—they're crooks. They got their hands in all kinds of funny business. Let's say it's not *only* about replacing Durazo with a drum machine. Let's say Rey found something out—something bad. He's pugnacious, ballsy—that's how his cousin described him, anyway. Well—I can't tell you how I know, but I *know* that Durazo was flat-out snooping on Bahari."

"So he stumbles onto something he shouldn't know and—"

"And he gets vocal—maybe he even threatens. I mean—he's part of this punker gang, he isn't afraid of shit, right? He talks back. And maybe this Bahari doesn't cotton to that. He shuts Durazo up for good and wipes his hands of the whole shebang."

"You check into the vitamin lab?"

"Yup—nothing there, it's a front. It looks *completely* bogus. And no address for Bahari either. It's like, midnineties he disappeared into the ether."

"Okay, okay," Fry said, contemplating. "I'll try to find out where this Bahari character lives. But meanwhile—you go home. And I mean straight home, lie low. Do not pass go, do not collect two hundred dollars. You got me?"

"Roger."

I signed off and caught a breath in the dark, then spun the car out of the alley and headed for Santiago Labs, ready to race home, park fast, skip up the stairs, into my room, and double-lock the door.

But as I pulled up, I spotted a car out front—one of those new-style beefy, boxy Arabian gray All-Wheel G-Class Benzos—a quarter-million bucks in a single ride. At first I didn't flinch, but as I got closer, their lights went on. I kept driving and they pulled out, turned, started tailing.

I cut up Cattaraugus and so did they.

I picked up the pace and so did they.

I tore onto Washington and so did they.

Now we were both pimp-slapping the speed limit, racing down the late-night boulevard, headed for nothing but the sea. On impulse, I peeled right into some residentials after Costco and completely fucked myself, cornered into a three-way cul-de-sac, game over. The Benzo screeched behind me—woman driver with dark Italian eyes was at the wheel—she shot me a sympathetic look. A slim blond man hopped out of the back seat brandishing the butt of a pistol in his jeans. He tapped my window. With great reluctance, I rolled it down. The night streets of Venice were dead silent.

Blond Man grinned. "The fuck you runnin' for, fraidy cat?"

I didn't answer.

"You're Zantz. True?"

I didn't answer.

"And you want to speak with Dr. Bahari—true?"

Our eyes met.

"That was quick," I said.

"Yeah, well," he said, "Doc's been eager to see you."

I took it in.

He thumbed west. "Follow us."

32

Rich car, poor car. I tailed them onto PCH and we shot up the silent coast, past Chautauqua, up Topanga, the dark beachside forest with its sloping, scorched earth, up-up-up the steep mountain. A wisp of night fog hung over heavy trees of mustard, violet, crimson—my tension mounted with every curve. I reached for the burner to call Fry but what could I tell him? I had no idea where the hell I was headed. The forest opened up into a forest ghetto of majestic hippie mansions, one after another, a whole village of 'em, on and on toward what seemed like the end of the line, a dirt dead end sloping off to a long, descending gravel driveway that led into darkness.

This road, this darkness—I was like a moth taking one last look at the flame before flying in.

But what else could I do? I tailed them down the rocky road.

Then the Benz came to an enormous wrought iron gate, they stopped, and Blond Man jumped out again, waved a hand for me to come out. Instead, I rolled down the window.

"What?" I said.

"Come on, chickenshit, I ain't gonna pluck your feathers. You want to see Dr. Bahari or not?" He pulled open the door to the Benz. "From here you ride with us."

The lady chauffeur shot me a worried frown as I got out of my car and into theirs. Blond Man shut the door, cut around and slipped in beside me, pointing his little black Glock at my belly. My hands crept up on instinct.

"What's dat for?" Lady Chauffeur said with a scowl in the rearview. "Put away."

"Zip it," he said. "I don't need this little dork to get any funny ideas about turning tail."

In disgust, she rolled her window and pressed the gate intercom.

"Hello"—a smooth man's voice.

"Yes, Marco, hi, this is Giuliana."

"You took care of that thing?"

"Dat's right."

"Nice." He sounded tentative. Then: "I'll get the doctor."

The gate began to open in slo-mo—with a giant lurch, we rolled forward on gravel. Up another short hill, we came to a loop—a spitting baby fountain stood before a behemoth log cabin, circular with twisting wooden staircases jutting over the mountain peak like a zoo habitat for monkeys. I took in the opulence, one eye on the gun. You see so many oversized homes in LA, but this was different, embedded in banana palms, unfurling into the raw nature that sloped down in every direction. One descending incline broke out into dark vineyards, perfect rows and rows of purple-green. I never knew you could make wine up here, but there was plenty about the wealthy I didn't know. Down in the middle of the vineyard sat a raised lookout house with glass walls. Inside was a round table surrounded by funky face chairs—Picassos. They looked as panicky as me in the night glare.

I looked over my shoulder—the gates were closing smooth behind us.

Giuliana parked in front of massive doors, cut the engine, and was about to get out when Blond Man said, "Ohhh no, sister, you wait here. This is *my* catch. And don't get any funny ideas about breaking ranks."

"What does this mean, *break ranks*?"

"You just stay put and keep your mouth shut."

The giant double doors opened and a bruiser with a conspicuous pistol of his own poking out of his sweats made his impatient appearance known. In a flurry, Blond Man got out, cut around the car, pulled me out. Only when my feet hit the gravel did it occur to me that I was at the highest peak for miles in every direction. I turned 360 in the high breeze—the ocean, the basin, the valley stretched out forever, city clusters cropping up like fingers of silver grasping for the sky.

The monster, Los Angeles.

Blond Man caught my one-second reverie, said, *"Move"* and gunned me to Bruiser who immediately frisked me again and yanked my wallet and keys. Then Blond Man tucked his gun and said, "Marco—apologies for the late intrusion," just as a slender man in a charcoal gray suit appeared at the door.

"Doesn't bother *me*. You caught the fish."

"A live one—for now."

Blond Man was trying to be funny but Marco didn't laugh. He turned on his heel, disappearing into the cavernous home. A few minutes later, Bruiser got a text. In a thick Israeli accent he said, "You coming with me."

"I'm coming too," Blond Man said.

"*Incorrect*. The doctor want only him."

"But my dad said—"

"Your dad says thank you and you go home now."

Blond Man seethed as Bruiser herded me into a high-ceilinged vestibule, through an enormous room with mustard couches, a giant oak table, a stone bowl of potpourri, and the longest fireplace I'd ever seen. Above it, an enormous painting covered one wall—the Rape of the Sabine Women, bodies tangled, terror-filled eyes. He whispered something to Marco that I couldn't make out. Marco took it in, sized me up, decoded the situation through a shield of agitation, then they disappeared down some piss-elegant oak passage.

Time passed. It might have only been ten minutes, but not all ten minutes are created equal.

Finally, Marco reappeared at the doorway, all business, brandishing a gun of his own. "Now—let's go."

Back out into the vestibule we went, down a long hall, through a kitchen fit to serve banquets, with industrial steel sinks and rows of ovens. Out a side door, we stepped back into the cold. Topiary, metal furniture, gargoyled separators—and in the dark distance, a flurry of wild turkey vultures moving through the trees, slow then frantically fast, ugly arched red faces zooming by like scalped skulls, the messengers of impenetrable fear.

"Fuckers keep me up all night," he said. "You can hear 'em hissing a mile away."

Marco opened a low garden gate and led me past a small waterfall bleeding into a long koi pond, then around the corner to a door—some kind of a dilapidated guest cottage, maybe the old service quarters. He unlocked the door—inside, a former office, piled high with junk.

"Go," he said with finality. "Wait here for the doctor."

I hesitated and he yanked me in. I steadied myself, looked around dumbly—a ratty old brown leather shrink chair and matching reclining couch, a busted green lamp, a busted moped lying on its side without a rear wheel, a golf bag without clubs, and stacks of old Playboys, rotting board games, precarious towers of musty books—Fromm, Perls, Cialdini—enough psych to choke a horse. A person could go crazy in a room like this—the moonlight blue damask wallpaper was unraveling in upside-down waves.

"Sit down," he said, wagging the gun at me, "or lie down, whatever. But you *will* be monitored, so don't try anything foolish."

"Like what?"

"Like if you try to run? I'll shoot you in the leg and drag you out back, let the turkeys peck you to death."

He gave me one last scowl for good measure, but just as he turned away, a beam of light hit us so strong my eyes watered. Coming forward, a distant silhouette, short, wide, hobbling on a cane, and I knew it was him—Dr. Aharon Bahari, PsyD. Behind him, Bruiser kept the flashlight on my face but Bahari waved him back—lights cut and Bruiser retreated into shadows.

Now from the dark, Bahari shuffled into focus in pearl-colored slippers, baby blue pajamas, pearl-colored bathrobe over his shoulders, cane in his grip, curious, scratching his beard, squinting, trying to make sense of the dim scene before him. He stepped forward and the contours of that tragic face came into the moonlight—white bearded and sad eyed and vulnerable. There was something powerful in his countenance, though, a mystery force that hit the space between all of us in an instant.

"What . . . in God's name is going on here?!" At the sight of the gun, Bahari flared with rage and in a single motion, yanked it right out of Marco's hand. "Give me that thing, you nitwit."

"But your son said—"

"I don't give a rat's ass what that hysteric said."

"But this is the one you were asking about, isn't it? He's been lurking around the warehouse."

"All right, *all right*," Dr. Bahari said, "cut the opera. Send them packing. And don't bug me for the next three hours. *Capisce*?"

He said, "Yes, Doctor," sounding relieved.

Then Dr. Bahari said, "Goodnight, Marco."

As Marco made himself scarce, the doctor turned to me, shaking his head, embarrassed.

"Idiots," he grumbled. "And the irony is I've been *hoping* you would pay me a visit . . . Adam—may I call you Adam?"

I nodded, watching Marco disappear, still wary. "How do you know my name?"

"Stanley and Roger," he said matter-of-factly. "Come, let's have a drink, you and me. We'll talk like civilized human beings, not gun-toting *mishugenas*." With a pointing wave of his cane, he turned and I followed, but at the pond, he stopped to cast a smile my way.

"My fish," he explained, gazing down upon his orange-white koi with sleepy-eyed intensity. "Good evening, my little soulmates. Daddy loves you."

33

There are people whose raw Zen state will disarm you quickly, and Dr. Bahari was certainly one of those, but as he picked up the polished Brazos cane and led me out across the property, breathing heavy, thudding on the night-gray of tennis court, I had to warn myself that a demeanor is not a soul and the Zen state is not the itemized bill. We came to a wine cave door—he knocked on the wood with his cane and said, "Anybody home?" but it was just for show—then reached into his bathrobe pocket and pulled out a key. "Pretty sure what you want's in here."

He opened the giant doors, got into the vestibule, and flicked on a light. In we went—down a short flight of stairs to a long, narrow cellar cave, dark with cold, wet brick walls, a giant King Arthur table, a bottle of Courvoisier the size of a basketball, and an ornate tin tray on which lay a neat pile of too-perfect joints.

Bahari hugged himself. "*Brrr, too cold*. I prefer a sauna." He grabbed two gold-laced goblets, stood at a barrel and turned the spigot—red poured. "Sit down, Adam, and tell me what's what."

I sat but I kept my eyes on him—as if that might stave off his powers to hypnotize.

"I'm here to learn about The Daily Telegraph."

"Here's a guy that gets right to the point. Comes waltzing

in at gunpoint and first words out of his mouth, '*Gimme the skinny.*' I like that too." He brought our drinks over and sat. "So, what's your connection? Tell me why you care."

"The guitarist Emil was . . . a family friend," I said cautiously. "His father is getting up there and he asked me to try to find out what really happened—he's . . . he doesn't have much time."

"What happened, as in . . ."

"Emil's father has strong reason to believe his son was framed."

I stared Bahari down. When he said nothing, I went on, counting fingers.

"No discernible motive, witnesses who were definitely with him the night of, best buds, no history of violence—it doesn't add up."

Bahari nodded knowingly, lifted his glass in a gentle toast and we drank. I didn't know good wine from bad, but this one went down easy as a parachute—nothing like the $4.99-ers I copped at Trader Joe's. Still, all this luxus wasn't making me trust him any more than I already didn't.

After swilling his creation, Bahari said, "And so . . . you came to me. Makes sense. Did you hear the demo we made?"

"I did."

"Not bad, right?"

"Quite a transformation."

Bahari drank again and said, "I'm glad you came. I don't have much of a memory these days—but I remember watching them record those songs like it was yesterday. It was a very exciting time for me."

"You remember where you saw them last?"

"As a group? I couldn't pin it down—maybe making the video? Emil I saw in prison, two days before he died. I went to visit, to try to help. Then—heartbreak."

I drank again and Bahari did too, studying the brick wall.

From out of the blue, he said, "Nothing I tell you tonight could explain how it made me feel, what happened to him."

"Yeah?"

"Yes, Adam. To this day I think of Emil Elkaim as the son I wished I'd had. Privately, of course."

"But . . . you had a beef—with Durazo."

Bahari frowned. "Who said that? I never even met the boy."

"You didn't?"

"Not even once—they'd already kicked him out. I worked with Devon the piano player, Geoffrey Grunes. And *Emil*—he was the big talent. We were two soldiers, he and I, we understood each other."

Bahari tasted a bigger sip and his wistfulness morphed into a kind of conviction—he pointed at me. "And I agree with his father. One hundred percent. I *know* Emil could not have killed . . . *anybody*. Not. A. Chance. And he didn't belong in that jail."

"You went to see him."

"Yes, we spoke. He cried to me from behind the glass. He was only eighteen, nineteen, for fuck's sake. Then it was my turn—I wept the whole way home." Bahari raised his eyebrows, his mouth went slightly crooked—half-bitter, half-throttled— and then he mumbled "we were soldiers" again.

I wanted to hate him, or at least sidestep his charisma, but it wasn't easy. In a matter of minutes, Bahari did have me hypnotized in a way—transfixed. The wine had taken the edge off my nerves, but inside the softness, I flashed that I could be in the hands of a true crazy—maybe that was the space from which his curious power emanated. This wasn't a street-level thug like Sandoz or even a Hollywood hustler like Roger Paulsen. This was a man driven by ideas, strange ones. Picking up on my concentrated static, his crooked grin disappeared and he said, "But you didn't come here to listen to me get sentimental. You want the facts. Salud—to Emil, may his memory be a blessing."

We finished our glasses.

I said, "I had no idea they made a video."

"Oh, it's marvelous—we'll watch it."

"Tonight?"

"Absolutely tonight."

Then he got up and ambled to a small, annexed room I hadn't noticed, a cramped office for the wine cave. He opened the door and ducked in, considering the file cabinets, trying to remember something. It's funny how he seemed to transform yet again at this distance, in this new, smaller habitat. Bahari obviously was an art collector, a brewer of wines, a breeder of fish, a wealthy bon vivant who knew how to party. And yet the man in the back room of a brick cave, rummaging in bathrobe and PJs, digging through an old file cabinet, a little confused, frustrated by fading memory, did not exactly look like a life enjoyer. In fact, he kind of reminded me of Lazerbeam—another wounded shlub trying to get in on the action.

"Aha!" Bahari pulled out one of those oversized old black VHS cases and jiggled it with triumph. "Pandora's box."

The sight of the video box made my pulse quicken—I had a gut sensation that it contained the secret key, the final puzzle piece. Bahari told me to pour some more and bring the glasses, then he motioned me to the far end of the cellar where he knelt to pull open a floor door. I peered down a long staircase disappearing into darkness.

"*Oh no,*" I said. "No thanks."

"It's my *screening room*, Adam. I'm not gonna chain you to the wall and whip you!"

Balancing one-handed on the cool brick wall, I followed him down.

34

With the flick of a switch, a blaze of crimson-gold beauty—a small-scale Mediterranean movie theater with three rows of overstuffed red velvet couches facing a ruffled red velvet curtain cascading down to a stage of polished maple, flanked by regal red-and-gold checkerboard walls with gold Greek columns stretching to the old-fashioned hand-painted red-and-gold tin roof.

I said what anybody would have said: "Holy shit."

Bahari said, "It's fun." Then he popped open the front of the stage—a half-dozen gizmos were in there blinking and waiting.

"Sit down, relax, please." As he fiddled with the bulky ultra-ancient JVC, he added, "You gotta be the most hypervigilant person I've ever met."

I snickered but took a seat in the second row, sinking into the plushness, looking all around. A person could get lulled way out of reality in a room like this. I tried to stay on track.

"So—Doctor. If you think Mr. Elkaim is right, who *did* kill Reynaldo Durazo?"

He popped the cartridge into the JVC—it closed like the mouth of a hungry alligator.

"Some crazy—obviously. There's so many out there you can't count 'em." When he saw that I wasn't satisfied with his answer, he turned to me and added, "That's really all I got, kiddo. Don't think I'm happy about it. Not a week goes by where I don't ask all the same shit you're asking." He shrugged. "It is what it is. All I can tell you is . . . I wanted to . . . have a band, be a part of the excitement. And then it all went to hell. *Veni, vidi . . . no vici.*"

"So you're telling me you just . . . *happened* to pick the wrong bunch at the exact wrong time?"

"You're being sarcastic, but it's not far from the truth. Indeed, I walked right into a tragedy." He started fumbling with a remote. "I can never remember how the hell you work this thing."

I waited, sunk deeper into the red plush, felt its taut smoothness. Four cone-shaped black Bose speakers perched at me from every corner in the room like faceless robots. I was a little drunker than I thought.

As the automatic curtains rose smooth, Bahari cracked his tilted smile. "Get ready to have your mind . . . *blown.*"

Then: a beam of light cutting through the darkness, just like creation.

A white screen, and then, in eighties digital type:

TELEGRAPH / "Big, Wide World" / MCA Records & Tapes

"They signed?" I said.

"Almost," Bahari said with a grunt. "*Music Cemetery of America*—we never inked."

"Did . . . Cinnamon know about the video?"

"The little manager girl?" He shook his head somberly and my belly tightened. *They burned their muse.*

On the movie-sized screen, old-school digits counted down—PICTURE START—8-7-6-5-4-3 —then one spin of the clock and the opening bars blared—too loud for two listeners.

On the giant screen, a Euro city scene, in that mushy '80s too-rich video color, made worse by being blown up to full movie screen—young Devon Hawley Junior, in dark shades and a suit with a full head of curly-blond hair, talking on a pay phone. Cut to a svelte brunette model type on the receiving phone line, trying to look Russian, but it was pre–Fall of the Wall, *fake* Russian, a wannabe Nastassja Kinski in red lingerie—she slams down the phone and now she's getting dressed up either for going to a discotheque or doing a top secret spy operation, I couldn't tell, but a fan blew her hair every which way in her apartment, typical '80s glamour shtick.

Cut to a long, slow-moving limo, Grunes at the wheel, hair combed back straight, looking awkward and bad actorly. He gets out, opens the door, as blond, suited, skinny-tied Hawley Junior gets in the ride—he's out on the town.

I watched like someone at a horse race, fixed on *it*, but Bahari stood to the side and his gaze was on *me*, measuring every impression. It was like he was trying to read my mind and control me by telekinesis and sell me the video all at the same time.

"Paris?" I said.

"We shot on the Columbia lot."

The motif was coming into view: super-suave international ultra-chic rock and roll spies. Oy vey.

Cut to Hawley and the faux Russian babe at *le outdoor bistro*, up comes the waiter—young Emil in a red bow tie, pressed white tux shirt, and black tux pants with the satin stripes, carrying a silver tray of espressos. My heart surged at the sight of him; I raised a hand to my mouth.

Cut to a private jet for no discernible reason.

Cut to Hawley letting the dame into the limo—classic flirtatious rock video back-glance. But no sooner does the limo door close, then we cut to them in bed, her naked back, his ecstatic face, still wearing sunglasses, she's on top.

Then the door flies open and it's . . . a bust of some sort—Feds, guys with cameras. The dame slips off Hawley wrapped in the sheet, revealing that he's chained to the bed. Cameras flash, Feds throw a trench coat around the temptress and they're gone, out the door, leaving Hawley Junior to thrash in slo-mo fade while the cameras flash.

I tried to tune my ears to the song, but in my drunky state, the volume and the spy flick conceit was so heavy, I could barely focus on it—the rhythm was assaultive, the riff forceful, *manipulative*, but even from my buzzed vantage, I knew it wasn't the music that was bothering me; I'd already heard it. No—it was the whole operation, a change in sensibility, from the human to theatric, life to larger-than yet also thinner-than, teenage experience to false innocence, and in a flashing swell of rage I hated them for it, all of them, Bahari and the band, hated them for this—and for betraying Cinnamon. Then the video came to a close, the screen went white, Bahari went subdued. Without exchanging a single word, he'd taken in the full range of my disgust, like it was written all over my face.

"I helped them go large," he said without apology.

"What . . . what does that *mean*?"

"It means I taught them to stop being *cowards*. I dared them to widen their scopes."

I drank from my full goblet. I was for sure drunk now, unmoored. I didn't want to be rude, but the wine had loosened my tongue. "Is that what you call that? A widened scope?"

"I gave them vision."

"More like . . . " I gave him the drunky smirk and wiggled fingers. "You hypnotized them."

"Hypnotize? Oh, you are a corny one, Adam. They came *begging* to be a part of all this, they were *dying* for success."

"Yeah," I said, "literally. So you, like, *axed* the drummer and sent the singer on his way."

"*They* wanted the drummer out," Bahari said, defensive now. "They said he could not keep time. And as for the singer—him I met. A totally unprofessional asshole. Or rather, what I should say is, he was a *professional* self-saboteur." Bahari pointed at the white screen. "He would've buried their career right at the starting gate."

"Who *is* singing on that thing anyway?"

"That's Devon, with the aid of some effects. We couldn't have Emil do harmonies, his accent was too strong—but his guitar playing was *ben zonah*."

"What's . . . *ben zonah*?"

"Hebrew—for son of a whore."

"Is that some kind of badge of honor, to be *ben zonah*?"

"Absolutely. The son of a whore . . . doesn't know from petty civilities. A son of a whore is a living byproduct of the bitterest truth—*sexual hunger*. Like the old song—*born free*, no unnatural code to uphold. Just life." Bahari pointed at me. "Emil Elkaim had the life force by the balls."

"Yeah, okay, I get it, I'll change my name to *ben zonah*, but that"—I pointed at the screen—"sorry, but that was false, that was . . ." I was frenzied, really buzzed now—the homemade wine was some serious liquor. "A sellout."

"*You got it, kiddo.* And that's why I wanted you to see it. Because I understand your struggle. And your disappointment. Your heroes, your precious idols—well, I got bad news for you." He pulled his bathrobe closed like a trial lawyer. "They were *desperate* to sell out. And had Emil not gotten caught up in all that ugliness, they *would* have succeeded." He looked up at the blank screen. "You know, I was furious at first—all my plans,

my hopes. After all, I made them, invested. I *owned* them, contract and all. And I could have sued the shit out of them—"

"So why didn't you?"

But Bahari wasn't listening, he was fiddling with the remote.
The red velvet curtain came down slow and smooth. Then he
turned to me in a gearshift down to grim.

"The real question is," he said, "why do *you* care about this
band so much? After all, Daily Telegraph is before your time,
isn't it? How old are you, anyway?"

"Thirty-seven."

"You're a pup. And the truth is I am *really very moved* that
you want so badly to understand all this. Don't forget, I *knew*
Emil Elkaim." He drank and I took another sip—the wine was
deeper, stronger in the second round. "Emil is not a figment to
me—the thought of his living being still tears me apart in the
middle of the night. Sometimes I think that's what's strangest—
not that he died, but that he ever lived."

"I do know what you mean, Doctor," I said, sounding buzzed
and desperate. "That's why I'm searching for the truth."

"Of course. But . . . if I had to guess, Adam, I would say that
you and I look at *the-search-for-the-truth* differently. See, there
is one thing of which I'm certain—" His voice went bolder,
direct. "In order to *understand* whatever happened to Emil
Elkaim, you are going to have to understand what happened
to Adam Zantz."

"Well—"

"No, not well. *Yes.* To look at yourself, *see* yourself. That is
your final truth, Adam, be certain of it."

"With all due respect, Doc, I didn't come here for therapy. I—"

"God, I hate that word—*therapy.* I never practiced *therapy.*
Hand lotion is therapy. Massage is therapy. I'm in the business
of helping people take the *lunge toward reality*—and that's
something you can use."

"Okay, but—"

"No, hold on, hear me out. You didn't just magically appear on my property. Uh-uh. You brought yourself to this place. You made a decision—to climb up or maybe fall down to the truth. Okay, it's admirable. But in the end, this isn't about Emil or his band *or* his father, it can't be. It's about *you*."

After a long pause, I said, "About me?"

He nodded comically.

"Fine," I said, "it's about me. I buy it."

The stentorian voice let out a goofy laugh-squeal that was part Egyptian, part Brooklyn. "I am glad you do. Because you don't look like a *dick* to me, a *private eye*. A real private eye is always . . . outside reality. Fact, that's what a snooper is—a kind of peeper, a coward on the fringes. But you're right in the middle of this one, kiddo."

"I am?"

"From where I sit?" He stared at me in silence—the wavy folds of crimson made a dramatic backdrop—a waterfall of velvet blood. Then: "I knew the family, you see. Herb Persky and I were close—"

"Cinnamon's father?"

"*Cinnamon's father*, a good man. Herbert was one of these fellows who wants to do right, who has a . . . a . . . *program* for healing the world—*the man with the message*. I cherished his passion."

"Was he your patient?"

"No. He was my lover."

"But he was married," I said.

"On paper, yes. To a very unfaithful woman. But in that mischievous thing called *reality*, he was married to me. And we split over what happened, the murders, and when Cinnamon died—it wrecked him. Wrecked *us*. For all time."

I stayed flat, killed my drink—I didn't believe for one second that he didn't know about Cinnamon, but I couldn't blow her cover either. Then I said, "Herb Persky died of a heart attack, right?"

"That he did," Bahari said. "But these are not the right questions, Adam, these inquiries into the past. To help *you*, we need to get to . . . the *why behind the why*."

We stared each other down in this cove of poshness. His words were getting pretzeled in my mind—*mischievous reality, the why behind the why*—and I couldn't tell if I had gotten too drunk now or something—I took the room in, the gold and red shimmering hard, then looked back at him—he was grinning.

"I'm sorry, Doctor, what were you saying?"

He raised a knowing eyebrow. "The why . . . behind the why."

"I . . . I don't understand. I . . . *I don't feel good*."

"Oh, you'll be all right. Anyway, *feeling good* is overrated."

He sipped and I went flush in lurches, tingly, hazed, half-dazed, and then I knew—"*Did you drug me?!*"

"I wouldn't call it *that*," he said with a Jewish shrug. "After all, I had some too. We just had a spot of The Empathy Mixture."

"The what? I don't feel good," I repeated dumbly. Woozy and more than a little pissed, I tried to stand up off the red velvet to move up the stairs and get the hell out of there, but the room tilted like a seesaw and I fell back into the velvet, panicky and full of rage. Bahari scurried toward me as if to comfort.

"Please, Adam," he said, "don't be frightened. Peace and love spoken here. Sharing, confiding. *Nobody* will hurt you." His weird cadence sent me from high to crazy high then way too high in three rock skips across a pond.

"You mean you dru—*I didn't come here for this*, I—"

"I know, I know—but I promise, this will *help you*. And your mission."

"I am fucking *spinning*, Doc," I said.

"You'll be fine. I vow it." Bahari had moved closer somehow; he was seated on the couch in front of me, but twisted, facing me. "I am here to help you—plain and simple. And for me to do that," he said softly, "we're going to have to start as close to the heart of the matter as we can. Forget about the long ago of people you barely knew for the time being. I'm going to ask you some personal questions now—get to know the real Adam Zantz."

35

A wave of woozy—Bahari stared me down, my psychic tour guide on a gnarly inside-out bad trip. "All I'm asking," he said, "is what keeps *you* up nights, Adam? What *hurts* you?"

"How the hell is that gonna help me solve this case?"

"It's pretty basic," he said, almost affronted. "I'm looking to discover what drives you forward." Then, after a pause, he said, "So come on, let me in. Close your eyes if it helps, lay down, stand on your head. I don't care. But let me in. You've come this far—all the way up the mountain just to have a gun stuck in your face, you already risked. So take me down your path—and maybe we'll discover the way forward."

"You are a nut," I blurted.

He said, "Takes one to know one," without missing a beat. And he watched me so patiently. Across the checkerboard walls, peacock feathers glistened electric—or maybe I was seeing that.

I said, "I heard you didn't believe in, uh, psychedelic whatever."

"Ha—where'd you read that? Wikipedia?"

"What's in my body right now anyway?" I said.

"One hundred percent organic and natural ingredients. You will not get sick, you won't *lose your mind*. The very worst thing that might happen to you tonight is you might feel emotions you have locked up for a long time. Believe me—it's a good thing." He grinned again and the room seemed to swirl with his mood—his company was more psychedelic than the strongest LSD on earth.

I looked to the exit—I wanted to get the hell out of there, but even if I could make it up the stairs, and I knew damn well I couldn't, my car was a million miles away.

As if reading my mind, he said, "If you don't *like* this, if it's too much, I'll call for Giuliana to take you home."

But I didn't answer.

"Try closing your eyes, Adam."

Reluctant, stuck, I closed them again and surged instantly with a strange, labyrinthine insecurity, self-disappearing into self-disappearing into self, like red-and-gold MC Escher staircases going up and down at the same time.

"Don't forget to breathe."

My heart rate normalized—the inner staircases broke open like a thousand floating streamers and then—

Faces: Emil and Cinnamon just before a kiss—

Faces: old men—Elkaim, Uncle Herschel—turning their sorrowful Jewish countenances upon me, then fading into dark—

Faces: the teenage boys in the canyon, posing for their shoot—solemn, sage—*they saw it coming*—

"Tell me what you see."

I groaned "faces" and hurt burst inside me like a superbubble, spreading its ache through my limbs. "I knew him," I confessed, "as a child."

"You knew Emil."

"Yes . . . I . . . looked up to him."

"I see. So presented with this case—"

" . . . to make my uncle happy. My late uncle."

"Your . . . dead uncle?"

"My dead uncle," I said, eyes still closed, clutching at a velvet throw pillow now, its softness throbbing in my grip like a beating heart. "He adopted me. *I don't feel good.*"

"Stay with me, Adam. What you are feeling is nothing more than extreme openness. And even that passes—you'll miss it when it's gone."

"Okay," I said. "Okay."

"Why . . . would your uncle adopt you?"

"My mother was arrested for vagrancy. Parent services intervened."

"I see. Did your uncle love you? Or was he just engaging in filial obligation?"

"He loved me."

"He did."

"Yes. Too much."

I felt speedy shivering from within, but Bahari's presence contained the dream-swirl, framed it like the movie-house walls.

"We . . . had a falling out," I said. "Uncle Herschel wanted me to be a winner."

"A winner at what? Not at detective work."

"Songwriting. But . . . I sucked. I didn't have what it takes, I bombed, I gave up. *We fought.* Then . . . he died. *But I don't see what any of this—*"

"Cause of death?"

The question had a businesslike quality I didn't quite like. *Nausea*—to snuff it, I blurted, "My uncle died of shame."

A grunt of approval. "Shame for what."

"For the way I let life blow me around."

"Say more."

"The way I got lost."

"*More.*"

"My lostness, my weakness. Is this going—"

"Weakness meaning—"

"*Everything I promised.* And didn't deliver."

"Hmm." It was a hum of inquiry that wouldn't let me budge, and I felt even more weak, immobilized—he had to see it. He said, "Lay *down*, Adam. Nobody's going to mess with you. You're safe here."

I lay back, why not? I wasn't going anywhere soon. But I opened my eyes. *Either-or.* It hardly mattered. The tin ceiling was alive like a bustling red-gold city—Hawley's miniature-land upside-down. The last piece of my resistance kicked in.

"Doc, I still don't see what *any* of this has to do with a pair of murders that happened thirty years ago. Laying here like a zonked-out blob—what the fuck? I may be amateur, but this ain't detective work."

"On the contrary, this is very much detective work."

"Well, I don't see it."

"No—no, you don't. Not yet. But I have a theory, Adam. You're a bright boy, I can see that. And I think there is a decent chance you may have a deep line into *why* all this happened—"

"The why behind the why?"

"Now you've got it. Problem is, right now your lens is too fogged up . . . with pain, resentment, the usual horseshit. And *that* anyone can see from a mile away—it's written all over your face."

"*I failed, okay?* I failed and broke my uncle's heart. You happy now?"

When he didn't answer, my eyes welled up, and I covered my face with the crook of my arm, and then he did something absolutely astonishing. He reached into his pocket, punched something into his phone, and the lights dimmed, just a hair, but it softened the room. It was the most graceful, compassionate gesture I'd ever seen a man do. Now all I could make of this curious, embarrassing moment were the shadows of red curtain, the tin ridged ceiling, the blurry black wrist of my hoodie in near darkness, stanching tears off my face. Bahari said absolutely nothing for a long time; I didn't either. Together, we let the kaleidoscope of sorrow spin.

When I regained my breath, I said, "I'm sorry."

"For what?"

"For coming here—waking you up."

He burst out laughing.

I said, "I made a mistake, okay?"

"*I disagree.* I say you came to the exact right place. The cosmos has asked you to solve the riddle of The Daily Telegraph, and the only honest person who can help you do that is me. Because I know that the only way for you to come even close is to circle around *your* motivation. Find your *inner Emil*—and you just may fulfill your mission after all."

"I think I understand you, Dr. Bahari. I've done a little therapy in my time. But I don't *believe* you. I wish I did."

"You promised to not call this therapy."

"Okay."

He said, "Let me explain it another way. *You are the son,* seeking the father, who is seeking the son. Really *trapped* in a cycle of guilt and retribution. Yesterday it was your dead uncle. Today you choose Charles Elkaim for a substitute. Tomorrow, you'll find another. *Ad infinitum.* You are looking to encounter Uncle's death head-on, but you can't, because the death is *inside you.* And you're stuck in the loop of it."

"I feel guilty, I—"

"*Guilt,*" he said definitively, "is a way of hanging on."

I sat up, eyes wet and wide open. Defensive, proud: "My uncle served in the 186th infantry; he fought the battle of Khe Sanh."

"Okay."

"He got a purple medal. He told President Nixon to fuck off. To his face."

Bahari chuckled. "Brave man."

"Right," I said. "Unlike me."

"Your uncle's context was his, yours is yours. And the war *you're* up against may be invisible, but that doesn't mean it isn't as tough as ole Dick Nixon."

We had a little laugh together—there was just no way to hate this guy.

I said, "Is there a way out—of the loop?"

"You *know* the way out, kid. Unleash the pain. Obviously. Otherwise, you'll be trying to placate an unforgiving ghost *for all time*. And it won't work. Uncle. Will never. Forgive."

My eyes softened to the darkness, a wash of patterns. I thought I might cry again but my lungs filled with sweet oxygen, and for a moment, all was calm.

I said, "How do you know so much about me? Like, so fast?"

"It's just what I do. Some people are good at making cupcakes. I'm good at helping people see what's already right in front of them."

I checked the wallpaper. "I still see swirls."

"Yes," he said, "I know. But behind the swirls?"

I closed my eyes again and, without any effort on my part, the patterns crashed into each other and separated, like the great pulling back of an inner velvet curtain in an old movie house. But the image revealed was tiny, microscopic, and detailed beyond belief. How did the mind do these instant vivid tricks?

"My uncle," I said, "alone in his backyard, digging, planting seeds."

"How is he feeling in the yard? And remember—it's all projection."

"Really?"

"Maybe not all, but you'd be amazed."

"Well, it's him. He's disappointed. Bitter. Life hasn't worked out as he'd hoped. He . . . it's *all* been a—" Big breath. "But me in particular, I'm—"

"Yes. *You.*"

"I'm like, a *symbol* of—"

"Say it."

"Disappointment."

A deep sob filled me, without tears, ricocheting in the zillion-dollar room. Bahari smacked his hands together.

"So you're a *symbol*," he said, the way a comedian might set up a joke. Then he laid out the punch line as flat and as matter-of-fact as a waitress repeating an order at IHOP: "A symbol of someone *else's* . . . failure." He thumbed the phone and the lights faded up. "Our work for the evening is done."

Bahari stood and turned and I straightened myself out, still high, bewildered.

The roof door creaked open. Marco traipsed down the red velvet stairs in tony orange sweats and black Nike slippers.

"Marco," Bahari said, "I want you to apologize to this young person for manhandling him. It just so happens he's a dear friend of the family."

"Yeah, well, Junior should have explained that," Marco snapped, then turned to me and said, "Sorry 'bout that," with supreme fakeness.

"I've enjoyed our chat tremendously, Adam. I know you didn't get *exactly* what you're looking for, but maybe in time you'll see that I have given you something of value in its place. I will never discourage you—but you deserve my candor, you've earned it. The bitter truth is, I'm not sure you can solve this riddle. I wish you could, but apparently, nobody can. I've tried for thirty years, others have too, and . . . nothing. Innocent teenagers died; it happens every day. We'll never *let it go*—but maybe we both need to . . . put it in its place."

I shook my head in groggy protest, weepy, bitter, spun out, disgusted, depleted, slashed up on the inside.

"It won't be long," he went on, "before Charles Elkaim is

dead. It probably won't be long before Marj Persky is dead. And it certainly won't be long before I am dead. You, on the other hand, have yet to learn how to live. Marco, give this guy something to help him sleep. Then get him off the hill—I don't want anyone sniffing around up here looking for him."

In one swift move, Marco was at me with a hypo in his hand. I got up to protest but Bahari held me back at the shoulders—either he was damn strong for a feeble-looking old man or I was still too buzzed to fight—I tried to kick, spit, wriggle, but nothing could hold back the needle; it hit my arm and pain spread like a bursting sun.

I glared at their unsmiling faces.

My eyes spun like Lotto balls.

The room tilted west.

California was falling into the jet-black ocean.

But the ocean was a warped LP, spinning forever and ever like a whirlpool of glossy vinyl blackness—

Put the needle on the record—I spun sideways, down into a whirlpool dream.

In this crazy dream, people were clocks.

Only they didn't *know* they were clocks.

That measured time by the half-life of the heart.

A new relativity—soul math.

36

Backseat, fetal. Parked in grass, a field at the edge of a marsh, ocean stretching out forever.

I know this stretch—north of Oil Piers?

Cool of morning. And warmth of sun.

My head throbbed again from the inside just as I caught my reflection in the car mirror: whoa, that's a hobo. Then I felt it in my grip—the keys, like I'd been clutching them all night. Smart man, clutch those bitches. Phone and wallet on the passenger seat. Some kindly soul put them there—remember to send thank-you email. Or text. No. Text too informal. Then again, happy as I was that they were there, I'd have to either stretch forward to get 'em, which was out of the question, or actually open the door, get out of the backseat and get behind the wheel, also out of the question.

Close eyes instead, more productive.

Something less than memory hovered. Bahari's theater—then, dragged somewhere, even carried, over a shoulder like a prize deer. Tennis court. Oh yeah.

Sudden pressure killed memory—I had to vomit. Like, now. *Not on the seat, for fuck's sake, you drive Lyft for a living*—that I remembered.

I threw the door open and leaned, let it rip. No tears left, eyes stung by salty sea air.

Wiped face, lean up, eyes closed again.

Try to remember—but it hurt my head, flashes getting lost in blackness.

I reminded myself that my phone and wallet and keys were keeping me company.

They would be by my side the whole way home. Strange comfort.

I let my burning eyes rest on the ocean sunlight, soak up its battery life.

Time passed—ocean time. It's slower. Somehow, some way, I made it out the door, into the driver's seat, behind the wheel. One random strange thing hit me as I tried to fasten my seat-belt—from nowhere.

Mickey Sandoz had been kicked out of the group—that I didn't know.

And I wasn't sure he did either.

Then, certain basic questions arose like trains running late: *Who got me to my car? And who got the car here? And where was here exactly?*

I opened Google Maps to see: marshes off Ventura—spitting distance to PCH. Hour and a half home.

I hit the ignition and drove carefully onto the highway, south along the whipping, merciless ocean. Pushing through an empty consciousness, I made the drive in just under an hour, heading for Tent Town, with Bahari's glow, his gait, his manner, his riches, his palace, his wine, his video, his words, his hypnotics all still ringing in what was left of my head.

The worst part was I knew he hadn't done it.

I parked a block from the 405 on-ramp and hoofed it to Tent Town, bracing myself for the dank angry eyes, the edgy hustle of it, but when I turned the corner—

Tent Town was gone.

Not a single tent or cardboard box, no shopping carts, broken bicycles, nothing. Only the spray paint remained:

EVERYTHING
YOU
WANT
IS
HERE

One straggler stood at the delta of the emptiness, begging for change with a cardboard sign that read: SEEKING HUMAN KINDNESS. It was like he hadn't gotten the memo. I fished a crumpled ten out of my pocket and gave it to him.

"Where'd everyone go?"

"You'd have to ask the shelter." His jaw did an involuntary vibration when he talked.

"The shelter—where's that?"

"Path—over on Cotner. That's P-A-T-H."

"What's it stand for?"

"Fuck if I know."

Eight minutes later I was standing in the waiting room of a clean pastel office. Behind a small desk, an older Hispanic woman in nurse gear manned a computer.

I said, "I'm looking for someone that's been living under the 405 up on Ohio. One of his colleagues said I should inquire here."

"You got a name?"

"Actually, I've got a few of them—he goes by Mike or Mickey, Karaoke Mike, Mickey Sandoz, Michael Sanderson."

She winced, checked her database, told me to hold on. Then she got up without a word and disappeared behind the swinging doors. I stood there for too long. A three-year-old pulled at my pants leg. I smiled at him, but his pregnant mom commanded him to sit down. Finally, the nurse came out with a slender man, balding, midforties.

"Are you a relative of the deceased?"

"The deceased?"

He froze for a moment, uncomfortable, exchanged a glance with the nurse, then pulled me aside.

"I'm very sorry, I thought you knew. They *think* they found Mr. Sanderson—but the coroner is still waiting for someone to identify the body."

"Found him how?"

"I'm . . . I'm really sorry, I really don't know the details. But even if I did, you'd have to get that information from the police."

A half hour later, with sand still in my shoes, I walked up the stairs to the Los Angeles County Department of Medical Examiner-Coroner on Mission in Boyle Heights. Odd-looking building—it could have been a train station or a high school, not the way station of death. The lobby was funeral parlor elegant too—burgundy leather sofas and marble walls—but the fancy-schmancy just rattled my shattered nerves even worse. I found an administrator, a slim, handsome Hispanic guy, who directed me to a computer, but in my typical foggy-headed fashion I couldn't figure out the online check-in. I walked back to the guy for help.

"I'm sorry, what's the difference between unclaimed and unidentified?"

"We know who the unclaimed are—they just . . . haven't been claimed."

"Right," I said. "Right. My guy, apparently they *think* it's Michael Sanderson, but they aren't sure."

He assisted me at the portal, scrolling the unidentified list—the number of just-recents was startling.

Gender: Male Ethnicity: Black Age: 20+ Date Found: October 16

Gender: Female Ethnicity: Unknown Age: 18+ Date Found: October 14

Gender: Female   Ethnicity: Hispanic/Latin American
Age: 18+   Date Found: October 14

Every gender, age, race was represented. When he hit Male Caucasian 50+ I stopped him and copied the case number.

About twenty minutes later, a kind-faced older Hispanic man wearing a yellow on black CORONER lanyard guided me down a cool hall, into a room with slab slots on either side—it resembled the storage space of a restaurant kitchen.

"Are you next of kin?" he asked.

"No," I said, "no, I'm not. Just a friend."

"It's good of you to come down. We've been trying to get an official ID for four days. The dad's up in Coulterville, he refused to make the trip." Without ceremony, the coroner stopped, used his keys, and pulled a slab—a body in a white plastic sheet lay on it, motionless.

Coroner said, "May I?" and I nodded.

With a quick zip and flap of the plastic, he revealed an unpeaceful face, eyes closed, hard-jawed, lost in frustrated dreams—or not.

I tightened up, looked away. "It's him."

Karaoke Mike, Mickey Sandoz, Michael Sanderson—the lead singer would sing no more.

Coroner nodded once, zipped up, and pushed the body back.

I said, "Can you—can you tell me what happened to him?"

Coroner forced a half-smile, to press comfort. "Well, we know he overdosed. We don't yet know that the overdose killed him."

"How do you mean?"

"The scabs on his arm tell us he was an experienced addict, and the blood levels of heroin were not quite lethal."

"Is it possible that—that someone . . . could have assisted in stopping his breathing?"

At this, the jolly fell off Coroner in an instant. "It's not my

job to speculate, but there were no signs of a struggle. That
doesn't quite answer your question, though. A big enough dose
of narcotics and a plastic bag over the head could kill someone,
even a seasoned user. We're still waiting for the histology on
the lungs."

"So you're saying—"

"Final autopsy is pending."

I staggered out of there, down the stairs and back into the
car in a fever nightmare, drove west like a man aching to return to innocence—but I knew the gates were closed. I parked
outside the Shalom Terrace and sat in the car for a while, listening to The Daily Telegraph CD, staring at the entrance. And
two brutal weeks had knocked it out of me. I'd been smacked
around, sucker punched, bonked, clobbered, drugged, and
dragged to the edge. I'd stared into the eyes of the dying and
the dead. Four band members . . . *gone*. But none of it was as
hard as what I had to do now—tell Charles Elkaim I'd hit the
brick wall.

I had nothing—and I was done.

I cut the music, got out of the car, and headed in.

Inside, I found Nurse Rosa at her station. "You are here to
see Mr. Charles?"

"Yeah. Hopefully I won't take much of his time."

"He's not in good health today. And he has a visitor."

I turned the knob softly—the room was late afternoon dark.
Charles was asleep, slightly curled and peaceful under the pale
brown blanket. In the chair at his side, lit only by the orange
curtain, Cinnamon Persky sat in her patchwork coat, hair up,
reading glasses on, a paperback at her knee—she took me in
without alarm and raised a finger to her lips.

37

She looked more alive than before, ignited and clear-eyed, and the glow of it doubled down on my shock. She was truly among the living now—even stranger here in this familiar dark, dank little corner.

In silence, she got up and motioned for me to follow.

She slid the glass door quietly and we passed through the curtains, into the gloomy nursing home courtyard by the ancient soda machine under dark afternoon clouds. Greek statue lady didn't pour water from her urn, but the sky threatened rain.

At first, we spoke in whispers.

"What are you doing here, Cynthia."

"I came down."

"I can see that. Have you lost your mind?"

"No," she said. "The opposite. I—I couldn't sleep, I couldn't stay away."

"Well, okay but—"

"I had to see him, be with him. After you told me—" She cast a strained glance to the sliding glass door. "He's almost gone."

"You must have freaked the living hell out of him."

"I think he thought he was dreaming at first. He smiled and reached out to touch my face."

"Okay but—isn't this dangerous being here? For you I mean."

"Adam, I don't care anymore."

"You could have sent him a message, through me, you could've—"

"No. That's not good enough." She studied me with all her piercing intelligence, and in an instant I saw her as she must have appeared to the band—fearless, determined, the true believer. "He's the only person who ever looked after me, Adam, do you understand? Ever. When nobody else would."

"Yeah, but that was a long time ago—you yourself said somebody really dangerous is out there right now, someone that seems to hate this band. Your band."

She didn't react.

I added, "Mickey Sandoz is dead."

She bristled. "Am I supposed to be surprised about that?"

"The coroner *thinks* it was an overdose."

"Which it probably *was*."

"Maybe. But I don't like it—and you—just being here, you're going to turn yourself into bait."

"*Good*." Our eyes met in the zone of the fatal. She recoiled a little from her own vehemence, then snuck back up on it. "Good. Whoever hurt Devon, whoever hates my boys, let him come for me. I wanna see his face."

"You're talking crazy, Cinnamon."

"I. Don't. Care." She cast another glance across the empty courtyard to the curtains behind glass. "And I'm not leaving."

"Did you tell your husband?"

She nodded.

"What did you say."

"I told him the truth, all of it. And I told him I was done living a fake life. Enough—time to set me free."

"Wow. How'd he take it?"

"Oh, he's an infant, he stormed off. But I can't mollycoddle anyone anymore—" She shook her head. "Adam—my whole fucking life has been one long impasse, running from this. Believe me, I have tried to let it all go—more than anybody could ever know."

"You mean . . . Emil?"

"Emil, all of it. I tried. To be someone else—like the band never happened. Well, it didn't work. I just kept on being me, stuck behind that . . . wall of toys. And now—" She motioned to the old man sleeping inside. "No. I'm done."

"So . . . what are you going to do exactly?"

"Nothing. Just be here, by his side. To the very end." Her parted lips breathed condensation in the cold. I couldn't tell if she was broken, mad, delirious, or bursting with joy. Maybe all of the above.

"Cin, I still don't think you get how dangerous this is. Things are way hairy right now. Somebody broke into my place, harassed one of my clients. I came to tell Mr. Elkaim . . . I'm out."

"What?"

"No, yeah, I give up."

"Do not do that, Adam, it will only hurt him."

"But I'm at a dead end, totally outta leads. I went to see Dr. Bahari. *Freak*."

She got somber. "Did he scare you off this? Did he hurt you?"

"Naw. He's a nut—but he's no killer."

"What did he say?"

"Swears he never laid eyes on Reynaldo—and I believe him. And he loved Emil, plain as day. I mean, he visited him in jail. Did you know that?"

She shook her head. For a second, I almost told her about the stupid video, how they double-crossed her, but just then it started to drizzle, and anyway it seemed so inconsequential now. I pulled the envelope from my inside pocket.

"I gotta do this, Cin. I came to give Charles his money back."

"Oh. So this is about the money?"

"No, of course not, but—"

"Adam. What do you think we're doing here?"

"In this courtyard?"

"No, not in this courtyard—in this life."

I didn't answer.

"You think it's just some kind of coincidence that Mr. Elkaim called on you? He picked you because he trusts you."

"Yeah, I'm honored, but—"

"This is a man that believes in divine purpose—and he gave you one. I knew it the second you showed up."

"Cin, I've got work to do."

"What work—carting around strangers? Living like a lone wolf. You are making such a big mistake. This will follow you wherever you go and you know it."

"Maybe. But I also know that *you* are risking your life for an old man who's going to die soon anyway."

"Not just some old man. The only man who ever treated me like a real father—the father of the love of my life." She stopped herself and gave me a compassionate look, just this side of pity. Then: "You got a love of your life?"

I hesitated at the funny question. "I don't think so."

"Well, if you find one, you are going to hold on to every last thing that connects you." I started to smirk and she said, "No, I'm serious, Adam. You will never know a minute's peace till you have peace with the people you love."

The rain picked up. I shoved the envelope back in my pocket and made for the glass doors, but she followed, grabbed my arm, and stopped me.

"Please. Let him sleep. Let him dream. He only wants his Emil back."

"I can't give him that."

"But you can give him hope."

"Hope for what?" My whisper went hard. "It isn't safe here, Cinnamon. You should go home."

Softly but firmly, she said, "This is home. I finally made it home." Then she pulled the sliding glass door and stepped inside.

I left her sitting by his side in the dark and backed out the door, closed it, and staggered down the gray nursing home hall, agitated, panicky, and confused. Ten steps and I stopped in my tracks, looked over my shoulder and almost ran back—to plead maybe—but for what? She was ready to face the music, the impasse, put everything on the line while I fled like a coward. I turned for the door and a silver drinking fountain down the long hall stole my gaze—a vision—the ghost of Herschel standing there, bent over the arc of water, bent on survival. He turned his phantom face to me and a memory surged, one of those strange interruptions so vivid, it throttled me as I pushed out the door and made my way back to the car and sat behind the wheel, paralyzed.

The impasse. *My* impasse. The last phone call.

I was twenty-nine—that sobering age—no idea Herschel's health was failing. I knew he was at the Shalom Terrace but visiting was out of the question—I wanted to spare him fresh bad news. I was broke again, flat broke, in debt and out of work. Maxed-out credit cards—for the weighted keyboard, the ProTools M Box, Logic software, eight-channel mixer, Carl's Jr., etcetera. Then the unemployment checks ran out. In a panic, I did the job counseling thing—the lady they assigned me had that Resting Judgy Face. In some kind of kamikaze move, I confessed my dream—to become a professional songwriter. She managed to translate this to mean *performer* and went on a twenty-minute spiel about how I needed to be willing to play birthdays and weddings and bar mitzvahs. When I said, "Will I need to buy a clown suit?" she faked a smile. She had me marked as one of The Doomed.

Now I sat in my car but could not turn the key, eaten alive by flashbacks. Bahari was right. I was Mr. Unfinished Business. The last phone call—I held it off.

Next memory came like chain lightning. From the defeat of career counseling, I got a real estate broker's license and entered the ninety-day New Salesman program at Keller Williams—the senior partner who came in twice a week to mentor had this odd verbal tic. "When the *person client seller individual* is seeking and desiring to unload their *home house domicile residence*—" A complete loon. But he was a closer. I, on the other hand, was not a closer. Every way a broker can, I dropped the ball. The office manager, overhearing me trying to make a phone sale said, "Jesus, Adam—stop being so damn gushing." But how could I be anything but? I was walking wounded, gushing blood.

And I had such ambitions! Crazy ambitions!

I was going to be Jerome Kern and Dorothy Fields or Lennon-McCartney, except in one person and during the twenty-first century. I was going to be Berlin, Porter, Dylan, Newman, and Buffet—the madman hubris of it, crazy enough to believe . . . no, not believe, to *talk myself into* believing. This was the primary business of my psyche—the talking oneself into. And I'd hit the wall, the place where you just *can't*. The selling off of my gear was painful—one guy offered to buy my portable Tascam DR-100MKIII stereo recorder for $170— half of what I paid. I met him at Echo Park Lake, handheld recorder in my grip, and he got there fifteen minutes late with six $20 bills—$50 short. I thrust the damn recorder in his hand and walked off with the cash. Rent was eleven days late and I'd gotten into a fender bender with insurance lapsed. I needed exactly $1,450 to stay off the street.

And so I did the unthinkable. I called Uncle Herschel at the Shalom Terrace.

Now, sitting alone in my car in the rain, the last phone call came to me as crystalline and uncontainable as the rivulets streaming down the window.

I called from a park bench.

A nurse picked up and went to get him. The wait was endless. In the background I heard television, coughs, the delirious anti-quiet of midafternoon nursing home life.

Finally, Herschel with that gruffness: "Hullo?"

The last time I ever heard that voice, that hello.

And I'd said to him, explained in my cloying way, that I was desperate, the real estate thing had not worked out, and was there any way he could float me—a bridge loan—until . . .

"*Genug.*" He shut me up quick and furious. "Enough. You and I both know I am going to give you the money, so come and get the check. But don't tire me with another story, Adam. Instead, ask yourself: *Then what?* These songs—you aren't a little boy anymore."

"What's that supposed to mean?"

"It means there comes a time when a man must face his limitations. A man—"

"Please, Uncle Herschel, don't. I just need a short-term loan; you don't have to dress down my whole character."

"What character? Character is dropping every job? Living in a shoe closet?"

"That's not what I mean. You don't have to insult my music."

"I am *talking* about your music—if you had what it takes you wouldn't be in this predicament. Time's up."

"You don't know that. You can't say that. People tell me I've got something, they say—"

"Adam, what is going to happen to you when I'm gone? Who are you going to borrow from then?"

"No, that's not—"

"Adam, I cannot stand here all day—I cannot stand to listen."

"Yeah?" I said to the man who raised me, who always came through for me. "Well, this is who I am, take it or leave it."

A pause, a millisecond that hangs in the ether for all eternity. Herschel said, "Then I leave it," and hung up.

I never went to pick up the check and I never spoke with him again.

Now I started the car, with a terrible, restless yearning—to see him, to be with him one last time, to apologize, mend the unmendable. Gasping for air—the memory of his final rejection only made me crave more, to connect, bond, bind for all time, but what could I possibly do with this violent frenzy of the heart? I could visit his grave, but the thought twisted me up inside like an old rag, and anyway I didn't even know where his grave was. I headed for Maya's, almost weeping again for the second time in twenty-four hours—I was losing it. I drove the freeway reckless. When I got there nobody was home—of course not. Steph was in elementary school; they were all at work. I knew they hid the key under the garage clicker, behind the pots. I let myself in and went upstairs, up into the attic, and knelt before Herschel's trunk.

The impasse.

I started digging through—old letters, postcards, a photo book—the wedding, Lydia in white, all that jet-black-and-white hair, the Semites. Herschel's diary—*tomatoes / Food King = $1.18*. There was a small, framed picture of my mom in there—I didn't have the heart to stare at it for long. Then I opened the trumpet case—the horn was beautiful, golden, engraved—*Fred Berman for Martin Custom, 1954*. I tried to blow a note through it but only got a little squeak. With great care I placed it back in the purple velvet.

I kept digging—tax returns, meticulous stapled receipts, a matchbook from Earl Scheib Auto Body. Then, at the bottom, wedged under the trumpet case, an old pad, foolscap, top page blank. I flipped it open. Marked-up drafts, of letters he wrote—most to Maya, one to his cousins in Cleveland, one to his bosses at the DWP, and then the last one, to Charles Elkaim, August 16, 2016—he was not yet in the home. I sat with the fanned-out pages on my lap, scanned the neat cursive, nervous for what I might find, then my name—

> *I remain worried about Adam. His innocence terrifies me. In fact, he is so much like me in my youth that I get a chill when I hear the foolish things that come from his mouth. ~~If only he had gotten my mother's genes but he seems to have been burdened with those of my father—another confused and absent-minded man that drove us all crazy, a luftmenschen we say in Yiddish.~~ Adam still wants to hit the big time. If only he knew I suffered just such a madness and threw away 18 years of my life. Can you imagine? 18 years I lost blowing hot air. Adam doesn't know the half of it, old friend. The story I told you, about auditioning for Stan Kenton, how I didn't make the cut, I don't dare tell him. It will only add fuel to his fire. I know this, because he is too much like myself, always with something to prove, and it is driving us apart.*

I closed the pad in a complete daze, looked around the room like there was somebody watching, but there was only quiet.

> *—auditioning for Stan Kenton, how I didn't make the cut.*

Poor Herschel. *Didn't make the cut*—such savage language, butchery. *Didn't make the cut.* The phrase followed me as I closed the pad, stashed it under the trumpet case, closed the trumpet case, and closed the trunk.
> *—didn't make the cut.*

The brutality of those four little words wouldn't leave my head—merciless. They gripped me as I locked up the house, turned toward my car. They hung over me as I got behind the wheel.

—*didn't make the cut.*

I drove home, showered off the long week, and slept the sleep of the gutted.

In the morning it hit me.

38

Forty minutes later, I was pulling into the cul-de-sac in Cheviot Hills under steady morning rain. I knocked on the door of Devon Hawley Senior. He stood there in terry cloth, smelling of hard liquor.

I said, "Good morning—hope I didn't wake you."

He grumbled. "I could use a visitor. Come on in."

Soon I was in a dark sunken living room with Tudor beams and a steel-grated fireplace black with soot. The faded orange couch covered in crocheted throws, the low oak table, the dim lamps and hanging needlepoint, and the unpolished silver suit of armor overlooking the whole scene all seemed to be stolen off an old Hollywood movie set, like the place hadn't budged since the days of The Daily Telegraph. A built-in bookcase was packed end-to-end with newer hardcovers though, mostly true crime and rugged masculine reads, lots of Grisham and Jack Reacher.

Hawley Senior said, "We got off to a bad start last time— can I fix you breakfast? You look wrecked."

"Mr. Hawley," I said, "you remember last time we spoke you told me about the amateur contest. And the yearbook photos?"

"Well, sure."

"I'd like to see it, the yearbook, I mean."

He paused, looked me over. "Why the hell not."

Around a gray chairlift, up the carpeted staircase, Hawley Senior hauled himself, clutching the banister, and I followed. Along these walls, framed family photos hung, all faded. Hawley Senior and Hawley Junior in matching conductor hats, operating a small outdoor train packed with little kids, then a portrait shot of the wife, a little rigid and depressive looking, then a framed Kodak of a three-person family picnic. They seemed lonely together, cul-de-sac'd in a cul-de-sac.

"What happened to your wife?" I asked.

"She died of Parkinson's eight years ago," he said.

"I'm sorry."

"Yeah, well."

At the end of the stairs, another work of art—a framed needlepoint that said LOVE IS . . . A RAINBOW. I'd been right—nothing had changed in this place since his wife had passed away. Maybe a cleaning lady came, that's it. Another mausoleum, another man stuck in time. Down the hall, first door on the right hung a kid's poster—cartoon firemen and the printed words DEVON'S ROOM. In uneven marker the word *Junior* was scrawled underneath.

Hawley opened the door, flicked on the light, and said, "After you."

One poster taped to the wall: Hendrix, *Axis: Bold As Love*. And out the window, a straight shot across the green lawn and over the hedges to the back of the Persky house—probably I was looking right at Cinnamon's window.

Soon, we were seated side by side on the hard old bed, looking over the pages of *Hamilton High Class 1983/1984*.

"Where the hell's that picture?" he said. "They played in the auditorium there. I helped 'em set up the speakers, AV stuff."

As he spoke, Hawley Senior thumbed page by page. There was something excruciating about high school yearbooks, even when they weren't your own. You felt the gloss of a bubble about to burst. Finally, he landed on a messy photo collage— Winter Talent Show. And in the corner of the page was a single blurry black-and-white stage shot scissored into a hasty blob, with a caption across the bottom in corrector ribbon white— *Daily Telegraph* with all the names listed.

"Here they are," he said, tapping the pic. "In all their raggedy-ass glory."

Impatient, I grabbed the book, looked closer.

It was not a great photo, taken longways from one corner of the stage. It was as if the photographer, Hawley Senior himself, of course, wanted to make sure you knew what kind of sneakers they were wearing. This put his son, Hawley Junior, at the far, far end of the stage, an apparition in a velvet tux, his face shrouded by a mop of blond curly hair, hunched over his old-time keyboard. Durazo was shirtless in the way back but Grunes you could see the most—staring at his fingers on the frets of his bass like they were his worst enemy. Sandoz was at the fourth wall, lurchin' like Jagger.

"Who's this?" I said. "On guitar?"

"That's Emil."

"Yeah?" I shook my head. "It . . . it doesn't look like him."

He grabbed the book back and looked closer, squinted. "It's a funny angle, that's all. This is them and they are it."

"Wait, hold on," I said, and yanked the book back. Then I fished out my cell to take a close pic. "Gimme a sec, we'll blow it up."

I took a pic of the page, did a quick stretch with thumb and forefinger. Hawley Senior had grabbed the yearbook back but I was focused on the cell phone now.

"See?!" I said, holding the phone out. "Who the heck *is* that?—'cause it's not Emil."

He stared at the phone, dumbfounded. His hungover eyes

did a little jiggle. He seemed to want to argue but then he said, "Got me."

Then I read the caption out loud. "*Daily Telegraph.* D. Hawly—no *e*, they misspelled it—Mike Sandoz. Ricky Durazo, Jeff quote Groony unquote Grunes, B. Appelfeld? And no Emil," I said. "Who the hell's B. Appelfeld?"

Hawley Senior grabbed the phone and stared, morphing from cocky authority to self-questioning and finally pale bewilderment. Then he said, "I don't know."

"Maybe . . . they let a friend join 'em," I mumbled.

He slammed the yearbook shut. "Or maybe it's just some jackass who wanted to hold the guitar."

From Hawley Senior's, I headed for DTLA, the Sophia T. Salvin School for Special Education. Walking down the glossy hall, I passed a female teacher squatting on her knees, trying to soothe a crying child with green-blue paint on his palms. I stepped into the administrative office. The lady at the front desk told me I had to wait another twenty minutes for Mr. Grunes's class to end. I had the perverse desire to ask her if she knew he was the former bassist for The Daily Telegraph, but I squashed it. When they finally called him in, he stopped in his tracks.

"Oh no, you gotta be kidding me, not you again. I haven't even had a minute to eat my damn lunch, for Chrissake."

"I won't be long."

"Yeah well, no visitors allowed in the teachers' lounge."

"So—can we go somewhere and talk?"

We hovered outside by his gray Prius under gray skies. While he ate a bologna sandwich and a bag of Pirate's Booty out of a tin lunch box, I showed him the pic on my phone. I said, "Hamilton High battle of the bands. Probably '82 or '83."

Grunes shot me a funny look and fished granny glasses from his pocket, leaned over and studied.

"Yup," he said. "Winter Talent Show."

"You remember it?"

"'Course I do—who loses an amateur contest and forgets?"

"Who's this?"

He adjusted his glasses. "Not Emil?"

"No," I said, "no, it's not. The caption says B. Appelfeld. So far, I haven't been able to track him down."

"Appelfeld? B . . . B . . . oh shit, that's Benji."

"Who's Benji?"

"Benjamin Appelfeld. *Total* nerd. Hawley was a dork, but Appelfeld was a *supernerd*—I think he rehearsed with us twice and maybe played two shows. Handsome guy, but . . . *so* awkward—definitely not, uh, rock star material, if you know what I mean."

"You mean like . . . he couldn't play?"

"Noooo, it wasn't that so much. It was like . . . he just—" Grunes did a little shiver of disgust. "—he just *telegraphed his neediness*, you know what I mean? Like, every fucking second. I pride myself on being a tolerant person, I mean—it's my job. But . . . I couldn't stand the guy."

"So what happened to him?"

Together we looked back to the photo—Sandoz in Jagger-pose on the mic, Mr. Cock of the Walk. Benjamin Appelfeld looked tame beside him—but there was something familiar in his eyes I couldn't place. Or maybe it was a common expression—the fated.

"*Man,*" Grunes said, grabbing a kiddie-sized Tropicana from his tin. He poked the straw in the box and said, "We were hurtin' *bad* after we lost—*serious* humiliation."

He took a sip and then—"Oh shit, it's all coming back to me now. Rey and Sandoz *fired* this guy. They told me about it. *Bragged* about it, really. How they were nervous—so of course they did like teenage boys do, right? They got stoned out of their minds. I think they maybe even dropped some acid. And they went over to Appelfeld's—his parents' place in the Palisades. They pull up, go past the white picket fence, lean on his door, like, on a Sunday afternoon and they're all there, giggling, gassed out of their minds. Suddenly the door opens and Appelfeld's *dad* answers. I remember this blew my mind, 'cause his dad was some kind of a heavy or something. Anyway, Benji is standing beside him, right? He knows what's coming, but he plays it off like he doesn't care. And Rey and Hawley're stammering, all like, '*Uh, well, uh, sorry, dude, but uh—you're out of the band!*' Then they ran away like little petrified schoolboys laughing their heads off."

"Not nice," I said.

"Yeah, I know," Grunes said, "but every band's got one—*the dissed and dismissed.*"

I said, "Wow."

"The Pete Best. Imagine being *the guy who was almost in the Beatles.*"

"I'd rather not," I said. "But—who knew him, this Benji guy, where was he from?"

Grunes shrugged. "You know—I think he was actually down with Rey in the beginning. Like, they had a gardening business together or pool cleaning or something."

My mind was racing. "Any idea where Appelfeld ended up?"

"Fuck if I know," Grunes said, finishing off his bologna sandwich, tossing the wrapper in the tin box and slamming it shut. "Probably went to go work for UPS or some shit."

I raced back to the marina, hopped on the boat.

Double Fry said, "You got something?"

"Crack the laptop."

39

The facts—they fall like rain.

Benjamin Appelfeld, b. August 3, 1963.

No current residence listed.

Hamilton High School, Class of 1984.

No college degree completed—one year at Santa Monica City College.

Then: A string of halfway houses and recovery groups.

Disability benefits, social security, institutional diagnoses.

No incarcerations—the internet's highest badge of honor.

Decades of sorrow—a lost soul.

With a sigh, Fry leaned back and made the educated guess. "Maybe this asshole never got over it."

He kept searching. The dad was easy to find. Robert or Bob Appelfeld, had an IMDb listing starting in '61 with cameos on *77 Sunset Strip* and ending in '74 with a role in the fourth installment of a Disney nature series I'd never heard of called *Adventures of the Mountain Family.* He was square-jawed, television handsome, a little remote looking in one of those red collarless jackets that were so rebelliously casual a million years ago. In '68, Bob Appelfeld starred in a teen surf comedy for American International Pictures called *Cali Sunshine*—this grabbed my attention. For a split second, I scrambled to see if

Globus / Columbia / Persky / Bahari / Elkaim could be traced to AIP and the *Cali* flick, but if there was a connection, I didn't find it. Anyway, the movie tanked. Appelfeld returned to television: *Love, American Style* and a semi-recurring role on *Marcus Welby MD*, playing a character whose only name was The Guy.

Fry said, "Formerly owned a home on Bowling Green Way in the Palisades."

"Right," I said. "The bassist's story sticks."

"We got the father but meanwhile, where's the son?"

Young Benji left a spare digital trail. Agitated, Fry hacked into a database of old Cedars-Sinai medical records—bizarre and grim. B. Appelfeld coughed up *148* entries. At the bottom of the list, a 4,078-page PDF including endless doctors' reports and a court deposition dated March 14, 1993, whose main objective seemed to be to substantiate that Benjamin Appelfeld ought to be entitled to receive live-in status at a county-funded mental health institution. Fry scrolled the monster mess of scanned xeroxes.

It made for a hell of a biography.

"Age nineteen," I said. "That's maybe two years after getting kicked out of The Daily Telegraph. What is it?"

"Looks like a note from a dental clinic on Wilshire stating that *'the patient will require taxi service following wisdom tooth extraction x4. Mother cannot attend this Thurs. aft.'*

"That's . . . not fatal."

But nine months and four teeth later, Benjamin Appelfeld checked into the Fielding Clinic on Venice Boulevard following a botched suicide attempt: wrists had been slashed "incorrectly," Thorazine administered.

"I didn't know Thorazine was still around then," Fry said. "But look at the warning—potentially serious side effects, including swelling, weight gain, blurred vision, and impotence. Patient must be withdrawn slowly."

"This pill may prevent or cause suicide—good luck," I said.

Fry kept reading: "Dr. Simpson notes that patient is diag-nosed with severe anxiety, paranoia, depressive symptoms; six months treatment of cognitive behavioral therapy is indicated."

"Looks like that was his first full-scale mental health diagnosis."

"First of many."

We kept reading. For the next ten years, Appelfeld was in and out of institutions, programs, and halfway houses, on and off a dozen different meds, and in and out of one-on-one and group therapies. He was a "cure junkie"—his rap sheet read like a walking history of twentieth-century psych: Gestalt, Primal Scream, cognitive-behavioral, existential-humanistic, sensory deprivation, and EMDR—he tried it all. But always, the final decree—*Patient reports that symptoms of extreme anxiety and depression have persisted.*

Fry: "Dude was a mess."

By page 1,367 of docs dating from 1998-ish, the suicide attempts seem to have decreased—he had learned to check himself in fast. In a Panel Qualified Medical Evaluation in the Field of Psychiatry dated June 19, 1999, Dr. Fakir Darshakian of Valley Village Medical declared the applicant "permanent and stationary"—i.e., without chance of improvement—with a whole person impairment rating of 23 percent, indicating moderate but recurring and unabated depression, anxiety, and paranoia "not due to PTSD." "*The applicant appears quite dysphoric,*" Dr. Darshakian wrote in the conclusions section of his report. "*He seems to have great difficulty securing and keeping gainful employment and is requesting that he be put on suicide watch despite no present suicidal ideation.*"

Page after page, the suffering, the cry for help, the dismissal, like a merry-go-round from hell. Appelfeld's address changed, but he stayed in a tight circumference—Culver City to Mar Vista to Playa Vista to Leimert Park—never moving east of La

Cienega. He moved a lot, though. Benjamin Appelfeld was lost in place.

Fry scoured records, page by page, on and on, redundant, cataloging and rehashing the same old miseries over and over and over.

I said, "This shit is numbing."

Fry said, "So imagine what the actual life was like—wait, look at this—"

A progress report from psychologist Dr. Mort Schulman of the bizarrely named Acute Care Mental Health Facilities, dated October 1, 1998. *"Patient states that he is 'still carrying a torch for a high school sweetheart who betrayed him and got him kicked out of his rock band.'"*

One little line, smack dab in the middle of babble mountain.

I read and reread that line ten times, my heart thumping.

Cinnamon never mentioned him, Sandoz never mentioned him, Grunes barely remembered him, but he nailed the salient fact: he was the hidden secret of every rock group that ever lived, The Guy That Got The Boot, the one that didn't make the cut.

Fry said, "You think he was really Cinnamon's guy?"

"No idea, but if he even *thought* he was, then she fell hard for Emil and rearranged the band all in one fell swoop—he must have really bad tripped."

We scrolled on, through endless fragilities, endless gripes, but by century's end, the records came to a dead stop.

B. Appelfeld did a stint working for Apple Temps—he was employed briefly by Nestle Corp in Glendale for a six-week engagement in the pet food department—and then, as if by some digital sleight of hand, he disappeared into thin air.

No obits, no records, no work history, no addresses, no nothing.

The fucker ghosted.

I air-dropped the yearbook photo and Fry opened it full screen. We stared at the washed-out image like two lunatics in a séance. Black pixels, Nice Guy with an uneasy smile, a scuffed white Stratocaster strapped around his shoulder, standing behind hunched Sandoz hanging on the mic.

To break the trance, Fry said, "1999."

"End of the century."

"Yeah but—the dad stopped doing his little cameos around the same time, November '99. Maybe there's a connection—Pops took a caregiver role?"

"Or a disavowal and Benji pulled a name change?"

"Or . . . else he died. But there's no record. Look—all we know is one way or another Benjamin Appelfeld disappeared, *poof*—gone."

Howard the cat strutted right across the laptop and looked at us, dead serious.

"He wants milk. I'll get you your milk, ya *noodnik*."

Fry got up, but I sat there transfixed, made dizzy by a wound—someone else's.

The spirit of Benjamin Appelfeld had invaded me—sorrowful, meandering, and so, so vulnerable.

And angry.

Very.

The father: a star. Ish.

The son: a rock-and-roll guitar-slinger. Almost.

Unfinished Hollywood business.

One lousy high school contest—he loses, gets dumped, the music, the inner music, the music of daily life comes to a crashing halt, and now he's turned loose out into the unforgiving world—*the Big, Wide World*—lost in the city maze, shadowed by that old devil, Daddy's dreams.

Fathers and sons.

Your ship . . . has sailed!

And . . . so has love—teen romance—it slipped through his fingers.

Cinnamon—linking a half-dozen hearts, the vortex in a paisley minidress.

Cinnamon—beckoning siren to desperadoes, dreams up in smoke.

Benjamin Appelfeld: Diagnosed, re-diagnosed, re-re-diagnosed.

> *The patient has a florid psychotic process involving either carelessness with language or bizarre preoccupations. Although he has resisted intervention, further psychiatric medication with monitoring is recommended at this time.*

Like Hawley Junior, he'd collapsed under the weight of teenage loss.

Unlike Hawley Junior, he had no model to build, no counter-dream to save him.

A teenager ungrown, desperate and lost in the city of the mind.

Could this three-time loser be the psycho hot on my trail?

And what did he want from the LP—*a record he probably didn't even play on?*

I circled back to the facts.

Someone named Benjamin Appelfeld played a high school battle of the bands with a group called The Daily Telegraph—then he got kicked out—it happens.

Drummer Rey-Rey and his gardening partner . . . could've been having a fling with Marjorie Persky.

Emil / Hawley / Grunes made a demo with Bahari—drummer Rey and singer Sandoz never even heard about it.

Then Rey-Rey got brained and tossed in the bushes behind the Perskys' garage.

Emil was accused—and killed in jail.

Cinnamon ran off, faked her own suicide.

Meanwhile: Appelfeld, the mystery man, in and out of institutions, a "lost cause," a caseload—*the replaced one, the unwanted.*

Who . . . *didn't make the cut.*

But would he rubberneck the band forever and ever?

Of course he would.

Would he know about Lazerbeam, the LP, Kip 'n' Rog, Bahari, the rest of it?

Of course he would.

Would he clock their every godforsaken move, seethe over every micro-win, plan his whole life around this one knot of hard resentment?

Of course he fucking would.

All the while, a riff was playing in my head, over a chord progression, sweet and hypnotic, louder and louder. The Jukebox Id was at it again.

I knew this riff . . . from the record. "Fair-Weather Freaks."

But the Jukebox Id was pressing hard, dragging me in— I'd heard it somewhere else too. Somewhere brightly lit, somewhere—

The nursing home.

I turned to Fry who was petting Howard on the edge of the boat while she lapped up the cool bowl of pure white goodness.

"Freiburger," I said, jumping to my feet, heading for the dock. "This guy, this Benji—I think I've got our man. And Cinnamon's in danger."

40

I tore into the alley behind Shalom Terrace and stuffed Hawley
Senior's Rock Island 9mm in my jacket pocket like kryptonite.
I didn't like guns, wasn't good with them, had barely handled
a pistol twice before—but I had a bad feeling about this dude.
He'd been hiding in plain sight, the crazy fuck, and the second
he saw my face, he'd know I was on to him. Cutting the windshield wipers and turning off the ignition, I bristled, hypnotized
with bottled rage—because he was the nicest guy you'd ever
hope to know, the most humble, generous, not one unkind—

But so what?

All that virtue was there to serve a monster wound, the ego-
devil *I-me-mine* fever, and once you saw it . . . *Your ship . . .
has sailed!* . . . you couldn't unsee it.

And it was too late to play Johnny Reasonable, the caregiver.
That was *his* game. I ditched the car and made for the Shalom,
rushed in through the glass doors across the gloomy mustard
carpet. Nurse Rosa was at her station, lining up pill bottles.

"Where's Mr. Elkaim?"

"In his room, where else?"

This time I cut in, found him at the edge of his bed in blue
pajamas and corduroy slippers, a little too happy to see me.

"Emil's love has returned," he said.

"I know, Mr. Elkaim," I said. "Where is she?"

"Then you saw her. This is a miracle."

"Yes, Mr. Elkaim, but where is she *right now*?"

"Why, you only just missed her. She went with Jensen to the market to—"

I pushed past him, out the glass doors into the rainy courtyard, past the Greek statue lady, frantic, out toward the back exit.

Just as I turned the corner, I saw them at the far end of the parking lot, under the back awning—I hid behind the soda machine, standing in the downpour. They were in some kind of heated exchange. Jensen was pissed. Cinnamon, rain drenched in black jeans and an army green parka and sneakers, was arguing with her hands, explaining something I couldn't make out over the rain on the tin. I wanted to race across the courtyard, accost them, *something*, but Jensen looked keyed up, he could panic and hurt her—situation unstable.

I stayed low so as not to startle them.

Under the rumble of thunder, I could hear him plead. "But where's the record?"

"Record? What record? There was none!"

"You fucking lying bitch, you recorded, in a studio, Rey told me—"

"Benji, it never came out. What the hell is this all about?"

Her tone was conciliatory, and it only fired him up worse.

"Well, who has the goddamn tapes?"

A silence, beating rain, the Fairfax traffic. I peered around the machine and watched their watery shadows.

"Tapes? I don't know where the fucking tapes are, Benji. You're talking about forty years ago—"

"Bullshit. Someone has a cassette, a master tape, something."

"Dev kept the masters," she said with a jittery shrug. "Why would you need *that*?"

"Don't worry about why—"

All at once he pulled a gun and pointed it right at her belly. "You just take me to the tapes. Now—get in the car."

"Benji, this is not—"

"Get in the car."

He tried to force her into the driver's seat but she turned, defiant.

"Benji, this is not going to help you."

I shuddered, tensed like a fever grip, almost stepped from the shadows, but he pressed the gun against her.

"Get in the fucking car, Cinnamon."

My pulse was whamming, eyes doing wide-awake REM as he gunned her into the Wagoneer—

Blind panic—as they pulled out and turned south.

I cut the corner, running through puddles straight for the Jetta and hit the ignition—catch-up time.

Next stop: Steam World.

Flash torrents came down now as I chased the Wagoneer through the city shrouded in gray. Afternoon was becoming night faster than anybody wanted or could handle. They hit the southbound on-ramp, sending back a fast wave of gutter water, and I followed, craning to keep tabs, they were maybe eight cars ahead. Then we hit the spiderweb that is Friday 6:00 p.m. rush hour 101/110/10, crawling around the downtown cyclone—I almost lost them.

Around Union Station they made for the exit, and I had to practically cut off a big rig to stay on their tail, but a traffic cop held me back, and I was blocked. They tore off and I slammed the steering wheel in a rage. Lights changed and I peeled out, rain-skidded, cutting the red light. I was way behind. By the time I pulled up to Steam World, the Wagoneer was parked out front. I parked on the lit side of the street, clutched the 9-millimeter in my pocket, ducked under the awning, and was about to bang on the front door, then thought better of it. I slipped around the back, rain streaming through the parking lot streetlamps.

The big metal door was up but the lights were out.

He was on to me, he'd set a trap—and she was in there, he had her.

41

"*Appelfeld.*" I stood at the mouth of the warehouse. "Come out and talk to me. Please . . . leave her alone, we don't need to do anything stupid."

Nothing but the sound of rain beating on aluminum, making fast rivers down the ridges.

"Turn on the lights," I said. "We should talk."

No answer.

Nothing to do but duck inside—pitch dark and meat locker cold. And I was drenched.

"*Appelfeld,*" I said to the emptiness, not shouting. "*Jensen. I can help you.* But you've got to let her go. And talk to me."

My words echoed in dead space, but he was there, she was too, I could feel them.

"I can help you," I said softer, walking backward to the center of the maze, where I fumbled for floodlights, gently bumped into a pole, steadied myself on it, clutching like I'd found the mast of a ship. But as I groped around, I realized I had no idea how to turn the thing on. My thumb felt a light switch—with a click a flood of green hit the models like a midnight nuclear flash.

"*Appelfeld,*" I said, squinting hard. "Talk to me."

First, a muted scream, his hand over her mouth, then a shrill one—"Adam, move!"

A shot cracked from behind the statue of Hollywood Hills—it boomed through the metal room—I dove down behind a table, cocked my gun, another scream, something fell, she wrenched herself free, scrambled.

Flash of a moving body, *his*, then another shot, her muffled "*No!*"—I cringed then aimed for his leg, squeezed—with a blast the HOLLYWOOD sign exploded into a white plaster of Paris dust bomb.

I rolled up like a pill bug under the table, clocked his Hush Puppies in the distance, squeezed off another shot; the gun almost flew out of my hand and a lamp exploded, sent a flash of glass fireworks tumbling over mini-PCH, then he aimed sloppy, another shot cracked hitting a foothill six yards from me, shredding its innards, mesh wires and plaster twisted every whichway. He was no marksman this guy. Neither was I, but I was small enough to hide.

He spoke firmly through the green smoky haze.

"You come out, Zantz—you get me that record and I'll let her live."

I said, "Drop your gun first—and set her free."

Maybe he saw me or maybe he flipped, but he took another shot, way wide of the mark, and that gave me the quarter second for better aim. I fired one right at the pair of jeans bent behind Hollywood and Vine and he flew back with a guttural yell, smashing into the Capitol Records building, grabbing for his folded knee, his gun flying *somewhere* into the rubble.

"Just keep your hands up," I said loud and firm. "And I'll come out to help you."

As I crawled out from under the table on my knees, Cinnamon moved frantically, out of the shadows into the green light—she knelt over him. Over her shoulder, she said, "Put that gun down, Adam."

"Cin, he's crazy, he's—"

"I said drop it!"

I placed the pistol gently on the plastic waters of Silver Lake, showed her my hands.

Hers were trembling as she tried to help Appelfeld up to a sitting position while he rocked and clutched at his leg.

"Benji," she said, "we're going to help you, we're—"

"Don't shoot me," he blurted.

"I can't *shoot* anyone," she answered with a high-pitched mix of panic and pity.

Appelfeld moaned and said, "I gotta get me some bandages," then Cinnamon looked up to me, and I moved to take off my hoodie, but in a crazed thrust, he yanked himself up using her shoulder, raging in the face, lunging for my gun off the fake Silver Lake as he threw his arm around her, clutching her like a wrestler.

Showing teeth, he threatened to gun-butt her.

"Benjamin!" she wailed.

"Don't *Benjamin* me."

He cocked the gun, moved it between us, back and forth, landing on her neck. "Now you shut your fucking trap or I'll put a bullet through you and stick this thing in his hand."

My heart was slamming but she was fierce in the eyes, jarringly unafraid—his leg was soaked brown-red right down to the sneaker, but he could stand. He pushed her chin up with the pistol. "Play this right, Cin, the two of us can run off together."

I watched them, hands up, newly grim. I wasn't sure I'd done the right thing following them, wasn't sure at all. She was pale, heavy-lidded.

Appelfeld said, "Whatta you say? We can make some new music. And this time, you'll have my back."

He leaned into her, pressed the gun deeper into her temple. And yet there was no shock in her eyes—like she knew all those years that this moment would come.

"Please," I said, measuring every syllable. "Please, Jensen. Shoot her and you've got nothing."

She tried to speak and he said, "Both of you—quiet." But the gun stayed in place.

"Shoot me instead," I said. "Right now, let her go. Or let me get you the LP, whatever you want. When Elkaim kicks, you'll get whatever's his, too. I'll talk him into it, I swear it. But let her go."

She looked to me like you might greet someone in a nightmare, silent, knowing. The puzzle had come together for her at last. For me too.

His face twisted and hardened with the full force of a half-century of hurt. Through gritted teeth, he said, "First the LP."

"Okay, okay," I said. "I promise."

"It's mine." He was corkscrewing himself up. I didn't trust him to not go off.

Softly, she said, "How . . . how is it yours?"

"How? You stupid bitch, those are *my songs*!"

I nodded in fake calm. "You mean—you wrote them?"

"Naw," he said, "naw, I *inspired* them."

"You inspired them."

"Oh yeah." He sang into Cinnamon's ear: "*Walk the plank, matey, 'cause your ship has saiiiiiiiled!*—that's *your* song. About me—isn't it, sister? That's *me* you were talking about, me they're making fun of. Admit it."

The white pallor of death warmed over her, all gravity. But she was no damsel in distress—she simply would not cave to fear.

"Benji," she said again, her voice reaching, resonating with the desire to soothe. "I can't turn back the clock." And then, with great tenderness. "We . . . we don't have that anymore, that time—it's gone."

"But I'm stuck!"

"I understand," she said. "I really do."

He pressed the gun. "Stuck!"

"But what could I give you, Ben?" she said. "What could I say that would stop the pain?"

"The truth! And nothing but."

"Okay. What truth?"

"That you told them to replace me. *You* set me up for the kill." He was crying now, she wasn't—but he had the gun. She considered his words, her lower lip almost trembled.

"No," she said carefully. "It wasn't like that, I—"

"You *angled*. To get me out."

"No, Benji, I—"

"You told them to dump me . . . in the worst possible way—"

"No, I—"

"Don't lie. Your mother spilled the whole thing."

"My mother?"

"Yeah, your mother. My *bitch*. She said *you* did it. No one else. You told them, *you* made it happen, admit it!"

Our eyes met—mine and Cinnamon's, then mine and Appelfeld's. Cinnamon, with a gun to her head, was utterly still now, held by some secret inner force, like she knew I knew: this was the final dead end—the inevitable.

And then she closed her eyes.

"I admit it," she said somberly. "I . . . admit it."

"You told them . . . to oust me."

She breathed deep. "I told them."

"In the worst possible way."

Something twitched in her without movement, a last piece of resistance, but she snuffed it.

"Yes. I told them. To let you go. And to make it final."

"Why?"

"To spare you."

"Spare me?"

"Yes, my . . . my mother, she—she said to . . . cut ties. She said it was merciful. She—"

"*Merciful?* They came to my door. They *mocked* me, laughing their asses off. In front of my dad."

"I know," she said. "They—didn't understand. They were children. We were all children, Benji. And I am so sorry."

He sneered, soaked in the confession, and for a split second, I thought it had penetrated him, softened him.

I was wrong.

He started laughing himself into a frenzy, jacked the gun up under her chin. "Yeah? Well, here's where I get merciful. First, I'm gonna redo that record in my name. Every fucking song. Then I'm gonna put it up on Spotify, take Elkaim's money, and promote the shit out of it. 'Cause I am The Daily Telegraph, the breaking news—*now where is it, Zantz?*"

He thrust the gun again as I was about to answer, but at that moment a lamp that had been dangling hit the ground with a smash, he turned and in the flash of distraction, I pounced, karated the pistol out of his hand, sending him in one direction, Cinnamon in the other. She scattered and fell back onto the floor as Appelfeld and I rolled on hard cement, punches flying—he grabbed at my hair, bashed me against some kind of car track, but I kick-toppled a table over him, sending him onto his bad leg, and he grabbed at the downtown skyline to balance.

I was down, trying to pull myself up onto the capsized table, then Cinnamon screamed as Appelfeld leapt up, ape-style, and went into a crazy jacked-up one-legged snort dance, looking for the gun, his shoulders bouncing. She was shivering full-on now, clutching onto the edge of the table. I thought she might throw up. I almost got up but slipped. He hollered like a banshee, lunging forward onto a skyline, up on his bloody knee with the tilted City Hall wobbling behind him. With determination he reached and broke the telegraph pole off the Wilshire Grand, its antennae as straight and sharp as coat wire, swishing and thrusting like a sword, thrashing the air as he came at me.

"*Your* ship has sailed, motherfucker!" He charged down at me, the sharp metal about to plunge into my gut and then—

A thundercrack, earsplitting loud—Appelfeld flew back and arched like origami and crashed onto the corded floor, the antennae flying as he clutched at his back.

Cinnamon seemed to shake from the gun wavering at the end of her skinny arms. She stared at it in horror, dropped it, and came for him, not to finish him off but to save him, and she threw herself over him as if to reach for a former safety long gone, cradling him under the busted Hollywood sign, the folded mountain range razed in green and brown. All at once, Appelfeld started heaving, he was still alive, a hunted animal curled under these ruins, a plastic paradise shattered all around him, his shirt going red, and she looked to me, dazed and shaken.

I hauled myself up on sore knees and said, "Call an ambulance—now."

She pulled her phone and started calling as I tore off my hoodie, ripped it and tried to tie off his torso. She pleaded to the dispatch operator, and then there was a grim chaotic silence, nothing but AC and the whirring of lights.

I said, "Help is on the way."

But I couldn't tell if he heard me—the wounded animal, considering a flight he can't actually make.

"Don't move," I said. "'Cause if I let go of this rag . . . you're toast."

He took it in, nodded, his lip curled.

Then, to my great surprise, Cinnamon took his hand, gazed upon him with patient tenderness.

Their eyes met. Something was exchanged, something only old friends can share.

Then, without rancor, she said, "Why'd you do it, Benji?"

He flashed with pain and shame, but he understood her.

"Why'd you hurt Rey-Rey?"

He winced.

"You could've gunned down the whole band," she said with a half-laugh. "But you picked the one guy, our little Rey—*why, Benji?*"

He didn't or couldn't or wouldn't answer. He panted. I held him in place—his blood was on my hands, and I couldn't let go. His eyes did a mini-REM, fighting the darkness. Then he exhaled sharply.

He mumbled, "I found him there, naked."

"Found him?" She was coolheaded, right here in the here and now.

"Your mom's studio, she was . . . under him." He snorted. "And when she saw me, she threw Rey off her and pulled the sheet."

Cinnamon nodded—one knowing nod—it was enough to keep him going.

"I . . . I went crazy, Cin. Yelling—how . . . how they burned me." He looked up at her, soldier to nurse. "Your mom, I loved her."

Cinnamon stiffened with barely veiled disbelief.

He whispered. "She'd said we were a team. She called us . . . the hotness trio."

Cinnamon took it in. "And . . . they cut you out."

"I didn't want to hurt anyone," he said with a whimper. "But Rey got belligerent, standing there naked. He *pushed* me, fuckin' naked midget, thinking he was gonna become some kinda big—he *pushed* me."

Appelfeld seized up and squinted like he'd just gotten pushed again—I tightened my grip on the hoodie but it was damn wet.

"I told Rey I knew all about the fancy producer and the

big-time deal. And Rey was like, 'You don't know shit, dude.'
And they just . . . cracked up, both of them, they were laughing too. They wouldn't stop. She was—so beautiful with the
white sheet like a Greek goddess, and him standing there with
his big old dong hanging out—they—I had to make it stop."

Cinnamon and I exchanged a side glance—Appelfeld closed
his eyes.

"I grabbed the lamp. I swung it—the . . . he just kind of
staggered there for a second, blood all over his face. And I . . .
I did it again."

Now he opened his eyes and stared at her blankly, but there
was remorse in there, way deep inside. And then it rose, burst
in a torrent of hoarse tears.

"I killed our drummer," he said, heaving with failing breath.
"I destroyed the band."

And it was so awkward, this final lie hanging onto the fantasy by its fingernails—my mouth parted to say something,
maybe to correct him, but no words would come and there
were sirens in the distance, getting closer—were they for us?
Time was turning to floating particles in the green light under crumbling cities and Appelfeld was letting go, not just of
the past but the present, fading to permanent and stationary
sleep—yet something kept him from completing the journey;
he was caught on a snag. Hand trembling, he reached for the
drawstring on Cinnamon's parka, but gentle. He had one last
confession to make.

"I . . . hated his guts. Just—" But he could not complete
the thought.

"Rey-Rey?" Cinnamon asked, with strained compassion.

He shook his head a little.

"Emil?"

"Mm-mm."

"Devvy?"

"*No*," he said, shaking his head once hard, eyes going wide, twisting up with the last of his powers. "*My dad*. Fucking loser. Complaining day and night about how the world did him wrong. How he was so great and he had fallen so far. Like just being our dad was such a disappointment, such a fucking punishment. I just . . ."

Now Appelfeld looked right through her—maybe to white light. Then he said, "But he *was* a star. To me, I mean. He was *the* star."

Their eyes locked in curious understanding. I clutched the blood-soaked cloth as if I was the one hanging on for dear life. Appelfeld smiled with a trembling hurt deeper than any gunshot.

"*And I wanted to save him. So bad.* Like, if I could be a part of the band, I could be a real star, and then . . . he would be a real star too." And then Benjamin Appelfeld took one last look at Cinnamon, and, as if to explain everything, he mumbled, "My dad."

She held his hand with supreme mercy and he shut his eyes for good.

42

"What are we doing here? We gonna try to crash the Playboy Mansion like ninth grade?"

Double Fry laughed, already standing at the door of the massive Tudor he grew up in as I hauled myself up the green slope and stopped to catch my breath. "Let's get this over with," he said, "before my mom comes back from her pro bono hustle." He pulled the key from under the crumbling lawn jockey and opened the massive doors. "Home sweet home—not."

The vestibule was cavernous, echoey. Fry's parents had been super-successful entertainment lawyers—now the house was occupied by his widowed mom and her full-time housekeeper. Fry yelled, "Marta?" and when nobody answered he said, "Good, the coast is clear. Follow me."

Fry, the black sheep in torn jeans, still kinda looked at one with all the opulence as he led me through the crystalline dining room into the den, across the shag carpet to a long, polished wooden stereo AM-FM record player-and-8-track cabinet with a full-on built-in bar stocked with winged corkscrew, ice bucket, Bombay Gin, Kahlua, Amaretto, and a long slim bottle of something Russian. He knelt and slid open the door, started flipping through the LPs—they looked like they hadn't been touched in years—Perry Como, *Bookends,* Tijuana Brass, *The Magic of Kauai.*

I said, "Are we about to throw a luau?"

"Yeah, a psych-out luau." Then he slid it out from the middle of the stack—the test pressing, lightly burnt, spotted, the dirty mad crazy beautiful relic.

> Customer: THE DAILY TELEGRAPH
> Title: DEL CYD
> Comments: PIONEER RECORDS
> Date: 11/14/83

I hadn't seen it in weeks, and the sight of it filled me with too many emotions to register. Like the hole in the record, my whole world had spun around this thing.

"Thought you'd want this back."

"I guess I gotta figure out who to give it to."

"Right," he said. "But maybe first let's play it."

"On *this* mammy-jammy?"

"Hell yeah."

Fry laid the black wax on the record player and carefully placed the needle. Then he clicked the volume. With a soft crackle the opening chords of "Runaway Sunshine" came through the giant cabinet speakers, deeper, warmer, more elegant, more surreal than I'd heard them before.

I said, "This is how they would have sounded if it was really the sixties."

Fry said, "It's kinda badass—somebody should release this thing." Then he flopped out on one of the big couches and I took the opposite—he started rolling a big funky-looking joint on the long glass table.

"I figure," Fry said, "might as well honor them with a little ritual."

"Won't your mom have a heart attack when she comes home and finds us here?"

Fry shook his head. "This is her weed, dog."

"Your mom's a stoner?"

"Helps her sciatica." Fry lit up. "Hey, what happened to the girl—the singer?"

"Endi?" I frowned. "We talked. She's moving back home."

"For real? So—no LA, no singing star?"

"She's marrying her ex in August."

"Wow, man, I'm . . . sorry to hear that—I thought she might convert you to actual grown-up. Hope she's okay."

He smoked, handed me the joint.

"Yeah, me too." I shook my head and smoked and did a long shrug—the international male signal for *I don't want to talk about it*. Good friend Double Fry took it in. I handed him back the joint and lay back and let the music play, washing over the sunlit, smoky room. The sweet hinky garagey clang of it held something else for me now—time and loss and the faraway-ness of Endi's smile. Into the second song, stony Fry sat up and started wagging his hands like a doubting rabbi.

"So this . . . Jensen, Appelfeld, whatever—he, like, *really* wanted to replace Emil?"

"Yup."

"Like, *at every level*."

"Totally. The second he got out of the loony bin, he tracked down Charles Elkaim and started playing substitute son, cozy-ing up. Anything to stand in Emil's shoes."

"Wow. Talk about holding a grudge."

I nodded. "It was like, '*You replace me? Oh no, I replace you.*'"

"That is fucking sick," Fry said. Then, out of the blue: "I gotta tell you, Addy, I never liked the guy."

"Oh. Really? *Now* you offer me this insight?"

"No, serious, bro. That time we went to the movies? I couldn't help but notice what a *gloomster* the guy was. The whole time, after you guys left, all through *Yellow Submarine* he was cursing under his breath, mumbling about '*the arrogance*.' I'm all, like, the arrogance? It's the Beatles, dude, it's supposed to be fun."

"Yeah, well, maybe next time share your hunches right away, okay?"

Fry laughed through closed teeth. "One thing I *still* don't get. Just how long was that jerk even *in* The Daily Telegraph?"

"My guess is barely. Sandoz told me they auditioned a lot of guitarists that didn't stick."

"But he played actual shows with them, right?"

"*One* show—an amateur contest they lost. Soon as Cinnamon brought Emil around, they forgot all about Appelfeld."

"But why'd he single out the drummer?"

"Well . . . the way I'm picturing it, Rey Durazo would have been especially vocal about kicking Appelfeld out—'cause he's the one who would've most wanted a clean break."

"Why?"

"The Perskys were just across the street from the rehearsal garage, right? He and Appelfeld had done some gardening work for Mrs. Persky. And she was sleeping with the both of them."

"*What?* Not at the same time."

"Yup, same time. High school boys." I started singing the theme to *Three's Company*—"*Come an' knock on our doooor—*"

"No. Way."

"Yes way. Ya know, early eighties, which came just after the seventies, which was also some kind of strange branch off the sixties—pre-AIDS and all that. Free love was still in the air."

"Nice pay for gardening services."

"I don't think it was an accident these two horny teenagers showed up with their rakes or whatever. They'd probably heard all kinds of rumors about Cinnamon's mom. I mean, the way Rey's cousin Professor Durazo painted it, Mrs. Persky was gunning for trouble. She ran with musicians, players—she was a scenemaker and she was crazy sexy—I mean, even her beautiful daughter felt outshined."

"That and she was married to a gay movie producer."

"Exactly—so Appelfeld and Rey and Marjorie had their little, uh, *after-school special*, and nobody got their feathers ruffled. But when Appelfeld got kicked out of the group, Marj knew she had to kick him out of the sack too—"

"Because sleeping with Pete Best is the ultimate groupie fail."

"So, she quote *fired her gardeners* unquote, canceled services. But Durazo was still in the band—" I threw a wide arm out. "—he rehearsed across the street. And then he came back for more. *Solo*."

"And Appelfeld caught them in flagrante?"

"Yup, and that's how Durazo got naked before he got dead. Then Appelfeld planted the bloody lamp in the trunk of Emil's MG."

"Brutal. All because Emil stole his slot in the band?"

"That and—they *really* humiliated him when they kicked him out, it was ugly."

"You think Marjorie helped the frame-up?"

"She might not have *participated*, but she kept her mouth shut."

Fry grew somber. "Why—why would she do that?"

"Appelfeld threatened her, for one. And maybe she was involved. But I have this crazy gut thing that she also didn't love Emil as much as she claimed."

"Why not?"

"Because her daughter found true love and a real family? Because maybe she even made a pass at Emil and got rejected?

I really don't know—it's a feeling. But I *do* know she practically sent Cinnamon away. I mean, really *talked her into* going on the lam."

"To set her free?"

"I'm not sure it was that innocent."

"Yeah—maybe not. Some moms just cannot bear to pass the torch." Fry cast a glance around the giant tomb of his mother's living room and sighed. "What'd you learn about the singer?"

"Mickey Sandoz?"

"Yeah—what did the autopsy say?"

"Inconclusive, last I heard—the coroner stopped answering my calls."

Fry took it in, smarted. "I guess," he said, "I guess either way, he got killed by rock-and-roll dreams."

Against the backdrop of the clanging, bright, arabesque melody, I shook my head in wonder. "You know what's really messed up? I mean, above and beyond this tragedy— here's this guy, Appelfeld, he's barely even in the band. He's running on pure fantasy—the dream of being a big star, a *rock star*—and, okay, he's nuts, obviously, he's a murderer. But *so* many people live under the weird pressure of that *same fucking dream*."

"The star thing?" Fry said. "Totally—everybody Twittering their balls off, Instagramming themselves to death. I saw something in *Forbes*—one in four gainfully employed white collar workers say they would quit their job to be famous. I'm talking med students, topflight engineers. No—they'd give it all up for more *likes*, more little red hearts."

"What's it really about?" I asked. "Like Bahari says, what's *the why behind the why*?"

"The dream of being a big star?"

"Yeah, man—why does it have so much force?"

"Well," Fry said, "it's about power, of course—*superiority*. I mean, I don't want to get all moralistic, but the whole fame thing—it's kinda got a touch of Nazi in it, right? *Bow to the superhuman!*"

"Like just being a human is somehow a curse," I said. "A lizard skin you gotta get out of."

We tripped on it together, the madness of it.

"I guess," Fry said, "*the why behind the why* is for some reason we all actually just feel *so* fucking small. The universe is shrinking us, the population is shrinking us, the robots are shrinking us—" Fry pinched an invisible point out of the air. "We're like that tiny dot on the old TV, right before it cuts to black."

"Ahhh, right—*that's* why these fantasies prevail. From small-ness . . . bigness. Yup. That's it."

Fry thumbed his joint and put it out in the crystal ashtray, shook his head, and raised a hand to his mouth like he was calculating something, but the dreamy music of The Daily Telegraph twinkling in the background took over, and then he looked at me and smiled. "This one's my favorite right here— *launch the lightning!—light up the sky!* Hell yeah."

I burst out laughing.

He pointed at me. "Somebody's gotta put this out."

43

There was no way to prove or disprove Marjorie Persky's involvement in the murder of Reynaldo Durazo. The next week, with Fry's help, I made the first of three attempts to present a request for inquiry, but both Lanterman and the two detectives who had been assigned to the case quashed it. The last time we went down to Newton Station to speak with the cops, they seemed gently annoyed that we wouldn't let it go—the thief who they thought had killed Hawley had been released, and as far as they were concerned, Marjorie Persky was an upstanding member of her community, an octogenarian. There was nothing to point to. Anyway, her daughter stayed by Charles Elkaim's side as she vowed and never contacted her mother once. I had to believe that, for Marjorie Persky, that was some kind of punishment enough.

I had just a few more things to do before walking away from the case once and for all, and so, on a Saturday afternoon, I parked at the Grove and made my way through the open mall, just as the Saturday night crowd was starting to pour in: Koreans, Persians, Mexicans, Black, white, everyone dressed for summer in bright colors and white things, hanging by the giant fountain as it spritzed in time to piped-in Sinatra while the trolley car ding-ding-dinged down the track. It was a funny collage of the past, but nobody would really mistake this for Olde Time Main Street, USA. The sense of the present was everywhere—people were here to shop, eat, laugh, love. The twentieth century was long gone, and far as I could see, nobody in this crowd cared.

Nobody except good ol' Larry Lazerbeam, that is.

He was waiting for me under the pagoda at the Farmers Market bar, nursing a Bloody Mary and clocking the Dodgers on the widescreen.

He smiled as he saw me saunter up. "Here comes Dick Tracy!"

I shook my head, laughing, and handed him a canvas bag. "For you," I said.

He reached in and pulled out the original acetate.

"*Wowie zowie.*" His grin went wide. "I thought you were gonna try to sell this baby on the black market."

"Naw. Far as I'm concerned, this is your piece of the rock. And it's yours to keep."

He placed it back in the bag with supreme care. "You wanna toast to the 'Graph before this planet goes kerblooey?"

I looked at the bar crowd, the game on TV, then down at my beaten red sneakers. "Why the hell not."

We ordered bad champagne and clinked plastic champagne glasses. About two sips in, Lazerbeam said, "You know what I'm gonna do, man? I'm gonna put this thing out on 180-gram vinyl. That's right. *Lost classics time.* This shit is gonna blow minds, I guarantee—"

But just as he was working himself up, his wife Marie appeared with two bags of veggies.

"There you are! I've been looking all over the damn market for you. Are you really talking about The Daily Telegraph *again*?"

"What the heck, Mare!" His voice pitched high. "You're embarrassing me in front of our detective friend over here—"

"Guys," I said, before they could escalate, "It's okay, I was just leaving."

She softened. "No, stay, I didn't mean to scare you off."

"I wish I could—I've got a test to study for, really. I just wanted to thank you for your help, both of you . . . and . . . I wanted to put this thing in the right hands."

Lazerbeam sulked, but he said, "Don't be a stranger, Zantz," and I said I wouldn't as I took one last look at them. They were a heartbreaker, these two keepers of the flame, a conundrum. Teenage senior citizens, cocky on the surface, but trembling in the face of mortality. They were not built for the future and they knew it, and everywhere they looked, the hyper-stim touchscreen Insta-world told them they were useless.

Nevertheless, *they kept the flame.*

The Daily Telegraph's shining rinky-dink masterpiece *Del Cyd* came out just two months later on Pioneer Records. I got a weird surge of pride by proxy when I looked on the back cover and read *Produced by Lazar Lawrence.* The deluxe release had a few awesome bonuses—a lyric sheet and a gatefold collage assembled from the photos I'd taken of Devon Hawley Junior's wall the night I broke in with Mickey Sandoz.

It just so happened that the very same week, Charles Elkaim called to tell me he received some documents he wanted to show me.

I drove over to the Shalom Terrace with a shrink-wrapped LP and found him eating lunch on his rolling tray. Cinnamon was there, bedside and faithful. She looked happy too, optimistic. It was the first time I'd seen her since the night with Appelfeld, and it was a little awkward between us out here in the light of day—her eyes gave me a gentle warning to not go there. Her almost-father-in-law looked a little weaker than before, but he had outlived the doctor's predictions and he was happy too—happy to see me, thrilled to show me the letter he got from the county.

"A court processor brought it over," Cinnamon said. "He thought he was under arrest!"

"For what?" I said.

"I thought maybe I forgot to pay a parking ticket twenty years ago," he said. *"Read it."*

The letter stated that Judge Maxwell R. Edler had vacated Emil Elkaim's thirty-year-old charges. New DNA tests revealed traces of Benjamin Appelfeld's blood on the original murder weapon, confirming the inquiry Fry and I had handed the county. Although Emil Elkaim had never been officially convicted, it was noted that he would be listed among the 1,281 recorded in the National Registry of Exonerations. *When an innocent person is deprived of liberty because of a wrongful conviction,* the form letter stated, *the government has a responsibility to do all it can to foster that person's reentry into society, in order to help restore some sense of justice.*

Well, it was a form letter, generated by a computer, and Emil Elkaim wouldn't be reentering society, but it was better than nothing. I handed the LP to Charles—it glowed majestic in his old hands, with Cinnamon looking over his shoulder, eyes instantly wet.

In a fit of passion, he said, "I want to show the record to Emil."

It had the ring of dementia—Cinnamon and I exchanged an uncomfortable glance.

"Aba," she said—but he was already up, grabbing his coat.

"We'll go to his grave. I don't believe Cynthia has ever seen her own grave. I'll hire you. You're a Lyfter, aren't you?"

I smiled and shook my head. "This one's a free ride, Mr. Elkaim."

A half hour later we pulled into Home of Peace. The afternoon was cool, and fluffy clouds were making their way across the blue. At a tin bucket chained to a faucet, Elkaim washed his hands and Cinnamon and I followed—neither of us knew the rituals quite right. Traffic hummed on in the distance as we got our bearings. Then Cinnamon and I each held one of Mr. Elkaim's arms and led him across the field to see his son's grave, and it dawned on me that it would probably be Charles Elkaim's last visit. Soon enough, he would join him. When we got to the plaques, Cinnamon ignored her own with tender dignity. Charles had her hold the record while he sang a Hebrew prayer in his low and mournful cadence, and then, with great care she laid the LP down between the graves—it made a crazy cacophony, the bright magenta and baby blue collage and the solemn granite with the green grass growing all around—but it was beautiful.

My eyes met Cinnamon's and some pure, helpless, sweet electricity passed between us—she almost blushed from it. Or maybe I did.

Then Charles said, "Don't you want to visit your uncle?"

"You know where he is?" I strained, embarrassed.

Elkaim pointed. "Over there, at the far end."

He pointed to a cluster of graves near the fence—just over the wall, you could see the orange-and-blue sign for Nuñez Building Supplies.

"That's a long walk, Aba," Cinnamon said.

"We must," he said. "Adam must say a blessing for the soul of his uncle."

I nodded and we made our way down the path, around the tombstones, ambling diagonal to the far end of the cemetery. I was apprehensive, but when I finally gazed upon my uncle's final resting place, it was all recognition and love and that same force of time I'd heard in those songs.

Herschel Berman
הרשל ברמן
1934–2017
Beloved Husband, Father, Grandfather, Uncle

"*He* insisted on including uncle—because he was *your* uncle."
Then Elkaim produced a little Kleenex packet from his pocket
and handed it to me. I thought he thought I might cry, but he
pointed at the plaque and said, "Needs a cleaning."

As I got down on my knees and gave it a good once-over,
a curious sensation came over me—that there was nothing
standing between me and life anymore, that I would have to
make my own way, without excuses, and I felt dizzy, weightless,
moving dirt off the grave. To get my bearings, I grabbed a few
small rocks from the grass and laid them across the plaque in
Jewish fashion—one for me and one for Maya.

And then something funny happened. The tiniest roly-poly
pill bug crawled out from under the plaque and hurried its busy
gray self across the granite surface.

"It's Herschel," Charles said. "Hello, old friend."

PLAYLIST

1. "This Can't Be Today"—Rain Parade (Words and music by Matt Piucci and Steven Roback)
2. "Too Late"—The Shoes (Gary Klebe)
3. "Suddenly Last Summer"—The Motels (Martha Davis)
4. "Private Idaho"—The B-52s (Kate Pierson, Fred Schneider, Keith Strickland, Cindy Wilson, and Ricky Wilson)
5. "She Talks in Stereo"—Gary Myrick & The Figures (Gary Myrick)
6. "As Real as Real"—The Three O'Clock (Louis Gutierrez and Michael Quercio)
7. "Down with Love"—Bobby Darin (Harold Arlen and E.Y. "Yip" Harburg)
8. "Colored Balls Falling"—Love (Arthur Lee)
9. "Dreaming"—Blondie (Debbie Harry and Chris Stein)
10. "Look Sharp"—Joe Jackson (Joe Jackson)
11. "The World We Knew (Over and Over)"—Frank Sinatra (Bert Kaempfert, Herbert Rehbein, and Carl Sigman)
12. "Find It"—The Carrie Nations (Stu Philips and Lynn Carey)
13. "I'm Insane"—Joe Cuba (Louie Ramirez)
14. "Who Are You"—The Who (Pete Townshend)

15. "We'd Like to Thank You, Herbert Hoover"—*Annie*, Original Broadway Cast (Martin Charnin and Charles Strouse)

16. "The Garden of Earthly Delights"—The United States of America (Dorothy Moskowitz, Joseph Byrd, and Ed Bogas)

17. "Voices Green and Purple"—The Bees (Tom Willsie and Robert Wood)

18. "The Beat Goes On"—Sonny & Cher (Sonny Bono)

19. "Song for Sunshine"—Belle and Sebastian (Stuart Murdoch, Stevie Jackson, Sarah Martin, Richard Colburn, Bobby Kildea, Chris Geddes, and Mick Cooke)

20. "Twilight Zone"—The Manhattan Transfer (Bernard Herrmann, Jay Graydon, and Alan Paul)

21. "It's Us Again"—Steve Lawrence & Edie Gormé (R. Ward)

22. "Any Place I Hang My Hat Is Home"—Helen Merrill (Harold Arlen)

23. "Message II (Survival)"—Grandmaster Flash & The Furious Five (Melvin Glover and Sylvia Robinson)

24. "Liar, Liar"—The Castaways (Dennis Craswell and James Donna)

25. "I'll Be Back"—The Beatles (John Lennon and Paul McCartney)

26. "My Mirage"—Iron Butterfly (Doug Ingle)

27. "Apples, Peaches, Pumpkin Pie"—Jay & The Techniques (Maurice Irby Jr.)

28. "Then She Remembers"—The Dream Syndicate (Steve Wynn)

29. "Lucifer Sam"—Pink Floyd (Syd Barrett)

30. "About the Weather"—Magazine (Barry Adamson, Howard Devoto, John Doyle, and Dave Formula)

31. "Green Fuz"—The Cramps (Randy Alvey and Leslie Dale)
32. "Grimly Forming"—The Salvation Army (Peter Van Gelder)
33. "A Question of Temperature"—Balloon Farm (Mike Appel, Ed Schnug, and Don Henny)
34. "Video Killed the Radio Star"—The Buggles (Geoff Downes, Trevor Horn, and Bruce Woolley)
35. "Mr. Soul"—Buffalo Springfield (Neil Young)
36. "Everybody Wants to Rule the World"—Tears for Fears (Chris Hughes, Roland Orzabal, and Ian Stanley)
37. "Southern Scandal"—Stan Kenton (Stan Kenton)
38. "The Battle of the Bands"—The Turtles (Jerry Douglas and Harry Nilsson)
39. "Hero Takes a Fall"—The Bangles (Susanna Hoffs and Vicki Peterson)
40. "Shaman's Blues"—The Doors (Jim Morrison)
41. "Time Has Come Today"—The Chambers Brothers (Joseph Chambers and Willie Chambers)
42. "Everything and More"—Dolly Mixture (Rachel Bor, Hester Smith, and Debsey Wykes)
43. "My Best Friend"—Jefferson Airplane (Skip Spence)

LINER NOTES FOR
THE DAILY TELEGRAPH'S *DEL CYD*

When people speak of "the Paisley Underground" they are usually referring to a handful of talented groups that helped reignite the spirit of the 1960s in a fresh punk and post-punk context: Salvation Army/Three O'Clock, Green on Red, the Long Ryders, Dream Syndicate, Rain Parade, the Last, the Unclaimed, and a handful of others. These bands left their mark, and they rightfully own the territory.

However the term itself is somewhat misleading because the Paisley Underground didn't happen in a vacuum.

There was a citywide spirit of *reclamation and rediscovery* in those years that stretched beyond any one scene. It was as if everybody who loved music willfully stepped into a time machine to embark on a wild journey, touching ground in *every* past era of rock and roll, just to see what we could gather and preserve . . . what we could use.

A full-scale rockabilly and roots revival was in swing with Levi and the Rockats, the Blasters, Top Jimmy and the Rhythm Pigs, Los Lobos, and the reappearance of old-timers like Italian-born Rockin' Ronny Weiser making the scene. The brilliantine was flowing, along with the taffeta and the unfiltered cigarettes.

Then you had the Gun Club fuel-injecting the blues in double-time and bringing Robert Johnson and John Coltrane to a whole new generation of hyped-up kids. The Mosrite surf guitar was also having something of a rebirth in those years, with the Cramps hitting their stride on *Psychedelic Jungle* and the Unknowns delivering their sublime one-of-a-kind surfabilly pop. When the Ventures appeared at Disneyland, rock and rollers from every corner of town descended on the park.

Then there were the devoted American mod/ska kids cruising to the On Klub or the Bullet in their fleet of Lambrettas and Vespas to see the Question, the Untouchables, early Fishbone, and others, decked out in parkas and buttons galore.

Then you had a slew of beatnik experimenters that were equally entrenched in the past, but perhaps wedded to no specific time—Phast Phreddie & Thee Precisions, the Romans, the Tikis, and others too countless to number.

Just what sparked this deep spirit of revival—which stretched not only coast to coast but US to UK to Australia and beyond—is anybody's guess and would probably require a degree in chaos theory to prove out. But the point is that *the past was everywhere*, from the clubs to the magazines to the used clothing shops along Melrose, spreading an infectious spirit right down to the high schools.

And that brings us to the Daily Telegraph.

You didn't read about them in *Bomp!* or *New York Rocker*, but you should have. One talentless *Music Connection* hack had the unmitigated gall to call the band, "another fish in the fish-eyed-lensed procession of current L.A. groups fetishizing the ‹60s." Well, rumor has it said writer (who shall remain nameless) is currently holding down a twenty-year-plus job in medical billing data entry, but that's another story. The fact is that they were not just another group—they were that rare but almost mystical thing: kids with a vision.

My husband Lazar first discovered "the 'Graph" when he went to see his friend Bill "Balloon Man" Morrison performing his special brand of philosophical comedy at the Natural Fudge. Lazar came home that night in a state of high ecstasy, not chemically induced, insisting that he had "seen the future of rock and roll." The very next day, their go-getter muse and de facto manager Cinnamon Persky called to invite us to see them perform—where else?—in somebody's parents' garage.

They were messy, they were green, they were half-shy, half-grandiose, and, at times, they were out of tune and nearly unlistenable—and yet, these five high school boys were totally invested in the original spirit of rock 'n' roll like nobody we'd ever seen. What they lacked in skills they more than made up for with drive and passion, each member bringing the force of his unformed but special personality to the table.

Drummer Rey-Rey was a kind of muscle-bound mini-man with a boyish heart of gold and he hit those things *hard*. It really stood out. Bassist Jeff "Groony" Grunes was an angel disguised as a porcupine, as methodical as Rey was wild. Keyboardist Devon was the daydreamer—every band needs one. Sometimes, mid-song, you could see him slip into a kind of trance, lost in song. Guitarist Emil was the heartthrob, fleet-footed, winking, but totally consumed by his axe. And lead singer Mickey Sandoz was a true shapeshifter, a trickster fox, a joker who lived to turn the room upside-down.

We knew they weren't ready, but we could not walk away. And so Cinnamon took it upon herself to work them tirelessly in the garage with Lazar at the helm, trimming songs, tightening up, epic rehearsals for whole weekends at a stretch. Like magic, the band tightened up, the music congealed, and inside a season, we were ready to roll tape.

That tape is just what you have in your hands—pure music, revealing the magic of time.

Across these miraculous tracks are the fruits of their labor—young people throwing themselves into psychedelic rock and roll with complete and total abandon, and discovering a space that is beyond the beyond.

Let's skip the details about what happened next. Suffice it to say that tragedy befell the group before they could come out from their own underground, and the record was subsequently shelved—a very real and personal heartbreak for many, my husband and I included.

The most bitter part, perhaps, is that their music could never be listened to again without this backdrop of pain. How a piece of magic so heartfelt and so innocent could get buried before it even got a chance to live? For many years, in darkest times, my husband and I would hold our single cassette of these songs up to the light and wonder if we lived in a just universe.

Well . . . it turns out that we do.

And the Daily Telegraph lives.

MARIE LAWRENCE, CO-FOUNDER, PIONEER RECORDS
INGLEWOOD, CALIFORNIA
2024

ACKNOWLEDGMENTS

First I would like to offer gratitude for the beloved memories of my father Shalom and my brother Moshe. Their spirits guide me every step of the way.

For believing in the continued adventures of Adam Zantz, my sincere gratitude goes to double-amazing agents Janet Oshiro and David Halpern at the Robbins Office, and to super-editor Carl Bromley at Melville House. Me and Zantz are lucky mugs.

Also very special thanks to the Duke of Earl, aka Michael Barson, for his savvy guidance, impeccable taste, black belt wisecracks, and unspeakable coolness.

And big love to Dennis Loy Johnson, Valerie Merians, and the supreme dream team at Melville House—Janet Joy Wilson, Ariel Palmer-Collins, Madeleine Letellier, Sammi Sontag, Pia Mulleady, Susan McGrath, Justin DeCarlo, Amber Qureshi, Michelle Capone, Mike Lindgren, Sofia Demopolos, and especially cover designer Beste Miray Doğan. And thanks to Kathy Robbins, Lucinda Halpern, Rishon Blumberg, and Michael Solomon for setting me on the path.

Thanks to H. W. Taeusch, Barbara White, Doug Magnuson, Troy Lambert, and my ninety-four-year-old mother Rama for their determined reads and brilliant editorial input.

Extra special thanks to Neil Normal of GNP Crescendo Records for the Seeds lyrics. Be sure to check out the mind-blow documentary *Pushing Too Hard* on Vimeo.

Once again, I'd like to thank the literary mentors and guides who showed me the way: Harvey Kubernik, Al, and Hud from Flipside; the late great Craig Lee; Gene Sculatti and Ronn Spencer; Daniel Shulman and Josh Schreiber; Jack Skelley; Steve Abee; Francesca Lia Block; Robin Carr; Amy White; Scott Sampler; Erik Himmelsbach-Weinstein; Lisa Rojany and late greats Larry Sloan and Leonard Stern; Rhonda Lieberman; Laura Nolan; Joan Leegant, Risa Miller, Allen Hoffman, the Shaindy Rudoff Creative Writing Program and Ilanot Review; Jill Schary Robinson and the Wimpole Street Writers; Ari Haddad, Jon Shapiro, Pablo Capra, and Kenneth Kubernik. And gratitude for the memories I hold dear—Ethel Rudbarg, Morris Rudbarg, Dave "Id" Hahn, Aviva Blumberg, Raina Nichelson, Bill Morrison, Natalie Werbner, Davin Seay, Roy Silver, Alan Grannell, Rita Davis, and Lenorah Hahn.

Finally, and most of all, love and gratitude to my wife Clover and son Max—my Skee-Ball players on the Santa Monica Pier.

ABOUT THE AUTHOR

Daniel Weizmann is a writer and editor whose work has appeared in the *Los Angeles Times*, *Billboard*, the *Guardian*, *AP Newswire*, and more. Under the nom de plume Shredder, Weizmann also wrote for the long running *Flipside* fanzine, as well as *LA Weekly*, which once called him "an incomparable punk stylist." He lives in Los Angeles, California.